Sleeping in the Ground

PETER ROBINSON

Sleeping in the Ground

HODDER &
STOUGHTON

First published in Great Britain in 2017 by Hodder & Stoughton
An Hachette UK company

1

Copyright © Peter Robinson 2017

The right of Peter Robinson to be identified as the Author of the Work has been
asserted by him in accordance with the Copyright, Designs and Patents Act 1988.

A CIP catalogue record for this title is available from the British Library

Hardback ISBN 9 781 444 78691 0
Trade Paperback ISBN 978 1 444 78692 7
Ebook ISBN 978 1 444 78693 4

Typeset in Plantin Light by Hewer Text UK Ltd, Edinburgh
Printed and bound by CPI Group (UK) Ltd, Croydon, CR0 4YY

Hodder & Stoughton policy is to use papers that are natural, renewable
and recyclable products and made from wood grown in sustainable
forests. The logging and manufacturing processes are expected to
conform to the environmental regulations of the country of origin.

Hodder & Stoughton Ltd
Carmelite House
50 Victoria Embankment
London EC4Y 0DZ

www.hodder.co.uk

Dedicated to the memory of my father

Clifford Robinson

31st December, 1923–27th May, 2016

And to me, though Time's unflinching rigour,
In mindless rote, has ruled from sight
The substance now, one phantom figure
Remains on the slope, as when that night
Saw us alight.

I look and see it there, shrinking, shrinking,
I look back at it amid the rain
For the very last time; for my sand is sinking,
And I shall traverse old love's domain
Never again.

Thomas Hardy, 'At Castle Boterel'

They are all gone into the world of light!
And I alone sit ling'ring here;
Their very memory is fair and bright,
And my sad thoughts doth clear.

Henry Vaughan, 'Silex Scintillans, Part II'

I

If the incident had been a scene in a film, it would have looked beautiful. The violence would have taken place in elegantly choreographed silence and slow motion. Perhaps it would have started with the wedding party milling around outside the picturesque country church, then the camera would zoom in on a rose of blood blossoming from the bride's white gown as she looks up, surprised, and floats serenely to the ground, arms reaching out, grasping for something too insubstantial to hold. She would toss her bouquet high in the air, pink and purple flowers against a backdrop of blue sky, and it would fall into the arms of a pretty bridesmaid. Then the bridesmaid's head would disintegrate. Strings of blood would snake through the air like drops of ink in water.

But the way Terry Gilchrist saw it – and he was there – it was as swift as it was brutal. A crack, loud enough to be heard above the church bells, was followed by a dull thud, then a patch of blood spread over the bride's chest. Her body arched, and she spun half around and crumpled in an untidy heap of blood-soaked white chiffon and lace, her mouth open, the scream for ever stuck in her throat. Another crack, and her groom fell beside her. A frightened child clung tightly to his mother's legs. The bridesmaids clutched their posies, eyes wide with horror. A third bullet hit the maid of honour before she could run for cover. She fell beside the bride and groom, half her face shot away. The men in their grey pinstripe suits and the women in difficult shoes and wide-brimmed hats bumped into one another as they ran around in panic and confusion. A bullet chipped the corner off an ancient tombstone and a sliver of stone entered the photographer's eye. A guest fell, clutching his thigh. The quickest to react reached the church door as another bullet slammed into the centuries-old wood. Someone managed to pull the heavy door open, and those who could rushed inside. They jammed the doorway, and another brides-maid arched backwards and dropped to the ground, blood oozing from her back. People trampled over her body in an attempt to get into the sanctuary of the church.

It was all finished in less than a minute.

Terry Gilchrist reacted as quickly as he could. He was no stranger to sudden death and violence. He had been under fire before, but nothing had quite prepared him for this. Even so, his soldier's instinct kicked in. He glanced up at the hill where he thought the shots were coming from and saw a dark figure scurrying away, over the grassy summit and down the slope.

Gambling that the assault was over and that there was no one else up there, Terry tried to shepherd the stunned and dazed stragglers into the safety of the church, desperately searching for Winsome. There were no more shots. The church bells stopped ringing. Tentatively, one by one, the birds started singing again.

Terry stood alone in the bright December sunlight and called the police and ambulance on his mobile. One of the fallen guests was moaning with pain. Nearby, a bridesmaid sat propped up against a gravestone crying, her hands pressed to her bloody midriff where something wet and shiny rested in her lap. Terry was no medic, but he had picked up some basic first-aid training in the military, and he visited all the fallen to see if there was anyone he could help before the ambulances arrived. The groom was his mate, Ben, and he had been shot just above his stomach, around the location of his liver. He was still alive, though barely conscious, and the best Terry could do was tear off and wad up part of Ben's bloodstained shirt and have him press it against the wound. Tears came to his eyes as he passed the dead bride and cast a glance down at her crumpled body. He knelt to touch her still-warm cheek and closed her staring eyes. It seemed that all he could see were bodies strewn around the graveyard. Then he turned and went into the church to find Winsome.

Banks left the crematorium ahead of the others, David Bowie's 'Starman' playing over the tinny PA system, and hurried away from the knots of people gathering behind him, down the gravelled drive to the iron gates.

'It always made her feel happy, that song,' he heard someone say between sniffles. Earlier in the brief service, a friend had read a Christina Rossetti poem: 'When I am dead, my dearest, / Sing no sad songs for me'. 'Starman' was certainly no sad song, but it still had people in tears. And even David Bowie was dead now.

Banks moved on quickly. He didn't want to hang around and make small talk about death and loss with people he didn't know. He had seen the mourners crying on the front row: two young couples, probably daughters or daughters-in-law, with small children, grandchildren, most likely; he had spotted her parents, father in a wheelchair, his head nodding and arm twitching. The others would be friends, work colleagues, nephews and nieces. The eulogy had mentioned the deceased's tireless work for Médicins Sans Frontières so some of the guests would be from that organisation.

But for Banks, this was *his* death, not something he wanted to share. He wanted to hold it to himself, to take it into him, if he could, let the grief become a part of him, and join with the grief of long ago.

The taxi he had ordered was waiting across the road. He slid into the back seat and told the driver to head for the train station. It wasn't a long journey, and it passed in silence. When he checked his watch against the timetable just inside the station entrance, he saw that he had almost an hour until the next train. He walked back to the street and scoped out the area. There was a Waitrose supermarket with a café to his left, but that wasn't much use. He didn't feel like a coffee or a cup of tea. Far more tempting was the Great Northern Hotel, almost directly opposite. It was a three-storey brick building with the ground-floor facade covered in white stucco, a black-board listing the daily specials stood by the door. Banks crossed the street, walked in towards the reception desk and saw the bar to his left. He didn't normally drink so soon after eleven in a morning, but after the funeral he felt in need of something to take the edge off. It sounded as if some sort of function was going on to his right. Banks could hear someone making a speech, punctuated now and then by hearty laughter.

The bar was almost empty. One elderly couple sat at a table sipping white wine and that was it, apart from the pretty brunette barmaid. There was a rugby game on the large screen TV at the far end of the room. Banks sat on a bar stool, from which he would be able to watch the game as he enjoyed his drink. He was about to order a pint but decided that he'd have wine instead. Less liquid. He had a two-hour train journey ahead of him, and the toilets on trains were generally a health hazard, littered with soggy paper and awash with spillage. Usually the taps didn't work, either, which didn't matter much as the paper towels were scattered all over the floor.

The barmaid smiled at him as he sat down. Banks ordered a large Shiraz and settled on his stool. He wasn't a great rugby fan, and he had no idea who was playing, but he did enjoy watching a game now and then. He'd played rugby union at school, had even been good enough to make the school team as fly-half, being wiry, slippery and reasonably fast. Nevertheless, sometimes he wasn't quite fast enough to prevent one of the hulking prop forwards from flattening him. He played once a week in regular games periods, and once on a Saturday morning for the school, no matter what the weather. Some weeks he was sloshing about in the mud, others slipping on the frozen earth.

It felt odd being back in his hometown and not visiting his parents, but they had sold the council house he had grown up in and moved into a private care home near Durham to be closer to Banks and their granddaughter Tracy, who lived in Newcastle. They were well into their eighties, and still healthy enough, but slowing down. Banks's father told him before the move that their cruising days were over; his angina bothered him and he had suffered a minor heart attack only a few months ago. Also, most of their friends on the estate had either died or moved away, so there was nothing to keep them there. Moving wasn't as much of a wrench as it would have been a few years earlier. With the money left to them by Roy, Banks's brother, they could afford the best care in a beautifully restored Victorian manor house with a fine view over the River Wear. They still had their independence. The one-bedroom flat had a large well-equipped kitchen, and Banks's mother still prepared the meals. They could come and go as they pleased, and there was always a registered nurse on duty, just in case. They said they had everything they needed and seemed happy enough, though Banks's father complained that some of the other tenants were either too posh or too gaga for his liking. He also wasn't much of a joiner and didn't sign up for quiz night, sing-alongs or exercise classes. Banks's mother got along just fine with the posh folk; she had always had aspirations beyond her class.

Just then, a small group from the party across the hall came in and clustered around the bar. A wedding group, Banks noticed. The men wore ill-fitting tuxedos with buttonholes, and the women were resplendent in lush cream satin gowns of ivory or peach. The bride and groom stood at the centre of the group. Someone ordered a round of pints and G&Ts. One of the men had a loud grating voice and, of course, he was the one who talked the most. The bride had a laugh like a braying horse. The loud-voiced man told a dirty joke and they all doubled up laughing. Someone else made a witty comment about the groom's mother-in-law, which raised more guffaws, especially from the mother-in-law herself, who seemed well in her cups. Fortunately for Banks, it was a short break. They downed their drinks quickly and headed back to the reception. The barmaid glanced at Banks and pulled a face.

Banks drank some more wine and saw that he had almost finished the glass. Checking his watch, he calculated that he had enough time to get another one down and asked for a refill. He took a long slug of Shiraz, and though his eyes were fixed on the rugby game, he wouldn't have said he was actually following it. He was thinking about those Saturday mornings long ago, towards the end of the sixties, when he still cared enough about being one of the lads to run around in the terrible weather week after week, risking a broken arm, cartilage damage or a wet rugby ball between the legs. It wasn't so bad, he reflected. You got a hot shower at the end of the game, and most Saturday afternoons he went into town record-shopping with his mates Dave, Graham, Steve and Paul. All dead now, except Dave. You could buy used 45s at a stall in the open-air market, he remembered, but the discs were recycled from jukeboxes and the middles had been punched out, so you had to buy flimsy plastic inserts which didn't always work. The 45s were often scratched, too, and they tended to skip. *Caveat emptor.* There was a second-hand book-stall in the market, too, where he had hunted down old Saint, Toff and James Bond paperbacks with lurid covers.

But the best thing about Saturdays back then was the nights. On Saturday nights he would usually go to the pictures with Emily: Emily Hargreaves, the first girl he had ever loved, the girl whose coffin he had just seen rolling towards the flames.

'It wouldn't be for long,' Ray Cabbot was saying. 'A week or so at the most. Just until I find somewhere suitable.'

Annie Cabbot put her knife and fork aside. 'I don't know,' she said. 'I mean, you know how small the cottage is.'

'I wouldn't get in your way, love. I promise. I wouldn't cramp your style.'

Annie laughed. 'My style? What's that supposed to mean? I don't think I have one. Anyway, it's not that . . .' But she *was* a bit worried about the effect a house guest might have on her relationship with Nick Fleming, a DI from County HQ. It was relatively new and had come after a lengthy drought. But she wasn't going to tell her father about that. 'What's wrong with the colony?'

'Nothing. I just feel like I'm getting a bit too old for all that sort of thing. These young turks.' He grinned. 'Nobody paints or sculpts any more. It's all concepts and attitudes. You could walk in an art gallery and piss on the floor and claim it was a work of art these days. Next thing they'll be wanting is a bloody lathe or a 3D printer for making installations. No, love, it's time to move on.'

'And you used to be so Bohemian, so avant-garde. Getting conservative in your old age?'

Ray Cabbot huffed. 'Everyone has to draw the line somewhere.'

'You're not in any trouble, are you?'

'What do you mean, trouble? Of course not.'

'It just seems so sudden.'

'Believe me, I've been thinking about it for some time.'

'Besides,' Annie added after a swig of beer. 'You're not old.' She thought Ray seemed a lot younger than his seventy-plus years.

'Thanks for saying that, love.' Ray ran his hand over his hair. It was silvery-grey, the same colour as his straggly beard, but he still had enough of it to wear in a ponytail. 'Maybe I'm just tired.'

'But why Yorkshire? You've always lived in Cornwall. It's home.'

'I know. It's just . . . well, you're here.'

'Don't be so soft, Dad.' It was rare that Annie called Ray 'Dad'. Ever since she'd been a little girl, after her mother died, she had got into the habit of calling him Ray, and he had seemed to like it. It was all part of the Bohemian atmosphere of the artists' colony outside St Ives, where she had grown up.

'It's true. You're all I've got, Annie. All that's left of . . . It's all right. I'm still fit and healthy. I don't have cancer or anything. There's nothing physically wrong with me. I'm not moving up here so I can use you as my nursemaid, if that's what you're worried about.'

'It's not. And I wouldn't make a good nursemaid.'

'No bedside manner?'

Annie grinned. 'That's right. It *has* been criticised, at any rate.' She picked up her fork and speared some more salad. They were having lunch in the Black Swan, in the village of Harkside, where she lived. It was a small, quiet pub behind its whitewash and timber facade. Annie didn't eat there often, but she had to admit that, as salads went, this one was a cut above the usual: avocado, quinoa, grape tomatoes. It didn't go with the pint of Swan's Down bitter very well at all, but that was something she could live with.

'When would you want to start this house hunt, then?' she asked.

'Soon as possible. Right away.'

Annie dropped her fork. 'You mean . . . like now? Today?'

'That's what right away usually means. Not today, perhaps, but after the weekend. Monday. Why? Is there some problem?'

'No. No. It's just that I could have used a little warning, that's all. I thought this was a preliminary visit. A recce, like. I mean, don't you have to go back and turn off the water or pack a bag or something?'

'Sorry, love. All done. At least until I find somewhere.'

'Can't be helped, I suppose. What about your paintings?'

'Zelda's taking care of them. I can trust her.'

'Zelda?'

'Long story. So it's OK, then? I can stay?'

'Of course you can. As if there was ever any question.' There was no way Annie could turn him away. He was her father. He had brought her up, had always been there for her – well, almost always – had loved her and cared for her, even if he hadn't made a lot of personal sacrifices to do so. He hadn't changed his lifestyle, for one thing, which had made her child-hood interesting, to say the least.

But her cottage was so tiny, and the walls were so thin. It would mean an end to nights with Nick until . . . well, who knew how long it would take Ray to find a suitable Yorkshire cottage? He was an artist, after all, and he would need a studio, somewhere the light was right, preferably with a fine pano-rama. He could be fussy, demanding and hard to please, despite his laissez-faire demeanour. It was a lot to ask, and it would be expensive. Still, she also knew that he was successful and not without funds. He did a brisk trade in Cornwall during tourist season – landscapes, seascapes and portraits – but his more serious Impressionist-influenced work hung in respectable galleries and fetched ever-increasing prices. At least he wouldn't be a financial burden.

'Of course,' he said, as if reading her mind, 'I could always afford a hotel or a B and B, if that's what you'd prefer?'

Annie thumped his arm playfully. 'Don't talk daft. I told you. You can stay at mine till you get somewhere.'

Annie's mobile rang, its 'Winkworth Gong' ringtone imitating the bell of a sixties' police car. 'Sorry, got to answer this,' she said. 'Work.'

She walked out into the street and put the phone to her ear. It was Chief Superintendent Gervaise, the Eastvale Regional Area Commander, and her voice sounded tight, urgent. 'We've got a serious incident. Shooting at a wedding. St Mary's church near Fortford. Nothing clear on how many casualties yet. All hell's breaking loose around here so you'd better get out there ASAP. And see if you can get hold of Detective Superintendent Banks. He should be on his way back from Peterborough by now.'

Annie could hear voices in the background, shouts, phones ringing, heavy footsteps. As she said, 'Yes, guv,' the only thing she could think of was Winsome. Her friend and colleague DS Winsome Jackman was supposed to be going to a wedding at St Mary's, Fortford, today.

Feeling light-headed and sleepy from the hastily consumed second glass of wine and early morning, Banks was glad to find that he had two seats to himself, facing forward. The previous evening, he had compiled a playlist on his computer and downloaded it on to his iPod for the train home. He leaned back, adjusted his headphones and cocooned himself in his own little world as he watched the landscape flash by through half-closed eyes.

He enjoyed the lush countryside of the English heartland. Even now, in December, the sun was shining on fields of stubble and distant rolling hills. Now and then the train would flash by a village, or he would catch sight of a steeple or squat Norman church tower in the distance, a stately home on top of a rise. Car windshields flashed in the sun. People walked their dogs down country lanes.

There was a stretch he particularly liked, a series of small lakes separated by grassy banks and copses, where he could usually spot at least two or three fishermen sitting far apart with their rods angled, lines far out in the calm water. The sight always made Banks want to take up fishing. There they sat like Buddhas, still and contemplative, waiting for the bite, the twitch, nirvana. Maybe they were thinking of the bills they had to pay, or the office girl's tits, but they always seemed so focused on the sublime, so at one with the elements. The only times Banks had been fishing, he had been bored silly, and he hadn't caught so much as a stickleback.

As the train sped by the ponds, Banks found himself listening to Andy Roberts singing 'Gliders and Parks', which he had included because it reminded him of the day he had met Emily in Hyde Park and she had ended their relationship. It wasn't so much the narrative as the mood the song created. That was followed by 'First Boy I Loved' by Judy Collins, then Roy Harper's 'I'll See You Again'. He knew he was indulging himself in gross sentimentality, not to mention nostalgia, but he didn't care. It was *his* death, *his* mourning, and he would cry if he wanted to.

But he didn't.

Memories of Emily didn't cascade effortlessly in his mind, though he could picture her standing before him, the little scar on her upper lip where she had fallen off her tricycle as a young girl, the way it twisted when she smiled; her pale, smooth complexion, waves of long blond hair tumbling over her shoulders. He had always told her that she reminded him of Julie Christie in *Doctor Zhivago*, and it was true that there had been something luminous about her, as if the light always favoured her eyes and lips. But Emily was no ethereal being; she could be earthy, impulsive, even crude. She laughed a lot, he remembered, but she could be serious, too. And she was moody, mercurial. There were times when it had been exceedingly difficult to get through to her at all, when she had remained a silent, aloof and enigmatic presence, especially towards the end of their relationship.

They had listened to *Ziggy Stardust* when it first came out, and he did remember that 'Starman' had been one of Emily's favourites from the beginning. He was stunned to discover she had still liked it enough that she chose to have it played at her funeral. But he hadn't known much about her recent life at all. He hadn't even known that she worked for Médicins Sans Frontières. If Dave hadn't clipped the death notice from the local paper and sent it to him, he wouldn't even have known that she had died. When your friends and lovers start dying, you begin to feel as if you have only narrowly escaped the reaper yourself, and that it's only a matter of time. Which, of course, it is. In the meantime, there's a version of survivor's guilt to deal with.

He found himself wondering if Emily's children would find anything of him when they cleared out her house. Would they find old photo albums and mementos of events and experiences meaningless to them? Rock concert posters? Ticket stubs? Love letters? Postcards? The Tibetan bracelet he had given her for her birthday? The silver ring?

The train stopped at Newark, then Doncaster. When the food trolley rattled by, Banks stirred himself and bought a cup of coffee and a Penguin biscuit, opened the tray by the empty seat beside him and set them down.

It always took less time to get from Doncaster to York than he expected, and soon after York came Northallerton. His stop. He switched off his iPod halfway through George Harrison's 'All Things Must Pass' and put it in his briefcase beside an anthology of English poetry he hadn't opened for a few days. The last poem he had read was Keats's 'Ode on a Grecian Urn', which he had enjoyed very much.

He had turned off his mobile for the funeral service and forgot to turn it back on again. Now, as he prepared to get off the train, he did so. The infernal thing practically exploded in his hand with urgent messages and texts. Something seriously bad had happened while he had been away. Juggling the phone in one hand and his briefcase in the other, he walked along the platform and listened to the first message from DI Annie Cabbot.

2

By the time Banks arrived in Fortford, the whole village was swarming with police, and the curious inhabitants had been strongly advised to stay in their homes. Naturally, they didn't, and the police community support officers had a job on their hands keeping everyone behind the police tape at the southern edge of the village green.

According to Annie, on receiving Terry Gilchrist's phone call at 1.03 p.m., the dispatcher had consulted with her control room inspector, who had ordered that no unarmed officers or emergency services personnel should attend the scene until given the all clear by Firearms Support Command, even though Terry Gilchrist had claimed that he had seen the shooter leave the hill.

Firearms support had sent their three closest armed response vehicles, and the officers had just finished securing the area around the church, about a quarter of a mile south of the village itself. Uniformed officers had then contained the scene and constructed designated pathways and meeting points so that the investigators could do their jobs and the paramedics could move in and out and take care of the injured. There were still no accurate reports on exactly what had happened in the churchyard, or how many people had been hurt.

Banks showed his identification at the second checkpoint, about a hundred yards from the church itself, signed the officer's log, then sprinted briefly to catch up with Annie Cabbot and DCs Doug Wilson and Geraldine Masterson, who were slightly ahead of him. Chief Superintendent Gervaise was Gold Commander, coordinating things back at Eastvale HQ along with representatives from the emergency services and firearms support.

A line of authorised firearms officers, resembling an invading army in their full personal protective equipment, stood outside the churchyard, facing the hill opposite. Banks could see a number of other armed officers moving about on the hillside itself. Each AFO carried a PR-24 baton, rigid handcuffs and CS spray, along with the Glock side arm and Tasers. Because of the seriousness of the incident, they were also carrying Heckler & Koch MP5 carbines, which they usually kept locked in the boots of their vehicles. They made a chilling sight.

'Any news?' Banks asked as he caught up with the others.

'Nothing yet,' Annie answered. 'How was the funeral?'

'As you'd expect. Winsome?'

'I've talked to Terry on his mobile. Winsome's been hit, but he couldn't say how serious it is. The AFOs have searched the hill area, which is where Terry said the shots were fired from, and they confirm the shooter's definitely gone. They think they've found the spot he fired from and secured it for forensic examination. Gold Command has instructed that everyone unharmed inside the church should remain there until the ambulances have cleared the dead and wounded. We've arranged coaches for the uninjured. Eastvale General's been advised to expect the casualties. So have James Cook Hospital and Leeds Infirmary. As far as anyone knows, there were about sixty guests in all. It was a bit of a local celebrity wedding. In the papers and all that.' She swallowed. 'It's a bloodbath, Alan, like nothing we've had before.'

'Media? You said it was a celebrity wedding.'

'We're not talking Madonna or royalty or anything. There were a few reporters and photographers, but they either ran away or took refuge in the church.'

'Pity for once the place wasn't swarming with them,' Banks said. 'It might have made the killer think twice, or one of them might have got some footage of him. What about the wedding photographer?'

'I don't think so,' Annie said. 'He caught a splinter of stone in one eye. But we'll be checking out all photos and videos taken at the scene. Terry said he's done what he can for the injured,' Annie went on. 'He managed to tie some tourniquets and staunch the blood flow on a couple of victims. He said it took ages for the AFOs to get here. It's been well over an hour since the shooting.'

Banks glanced at his watch. 'I know,' he said. 'I was just getting off the train when I got your messages. I drove as fast as I could from Northallerton. I'm sorry my mobile was turned off earlier.'

'It doesn't matter. There's nothing you could have done on the train except fret. We've only just been permitted to approach, ourselves. Before that, it was armed personnel only. We couldn't get near the place. The first armed response vehicle didn't arrive until 1.41 p.m., and they had to search the area and make sure the shooter wasn't still around. Some of the paramedics and doctors are really pissed off. They say people could have been dying up here while they were tied up in red tape.'

The four detectives walked through the lychgate into the old country churchyard. Banks saw the wounded sprawled here and there, sobbing and clutching torn bits of shirt or dresses to staunch their bleeding. He could hear more ambulance sirens in the distance, and already paramedics were making their way around the churchyard along the common approach path designated by bright yellow plastic squares, like garish stepping stones, marked out to avoid people contaminating the scene. Peter Darby, the crime-scene photographer, was already hard at work amid the carnage. These were the 'golden hours', the period closest to when the crime had taken place, and evidence would never be as fresh or as plentiful as now. Dr Burns, the police surgeon, glanced up as Banks passed. Banks had never seen him so pale.

One beautiful young woman in a coral-coloured dress sat propped up against a gravestone shaking and whimpering, 'Help me. Please.' Her lap was soaked in blood and her hands were clutched around her stomach, as if she were trying to hold her insides in. With her long blond hair and her pale heart-shaped face, she reminded Banks a little of Emily Hargreaves. A doctor hurried past him towards her. Another girl lay on the grass with half her head missing. She resembled an actor from that zombie TV programme wearing a realistic prosthetic.

'How many victims?' Banks asked.

'Seven or eight, according to Terry. It's not official yet.'

'Adrian Moss here?' Moss was their media liaison officer, and he would soon be much in demand.

'Not yet.'

Banks noticed that Gerry Masterson, the newest and youngest team member, had turned white. She was slowing to a halt, as if marooned on one of the yellow pads, staring at the girl holding her stomach by the gravestone. Banks thought he could see Gerry start to shake. Quickly he went over to her and grasped her arm. 'Come on, you'll be OK,' he said. 'Look at me. Deep breaths. One. Two. Three.'

Gerry turned towards him, her nostrils flared, eyes wild, then she gave a slight nod. Her shoulders stiffened, and he could see the effort she made, slowing her breathing, staring fixedly straight ahead at the church doors. 'I'll be all right, sir,' she said through gritted teeth.

Banks could hear children crying the moment he stepped through the doors, but it took a while for his eyes to adjust to the gloom inside the church. There were people everywhere, some silent, some crying, some just talking. Banks saw a flower girl, with her hair in ringlets, holding her bouquet and sobbing. She had blood on her dress and her face, but he didn't think it was hers. A little boy in a smart suit had his arm around her and was trying awkwardly to get her to be quiet. Next he saw the vicar sitting on the worn stone step by the altar, hunched over, head lowered, hands clasped in prayer, mumbling to God. Then he spotted Terry Gilchrist holding someone in his arms, leaning against a stone column.

Banks hurried over to Terry and saw, as he had expected, that it was Winsome he was holding. Her arms were wrapped around her raised knees, clutching them tightly to her chest. There was blood all over the front of Terry's shirt as well as on his suit and face. Winsome's peach satin dress – the one she had been so thrilled to find on sale – was smeared and stained with blood, too, and he noticed a bloody streak running across the top of her bare left shoulder. Something had made a furrow in her skin. The cut wasn't bleeding much, a superficial flesh wound at best, but she had come *that* close. Winsome was trembling; her tear-filled eyes seemed unfocused, directed inwards, unaware of her surroundings.

'She's in shock,' Terry said. 'She needs a doctor, but there are people far worse off. You've seen what it's like outside.'

'You were out there when it happened?'

Terry stood up, but he didn't take his eyes off Winsome. Annie took his place beside her. 'I did the best I could. I tried to get everyone inside to safety. The shooter nicked Winsome's shoulder. She's lucky. I think the bastard was using hollow points, judging by the damage he's caused. I saw him leave the hill over the road, heading south. I think the waiting was the worst. People were crying everywhere, screaming in pain. We could have got the ambulances and paramedics in much sooner, they were just waiting for the word, but the firearms officers wouldn't let anybody past, and it had taken long enough for *them* to get here. Christ, Alan, people were *dying*. Winsome could have died. The bastards just wouldn't take my word for it that the shooter had gone.'

Banks touched him lightly on the shoulder. 'You did the best you could, Terry. Remember, I know your military background but the others don't. They had to follow procedure. Don't worry, we'll get Winsome some attention soon enough. She'll be fine. What about you?'

'I'm OK.'

Banks stood up and surveyed the scene. Gerry and the others were squatting on their haunches, talking to witnesses. The sirens he had heard out in the churchyard stopped suddenly, and then more paramedics and doctors rushed into the church bearing stretchers and medical supplies.

Banks stood on top of the hill opposite the scene and watched the activity in the churchyard. Tiny figures, like a Lowry painting. The hillside sloped gently down towards a field full of sheep across the road from St Mary's. They were grazing innocently, as unaware of what had happened as the horse scratching its behind on a tree in the Auden poem about the fall of Icarus. To his left, he could see the village of Fortford, at the junction with the Helmthorpe Road, a cluster of stone cottages with flagstone roofs huddled around a village green, the familiar Roman hill fort, the whitewashed facade of the Lamb and Flag. Behind him stretched the moors, a tangle of bare heather and gorse, like coiled barbed wire among the rocky outcrops. On the other side of the road, behind the church, a similar hillside sloped up to similar moorland. It had been a perfect sniper's day, not even a hint of a breeze nor a drop of rain, but now the wind was whipping up again and the rainclouds were gathering fast. It was close to four on a Saturday afternoon in early December, and it was already getting dark, a chill creeping into the air from the north.

Banks was joined by Stefan Nowak, crime-scene manager, and Superintendent Mike Trethowan, head of the firearms cadre. The three men stood by a section of the hilltop surrounded by police tape, inside which two CSIs were busy erecting a makeshift canvas tent over the area where the shooter had lain.

'Find anything yet?' Banks asked.

'Ten shell casings,' said Trethowan. 'They've gone to ballistics.'

'Anything else?'

'Not yet,' Nowak answered. 'The grass is clearly flattened, as if someone has been lying there. No doubt there'll be other traces when we organise a full search. Fibres, most likely. Who knows, maybe he smoked a cigarette and left us a nice DNA sample.'

Trethowan pointed to a rough path leading diagonally down the hillside to their right. 'Mr Gilchrist said he saw the shooter head down there,' he said. 'We've already got road blocks up. Alerts have gone out all over the county. If only we knew what we were looking for. We're still waiting for the sniffer dogs up here.'

'Vehicle?'

'We don't know. I assume so. Plenty of spots to park it out of the way nearby. They're all being checked out. It's not a busy road. And there's no CCTV for miles.'

Banks knew the road well enough. It was a pass that cut sharp south from the main east–west Helmthorpe Road. After climbing then winding through a long stretch of wild moorland beyond the youth hostel, it dropped slowly into the adjacent dale. From there, anyone could easily get to Harrogate, York or Leeds, and from there to the M62 or M1. The killer had a good start. He could be well on his way to London by now, and they would be none the wiser as they had no vehicle description to go on.

That was, of course, assuming the killer wanted to get away.

Banks glanced back down on the scene. It was hard to believe that such a horror could have taken place in broad daylight, on such a joyous occasion and in such a beautiful spot. The squat Norman church, originally built in 1174, had the traditional square tower with clock, and the limestone was a greenish grey colour in the dimming light. Many of the tombstones stood at precarious angles, and most were spotted with lichen or overgrown by grass. The more recent ones seemed well tended, with vases of bright flowers placed before them.

St Mary's was one of the best known and loved churches around, and it had once been the place for all burials in the dale. Inhabitants of the more remote western villages and farms had carried, or brought on carts, the bodies of their loved ones along the 'Corpse Way' for Christian burial there, as there was no closer church that could accommodate them. Like St Andrew's in Swaledale, it had become a sort of 'Cathedral of the Dale'. Now this.

'What about the risk factor?' Banks asked.

'I'd say it wasn't very high,' Trethowan answered. 'It's a clear day, yes, for once, but that's more a matter of good fortune than weather forecasting. It was supposed to rain, and you can see that's coming, but we got a brief stay for some reason.

You wouldn't necessarily get a lot of walkers up here at this time of year, though. Besides, the other side of the valley is more popular, more scenic. I'd say he probably worked it out in advance, chose his spot well.'

'But if he was lying there in the grass overlooking the church, there's a chance that someone might have spotted him, isn't there? A dog-walker, someone like that.'

'There's always a chance, Alan. Always an element of risk,' said Trethowan. 'But if a dog-walker or a couple of ramblers had come along, he'd probably have shot them, too.'

'Fair enough. Why did the ARVs take so long to get to the scene, Mike?'

'Oh, for Christ's sake. Not you as well.'

'What do you mean? You know it's going to come up. And I'm in the bloody hot seat here.'

Trethowan sighed. 'We're well trained, but we're not used to firearms incidents in these out-of-the-way parts, as you know. The nearest ARV was in the Middlesbrough area. They got here as quickly as they could. Traffic was heavy. They could hardly sprout wings and fly.'

'And in the meantime there were people wounded and dying here.'

'I'd like to know how we can do any better with the resources we've got. Most of our firearms officers and support units have been targeted towards cities and towns where there's more risk of terrorist threats. Shopping centres, sports and music stadiums, that sort of thing. We've got hardly anyone left in North Yorkshire.'

'I understand that, Mike, but Terry Gilchrist told you he'd seen the shooter leave but you still wouldn't let the medics through.'

'There might have been more than one. Or he might not have gone very far. Or Terry Gilchrist might have been mistaken. We had no idea how reliable he is. There arc any number of problems with a vague witness opinion like that. You can't trust it. You know we're supposed to be on the scene to protect unarmed police officers as well as emergency services personnel. Who gets the blame if a civilian or a paramedic gets shot? We do, that's who. So nobody approaches a shooting scene until we've cleared it and given the OK. That's how it works. Besides, I don't even know why I'm bothering to defend the action. It wasn't my call. Talk to the Gold Commander.'

'I'm just saying it'll come up. Forewarned and all that . . .'

'Don't I know it?'

'What's the distance, do you think? Here to the churchyard.'

'Between three-fifty and four hundred metres.'

'What's that in English?'

Trethowan snorted. 'Luddite. About a quarter of a mile.'

'It's a long way. What kind of weapon would he need to shoot accurately that far?'

'We don't know how accurately he shot,' Trethowan said. 'He was firing into a crowd. We don't know what, or whom, he was aiming at, other than the crowd. According to Terry Gilchrist, he shot the bride first, then the groom, then the chief bridesmaid, and it gets a bit confusing after that. But even if he was simply aiming in that general direction, the odds are that he'd have hit *someone.*'

'Seven or eight people were hit, I've heard.'

'Sounds about right.'

'Scope sights?'

'Most likely. That would certainly have given him a chance of being more accurate, if he had specific targets.'

'Any idea what sort of weapon the shooter used?'

'Don't quote me on this,' Trethowan said, 'but I'd put my money on the Armalite, an AR15. What they call the "Black

Rifle". The cartridge casings we found bear this out. They're .223 Remington, the same kind the AR15 takes in a twenty- or thirty-round clip. Of course, there are other rifles that use the same ammo, but . . . well, the AR15 is the most common. You asked what I thought.'

'Illegal, I should imagine?'

'Not at all. Very popular with enthusiasts. But it's available to competition shooters only as a straight pull version.'

'Meaning? It's a long time since I took a firearms awareness course.'

'You have to pull the bolt back to empty the chamber and reload.'

'So it takes time? Could he have done that quickly enough to get off as many shots as he did?'

'Ten? Yes. Easily. And he obviously did. It would have taken less than a minute. From what Mr Gilchrist told us, it was definitely straight pull, not semi-automatic fire. And he should know his stuff, with his military service. If it had been an illegal firearm, a semi-automatic, say, there would have been a lot more people killed.'

'Bullets?'

'You'd best ask the pathologist about that when he digs them out.'

'Terry thinks they were hollow point.'

'And he could well be right.'

'Would the killer need a military background?'

'Not necessarily, but I wouldn't rule it out. There are plenty of rifle and pistol clubs and people who enjoy competitive shooting with a wide range of weapons. Or hunting. He might simply be a good shot.'

'Any chance it was a terrorist attack?'

'Always a possibility, something like this,' said Trethowan. 'Even here. The experts are on their way and they'll be digging deep. But off the record, it's not really terrorist style, is it? A lone gunman, as far as we know, with a legal weapon, shooting from a distance. A country wedding in an out-of-the-way place. Where's the cachet in that?'

'That they can hit us anywhere, anytime they like, and our customs and ceremonies mean nothing to them. They've been going for a lot of "soft" targets recently. Paris, Brussels, Nice, Istanbul.'

'Well, if you put it like that . . .'

'No, I agree with you, Mike. It doesn't have the feel of a terrorist attack. They could have done far more damage sending a man or a woman in the church with an automatic weapon, or strapped with explosives, though I don't suppose you can always find a keen suicide bomber when you want one. I'm just keeping an open mind.' He paused. 'If the gun was legal, we should be able to trace it through the firearms certificate, right?'

'Ostensibly,' said Trethowan. 'The checks to get a certificate are pretty thorough, but people do slip between the cracks. Remember, I only said that guns modified in that way are legal to own. I didn't say this one was obtained legally.'

'OK. But criminals make mistakes, get overconfident. How many certificates might we be talking about?'

'The last I heard there were about seven hundred thousand gun owners in the UK and almost two million licensed firearms.'

'Two million?'

'Easily. About sixty thousand in North Yorkshire alone.'

'A lot of those would be shotguns, I assume?'

'Uh-huh. Typically, in rural areas.'

'So there would be fewer AR15s?'

'Far fewer. We can narrow it down a lot. It shouldn't take us that long to sort them out.'

'The sooner we get started, then,' said Banks. 'Tell your team to start with those living closest to the scene, then work their way out. You know the drill.'

'I'll be sure to advise extra caution, too. If a man uses a legal firearm to commit an atrocity like this, he's got to be expecting a visit from us before long.'

'Maybe he doesn't care,' said Banks.

'That's what I'm worried about.'

Banks could see the news vans arriving, and there were two TV helicopters already overhead, along with the Dales search-and-rescue teams the police had co-opted to scan the moors for the killer. This would be a big story. All eyes would be on them for the next while, however things developed. If a reporter discovered how long it took the ARVs to get to the scene and secure it while people were dying there, and how long it was before they let in medical help, heads would roll, despite the orders to redistribute personnel to urban areas more vulnerable to terrorist attack. And the media *would* find out. Someone always blabbed. Adrian Moss, the MLO, would have his work cut out for him. If a Paris- or Istanbul-style attack occurred in a tourist beauty spot such as the Dales, the Cotswolds or the Lake District, then the terrorists would have all the time in the world to do whatever damage and kill as many people as they wanted before anyone could even attempt to put a stop to them. Talk about soft targets.

Banks heard a rustling sound and turned to see two officers leading sniffer dogs to the site. Mike Trethowan's police radio crackled. 'Sir,' the voice said over the static. 'I've been instructed to ask you if Detective Superintendent Banks is with you.'

'He is,' Trethowan answered.

'His team has just had a call from the youth hostel, sir. Seems somebody up there knows something. One of his officers is already on site. He's been asked to drop by. There's a car waiting at the bottom of the hill.'

Banks nodded to Trethowan and set off down the hill.

Banks got out of the patrol car outside the youth hostel and asked the driver to wait. He looked up at the nineteenth-century manor house with its distinctly Gothic facade, as if the builder had been a fan of Bram Stoker and Ann Radcliffe. It was built of local limestone, like the church, with added wings, gables and a gargoyle or two stuck on for good measure. In the gathering late-afternoon darkness, against a background of heavy rainclouds, with only a few lights showing in mullioned windows here and there, it resembled a spooky old house from a black-and-white horror film. *The House on Haunted Hill*. All it needed was thunder and lightning.

The front door was open, and the woman at the reception desk directed Banks towards the common room and asked if he would like a cup of tea. He thanked her and walked down the vaulted passage. Several armed officers were already conducting a search of the building, as it was only about a quarter of a mile south of St Mary's.

The common room was a cold, high-ceilinged lounge with a huge bay window and a glittering chandelier. Battered armchairs were scattered around, some next to shaded reading lamps. Pop music played quietly in the background, some group he didn't recognise. The room was empty except for DC Masterson sitting opposite a lanky blond boy by the window.

'How are you doing?' Banks asked Gerry when he reached them.

'Fine, sir. I just got here.'

Gerry was all business now, long legs crossed, hair tied in a ponytail trailing down her back, bottle green jacket and black jeans, black polo-neck jumper. She had also regained a bit of colour and a lot of composure, and, judging by the way she averted her eyes, Banks could tell that she felt embarrassed by the earlier episode in the churchyard. That would pass, he knew, but the deeper feelings would remain. He certainly couldn't blame her for such a reaction; it had probably been the worst thing she had ever seen in her life. It could haunt her nightmares for years to come.

It was hardly water off a duck's back to Banks, either, and would contribute significantly to the nightly *danse macabre* that was his dream world. But it wasn't his first scene of carnage: he had seen the young girls' bodies in the cellar of Terence Payne's house; he had been on the spot to help the maimed and dying in the immediate aftermath of a terrorist bombing in London; and more recently he had picked his way through mixed human and animal body parts strewn along the bottom of the Belderfell Pass. All had taken their toll. It wasn't so much the number as the details that stayed with him, like the bridesmaid in the churchyard holding her intestines inside.

'This is Gareth Bishop, sir,' Gerry said. 'He says he's got some interesting information for us. I thought you'd like to be here.'

The gangly youth half stood and shook hands with Banks, then they both sat. Gerry took out her notebook. The woman from reception came in with a tray of tea and set it on the low table between them. 'Give it a minute or two to mash,' she said, then left.

'OK, Gareth,' said Banks. 'What is it you saw?'

Gareth Bishop swallowed. He had a prominent Adam's apple and a shock of fair hair hanging over his left eye. 'I saw a man hurrying down the hill across from the church and getting in a car parked in a lay-by about fifty metres further up the road, towards this place.'

'Just one man?'

'Yes.'

'Was there anyone waiting in the car?'

'Not that I could see, but the windows were dark.'

'Where were you? How far away?'

'I was up on the opposite hill. You have to walk right along the edge on some sections of the footpath. It's quite high up and far back, maybe four or five hundred metres from where the car was parked.'

'So you didn't get a close look?'

'No.'

'How do you know the figure you saw was a man?'

'His shape, and the way he moved,' said Gareth. 'I mean, girls ... they move ... You can just tell. No woman would walk or run like that.' He glanced nervously at Gerry, blushed and put his hands to his chest. 'Or be that shape. He had no breasts.'

Banks saw Gerry smiling to herself as she wrote in her notebook. She probably wasn't in the least surprised that a teenage boy could spot a pair of tits, or the lack of them, at four or five hundred metres. Banks had seen plenty of women with very small breasts, but there was no point telling Gareth that. The lad had a point about the way the men and women moved differently.

'Was he fat or thin?'

'Sort of ordinary, really. In the middle. Not fat, but not skinny. Slim, I guess.'

'Could you see how tall he was?'

'Only in comparison to the car. Not really tall or anything. I'd say he was medium height, about 175 centimetres.'

'What's that in—'

'About five foot nine or ten, sir,' said Gerry, with a patient smile.

Banks poured them all tea. 'I don't suppose you saw his face?' he asked.

'No. I was too far away to see that kind of detail.'

'White?'

'Yes. I think so.'

'What time was this?'

'I'm not certain. I don't have a watch, and I had no reason to take out my mobile. Perhaps about one o'clock, a bit after?'

The timing was right, Banks thought. 'Did you hear anything before you saw this figure?' he asked.

'Yes. I heard the church bells ringing, and some bangs. Not very loud, not from where I was, at any rate. The footpath dips behind the edge for a while and blocks off the view of the road.'

'How many bangs?'

'Dunno. A few. I wasn't counting.'

'Gunfire?'

'I suppose it could have been. You hear guns often out in the country and think nothing of it. Shotguns, usually. Now I know what happened, I could kick myself for not recognising what it was, but . . .'

'Don't beat yourself up, Gareth. There's nothing you could have done without risking getting yourself killed, and, as it happens, you're turning out to be much more useful alive. You're the first person we've come across who saw the car.'

'I am?'

'Yes. What can you tell us about it?'

'It was one of those SUVs, a people-mover. That Toyota you see advertised a lot.'

'The RAV4?'

'That's the one. It had the hatchback and everything. That was where he put whatever it was he was carrying. His gun, I suppose. It opened sideways, like a door.'

'He opened the hatchback and put the weapon in there?'

'I didn't know it was a weapon, but it wasn't long enough for a golf club. I suppose it could have been a fishing pole. They come apart into sections, don't they?'

'What did he do next?'

'He got in the driver's side and drove off.'

'Which direction?'

'South. Away from the village.'

'What colour was the car?'

'Black.'

'Are you sure?'

'Well, I suppose it could have been dark green or blue, but it looked black to me.'

'OK, Gareth. You're doing really well. Where were you going when you saw all this?'

'I was heading along the edge, back towards the hostel. I'd been for a long walk in the morning and stopped off at the Lamb and Flag in the village for a sandwich and a pint.'

'So you were on the section of the hill between St Mary's and here?'

'Yes.'

'And you thought you heard some bangs, then you saw a man get in a people-mover, maybe a black RAV4, but you didn't see the church below, what was going on down there? You didn't hear any screams or anything?'

'No. Like I said, the path only comes up along the edge when I saw him getting in the car, about a hundred metres south of the church. Before that, I couldn't see or hear anything very clearly down towards the road, except the bangs and the church bells. But even they sounded distant and muffled.'

'How long have you been staying here at the hostel?'

'All week. I head home tomorrow. Southampton.'

'You're on your own?'

'Yes. A walking holiday. Sort of compensation. I'm . . . well, I just split up with my girlfriend.'

'Sorry to hear it. So you've been out and about a lot this week, then?'

'I suppose so.' He grinned. 'Walking away the pain, you could say.'

'Have you ever seen either the man or the car before?'

'Not the man, no, but the car was there on Thursday.'

'Thursday? Two days ago?'

'Right.'

'Same spot?'

'Yes.'

'Are you sure it was the same car?'

'I never saw the number plate, so I can't be a hundred per cent certain, but I think so. It was the same colour, and it was an SUV.'

What were the odds of another black SUV being parked in the same remote lay-by two days earlier, Banks wondered? Probably very small. So the shooter had been out on at least one recon-naissance mission. He must have heard about the wedding some-where, or read about it in the local press, specifically targeted it, picked his spot, checked out the lie of the land. Annie had said it was something of a celebrity wedding. Could that be a motive? A stalker of some sort? There were still many lines of inquiry to pursue, but Gareth's information had given Banks a degree of focus he hadn't had before. Now he knew at least that the killer had *driven* away from the scene in a black people-mover, rather than heading for a bolt-hole on the moors, which agreed with what Terry Gilchrist said about seeing him hurrying down the hillside. It didn't mean they could call off the search of the moors completely, as he could have dumped the people-mover and struck out over open country, but they could probably afford to scale it down and concentrate on tracking the vehicle.

'OK.' Banks gestured to Gerry, who closed her notebook, then he turned to Gareth. 'Thank you for your time. You've been very helpful.' He handed the youth his card. 'If you remember anything else, however minor you think it is, please call me.'

'Do you know . . . how many?' he asked.

'We don't know yet.'

Gareth hung his head. 'It feels terrible, you know. To have been so close and not known, not been able to do anything.'

Banks stood up and rested his hand on Gareth's shoulder. 'You should think yourself lucky you were over the ridge, out of the way. A walking stick isn't much use against a powerful rifle. Take care.'

As they walked to the car, Banks asked Gerry to check Gareth Bishop's story. 'I know he seemed honest,' he said, 'but stranger things have happened than killers interposing themselves into the investigation. We'd look like a proper pair of ninnies if it turns out he did it all along. I'd like you and Doug to check his alibi at the Lamb and Flag – find out what time he arrived and how long he was there – then check the walk he says he did just to make sure he isn't lying about what he could and couldn't see or hear. Get him to show you it tomorrow morning, if you like. Tell him it's a re-enactment.'

'What about his room at the hostel, sir?' said Gerry.

'The search team will get to it. They're doing the whole place. Though if Gareth did have anything to do with the shooting, he's no doubt got rid of the gun by now.'

Back at the mobile incident vehicle parked beside the church, Banks asked if there had been any developments. There hadn't, and the only comfort Banks could take from that scrap of news was that nobody else had been shot.

3

Banks arrived at the boardroom in Eastvale Regional HQ just before eight o'clock that Saturday evening and found the whiteboards already plastered with photographs of the victims. The ancient wool merchants with their purple-veined noses, whiskers and roast-beef complexions, staring down from their gilt frames on the walls, would probably wonder what on earth was going on. Because of the nature and scale of the crime, the usual team had been augmented by staff from county HQ, civilians as well as police officers. All the chairs around the long polished oval table were taken, and someone had brought in some folding chairs for the people at the back. The shooting was now of national concern. People were scared. An armed killer was on the loose, and nobody had any idea who he was or where he might strike next.

The only new development was that the sniffer-dog's trail had stopped at the lay-by where Gareth Bishop said he saw a man get into a black people-mover. Stefan Nowak's team was working the lay-by, intent on drawing even the tiniest amount of trace evidence from it. They had found a partial tyre track that Stefan believed could belong to a RAV4, so that was a start.

Banks had called the meeting to get a fix on who the victims were and to steer the investigation in the most fruitful direction. He wished he knew what that was. He felt the weight of responsibility, and he couldn't afford to be wishy-washy; the team was depending on him for leadership and authority. Most of them wouldn't get to meet the higher ranks who moved the pieces behind the scenes, but Banks was the senior investigating officer, and he was on the front line with his troops.

Banks stood by the whiteboards and faced the crowd. He already knew that there were three dead and six wounded, including Winsome. Ten shots, nine casualties, one bullet in the church door. Was that precision marksmanship or simply shooting fish in a barrel, as Mike Trethowan had said? Three of the wounded, including the groom, were in critical condition.

Banks summarised what they already knew about the shootings then walked over to the board of photographs, where he went on to share what he knew about the victims. He pointed to the first photograph. 'Let's start with the dead,' he began. 'As many of you already know, it was a fairly high-profile wedding for these parts, and it got a fair bit of coverage in the local media. First victim: the bride. Her name is Laura Tindall. She was a successful model, then she switched to running an agency. Laura was in the process of moving from the Docklands area of London to a country home near Lyndgarth with her husband-to-be. One bullet to the heart. She died instantly.' He moved on. 'Second, we have Francesca Muriel, her maid of honour, who also lived in London and was a work colleague at the agency and a close friend of Laura's. Head shot. Thirdly, there's Charles Kemp, father of the groom. Bullet wound to the chest, puncturing his right lung. He ran a software development company on the outskirts of Northallerton. Those are the dead. Dr Glendenning and his assistants will be carrying out the post-mortem examinations as soon as possible. I'd like to add that many of the survivors are in poor psychological shape, as you can imagine, and we may not be able to talk to some of them for a while. Also, Chief Superintendent Gervaise has arranged counselling for those who need it – and that doesn't only mean the wedding guests.

'Now the wounded. Benjamin Kemp, bridegroom. The bullet hit his liver. He's in intensive care. After he left the military, Benjamin went to work for his father's company and lived in Northallerton. Diana Lofthouse, bridesmaid, an ex-model and another close friend of Laura's, was shot in the back. She should survive, but she's unlikely to walk again. Next, Katie Shea, another bridesmaid. Shot in the stomach.' Banks glanced at Gerry, who looked down at her clasped hands on her lap. 'She has extensive internal damage. It's touch and go. In addition, there's David Hurst, a wedding guest, friend of the groom, with a leg wound, the photographer, Luke Merrifield, who may lose an eye, and our very own DS Winsome Jackman, friend of the groom, who was lucky to escape with a minor flesh wound to her shoulder. Winsome, I'm happy to say, has already been released from hospital and is resting at home with her fiancé, Terry Gilchrist, the hero of the day. Winsome is under mild sedation for shock and pain, but I'll be talking to both of them at some length tomorrow. And that, ladies and gentlemen, is the tally. The bride's parents, Robert and Maureen Tindall, were uninjured, as was the mother of the groom, Denise Kemp.'

'Why?' Banks heard someone ask. 'For Christ's sake, *why*?'

'A good question,' Banks said. 'One thing we have to accept is that we may never know. Alternatively, we may find out, but we might not be able to understand. It may seem like a madman's reasoning to us. But if we are dealing with a rampage killer, we may discover what triggered him, and we may also find that the wedding was simply the most convenient or dramatic way he could find to express his sick needs. Don't expect any easy answers. All we have right now are theories.

'I want to know everything you can find out about the victims, especially those who are deceased. Start with their movements over the last twenty-four hours, including what they ate for breakfast this morning and who they stopped and said hello to on the way to the church. Nobody knows what trigger sets off an event like this. We have information that leads us to believe a certain amount of forethought went into this shooting, so you may find yourself going back beyond those twenty-four hours. Use your judgement. If you come up with anything you think is the remotest bit relevant, tell me. We've already got plenty of officers out there canvassing the dale, and all shooting clubs and legal gun owners are being contacted through information from their firearms certificates – especially owners of AR15s.'

A hand went up. 'Isn't it possible we're dealing with terrorists, sir?'

'It's a possibility, and one we overlook only at our peril. We already have counter-terrorist officers working the case up here. Special Branch and MI5 are involved, too, I understand. I'd advise you all to stay well out of their way, as they're a none-too-friendly bunch. All I do know so far is that there has been no chatter, and that no group has claimed responsibility. But you know as well as I do that doesn't necessarily mean anything. Any more questions?'

There were none.

'OK.' Banks checked his watch. 'Unless you have already been given a specific duty or action to perform, you'd better get home and get some rest. I'll want everyone back in early tomorrow morning, and if we don't get a break soon, you can look forward to a few sleepless nights. I know it's Sunday tomorrow, a tough day to track down leads. You won't find a government office open on a Sunday, for example, even if it were Armageddon, but there's still plenty to be done. You may also have already noticed we're inundated by media. I'm sure you don't need me to tell you this, but keep your mouths shut. Everything goes through our media liaison officer, Adrian Moss. Area Commander Gervaise has scheduled a press conference in an hour, just in time for the ten o'clock news. That'll have to be enough for them right now. And it goes without saying that all leave is cancelled until we catch this bastard.'

It said something of the way everyone felt about this crime that not one groan rose up from the men and women gathered in the boardroom, and that there was no usual rush for the door to be the first one out.

'Quick coffee before the press conference?' Banks asked Annie in the corridor outside the boardroom.

'Not tonight, thanks.'

'Hot date?'

'Chance would be a fine thing.'

'What about Nick Fleming? How are things going?'

'You know about Nick?'

'It's my business to know everything.'

'Sure. Well, it's fine. What about you? How's your poet?'

'Linda Palmer? Just a friend. She's teaching me about poetry.' Banks had been looking forward to talking with Linda about Hardy's *Poems of 1912–1913*, but he hadn't read them yet and doubted he would get the time. Suddenly Keats's Grecian urn seemed a long way away and a long time ago.

'Is that the literary equivalent of come up and see my etchings? Come up and see my odes?'

Banks laughed. 'Don't be cheeky.'

'Anyway,' Annie went on, 'it's not a date. It's Ray. He's thinking of moving up here, and he wants to stay at mine until he's found somewhere suitable.'

'Is everything all right?'

'Yeah, it's fine. He's fine. It's just . . . he wants to stay with me while he's house-hunting.'

'Is that a problem?'

'Alan, don't be thick. You know how tiny my cottage is. It's like living in a bloody thimble, even on my own.'

'True,' said Banks, remembering his days and nights at the little terraced cottage in the centre of the labyrinth. It was years ago now, but he still had good memories of the brief time when he and Annie had been lovers, before work and careers got in the way.

'He can come and stay with me if he likes,' said Banks. 'I've got plenty of room.'

Annie's eyes lit up. 'Really? He'd like that.'

'Of course. We get along well enough.'

'Well, you like the same music and stuff. I mean, he was listening to Bob Dylan when you were still wearing short trousers.'

'I was listening to Bob Dylan when *I* was still wearing short trousers.'

'You know what I mean. You're about the same generation, so you should have something in common.'

'Same generation? He's got at least ten years on me.'

'Doesn't mean so much when you get to your age, though, does it?'

'Less of your lip, or I'll change my mind.'

Annie held her hand up, palm out. 'All right, all right. I'm sorry. He might as well stay with me for the weekend, then I'll send him over to you on Monday, if that's OK? And I'll be eternally grateful.'

'You'd better be.' Banks reached into his pocket and worked one of the keys off his chain. 'That's a spare,' he said. 'He knows where I live. Tell him to make himself at home. He'll probably need to get some food in. And I'll most likely be late. And if you want rid of him sooner, tell him it's folk night at the Dog and Gun tonight and tomorrow, if he's interested. With a bit of luck, I might just make it tonight myself.'

Annie rolled her eyes. 'I'll be sure to tell him to take his anorak along.'

Banks arrived at the Dog and Gun just in time for last orders and joined the crush at the bar, but he didn't see Ray there. After the kind of day he'd had, he didn't feel like going straight home to a dark and empty house. He wanted people, noise, music, perhaps even company, a bit of harmless blethering to take his mind off things. Finally, pint in hand, he edged his way out of the crowd and found space to lean against the wall. He spotted a few people he recognised, said hello, exchanged a brief pleasantry or two. It might have been his imagination, but he thought he sensed a stunned, subdued atmosphere about the place, which no doubt had something to do with the tragic and bloody events that had taken place only a few miles down the road.

The press conference had gone about as well as could be expected, the best part of it being that Banks himself had hardly had to say a word. Chief Superintendent Gervaise and Adrian Moss had done most of the talking. After the short announcement, which said nothing, but said it quite eloquently, the usual questions tumbled out, many Banks would have asked himself, had he been a reporter. Terrorists. Nutters. Mass murderers. As expected, news of the delay suffered by emergency services had leaked, and the most persistent inquisitors demanded to know how much time had been wasted and how many people had died because of a lack of trained firearms officers. As Banks had expected, that progressed to, 'Shouldn't more police be armed?' which then led to, 'Shouldn't *all* police be armed?'

And so it went on, comparisons with American school shootings, with Raoul Moat and Derrick Bird, even insinuations that refugees, migrants or asylum seekers might have been involved. Banks had been glad to get out of there, which he did as surreptitiously as he could, when the subject turned to how the NHS was coping with the A & E overload and what the waiting times for victims were.

The band finished their instrumental, and the guitar player introduced the final song, a solo by singer Carol Langland. She seemed very young, hardly older than eighteen, with short, spiky blond-and-pink hair, more punk than folk, and a ring through her right nostril and stud through her lower lip, wearing a black KURT COBAIN T-shirt and jeans torn at the knees. Banks hadn't noticed her at first, as she had been standing in the shadows while the band played, but now the musicians all walked offstage and left her there alone.

A hush fell on the audience and Carol Langland started singing an unaccompanied version of 'Farewell, Farewell', Richard Thompson's words set to a haunting traditional melody. You could hear the proverbial pin drop, and there was little doubt in anyone's mind, Banks thought, that the farewells were for the dead of St Mary's. Carol's voice was a pure and clear contralto, with just a hint of husky tremor, though not so much that she sounded like Sandy Denny.

Banks leaned against the stone wall sipping his pint of Daleside bitter and let the music wash over and into him, stilling some of the day's anguish and confusion. His head ached, and his stomach felt permanently clenched, but her voice was so full of youthful yearning and the poignancy of experience beyond her years that it touched him through his pain. He felt the muscles in his neck and shoulders relax and the tension headache disappear. The voice, the melody, the words sent tingles up his spine and brought hot moist tears to his eyes. Tears for Laura Tindall, Francesca Muriel, Charles Kemp, Katie Shea and the rest of the wounded who were lying in hospital beds not knowing whether they would see tomorrow. Tears, too, for Emily Hargreaves, who definitely wouldn't.

'Farewell, Farewell' was followed by 'We Bid You Goodnight', and most of the audience started to drift away. It was close to eleven o'clock and starting to rain by the time Banks pulled up outside his cottage at the edge of the woods, and the house was pitch dark, as he had expected. Banks used the light of his mobile phone to fit his key in the door, which opened directly into his old living room, now a small den where he kept his computer, a comfortable chair and reading lamp. He had left before the post came that morning, but all he found on the floor was a circular about boilers addressed to 'The Homeowner' and a postcard that read 'Having a great time' from his son Brian, who was recording with his band in Los Angeles. The picture on the front showed a long curving vista of Santa Monica Beach and pier. Needless to say, the water was blue and the sun was shining. Banks sighed and set it down on the little table by the door, where he piled the mail he didn't need to answer. He dropped the circular in the recycling box.

When he walked through to the kitchen, he realised that he hadn't eaten since his sardines on toast for breakfast, unless he counted the Penguin biscuit on the train. One disadvantage of living in such an isolated place was the lack of takeaways that stayed open late. The Dog and Gun didn't serve food on an evening, and there was nowhere else open in Helmthorpe after eleven o'clock at night. Banks checked the fridge and found, as he had expected, nothing but a few hard heels of cheese. There was, however, a tin of baked beans in the cupboard over the sink, and as far as he could tell, the one crust of bread left in the bag hadn't developed any green spots of mould yet. Beans on toast it was, then.

After putting the beans in the microwave and slotting the bread in the toaster, he plugged in his mobile to recharge, then went into the entertainment room to choose some music. The Dog and Gun had helped, but he still felt jittery and not in the least bit tired. The twists and turns of the St Mary's shooting were already wearing furrows in his brain, and Emily's funeral lay like a heavy weight on his heart. More music would help. It could be nothing overly busy or emotionally heavy tonight, no Shostakovich or John Coltrane, just cool jazz or gentle chamber music. In the end, he went for Tabea Zimmermann's *Romance Oubliée*, music for viola and piano, and he knew as soon as he heard the opening melody of Hans Sitt's 'Albumblätter' that he had made the right choice. He turned up the volume a notch or two.

Back in the kitchen, he examined his wine rack and settled on a bottle of Primitivo he'd bought on sale at M & S a week or so ago. He poured a large glass and took a swallow. When the microwave beeped and the toast popped up, he plated his baked beans on toast and settled back down to eat in his wicker chair in the conservatory.

He still found it hard to accept that Emily was gone for ever, even though she had been no more than a memory to him for the past forty-five years. And now that lithe, soft, youthful body had first been ravaged by pancreatic cancer, and was now burned to ash. It was a morbid way to think of Emily, he knew, but he couldn't help it when he remembered her smile, the tilt of her head and serious expression on her face when she was listening to a song she particularly liked, the sound of her laughter, the scent of Sunsilk shampoo in her hair. How easily something you thought was safely buried in your past could suddenly come back and cut you to the quick.

He drained the glass and put it aside. It would have to be his last one for tonight, though if truth be told he felt like getting blotto. But the phone might ring at any second. He was no longer simply a detective working a case; he was SIO of a very big, high-profile case indeed, and he might not get a full night's sleep or a proper meal until it was over. The need to turn off like this for a while was vital, but so was the ability to snap back into action quickly. Fortunately, his mobile didn't ring, and he was able to finish listening to *Romance Oubliée* and lose himself in sun-dappled memories of Emily Hargreaves and the golden days of his lost youth.

4

It was still dark the following morning when Banks showered, shaved and dressed for work between gulps of freshly brewed black coffee. He had awoken from a bad dream in the wicker chair in the middle of the night with a crick in his neck and his heart racing fit to burst. He couldn't remember the details of the dream, but it involved Laura Tindall in a bloody white bridal gown. Only he knew that she was really Emily Hargreaves, and she was telling Banks that she was sorry someone was dead, but that it wasn't her fault. After that, he had somehow got himself up to bed, but he had slept only fitfully and still felt stiff and aching when he got in the shower. There was no food in the house, not even bread, sardines or baked beans, so coffee would have to do until he got to work. Then he remembered it was Sunday, and the canteen would be closed. There would be something open in the market square. Bound to be. Takeaway roast beef and Yorkshire pud, maybe.

The Porsche started as smoothly as ever, and he set off, headlights piercing the darkness of the deserted Helmthorpe Road, scaring the occasional wandering sheep back into its meadow. His mobile sat in its cradle, hooked up for hands-free communications.

His first port of call was the incident vehicle at St Mary's, where he found a number of tired CSIs slumped over, heads on the desks. They had been working most of the night. The arc lights were still flooding the churchyard. AFOs stood here and there, Heckler & Kochs cradled in their arms, guarding the area. It was unlikely that the killer would return, but the possibility couldn't be ruled out. Banks had a brief word with the counter-terrorist unit's second in command but learned nothing. Still no chatter, still no claiming of credit, no evidence of terrorist activity.

When he got back in his car, Banks slipped *Ziggy Stardust* in the CD player and turned up the volume. 'Starman' had been playing over and over in his head since he woke up, so he thought he might as well use fire to fight fire and try and exorcise it. His plan worked, but 'Starman' had been replaced by 'Moonage Daydream' by the time he reached the station.

'Alan.' Chief Superintendent Gervaise turned to Banks from the duty sergeant at the front desk. She looked as if she had been up all night. 'I was wondering when you'd be getting here. Follow me, there's someone I want you to meet.'

Puzzled, Banks followed Gervaise upstairs and along the corridor to her office. She opened the door and bade him enter first. Someone was already sitting at the round conference table, cup of coffee in front of her, and when Banks entered, she smoothed her skirt, smiled and said, 'Hello again, Alan. Long time no see.'

Banks could only stand there rooted to the spot, gobsmacked, and hope that his jaw hadn't dropped as far as he felt it had. Gervaise managed to squeeze through the door past him and introduce her guest. 'Detective Superintendent Banks, this is Dr Jennifer Fuller, forensic psychologist. Dr Fuller has very kindly offered to come in and help us out on the case. We're lucky to have an expert of such sterling reputation, especially so early on a Sunday morning.'

Bloody hell, thought Banks. *Jenny Fuller*. Was today going to be as full of surprises as yesterday?

★   ★   ★

Once Banks had taken a couple of seconds to get over his initial shock at seeing Jenny Fuller again, he walked over to her and she tilted her head for him to kiss her cheek. Banks knew it wouldn't take Gervaise more than a few seconds to figure out that the two of them were already acquainted. Why hadn't Jenny told her? Banks wondered. No doubt to surprise him. She could be mischievous that way. But why hadn't she even told *him* that she was back in Eastvale? He could see by the gently mocking smile on her face that his discomfort pleased her; she had always liked to catch people off guard and, as he remembered, she did it very well. Jenny Fuller was the one woman in Eastvale he had come perilously close to committing adultery with. Then she was gone. Off around the world. America. South Africa, Singapore, New Zealand, finally settling to teach in Sydney, Australia. The last he had heard, she was happily married to an Aussie economics professor.

His first impression was that she hadn't changed very much since he had last seen her more years ago than he cared to remember. It was an uncanny feeling, losing Emily and suddenly finding long lost Jenny again, as if he were leaping through time and space like Doctor Who. True, there were a few more wrinkles around her eyes and mouth, but not many, and they only made her that much more attractive, as did the tan. Her pale pink lips were as full as ever, and her eyes still sparkled with mischief, though he fancied he could sense a sadness in them now, something that hadn't been there all those years ago. The short page-boy hairstyle suited her, but the light brown colour was not as he remembered. As far as he could see, her shapely figure had hardly changed at all. Unless she was as lucky in her metabolism as he was, she must have worked to keep it that way.

'I've brought Dr Fuller in to give us some sort of profile on our killer,' said Gervaise. 'I realise there's very little for her to go on so far, but I'm hoping we can at least make a general start and then build up an even stronger individual picture as more information comes in.'

Jenny yawned. 'I'm sorry,' she said, putting her hand over her mouth. No rings, Banks noticed. 'Haven't got over the jet-lag yet.'

'Sorry to call you in at such short notice,' said Gervaise. She turned to Banks. 'I got in touch with a friend at the University of York, and she mentioned that Professor Fuller had just returned from abroad and recommended her.'

'Just?' said Jenny. 'I'd hardly got in the door. Still, needs must, I suppose.'

'Have you had a chance to read the file I sent over yet?'

'Over coffee this morning. So don't expect too much from me. I'm afraid you'll probably get little more than the text-book version.'

'Talking about coffee . . .' Gervaise refilled Jenny's cup and poured some for Banks. 'Now let's get started.'

Banks felt his stomach rumble and hoped they couldn't hear it. Jenny cleared her throat and took a pair of tortoiseshell reading glasses along with a buff folder from her briefcase. They were the kind of glasses you bought off the rack at Boots or Marks and Spencer's, the same as he used, but they gave her a studious appearance. He could imagine her standing at a podium lecturing a class of randy young students.

'First off,' Jenny said, 'I trust you've made arrangements for psychological counselling for the survivors and any of your officers who may need it?'

'Yes,' said Gervaise. 'It's hard to come up with enough counsellors, but it's under control.'

'Good,' said Jenny. 'Well, as far as classification goes, I suppose we'd have to categorise this one as a rampage killer. That statistically makes him far more likely to be a man, so I'll use the male pronoun from now on. Men are more prone to violence. We don't know for sure why, but it seems to be the case. It may be evolutionary, in that men have throughout history been rewarded for aggression. To the victor, the spoils. James Bond always gets the girl. Also, if you consider animal behaviour, you'll find any number of aggressive contests for the privilege of taking a mate, or mates, mostly performed by the males of the species.'

'*Could* it be a woman?' Gervaise asked.

'It could be,' said Jenny, 'but I think it would be more helpful at this point to rule out the more unlikely possibilities along with the traditional list of red flags. A "nutter", for example. People who are mentally ill rarely kill, especially like this, though of course many would say a person would have to be insane to commit such an act. However, that doesn't make for a very scientific argument, or for a useful method of approach to an investigation.' She glanced from Banks to Gervaise over her glasses. 'While it's quite true that the killer may well have a long trail of antisocial acts and psychological problems in his background, from abusive parents and pulling the wings off flies to arson, sexual assault, lack of conscience, outbursts of irrational rage and so on, there are many more individuals who have a similar history but never graduate to mass murder. It's not a natural progression, the way many doctors argue that the route from soft to hard drugs is. I think when you find your man, he *will* have a history of violence and abuse, and he's very likely to have served time in prison or been incarcerated in a mental institution. But so have a lot of other people, and that's not necessarily what will lead you to him. Too many false starts and blind alleys there. That's why it's impossible, even armed with all the facts, to pick out the next mass murderer from the millions of other disaffected individuals. A sad comment, but it's true.'

'We're still considering terrorism as a possibility,' said Banks. 'Even though the investigators haven't got anywhere yet.'

Jenny nodded. 'As you should be. But if that's the case, you won't need me. Most of what I say won't apply if someone kills for ideological reasons, or because he's under the influence of a powerful personality, though it's sometimes surprising when you look deeper into the backgrounds of some of these terrorists. You often find the same pattern that you find in other mass murderers.'

'What *will* lead us to him?' Banks asked.

'I think first you need to know what set him off, what tipped him over the edge. The trigger. This could have been building up for years. He could have felt slighted, humiliated, envious, abused, any number of things – but something pushed him over the edge. Perhaps more than one thing. A combination.'

'How do we do that?' Gervaise asked.

'For a start, we try to push the stereotypes and lists of traits that usually confound cases like this to one side, and then we go from what we know. All I can do is take whatever information you give me and analyse it in the light of scientific and statistical knowledge. It's not perfect, but then profiling isn't an exact science, and I won't try to tell you that it is. Basically, a rampage killer is an umbrella term for a spree killer or a mass murderer. And when we get right down to it, the differences between a spree killer and a mass murderer aren't great, especially in terms of motivation and criminal history. A mass murderer usually commits his acts in one place. A spree killer kills a number of people in two or more locations, a sort of mobile mass murderer, if you like, before either shooting himself or inviting the police to do it for him.'

'So we're dealing with a mass murderer here?' said Banks.

'Not necessarily. Though a spree killer operates at two or more locations, there can under certain circumstances be a cooling-off period of up to seven days between killing sprees. Raoul Moat, for example, up in Northumberland in 2010. He shot three people, one of them his ex-girlfriend, and went on the rampage in the countryside. It was seven days before he was found, and then he shot himself.'

'So our man might not be finished yet?' said Gervaise.

'And we have to wait seven days to see if he does it again?' Banks added.

'Unless you catch him first,' said Jenny. 'Yes, it's a possibility. But you won't just be sitting here twiddling your thumbs, will you? A lot can happen in seven days. And it's not written in stone. He may kill again today, tomorrow, or not at all. He may be a mass murderer who's finished his work, or a terrorist who's melted back into the darkness. Moat obviously made a run for it and survived out there for days, but in the end, when it came to the choice, he took his own life rather than face prison. Remember the Hungerford Massacre in 1987? Ryan killed sixteen people and wounded fifteen in and around the Berkshire village of Hungerford. We don't know why. We assume he had his reasons, but they were explicable only to himself. He also shot himself after being run to ground in a classroom in his old school. You could read all sorts of things into that. And what about Derrick Bird, the taxi driver? Same year as Moat, not far away, in Cumbria. He shot and killed twelve people and wounded eleven more, starting with his twin brother after an argument over a will and tax issues. Then he starts driving around and kills ten people in a forty-five-mile rampage. This all happened on the same day. Bird also shot himself before capture. Or the Dunblane school massacre, sixteen children and one teacher. The killer took his own life. That's the main thing these killers have in common, except for shooting large numbers of people. They shoot themselves in the end when cornered.'

'So what would our man do next, assuming he hasn't shot himself already?' Banks asked. 'Where would he be likely to hide?'

'Good question. I wish I knew the answer. From what I've read, he was cautious enough to visit the site in advance of his act, which shows a more than usual preoccupation with escape. Most of these sort of events happen in America, as I'm sure you know. To the degree that some sociologists are labelling mass shootings a contagion there. Schools, workplaces, shopping malls, that sort of thing. Shootings distinct from terrorist acts. Loners, outsiders, disgruntled employees. Rarely do they go in with an escape route planned. If your killer was so concerned with escape, and he hasn't killed anyone else except the people at the wedding, then it's logical to predict that he had somewhere to escape *to*, wouldn't you agree?'

'A bolt-hole?' Banks suggested.

'Something like that. Somewhere he'd feel safe. Somewhere he'd believe you couldn't find him. He's clever and obviously not lacking the nerve to take risks. He could even have gone home, on the assumption that you're not smart enough to find out who he is or where he lives.'

'He may well be right about that,' said Banks.

'Exactly,' said Jenny. 'But it's good that he thinks he's smarter than you, and that he likes to take risks. It gives him a far greater chance of slipping up, and you a far better chance of catching him when he does. He could even be doing a "purloined letter" and living next door to the police station. That's just a frivolous example, by the way. I'm not suggesting you should dash out and check up on it. But do you see what I mean? The level of premeditation, of planning, makes his actions a bit different from the run-of-the-mill rampage killer.

And whether he's finished with the killing or not, he still has to hide out somewhere unless he wants to get caught, and so far I wouldn't say that he does.'

'Could he already be overseas?' asked Gervaise.

'I suppose it's always possible,' Jenny answered. 'It's true that he could be anywhere, as none of us know who he is or what he looks like. If he's as organised as he appears to be, he no doubt had a change of clothing stashed somewhere, perhaps a passport, too. He could be in Paris wearing a business suit and carrying a leather briefcase by now, for all we know. But let's not get ahead of ourselves. If you start assuming things like that, it tends to affect the investigation, sap confidence, lower morale. All we can do is work with what we've got. You'd have to ask a geographical profiler for a more detailed analysis – that's not my area of expertise – but spree killers generally start close to home. They may travel some distance over the course of the spree, but the starting point, and returning point, if they get that far, is somewhere close to home. Remember Ryan and his old school. We don't know for certain that our man's a spree killer yet, but the same applies to most rampage killers. So let's assume he's not operating too far from home. Unless he is a terrorist – and I'm sure you have experts in that field working with you – there's a very good chance that he'll stick to what he knows, where he knows, where he feels comfortable. Remember, he's not infallible, no matter what he thinks. He will make mistakes. And you have to believe that even if he has fled overseas already, you'll still bring him to justice in the end.'

Banks could follow the logic in Jenny's arguments and accept pretty much everything she said, but he could also see why many police officers were suspicious of psychological profilers. After all, she hadn't told them where to find the killer or how to go about tracking him down. Pep talks were all very well, but how much further ahead were they? 'Can you be more specific about any of this, Jenny?' he asked, trying to word his thoughts as diplomatically as possible.

'Name, address, National Insurance number, you mean?'

'That sort of thing would be useful.'

Jenny laughed. 'Sorry. I warned you not to expect too much or you'd be disappointed.'

'I'm not disappointed, just frustrated.'

'Well, Alan, I don't know if it's in my job description to do anything about that.'

Banks noticed that Gervaise was following the exchange with great interest, and it was hard to miss the sparkle in Jenny's eyes. He felt himself redden. 'Same old Jenny,' he said. 'Batting the ball back and forth.'

'Not so much of the old.' Jenny put her folder down, leaned back in her chair and removed her glasses. 'I know how frustrating this must be,' she said. 'I've been through this sort of thing many times before. Many, many more than I had last time we worked together, Alan. Things have come a long way since then. Certainly profilers have and, in some cases, the police attitude towards us has become somewhat more enlightened, but we're still not miracle workers.'

'I didn't mean to be critical,' Banks said. 'I'm just thinking about this specific crime. So we've got a mass murderer and not a spree killer, maybe, unless he kills again within seven days. That's useful to know, but it doesn't help us, it just puts a ticking clock into the equation.'

Jenny raised an eyebrow. 'I'd say you had that already, wouldn't you?'

'Point taken.'

'Anyway,' Jenny went on. 'I was getting to that, to this specific crime. There are some details I find interesting, in addition to the recce and the planning of an escape route.'

'Such as?' Banks asked.

'Such as the occasion. Why target a wedding? As I said before, in America, schools and workplaces are the main targets. At one time post offices seemed such a breeding ground for mass murderers that it was called "going postal".'

'So what does our killer have against weddings?'

'Not even that,' Jenny said. 'His thinking is unlikely to be so linear. But there's something in there. Something in why he chose a wedding. Perhaps even why he chose that particular wedding. There's all the usual stuff in his behaviour, of course, anger against women, or a particular woman, perhaps a failed marriage in his background, but you need to examine it from all angles. Revenge and envy are often strong motives for mass murderers. They've often failed and are envious of those who appear to have succeeded, or they're avenging some real or perceived slight, perhaps from years ago. Something that might seem quite insignificant to us.'

'The wedding got quite a bit of publicity around Eastvale,' Gervaise said. 'Minor local celebrities and all that. Model. War hero.'

'That's the sort of thing I mean,' said Jenny. 'Anything like that could have set off some dormant desire for revenge. A war hero, for example, could have been a symbol of something he wanted to destroy, maybe because he was a coward, or he thought he should have been given hero status himself but was overlooked. Envy and revenge.'

'Why does it have to be a symbol?' asked Banks. 'Why couldn't it have been that actual wedding itself he wanted to destroy? Or a particular person who was there? The bride or groom, for example. Both were hit. One killed. Could he have been after a specific person? Isn't a cigar sometimes just a cigar?'

'I haven't jumped to any conclusions yet,' said Jenny. 'It's an interesting idea, and of course he could have been after one or more people in particular, people he thought had ruined his life, but I'm afraid I don't have enough to go on to take my analysis any further than that. If it was a terrorist attack, then perhaps a large social gathering was enough of a target. You also mentioned that the groom was a war hero. There could be something in that, too. A military connection. A number of mass murderers were found to have military backgrounds. You should certainly look at the soldiers who were with him in Afghanistan.'

Banks had already thought of that and mentioned it to the counter-terrorist investigator.

'What was the order of killing?' Jenny went on. 'Did that mean something to him, or was he just firing randomly into the crowd? As far as I could make out, there were more female victims than male. Was that simply because they were wearing brighter or light-coloured clothes that stood out more from his perspective up on the hill, or was it deliberate? It would be pretty easy for him to have picked out the women from a group like that.'

'We're not sure of the order yet,' Banks said. 'And the victims weren't all women.'

Jenny consulted her file. 'Five of them were.'

'But there were four men, too. Anyway, we don't know the answer to any of those questions yet,' said Banks. 'We're still trying to piece it together from ballistics and witness reports. We should be able to talk to more of the guests today. Naturally, everyone was pretty much in shock last night.'

'Of course. Be sure to let me know when you have some answers,' Jenny said. 'It might be important.'

'Will do.'

She packed away her folder and glasses in the briefcase. 'If it's OK, I'll head out and try to catch up on a bit of sleep now,' she said. 'Or I'll be even less use to you next time than I am already.'

'You've been very helpful, Dr Fuller,' Gervaise said.

Banks got to his feet. 'Can I give you a lift?'

'No thanks. My car's outside.'

And with that, she was gone.

'Well, that was interesting,' said Gervaise. 'I take it you two have some history?'

'Many years ago,' said Banks. 'In fact, Professor Fuller worked with me on my very first case up here, after London. A peeping Tom. She was very good at her job, even back then, and that was before *The Silence of the Lambs* came out.'

Gervaise hesitated, then went on. 'Alan, I know it's none of my business, but I know where you were yesterday, and I never got the chance to say how sorry I am. Losing a friend is a terrible thing, the memories it shakes loose, even if you've drifted apart. The panicky feeling that you're losing bits of yourself.'

Banks thought she spoke as if she knew what it was like. 'Yes,' he said, hand on the doorknob. 'Yes, it is. Thank you.'

'Childhood sweetheart, was she?'

'Something like that. Yes.'

'Just don't lose sight of the good memories. That's all.'

'I'll try not to.'

'How's the invalid?' Banks asked Winsome when Terry had let them into his house near the village of Drewick, on the eastern side of the A1. Winsome still kept her flat on the fringes of the Eastvale student area, but now that she and Terry were engaged, she was spending more time at his place. Banks had marvelled more than once at how falling in love had loosened the grip of her previous morally strict and strait-laced approach to life. That morning, she lay on the sofa, half sitting up, with a tartan blanket draped over her.

'I'm fine. Really,' Winsome said. 'It's nice to see you, Guv. Annie.'

Annie leaned forward and gave her a quick peck on the cheek.

Terry Gilchrist clapped his hands together. 'Tea, everyone?' Then he went into the kitchen to put the kettle on and leaned in the doorway while it came to a boil.

'How's the shoulder?' Annie asked.

'It's nothing. Just a scratch.' Winsome bit her lower lip. 'It's the other stuff that's most upsetting. I still can't take it in.' Her eyes filled with tears. 'Those people were our friends.'

'I know,' said Annie. 'We're trying to sort out exactly what happened. It's not easy. We're hoping you and Terry will be able to help us put together a sequence of events.'

Winsome glanced at Terry, who came and perched beside her on the sofa, taking her hand between his. 'Terry was more involved than I was,' she said. 'I was inside the church a good deal of the time. Everything was chaos. I didn't know what was going on out there.'

'But not at first,' said Banks.

Winsome fingered the tassels on the edge of the blanket. 'No. Not then.'

'We've even brought in a hotshot profiler from Australia,' Annie went on. 'Seems she's an old flame of Alan's.'

The kettle started to whistle, and Terry went back into the kitchen.

'Before your time,' said Banks. 'Both of you. Believe it or not, I was young once.'

'And married,' said Annie.

'I told you. Nothing happened.' Banks felt his cheeks burning.

'Methinks he doth protest too much. What about you, Winsome?'

'Oh, leave him alone,' said Winsome, smiling. 'Is it true?'

'Is what true?' Banks asked.

'That she came all the way from Australia.'

'Yes. She's taking up a teaching post at York again, where she started out.'

'And you're not married now, Guv,' said Winsome. 'You're free as a bird.'

'But she may not be.'

'Isn't life unfair?' said Annie, with a wink.

Terry returned with a pot of tea and four matching blue mugs on a tray, which he set down on a low glass table in front of the sofa. He still walked with a slight limp, but had shed the walking stick he had used when Banks first met him a couple of years ago. He was a tall, fit young man in his early thirties, maybe a year or two older than Winsome, with a strong jaw, clear blue eyes, close-cropped fair hair and a boyish grin. His beagle, Peaches, lay content in front of the crackling and spitting log fire. Banks could see the garden all misty with drizzle through the window.

Once they each had a mug of hot tea warming their hands, Banks asked Terry if he would recount what happened.

'Of course.' Terry sat on the edge of the sofa, set his tea on the tray and kept hold of Winsome's hand while he talked. 'The service ended and we all piled outside. Well, some of us did. The photographer was trying to get everyone from the main party organised into groups for the photos, but you know what it's like. Some people were chatting. A couple lit cigarettes. He was getting frustrated because everyone was having a bit of a laugh instead of standing in their assigned groups, and it was taking so long.'

'Do you remember the first shot?' Banks asked.

'I was about five feet away, kneeling to chat with Megan, the flower girl, when I heard a crack and I saw Laura spin around and fall in a heap. I didn't realise it was a shot at first because the bells were so loud, but I could see blood on the front of her white dress, and I then knew what had happened.' He paused and shook his head slowly. 'It was as if I'd never been away. For a moment, I was right back there in Helmand. I think everyone just froze for a split second. Of course, we didn't know to expect more shots, or what. All I knew was that Laura had been hit. Bad, by the looks of it. Then I suppose my training kicked in about the same time as someone started screaming. My first thought was to get everyone back into the church in case he fired again. I thought they would be safe in there. Before I could even begin, though, while most of us were still rooted to the spot, there was another shot.'

'Can you remember who was hit next?'

Terry closed his eyes. 'Yes. The second shot hit Ben. That's Benjamin Kemp. The bridegroom. My friend. My God,' he said, putting his free hand to his mouth then wiping his eyes. 'I'm sorry.'

'It's OK, Terry,' Annie told him. 'Take your time.'

'He's right so far,' said Winsome. 'It was Fran next. Francesca Muriel, Laura's maid of honour. I was talking to her at the time, telling her to head for the church. It was . . . I don't know . . . her head . . . it just . . . cracked open, disintegrated. Like Terry says, we hadn't really had time to react to what had happened yet. I turned to run back to the church, trying to urge people on before me. That's when the bullet grazed my shoulder. So I think I may have been the fourth victim.'

'The photographer was hit around then, too,' said Terry. 'And Dave Hurst, one of the guests.'

'So the two of you were directing people towards the church?'

'They were completely freaked out,' said Terry. 'Running around like . . . well . . . you know, chickens. I suppose I was thinking more professionally then, and I knew by the spaces between the shots that whatever make the gun was, it was a single-bolt, not an automatic, and we could be thankful for that. It gave us a bit more time. I remember glancing up at where the shots had come from, but all I could see then was a sort of small black smudge on the edge of the hill. A sniper, or so I thought.'

'By this time,' Winsome said, 'people were starting to get the picture and rush back towards the church doors without my having to tell them. There was a bit of a jam, and I think the next victim was Diana. Diana Lofthouse, another one of the bridesmaids.'

'Yes,' said Terry. 'He shot her in the back just as she was getting near the church door.'

'That makes seven shots,' said Banks. 'There were ten in all. Do you remember who was next?'

'Charles, I think,' said Terry. 'Ben's father.'

'I saw none after Diana,' said Winsome. 'I was too busy trying to get people into the church. The problem was that there were even a few people who'd stayed inside now trying to get out again to see what was going on. It was a bottleneck.'

'Did you notice the next victims?' Banks asked Terry.

'Not clearly,' he said. 'Not by then. Like Winsome, I was too busy trying to get people out of the way. I had little Megan, the flower girl, in my arms, and she was crying. I think I saw Charles go down next – that's Ben's father – then Katie, but I couldn't swear to the order. Katie was just standing there, frozen to the spot. I was on my way over to her. She took one in the stomach and fell back against a gravestone. I don't know if she'll make it. She'd lost a lot of blood.'

'Katie Shea's still critical,' said Banks. 'Same with Benjamin Kemp.'

'I know there were others hurt,' Terry went on. 'David, I think, was shot in the leg quite late on. The photographer was hurt, too. He was holding his eye and it was bleeding. Others had just frozen, like Katie. They couldn't move. Laura's mother, Maureen. I had to go back and pick her up and carry her in. And Denise was kneeling beside Charles, her husband. She didn't want to leave him, but I managed to get her inside. I knew he was dead.'

'You saw the shooter running away, right?'

'I saw a dark figure running diagonally down the hillside towards the south, yes. But he was too far away for me to see any detail. He was carrying some sort of long object at his side. It could have been a rifle.'

'You're sure it was a man?'

Terry wiped the back of his hand across his eyes. 'Sorry. I'm jumping to conclusions. He was a fair distance away. But what kind of woman would do a thing like that?'

'I'm sure you're right,' said Banks. 'A lad from the youth hostel saw the same figure – at least, we're pretty sure it must be the same figure. He seems quite certain it was a man. Something to do with the way he moved, his shape.'

'I couldn't see where he went, or any car. I know what your witness means about the way he moved, though. I think that's one of the things that made me assume it was a man. There were no more shots after I saw him run off, so he must have been the shooter.'

'Anything to add, Winsome?'

'Nothing. I was inside the church while all this was going on. I just remember hearing another two or three shots after I got the door closed. It's still all jumbled up in my mind. Someone made them stop ringing the bells. It was terrible, the noise, and the shots. Terry came in after a while and found me. He told me the shooter was gone and he was going to help the people who'd been hurt out there, that I should stay with the people inside. Maureen took care of me. Maureen Tindall. That's Laura's mother. She was in a bit of a trance, but she used to be a nurse. She sort of went on automatic. I'm sorry, but that's about all I can remember. Terry was in and out a few times, checking on me and the others, then trying to tend to the wounded in the graveyard until the paramedics arrived.'

'Terry?'

'Same here.' Terry finished his tea.

'So let me get this clear,' Banks said. 'You're both pretty certain that Laura was the first victim, then Ben, then Francesca, then possibly the photographer Luke Merrifield, Dave Hurst and Winsome, then Diana, Charles Kemp and Katie Shea?'

'I can't be a hundred per cent sure about Katie and Charles,' said Terry. 'I was more concerned with getting people to safety by then.'

'And I saw none after Diana, as I told you,' said Winsome. 'I was inside the church by then. Do you think it means something? The order?'

'I honestly don't know,' said Banks. 'Ten shots. Nine people hit, including you. Five women, four men. Three dead, six wounded. We found two bullets in the church door, probably the one that nicked you and the wild shot.'

'Whoever did it had to be pretty cool and collected,' said Terry. 'I've known snipers. They're a strange breed.'

'You think this shooter was a sniper?' said Annie.

Terry glanced towards her. 'Well, he certainly acted like one yesterday, even if it was his first time. He stayed in a concealed position and pulled off his shots then made a speedy exit.'

'True enough,' said Banks. 'Special Branch and MI5 will be looking into any possible military or terrorist connections. But whatever the reasons for what happened, we still need to find out as much as we can about the victims. You two can help us with that. If someone hated one or more of them enough, someone unstable, with access to a weapon, then . . . who knows.'

'No,' said Terry. 'No. I can't believe it. Not Laura and Charles and Francesca and the others. I've known Ben since I was in Afghanistan, and I've known Laura, Katie and her friends for as long as Ben did. Laura and Ben had just bought a house not far from Eastvale. She was staying with her parents until after the wedding. They're all just decent, ordinary folk. Nobody could possibly have a reason for wanting any of them dead.'

Winsome rested her hand on his arm. Terry looked at her and swallowed. 'I'm OK,' he said. 'I just can't . . . I mean, these people were our *friends*. And now they're dead. Why?'

Banks paused to let Terry collect himself, then went on. 'What about any previous boyfriends Laura had? She was a beautiful woman, a model. So was Diana Lofthouse. They would have attracted all sorts of men. Anyone madly jealous, a stalker, anyone who felt Ben stole Laura away. Anyone strange in Diana's life? Any incidents from her modelling days?'

'Not that I know of,' said Terry. 'Though I didn't know her then.'

'Any strong political connections?'

'Laura? No way. And Ben's family was just typical North Yorkshire conservative.'

'What about a connection with Francesca, the maid of honour? Or one of the bridesmaids? Diana? Katie? Any trouble, any boyfriend problems lately?'

'Nothing comes to mind,' said Terry. 'Besides, I should think that if someone did want to kill Laura or any of the others specifically, then it would have been a lot easier to do it some other way.'

'You'd think so, wouldn't you? Except that the wedding was the one place they were all together, and the person we're dealing with doesn't think in the same way as we do. It may make sense to him, seem logical, but not to you and me. And I'm not saying he did have a specific target. I'm just asking if you know of anything, Terry, that's all. Then there's the terrorist angle. Both you and Benjamin Kemp were in Afghanistan—'

'So were some of the others. Wayne was there, too. Wayne Powell, the best man. And he was uninjured.'

'Fair enough. But there *is* a military connection. You mentioned snipers earlier.'

'Just because of the method.'

'Yes, but the killer had a military-style weapon – even if it's one that's been adapted to make it legal over here – and he knows how to use it.'

'So you're suggesting there might be some connection with the war? With Afghanistan? Or that we were somehow symbols of oppression, to be made an example of by IS?'

'I'm not sure what I'm saying. Only that there are plenty of military people with some sort of expertise in shooting. But could there be a connection? Maybe even someone you knew. I'm just asking you if you can think of anyone from those days. Any incident. Anyone go off the rails, have a grudge against Benjamin Kemp? Anything from your military time, from Benjamin's military time, that could be in any way connected with yesterday? We know that war can do terrible things to a man's mind. Maybe someone you served with just lost it for some reason. PTSD, for example. What happened was not necessarily a *rational* response to anything.'

Terry ran his hand over his head. 'Yes, but people who suffer from PTSD don't usually go around committing mass murder. I'm sorry, I can't think of anything or anyone offhand, but I'll give it some thought, see if anything comes up.'

'I understand Benjamin is something of a war hero?'

Terry laughed. 'Sorry. He always laughed about it. Said it was more of a media invention than anything else. It was, really.'

'Even so, he did get a fair amount of publicity at the time, didn't he? I wonder if it was enough to make him a target.'

Terry got up, put his mug down and went upstairs. Banks glanced out of the window and saw that it was getting dark. When Terry came down he was carrying a large scrapbook. He went over to Banks and Annie and opened it to a newspaper clipping. It showed a front-page picture of Benjamin Kemp standing outside a burning ruin holding an Afghani boy of about five in his arms. The boy was staring into the camera and tears were running down his dirt-streaked face. Kemp seemed merely determined, his jaw set firm.

'That was what it was all about,' Terry said. 'Ben rescued a young lad from a bombed-out school, under fire, and there was a war photographer on the spot, ready to capture the event. There were about twelve of us involved in that operation. We'd all been in and done our bit. A few minutes earlier, one of our mates had come out with two boys, one under each arm, but the photographer wasn't ready. You know what's so funny about the whole thing? Well, not funny ha-ha, but ironic, I suppose you'd say.'

'What?'

'It turned out it was the Americans who bombed the school in the first place. By mistake. They killed fifty-six children and we managed to pull out seven alive. The Taliban fighters were in another building less than a hundred yards away, shooting at us. We cleared them out later. They'd booby-trapped the building they were in, and there's where I got . . .' He tapped his leg.

'You got a medal, too, didn't you?'

'We all did. But there was no photographer present to capture the moment.'

'Was there anyone involved in that day's operations you think may have taken against Benjamin Kemp? For any reason. Envy. Feeling slighted. Side-lined. Anything that could become warped and exaggerated into an event like yesterday's?'

'Envious enough to shoot up his wedding? No way. We were all just doing our duty. And we were mates. We depended on one another for our lives. I'm not saying events like that happened all the time – it was a pretty intense day, as I remember – but it was wartime, and you did your duty. Everybody thought it was a bit of a laugh that Ben got his picture in the paper, all Rambo.'

'Maybe somebody didn't,' said Banks.

Banks was still not used to his new office. It felt like a suit two sizes too big for him. He had tried to fill the bookcases, but even with a few ornaments, bulky poetry anthologies, forensic texts and orange-covered Penguin paperbacks from the Oxfam shop, there were still too many gaps and not enough family photographs to fill them.

The view was the same as from his old office, only one floor higher up. That Sunday evening, the rain was sweeping down the windowpanes in torrents and bouncing on the cobbles in the market square. The lamps were on in the pubs and shop windows, and Christmas lights and decorations hung all around the square, giving the scene a distinctly Dickensian aspect. Banks could see a few distorted figures shuffling about under umbrellas, and the crowd of reporters, who had set up camp outside the police station. They must be bored, as nothing new had happened during the day.

The office was well enough appointed. Banks's desk was large and solid, he had a small flat-screen TV attached to the wall, on which he could watch relevant breaking news stories and police press conferences on cases with which he was involved, and there was a low round table for small, informal meetings. He also had a Nespresso-like machine, a promotion present from his Homicide and Major Crimes Squad team, and Annie had made it clear when she presented it to him that she and the others expected to be allowed to nip in for a cup of coffee whenever they needed one. Banks had brought in his own Bose mini sound-dock, with a Bluetooth facility for his Nano. The little iPod didn't have much memory, but he rotated its contents fairly often from the large music library on his computer at home.

He was reading over the statements taken so far and listening to the Brahms 'Clarinet Quintet', whose melancholy edge seemed nicely attuned to the weather outside.

Just as Banks was about to tidy up his desk and go home to enjoy one final night of peace and quiet in Newhope Cottage, the sound of his telephone startled him. It was going on for ten o'clock. He picked up the receiver. It was Chief Superintendent Gervaise.

'Still at it?'

'Yes, ma'am,' said Banks. 'As a matter of fact, I was just about to head out.'

'How do you fancy a pint over the road? On me?'

Banks almost dropped the receiver. He had never been for a drink with Catherine Gervaise before; she had always kept a professional distance. He wondered what it was about. 'Of course, ma'am,' he said.

'On one condition.'

'Yes?'

'That you don't call me ma'am.'

The Queen's Arms was almost deserted at that time on a wet Sunday night. Cyril himself was working behind the bar, and true to her word, AC Gervaise folded up her umbrella, went up and bought two pints of Timothy Taylor's Landlord Bitter, one for herself and one for Banks.

'I understand this is one of your favourite tipples,' she said, setting the glasses on the table. She had changed out of her uniform and wore a simple cream blouse and navy skirt with a matching jacket.

'To what do I owe this honour?' Banks asked.

Gervaise said nothing, just shuffled in her seat and made herself comfortable. Banks drank some beer. Cyril had one of his interminable sixties' playlists going, and Gene Pitney was singing 'That Girl Belongs to Yesterday' in the background.

'It's something I wanted to tell you in person,' she said. 'It's been a trying two days, and I'm afraid I'm not going to make things any better.'

'Oh?'

'I just got a call from James Cook Hospital in Middlesbrough. Katie Shea died on the operating table at five past nine tonight.'

Banks felt the beer turn to lead in his stomach. His teeth clenched and his chest tightened. He felt like standing up and kicking the table over, throwing a chair through the window. Instead, he took several deep breaths, only vaguely aware of Gervaise's hand on his forearm.

'I suppose I knew it was bound to happen,' he said eventually. 'Gerry will be devastated.'

'I heard about DC Masterson in the churchyard,' said Gervaise. 'She'll be fine, Alan. She's young and resilient. It's you I'm worried about.'

Banks gave her a flicker of a smile. 'Me being old and weak?'

'You having had rather too much misery for one weekend. I wasn't there, but I understand Katie Shea was in very poor shape.'

'She was holding her guts in with her hands and a bit of material Terry had found for her,' Banks said. 'Begging for help, but the bloody gunslingers didn't get there for three-quarters of an hour, and it was almost as long again before they let any medics in.'

'You know that's the protocol, Alan. It was nobody's fault. Certainly not the AFOs'. Nobody but the killer's.'

'Even so . . .'

'You'd like to throttle someone. I understand.'

Banks drank some more beer. For the second night in a row he felt like getting rat-arsed, but he couldn't. He had a feeling that no matter how much he drank, it would have no effect on him, anyway; it wouldn't take the anger and sadness away, would hardly even dull it. A sudden image of Katie Shea propped against the gravestone flashed through his mind. The expression on her face, the fear, pain and despair there, as if she *knew* what was going to happen, *knew* she was down to her last few sacred minutes on earth. Perhaps he was being fanciful, but that was what he had felt. A young woman who not long earlier had her whole life ahead of her was now facing certain death, and she knew it. He didn't know whether Katie had any religious faith. That might have given her some comfort towards the end. Banks hoped so, for her sake, though he had no such faith himself. He remembered, too, the look on Gerry's face. She had seen death before, but nothing quite like Katie. It had shaken her to the core. Yes, she was young and resilient, but she wouldn't forget that day in St Mary's churchyard; she would carry it with her always; it would change her.

'Don't make it personal,' Gervaise went on. 'Your old sweetheart's death is personal, but this is what your job is about. It wasn't only Katie Shea. Laura Tindall died from a gunshot wound to the heart. Her maid of honour had her head almost blown off. Need I go on?'

Banks shook his head and finished his drink. Gervaise had about three-quarters of a pint left.

'Want another?' she said. 'Or a whisky perhaps?'

'Are you trying to get me drunk, ma—' Banks managed to stop himself before he got the title out.

'Furthest thing from my mind, but you've got an empty glass in front of you, and you're not going anywhere yet. Don't worry about driving. Leave your car and I'll drop you off home.' She pushed her beer aside. 'I don't even want this. I'm a white wine spritzer girl, myself. So what's it to be?'

'Macallan, please,' said Banks. 'If that's OK.' He couldn't face another beer.

With that, Gervaise went to the bar and got him another drink. 'Cyril said it's on the house,' she said when she got back. 'Double. Says you look as if you need it.'

Banks glanced over at Cyril, who gave him a nod and a wink. 'Taking bribes from the publican,' he said. 'What will it come to next?' The song changed. Skeeter Davis, 'The End of the World'.

'You don't have to worry about me,' he went on. 'But thanks for telling me in person, not over the phone, and thanks for the drinks. That makes four dead now, right?'

'Yes. And Benjamin Kemp is hanging on by a thread. They don't think he'll make it through the night.'

'What about Diana Lofthouse?'

'The spinal cord was severed. There were other injuries, internal organs, but that's by far the worst. It's unlikely she'll walk again. As yet, they're not sure if she'll be a quad or a para.'

'What a bloody mess. And we've no leads at all so far yet.'

'It's early days,' said Gervaise. 'There is one more thing, though, and it might be something of a development. When the surgeons were working on Katie Shea, they discovered that she was pregnant. The foetus was unharmed by the gunshot, but, of course, it didn't survive. She wasn't married – not that that means anything these days – but there has to be a father somewhere.'

'And we'll find him,' said Banks. 'How far along was she?'

'I don't know all the details yet. Dr Glendenning will be doing the post-mortem tomorrow morning, so we'll no doubt find out more then.'

5

'There it is for you,' said Dr Glendenning. 'The tally. Nicely laid out in layman's terms as close as I could get to the order they were hit in, according to your notes.'

Banks read the list clipped to Dr Glendenning's post-mortem reports. Ten bullets, nine hits:

Laura Elizabeth Tindall, age 32, bride. Residence:
   London. *Deceased.*
Benjamin Lewis Kemp, age 33, groom. Residence:
   Northallerton. *Critical.*
Francesca Muriel, age 29, maid of honour. Residence:
   London. *Deceased.*
Luke Merrifield, age 42, photographer. Residence:
   Eastvale. *Damage to right eye.*
David Ronald Hurst, age 30, guest. Residence:
   Harrogate. *Minor flesh wound.*
Winsome Jackman, age 33, guest. Residence:
   Eastvale. *Minor flesh wound.*
Diana Lofthouse, age 30, bridesmaid. Residence:
   Ripon. *Spinal cord injury.*
Kathleen Louise Shea, age 30, bridesmaid. Residence:
   Leeds. *Deceased.*
Charles Morgan Kemp, age 59, father of groom.
   Residence: Northallerton. *Deceased.*

'So Benjamin Kemp is still alive?' Banks said.

'For now. His liver's done for. If I were a gambling man, I wouldn't give much for his chances.'

Dr Glendenning seemed tired, Banks thought. It was hardly any wonder; he was getting on in years, and he had been bending over dead bodies almost non-stop since Sunday afternoon. He had help, of course. His chief anatomical pathology technologist Karen Galway and two trainee pathologists were working with him, all of them still busy at the stainless-steel tables in the autopsy suite next door. Even so, the long hours showed in his watery eyes behind the black-framed glasses and in his drawn, pale flesh. His white coat had been smeared with blood and worse when Banks had arrived, and he had removed it and dropped it in a bin before sitting behind his desk. He wore a white shirt and maroon tie under his herringbone jacket.

'Finished?' Banks asked.

Glendenning raised a bushy eyebrow. 'With the dead? Aye. For now.' He took a packet of Benson & Hedges out of his waistcoat pocket and lit one. Smoking was strictly prohibited in the building, but no one dared tell him that. He was more careful these days, though, Banks had noticed, and he didn't actually smoke while he was working on a body. Watching Glendenning light up brought on one of Banks's own rare cravings, which surprised him with its urgency and power. He fought it back.

'It's not strictly my business,' Glendenning went on, 'but you've got a lot of psychologically wounded people out there. What are you going to do with them?'

'Most of them have friends and relatives already with them. There's also counselling sessions going on.'

'Poor sods. You come to a wedding and it ends up a funeral.'

'I know,' said Banks. 'There's something not quite right about that.'

Glendenning scrutinised him. 'I may not be the picture of health myself, but you certainly seem the worse for wear. Been sleeping properly?'

'Not much.'

'Eating?'

Banks was beginning to regret the stop he had made for the full English at the greasy spoon on his way to work that morning. Bacon, eggs, mushrooms, baked beans, fried bread and a slice of black pudding probably wasn't the sort of breakfast Dr Glendenning would approve of. 'Plenty,' he said.

'Well, cut out fatty foods. Drinking?'

'Now and then.'

'Thought so.' Glendenning rummaged in his drawer and tossed Banks a foil strip of tablets. 'Take one of these with two fingers of good whisky every night,' he said. 'Only two fingers, mind. And good whisky. That means Highlands. None of that Islay rubbish. I don't want to come in to work one morning and find you laid on a table out there.'

Banks pocketed the tablets. 'Thanks,' he said. 'Am I likely to become addicted?'

'If they make you feel better, you'll probably become addicted,' said Glendenning. 'Why wouldn't you? But don't worry about it. It won't last. And you won't be getting any more from me.' He sighed and slouched back in his chair. 'Days like this,' he said, 'I sometimes think junkies are the only ones with the right idea. You know they say that sometimes heroin feels so good you don't even want to hang on to your life any more. It's better than breathing.'

'If I hadn't seen so many dead junkies – most of them kids – I'd probably agree,' said Banks.

'Oh, don't mind me. I'm just grouching.'

'So what have you found?'

'Four corpses, so far,' said Glendenning. 'And from what I hear from my colleagues at James Cook, there's one poor wee lassie in a wheelchair.'

'Diana Lofthouse,' said Banks. 'Anything unexpected show up in your post-mortems?'

'No. They all died from gunshot wounds. Hollow-point .223 ammo, as a matter of fact. Nasty way to go. The bullet expands when it enters the victim, as I'm sure you're aware. Causes massive tissue damage. Young Winsome's lucky the bullet didn't enter her flesh, but only grazed her shoulder.'

'Who would have access to such ammunition?'

'That's one for you to answer,' said Glendenning. 'But everything's available if you want it badly enough. You should know that. Some people use them for greater accuracy in target shooting, and apparently, they reduce smoke and exposure to lead vapour. And I have a friend who tells me deer hunters use hollow-point ammo, so you can obviously get a special dispensation of some sort. Of course, lots of shooters prefer to make their own bullets. I don't think the source would be much of a problem.'

'Still,' said Banks, 'it's a bit unusual. It might help us narrow down the field.'

'They make for a very ugly wound. I can tell you that much. That's another reason the doctors don't hold out much hope for Benjamin Kemp. The damn bullet expanded and turned his liver and half a kidney to mush, to use a technical term.'

Banks swallowed. 'And Katie Shea?'

'Aye. A regular bullet and she might have survived even the blood loss. But her insides resembled a plate of spaghetti Bolognese.' He pointed towards the post-mortem suite. 'She's still on the table. The students are sluicing her down and sewing her up.'

Banks knew he would always remember the pretty blond girl in a coral-coloured dress slumped against the gravestone, the one who reminded him of Emily Hargreaves. Even AC Gervaise had intuited some sort of connection the previous evening when she told him about Katie's death. *And not just her own death*, he realised. Not just Katie Shea holding her bloody guts in, keening and wailing and begging for help. But pregnant Katie Shea. Perhaps, in her mind, it was her baby she was cradling on her lap.

'I don't know whether anyone's told you this already,' Glendenning went on, 'but one thing they did find out at the hospital was that she was pregnant.'

'AC Gervaise told me last night.'

'I have to say, though, it was a hell of a job making sure. The bullet missed the foetus, but there was plenty of damage in the general area. But the tests came out positive.'

'OK,' said Banks. 'OK. I get the picture.' And he did, all too clearly. In full colour, with sound. He felt his breakfast repeat on him, tasted bile and felt the anger surge inside him again. Just like last night, he wanted to lash out at something, anything.

'Calm down, laddie,' said Glendenning. 'You'll have apoplexy.'

Banks gritted his teeth. 'How long?'

'Not long at all. Six weeks, maybe eight. Do you know how tiny a foetus is at that stage?'

'No idea.'

'The size of a blueberry.'

'Would she have known?'

'I should think so, though I'm not a mind-reader, especially when it comes to corpses. For a start, she would have missed her period. She would also probably have experienced mood changes. Aches and pains. Even morning sickness. Loss of appetite. Increased urination. She may even have noticed her breasts and waist increasing in size. Does it make a difference?'

'It could provide a motive,' said Banks. 'First we'll have to find out who the father was. I'll put DC Masterson on it.'

Glendenning managed a thin smile. 'Well, I doubt it was an immaculate conception, though I'm afraid even my advanced pathological skills don't stretch to that kind of judgement.' He paused. 'Alan, you know I'm no great fan of this psychological gobbledygook, but don't you think you might benefit from a bit of this counselling yourself?'

'I'll be all right,' said Banks. He took a deep breath and let it out slowly. 'It's just that I noticed her specifically, that's all. You know how they say it's hard to relate to the deaths of thousands in a flood or on a battlefield, but if there's just one, it tends to stay with you. Katie Shea was the one. Out of the whole massacre, it was seeing her that stuck in my mind the most. She reminded me of someone I once knew. And now . . .'

'Aye,' said Glendenning. 'Well, she would have been a bonny lass when she was alive, that's for certain.'

'I never knew her.' Wearily, Banks got to his feet. 'Thanks, doc,' he said. 'If you come up with anything else, you know my number.'

'I do. And think about that counselling gobbledygook.'

Banks turned at the door, nodded briefly and left.

'And don't forget the pills and whisky, either,' Glendenning called after him.

'I'm sorry to be the bearer of bad news,' said Gerry Masterson at the opening of the briefing later that Monday morning, 'but I just heard that Benjamin Kemp died during the night. Along with Katie Shea, that makes murder victims four and five.' As she spoke, Gerry was uncomfortably aware of some of the male detectives undressing her with their eyes. She had dressed conservatively for work in maroon cords and a pale green jacket buttoned up over her white polo-neck top. She had even tied her long hair in a ponytail as she usually did at work. Still they undressed her. No matter what she did, there was no escaping the fact that she was an attractive young woman, and some men were going to ogle her rather than listen to what she had to say.

Gerry loathed standing in front of an audience like this, but she could hardly say no when Detective Superintendent Banks had asked her to, not if she valued her career prospects. It would be good experience, he had said. An experience in terror, more like, she thought, aware of her hands trembling and her neck stiffening as she tried to stop her head from shaking, too.

Banks was sitting in the front row, but she didn't feel that he was undressing her. She was aware of her face flushing, but she carried on, casting her gaze to the people at the back of the room, doing her best to concentrate on what she was saying. What made everything worse was the news Banks had given her about Katie Shea. Gerry would never forget witnessing her agony, her courage. All for nothing. And now the baby, too.

Banks had tried to persuade Gerry to go for counselling, but she didn't feel that she needed it. Besides, however much things had improved over the years, there was still a stigma attached to cops seeing shrinks. Many male officers thought it was a sign of weakness, and it meant you weren't up to the job. As a woman, she didn't want or need to invite that kind of attention. She could handle this herself. Yes, she was upset and unnerved by what had happened – who wouldn't be? – but she could function. She hadn't slept last night, but she'd had a lot on her mind.

Gerry shuffled her papers. 'First, a few nuggets we've dug up so far, mostly from some of the survivors of the shootings who were able and willing to talk yesterday. Laura Tindall and Benjamin Kemp had known each other for two years and had been engaged for the last six months. They had recently bought a house near Lyndgarth, and Laura was planning to live there with Benjamin after the wedding. Laura's father Robert is a retired banker, so there's always a possibility we're after someone who had a thing against bankers. But, I mean, who doesn't?'

Gerry was surprised but pleased by the murmur of polite laughter.

'Maureen Tindall, the mother of the bride, grew up in Leeds, but the family moved down south to Aylesbury when she was in her mid-teens. She trained and worked as a nurse until she met Robert in 1982 when he came in for a routine X-ray after a minor car crash. She married him in 1984, gave up nursing and devoted herself to keeping the house and later to taking care of Laura, their only child, born in 1985. The only interesting fact I've been able to dig up about her so far is that her best friend Wendy Vincent was murdered in Leeds when they were both only fifteen years old. That was over fifty years ago, however, and the killer recently died in jail, so I doubt it's very relevant, but it might account to some extent for her poor psychological state. We won't be able to talk to her for a while yet.

'Laura briefly attended the University of Manchester from 2003 to 2005, but gave up her history degree for a modelling career at the end of her second year. Eventually, she decided to retire from that life, and for the last three years she's been involved in recruiting and training for a West End modelling agency. She planned to keep on working after her marriage, mostly from home. She met Benjamin Kemp at a party in St

John's Wood thrown while he was in town on business for his father's company. Ben and Laura hit it off, and the rest, as they say, is history, or would have been had it not been for Saturday's shootings. Benjamin Kemp worked for his father's software development company just outside Northallerton, where the Kemp family has lived for over twenty years. He also planned on continuing with this work after the wedding.'

Gerry noticed someone near the back raise her hand in the air. 'Yes?'

'Are you saying there may be a rational motive somewhere in all this? Revenge, for example?'

'I'm saying it has to be considered, however outlandish it may seem. In the same vein, it's important to remember that we're dealing with some very young victims, and there are ex-boyfriends and ex-girlfriends out there. None of them has exhibited any odd or violent behaviour as far as we know, but they need to be checked out. Laura Tindall did have a cyber-stalker a few years back, but he's in New Zealand and there's no way he could have been in Fortford last Saturday. We'll be looking into him, anyway. I've already asked the Auckland police for their help. Other than that, she didn't seem to have any obsessively jealous lovers that we know of, but that's an avenue we will also have to pursue further as the inquiry continues. She was in the public eye, so it's quite possible that there could have been someone who had active fantasies about her of which she knew nothing. She could even have been stalked without her knowledge. We'll have to carry out a thorough examination of her computer and see where that leads us. But let's also remember, this wasn't a sex crime.'

'So are you saying there's no specific line of inquiry yet?' the speaker asked.

Gerry began to feel flustered. She wished she could pass the briefing over to Superintendent Banks or DI Cabbot, but she struggled on, determined not to show weakness. 'I'm saying that we need to keep an open mind. I'm sure our profiler Dr Fuller will have more to say about all this when she produces her report. We're certainly not ruling out the military connection, even though it was three years since Benjamin Kemp's last tour of duty in Afghanistan. Kemp also had a steady girlfriend until two and a half years ago, when they split up. It sounds as if he might have taken up with Laura quickly afterwards. The girlfriend will need to be interviewed, along with any other exes of Ben, Laura and the rest of the victims.'

Gerry held up some stapled sheets. 'I have details on all this here, by the way, and DI Cabbot and I will be handing these out with the TIEs and actions when we've finished here. You will need to talk to more of the uninjured wedding guests as they become willing and able, and track down family and friends of the deceased. I don't need to tell you to tread softly here. These people have just lost loved ones. Two bridesmaids went uninjured, Lucy Fisher and Danielle Meynell, along with the best man Wayne Powell. They're still in shock but will also need to be interviewed as soon as the doctors declare them fit. I wish I could be more specific in telling you what to look for, but the previous questioner was right. There is no certain line of inquiry yet. Right now we're still working more or less in the dark. Some of you have already been checking on firearms certificates and local shooting clubs. There's plenty more of those to get through. Some of you have been assigned to track down all local black- or dark-coloured RAV4s and similar vehicles. We're still trolling the records for anyone with a history of violence, especially involving firearms, of making threats, or anything of that kind. Keep your eyes and ears open. We have messages out in all the media for members of the public to get in touch if they know or suspect anything, so be warned. There'll be plenty of attention-seekers and just plain weirdoes calling in. Psychics and people who want to confess, too. Of course, the trouble is that once in a while one of these actually has something of value to tell us. There's also a massive manhunt going on, though it's being severely hampered by the weather. According to the most recent forecasts, we can't expect much change there. In fact, the rain is only expected to get worse, which shouldn't come as a surprise to any of you who grew up in Yorkshire. CSM Nowak will be bringing you up to date on all that soon, along with any forensic evidence discovered so far.

'I can tell you one final thing, though. I've checked most of the local media reports on the wedding coverage, and the only people mentioned in the articles, or shown in photographs, were the bride and groom and their parents. That means if our killer is local, and if he found out about the wedding from the local media, then he would probably have no idea who else was going to be there. Therefore, it's not a bad idea to concentrate on Laura and Benjamin and their parents first. As only Laura Tindall and Charles and Benjamin Kemp of this group were killed, that might cut down the possibilities even more. But don't forget, this is just a rough guide. The main thing not to forget is that we've still got a killer out there, and he might strike again at any time.' She glanced at Banks, who tapped his watch and gestured to her. Time to wrap up and get back to the search for the father of Katie Shea's baby. 'Thank you.'

Gerry sank gratefully into her front row chair, exhaling a deep sigh of relief. Stefan Nowak got up to speak next. Banks leaned over to Gerry and whispered, 'Well done, DC Masterson. I told you it was a piece of cake.'

Gerry could only stare at Banks. She was still trembling inside. When she found her voice, she felt as if it was trembling, too. 'Yes, sir,' she said. 'A piece of cake.'

★   ★   ★

'We're very sorry for your loss, Boyd,' said Banks as he sat down beside Annie at the low round table in his office that Monday evening. Farrow wasn't a suspect yet, so they had no reason to have their chat in an official interview room. As it turned out, Farrow wasn't so much a boy as a fortyish man in a light grey Hugo Boss suit carrying a leather designer brief-case. A good fifteen years or so older than Katie Shea, he was handsome in a chiselled kind of way, with short dark hair, a strong square jaw, a slightly overlarge nose and a fleshy mouth. Nobody Gerry had talked to had known that Katie was preg-nant, but Gerry had identified and tracked down Boyd Farrow through several emails discovered on her mobile.

'I can hardly believe it,' said Farrow. 'Katie. Dead.'

'Didn't you know about the wedding this weekend?'

'I knew she was going to a wedding, but to be honest I didn't pay a lot of attention to the details.'

'You weren't invited?'

'I had a business meeting.'

'On Saturday?'

'I'm self-employed, Mr Banks. I take my meetings when I can get them.'

'What business are you in, if you don't mind my asking?'

'Not at all. I'm in website design and social media.'

'How did you meet Katie?'

'She's with a small publishing firm in Leeds, and they wanted to up their profile. The full package. Website, Facebook page, Instagram and Twitter accounts. We met, we hit it off . . .' He put his head in his hands. 'My God. *Katie*. What am I going to do?'

'How long had you been together?'

'Not long. Just six months.'

'Did you live together?'

'No. We hadn't got to that stage yet.'

Banks glanced at Annie, who raised her eyebrows. He shook his head almost imperceptibly. *Not yet.*

'So Katie had her own flat and you have yours?'

'Katie rented a flat, yes. I own a house. Well, a mortgage, I should say.'

'And you lived separate lives?'

'We spent as much time together as we could, but . . . well, she had her work. I'm afraid I don't know many of her friends. We preferred spending time together rather than socialising.'

'Of course.' Banks paused. 'My DC tells me that you seemed rather reluctant when she offered to drive down and talk to you in Leeds.'

'I don't mind the drive. It can be relaxing after a day at the office.'

Banks gave Annie the most discreet of signals.

'Did you know that Katie was almost eight weeks pregnant?' she asked.

Farrow spluttered and seemed set to deny everything, then he folded in on himself. 'Yes,' he whispered. 'She told me.'

'When?'

'Ten days ago.'

'A joyous occasion?' Banks asked.

'Not exactly.'

'You mean you didn't want children together?'

'This has absolutely nothing—'

'Please answer the questions, Mr Farrow,' Annie said. 'It'll be over sooner that way.'

'But why aren't you out there catching Katie's killer?'

'Believe me,' Banks answered, 'there are more than enough people out there after Katie's killer. They've been out there in the wind and rain since Saturday afternoon. Besides, according to most of the TV cop programmes I've watched, it's almost always someone with something to hide who asks that question. What is it you have to hide, Mr Farrow?'

'I'm sorry, but I just don't—'

'The baby, Mr Farrow,' Banks went on. 'You didn't want it? Neither of you?'

'Katie ... she ... perhaps more than me. But she saw it couldn't be. Not yet. We weren't ready. She understood that.'

'It doesn't sound as if you were ready for anything. I should imagine you could have made a few adjustments to your lifestyles if you'd tried. You certainly can't claim you were too young for such a responsibility.'

'You don't understand.'

'What am I missing?'

Farrow stared down at the table. 'It just wasn't possible, that's all.'

'Why not?'

'Oh, come on, man, isn't it fucking obvious? Because I'm married, that's why. That's what you've been wanting me to say, isn't it?'

'I've been wanting you to tell me the truth, Mr Farrow,' said Banks. 'So you were having an affair with Katie Shea?'

'It wasn't a ... it wasn't sordid like that. We were in love. We were going to get married as soon as I divorced my wife.'

'And when were you going to do that?'

'I'd been trying to broach the subject, then this came up.'

'How bloody inconvenient,' said Banks. 'So what were you going to do?'

'Well, we couldn't have the baby, could we? Not yet. Not when things were like they were. Katie was going to have a termination.'

'Well, she's certainly had one now, hasn't she?' said Banks.

He noticed out of the corner of his eye that Annie gave him a puzzled and concerned glance. Farrow reeled as if he'd been thumped and started whimpering and chewing on his thumb. 'That's cruel. That's not fair.'

'I'll tell you what's not fair,' Banks went on, 'and that's a married man getting a young girl pregnant then persuading her to have a termination. I'm assuming it was your idea? And that you were paying?'

'She didn't want the child, either!'

'How do you know that? She obviously wanted to please you. I suppose she believed you when you said you were going to ask your wife for a divorce so you could marry her?'

Farrow slapped the table. 'It's true.'

'Bollocks. It's the oldest trick in the book. You had no intention of asking for a divorce, did you?'

Farrow hung his head.

'How many children do you and your wife have?' Banks went on.

'Two.'

'How old?'

'Seven and five.'

'The last thing you wanted was another, wasn't it? You'd already been through it with two. Even if you did plan on getting a divorce and marrying Katie, which I doubt, you weren't signing up for dirty nappies and sleepless nights, were you? But I'll bet she wanted children, didn't she?'

'You don't know what you're talking about. It's none of your business. She was no angel. She knew what she was doing. What are you, pro-life or something?'

'That takes the bloody biscuit, that does,' said Banks, standing up. 'If you'd seen just half of what I've seen these past two days ... And that included your Katie, the woman you say you love, sitting propped—'

'Alan, that's enough!'

It was Annie. Banks was so shocked by her sharp tone and the way she was glaring at him that he stopped mid-sentence and turned to face the window, arms folded. His breath was coming in short sharp gasps, and he was certain his blood pressure had gone way over the limit. He could feel his heart thumping in his chest. He took a few paces and looked out over the dark market square. Car headlights reflected in the puddles among the cobblestones. He'd lost his cool, and he knew it.

After an uncomfortable silence, Annie picked up the questioning in relatively gentle tones. Banks didn't trust himself to turn around just yet. He had not felt such anger, such revulsion for someone, in a long time. He wanted to pick Farrow up by his neck and shake him. Slowly, his heart rate returned to normal.

'Did your wife know about the affair?' he heard Annie ask.

'She suspected that I was seeing someone else. I think she might have followed me once and seen us meet up.'

'She never broached the subject with you?'

'Rosie doesn't work like that. She stores it all up until the dam bursts, and then there's no stopping her.'

'But she hadn't reached that stage yet?'

'No.'

'Though you think she knew?'

'Suspected.'

'Boyd,' Annie said. 'This isn't a personal inquisition into your morals. It's a murder inquiry. Do you think Rosie knew enough about the affair, was angry enough about it, to harm Katie?'

'Good God, no. She wouldn't do anything like that. If anyone was going to suffer for it, it would have been me.'

'OK. Where was she on Saturday?'

'At home with the kids. Like I said, I had a business meeting. It was in Wakefield, by the way, and I can tell you the names of the clients. You can check.'

'That might be useful,' said Annie. 'And we'll need some corroboration of your wife's whereabouts. Would anyone else have been there? Might she have taken the children shopping or to the playground? Would anyone be likely to have seen her?'

'It's possible. I'm sure someone would, but . . . oh, God . . .' He buried his face in his hands. 'You're going to have to ask her, aren't you? You're going to have to tell her everything. I've lost Katie, and now I'm going to lose Rosie and the kids. Please can't you—'

Banks couldn't tolerate any more. He walked away from the window and left his office. He didn't trust himself to stand there and listen to Farrow's cringing self-pity. When he found himself out in the corridor, he didn't know what to do, so he just stood at the far end looking out over the car park at the back of the station.

He didn't know how long he'd been standing like that when he heard his office door open and shut behind him. He turned to see Annie standing there with Farrow. A few seconds later, a uniformed constable entered from the stairwell to show Farrow out.

'What the hell was all that about?' Annie demanded, following Banks back into his office.

'Don't you start, Annie.'

'What you do you mean, "don't you start"? What the hell did you think you were up to?'

'I was trying to push him,' Banks said, sitting behind his desk.

'You mean you seriously think he had something to do with the massacre?'

'I'm not saying that. I—'

'You were out of bounds, Alan.' Annie's tone softened. 'No matter what you think of him, Farrow is a witness and a victim, not a suspect. You had no right to treat him like that. I don't know what it was all about, what's going on in your mind, but you were way out of bounds. What were you thinking of?'

'I don't know,' said Banks. 'He just pushed all the wrong buttons.'

'Oh, bugger it, come here, you daft sod.' Banks stood up and walked over to her. She took him in her arms and gave him a firm hug then held on to his shoulders and faced him.

Banks felt himself relax a little. 'I'm sorry,' he said. 'You're right. I lost it in there. Is Farrow planning on making a formal complaint?'

'No. He feels far too guilty for that. And I think I managed to calm him down after you'd left the office. In the end, he was more worried about what he was going to say to his wife when he gets home than about anything you might have said to him. You surprised me, though. You were cruel, Alan. I never thought of you as cruel.'

'I suppose we can all act a little out of character at times. Forgive me?'

'Of course.' Annie went over to the coffee machine. 'Want some?'

'Please.'

'Feeling OK now?'

'Much better.'

Annie handed him the coffee and they sat down at the glass table again. 'Farrow might be a creep,' she said, 'but he didn't do it. Or his wife.'

'I know that. It's just . . .'

'What?'

'Oh, never mind.'

'You never struck me as being the moralistic kind. I mean, he's not the only married bloke to have an affair. I've been with a married man or two in my time, and you—'

'It was once, before I came up here.'

'I know. You did it, though, didn't you?'

'You're saying people in glass houses . . .'

'Or "let him who is without sin . . ." Pick your cliché.'

Banks laughed. 'It's a fair cop.' He put his coffee cup on the table. 'And thanks for the pep talk. I wasn't being moralistic, really, though. I was trying to get his goat. I'm sorry, I just lost it. It won't happen again. And now I think I'm going to go home and have an early night.'

'Not if Ray has anything to do with it, you won't,' said Annie.

When Banks got home to Newhope Cottage later that evening, the rain was still pouring down, and Gratly Beck was close to full spate. Normally a steady, soothing trickle of water over the terraced falls outside his cottage, tonight it roared down the daleside, swollen with the flow of countless becks, burns and rills from higher up in the hills, flecked with foam that caught the light of the half moon like whitecaps out at sea. But the beck was deep and its banks were high. He knew he would be safe from flooding here, so far up the side of the valley, but Helmthorpe and The Leas below might have serious problems. It wouldn't be the first time. The worst his cottage had ever suffered from protracted wind and heavy rain was a leak where the conservatory joined the older part of the building, which he had caulked the previous spring, and a little dampness had managed to seep its way through the thick stone walls to darken the bedroom wall in patches. After the previous winter, he'd had one of the local handymen around to fix a few gaps in the flagstone roof and spray the back wall with silicon, which was supposed to seal the porous limestone against the elements. The way things were going, he would soon find out whether it worked.

The cottage felt more welcoming than it had on Saturday night, with smoke coming out of the chimney, a light visible from the entertainment room and Ray's ancient Honda Civic parked outside. As soon as Banks got inside, he could hear Billie Holiday singing 'Lover Man'. Even though it was his own home, he tapped gently on the entertainment room door before entering, so as not to surprise Ray if he happened to be asleep or lost in thought.

'Alan, nice to see you,' Ray said, rising and shaking hands. 'As you can see, I'm making myself at home. I do appreciate this. I'm not a particularly large man, but I must confess that in Annie's place, I felt rather like Alice when she was ten feet tall after taking that pill.'

'No problem.' Banks dropped his keys on the sideboard beside an open bottle of Laphroaig. Ray must have bought it, he realised, as he hadn't had any in the house for ages. Ray had also managed to light the wood stove, and the room felt warm and cosy.

'Why don't you join me?' Ray said, pointing to the bottle. 'Nightcap.'

Banks hesitated. He had lost his taste for the peaty whisky since he had come to associate it with a fire at the cottage, but he had tried a drop now and then over the past couple of years, and his tolerance was improving. Besides, after the day he'd had, he felt he needed a drink or two to help him unwind. He helped himself to a wee dram and topped up Ray's glass.

'*Slainte*,' Banks said, clinking glasses.

'*Slainte*. Hope you don't mind the music.'

'Billie? Never,' said Banks.

'They said she could tell a story in a song, but as far as I'm concerned she can tell a story in just one note.'

'She had what it takes,' Banks agreed.

'Frank Sinatra said he'd once kissed her as she ought to be kissed,' Ray mused. 'I've often wondered what that was like.'

Banks flopped down in his armchair. 'Perhaps a mixture of bourbon, gardenias and cigarette smoke.' He tasted the Laphroaig, and it burned nicely as it went down. Billie Holiday was singing 'Solitude' now in her husky, booze-soaked late-career voice, the one Banks loved best, the one that expressed clearly in every broken note how much she had lived and loved and suffered, but also how she had come through, survived. He inhaled the peat and iodine fumes from his whisky and revelled in the music.

'Tough day?' Ray asked.

'Yes, it was tough.'

'Want to talk about it?'

It was strange having someone else in the house. Banks knew Ray reasonably well from previous visits, but he wouldn't say they were especially close friends. And he wasn't one for talking things through. Oddly enough, though, he felt like talking to someone tonight. 'And I was at a funeral on Saturday,' he said, 'just before . . . well . . . before the shit hit the fan up here.'

'That must have been hard. Someone close?'

'No. Not for years. That's the thing. I can't seem to stop thinking about her, even with all this chaos going on up here. We went out together for a while when we were kids back in Peterborough. You know, just a bit of necking on the back row, reaching for a blouse button and getting your hand slapped. That sort of thing. Then we met up again quite by chance a few years later, when I was at London Poly and she was at the university. It was the early seventies, and we were both away from home for the first time, footloose and fancy-free.'

'Exciting times. And it developed into something serious?'

'It did. Yes. But for Christ's sake, that was over forty years ago, and I haven't seen her since. My children are older now than Emily was when I knew her. It just all came rushing back at the funeral.'

'Doesn't make it any easier, though, does it, the passage of time?'

'You were pretty young when your wife died, weren't you? Annie's mother. That must have been hard.'

Ray slugged back some whisky. 'Hard? I was thirty-seven, and Annie would have been about seven. I don't know how we made it through those first few years, to be honest. The colony, I suppose. People took care of each other. Without the others . . . I don't know. I do know Annie's never got over losing her mother.'

'You never thought of remarrying?'

'Me? No. Oh, maybe once or twice.' Ray grinned. 'Fleetingly. I'm not saying there haven't been other women, but I've never been able to *give* myself to any of them the way I had with Judy. I've always held something back. The part of me I probably shouldn't have held back if I wanted any sort of meaningful relationship. The part that won't let you get close to anyone ever again because you know you're going to lose them, and you know how bad it feels. Because they're going to die.' He waved his glass. 'Maybe that's why I've been a bit distant from Annie over the years, too. Not because I associate her with Judy's death, or blame her, or any of that psychological claptrap, but because I don't know if I could take that sort of blow again. When she got shot . . . well, you remember what it was like. Lovers leave you, and it hurts, of course, but you can get them back, sometimes, if you try, if you want to, if you know how. But death's the final thing. At least, *I* think it is. I don't know about you, maybe you're religious, but I don't believe there's anything after death. I reckon you *should* think about your first serious girlfriend. It's a major emotional turning point in your life. Remember her. There's not a day goes by when I don't think about Judy, no matter how many years have passed. But if you can take a bit of advice from an old fool like me, save your best efforts for the living, because one day they'll be dead, too, and you'll end up feeling guilty for neglecting them while they were alive. That's the paradox. Damned if you do and double-damned if you don't.'

'It never stopped you from loving Annie, though, did it, all this fear of one day losing her?'

Ray grunted. 'No. I suppose not. But she's my daughter. It's different.' He knocked back his whisky and laughed. 'Listen to me. Sorry, mate. What a fucking old bore I must sound talking about lessons learned. And me a guest in your home. Must be the whisky talking. Much more of this and you'll be kicking me out on my arse before I've even spent a night under your roof.'

'Don't worry about that,' said Banks. 'I'm glad of the company, to be honest.'

'Thanks. I appreciate that. I was worried about being a burden. Fancy a quick spliff?'

Banks smiled. 'No, thanks. Better not.'

'Maybe I'll go outside later. You won't arrest me, will you?'

Banks laughed and drank some more Laphroaig. He could get used to the peaty taste again very easily, he decided, despite Dr Glendenning's words of derision. 'Is there any particular reason you want to move up to Yorkshire?' he asked.

Ray shuffled in his seat. 'Something about the light up here,' he said. 'Hell, if Hockney could do it, I don't see why I can't.'

'Tired of the light in Cornwall?'

'It's not that. I've spent most of my life there. I love the place. Always will. But it's getting to be a young person's world now, the colony. I feel like an intruder, an old fogey. And it's what we've been talking about. Mortality. Like I said, I feel I've neglected Annie. I may have had my reasons, but they don't count for much now. It's something I've been thinking about since that time we almost lost her. She's my only child, after all. The most beautiful thing I've ever created, or helped to create. All that's left of Judy and me. Oh, fuck, I'm getting morbid and sentimental now.'

'Is there something wrong? Are you OK? I know you told Annie you are, but—'

'Physically? No, there's nothing wrong. No cancer or anything, just the same ticking clock we all have. I'm fit as a fiddle. Well, as fit as can be expected for a man my age who's led the sort of life I've lived.' He tapped his temple. 'It's in here, Alan. I mean, let's be honest. I turned seventy a few years ago. How many more good years can I expect? Ten? Five? I may be feeling my age, but I'm going to have a bloody good time for as long as I've got left. And I want my daughter to be part of that. There. Is that so strange a reason?'

'Not at all,' said Banks, thinking of his own grown-up children, Brian and Tracy, and how far he felt from them at times. They had their own lives to live, he told himself; they didn't want to be bothered with him and his problems.

'Let's have some loud rock 'n' roll,' Ray said, walking over to the stereo and changing discs. 'I picked this one out earlier.' And he put on Jimi Hendrix's *Rainbow Bridge* then went for the bottle. The level was getting dangerously low. He was moving unsteadily. 'Should we . . .?'

They were well into their next glass and 'Hear My Train A Comin'' when Banks thought he heard his mobile play its blues riff. He left the room, pressed the talk button and put it to his ear. 'Banks speaking.'

It was Annie. 'I hate to drag you away from your old fogey's sleepover with Ray,' she said. 'I should imagine you're having a nice semi-drunken reminiscc right now. I hope you can hear me over all that racket. What is it, best shags or best albums? And I hope you haven't lit up that spliff yet. We've got developments. Major developments, we think. A strong lead. In fact, it's strong enough that we might even have the bastard before the night is over. Interested?'

'Where are you?'

'Not far away. Put your glass down. I'll pick you up in a few minutes.'

6

'It's just beyond Swainshead village,' said Annie, leaning forwards and squinting at the road ahead as she drove. The rain had eased up somewhat, and the windshield wipers were keeping up with it, but outside the beams of Annie's head-lights the landscape was pitch black. She had her foot down hard, and Banks noticed that the speedometer was edging up towards fifty. Madness on this road. He hung on to the door handle tightly.

'His name is Martin Edgeworth,' Annie was saying. 'Lives alone. Retired dentist. Used to have his surgery on Market Street about a mile south of the square.'

'I remember it,' said Banks. 'It was that big old house on the corner, just over the zebra crossing, I used to walk past there on my way to work every morning. Wasn't there someone else in the practice with him?'

'I almost forgot you used to live near there,' said Annie. 'Yes, he had a partner. A bloke called Martell. Jonathan Martell.'

'That's right,' said Banks. 'I remember the brass plaque beside the door.'

'Was he your dentist, then?'

'No.'

'Why not? He must have been the closest.'

'I didn't need a dentist,' Banks muttered.

'You were scared, weren't you?' Annie said. 'Scared of the dentist.'

Banks scowled at her. 'There's no need to make a big deal out of it. Lots of people are nervous about going to the dentist's.'

'Scaredy-cat.'

'Get on with it.'

Annie grinned. 'He's fifty-nine. Fits the description, as far as it goes. Medium height, slim. Been retired three years now. That's all we know about him so far. Except he has a Firearms Certificate for an AR15, along with one for a Taurus pistol, he drives a black RAV4 and he's a member of the Upper Swainsdale District Rifle and Pistol Club.'

The right turn came up faster than Banks had expected. Annie turned the wheel sharply, and the car skidded, tyres squealing, as she made the bend on to the minor road that led through the village of Swainshead. Banks hung on for dear life as she regained control and drove on past the triangular village green, squat church and whitewashed pub, blurred images in the dark through the rain-spattered car windows.

The road they were on, which cut north from the main east–west road, narrowed beyond the borders of the village. Though they were invisible in this weather, Banks knew that the valley sides rose steeply on either side of the road. From this point on, there were very few dwellings, all of them off the beaten track, if you could even call the road they were on beaten, or a track.

'You feeling all right, by the way?' Annie cast him a sidelong glance. 'I mean, I'm not going to have to carry you, am I?'

'I'm fine,' said Banks.

'Not had too much to drink? Or smoke?'

'Hardly got started drinking even.'

'Good.'

'There.' Banks pointed towards the left, where flashing police lights were just visible down a driveway. Annie turned, travelling more slowly this time, and they came to a halt beside the two ARVs that had been first at the scene. The large house at the end of the gravel drive was a dark silhouette against the darker daleside.

Banks and Annie were already kitted out in raincoats and wellies, and they made a dash from the purple Astra to the first Volvo T5 estate car parked ahead of them. Banks recognised both of the officers from St Mary's leaning against the car.

'Evening, sir,' said the driver, a DS in the firearms cadre, whose first name was Keith. 'No activity so far.'

'You've checked out the premises?'

'Outside only. As best we can. There's a black RAV4 in the garage. Thought we'd better wait for you to arrive. All doors and windows appear to be securely locked. No lights on. No answer when we knock or phone. Unless he's lying extremely low, I'd say the place is empty.'

'So how do you want to play this?'

'Safely, sir. By the book. Just in case he is lying low in there, armed to the teeth. We go in first, then we give you the all clear.'

'Have you got enough men surrounding the house, just in case?'

'First thing we did. Called for backup. It's kettled tighter than a . . .' He glanced nervously at Annie. 'The area's secure, sir. Nobody's getting away from here. Not even in the dark.'

'Good to know. After you.'

The two armed officers left the car, one of them carrying a red battering ram, which he used to splinter the door. Heckler & Kochs slung around their shoulders, Glocks in one hand, torches gripped like overhead handrails, the two officers advanced slowly into the dark house to begin their sweep. One by one, the lights came on. Banks could still hear little but the wind whistling and moaning as it encountered the solid stone, and the different sounds of the rain tapping against slate, glass and metal.

It seemed to take for ever, but the all clear came eventually, and they were able to enter the house. From the vestibule, with pegs and a cupboard for hats and coats, and racks for muddy boots and shoes, they went into a large kitchen with rough natural stone walls, a big red Aga and a flagstone floor. There was a central island, granite-topped, and beyond it, a stainless-steel fridge and freezer unit stood beside wall cupboards, a double metal sink and a dishwasher unit. Everything was sparkling clean.

'Nice set up,' said Banks.

'Not your run-of-the-mill mass murderer,' Annie added.

The rest of the downstairs was well appointed, but not ostentatious. The living-room furniture was solid and service-able, nice on the eye, with beige leather sofas, walls painted light pastel shades. There were the usual items: cocktail cabinet, sideboard, large screen TV, Blu-Ray player, book-cases mostly full of paperbacks and illustrated hardcovers on military history, along with a selection of Ordnance Survey maps and local guides. There was also a glass-fronted cabinet in which stood a number of cups and plaques. When Banks looked more closely, he could see that they were awards for shooting competitions. A wood-burning stove filled the old fireplace, and a set of andirons stood on the hearth next to a box of kindling and a stack of firewood. Banks went over to the stove and opened the door. Everything was cold. Cold and clean.

A quick glance upstairs revealed a large bathroom and toilet, equally clean, and four bedrooms, only one of which was used for sleeping, with an en suite walk-in shower unit. Another was clearly an office, with desk, computer, printer and more bookcases, the third a guest bedroom, and the fourth was filled with boxes. They went back down to the main floor and met Keith coming up from the cellar with a grim expression on his face.

'You may want to check out down there next,' he said.

Banks and Annie followed him down the wooden steps. It was a dank, musty-smelling cellar, with whitewashed walls and a bare bulb overhead. One of the AFOs must have jogged it somehow, as it was swinging back and forth, casting shadows across the still figure that slumped against the far wall. The whitewash above his head was splattered and speckled with dark blood. Banks saw the gun in the man's right hand, where it had fallen into his lap. The black AR15 was lying next to a pile of neatly folded outdoor clothes beside him on the floor.

'Martin Edgeworth, I presume,' Banks said, then turned to Keith. 'Call Dr Burns, would you, and bring in the CSIs and a search team. I hate to spoil their beauty sleep, but I think we've got our man.' Then he turned to Annie. 'Let's go upstairs and ring the boss,' he said. 'She's going to want to know about this, too.'

Chief Superintendent Gervaise joined them at the scene in less than an hour, and after a quick poke around as they brought her up to speed, she left for Eastvale HQ, where she said she would put on a pot of coffee and make some phone calls, including one to Adrian Moss. By two o'clock in the morning, the house and grounds were lit up by arc lamps, and there were so many people coming and going that anyone might be forgiven for thinking there was a big party going on, albeit a quiet one, without music or dancing.

Stefan Nowak's CSI team went methodically over all the surfaces, taking fingerprints and trace evidence, while skilled searchers went through the drawers, cupboards and appliances, loading everything from letters and bills to kitchen knives into transparent plastic crates, which they carried out under a makeshift canvas awning to the waiting van outside.

A special team was assigned to the garage where Martin Edgeworth's black RAV4 was parked. They would pick through it for anything of interest before getting it on a trailer and driving it to the police forensic garage when the rain stopped. They wanted to preserve the exterior of the car as best they could, so someone was sent to find a tarpaulin or some plastic sheeting. For one thing, they would probably be able to match soil samples from the tyres with those from the lay-by where the killer's car had been parked.

The rain continued to fall steadily, and officers whose duties kept them outside wore bright yellow capes slick with it, the shiny black peaks of their caps glistening in the lights. Inside, after the body had been examined *in situ*, photographed extensively and taken away in the coroner's van, someone had managed to get the central heating working, and the radiators banged and rattled as they came to life. At some point, nobody seemed to know quite when or how, ham and cheese sandwiches materialised.

There was no need for Banks and Annie to stay on, they knew, but as neither felt that there was much chance of sleep by now, they made valuable use of their time. Ray would be fast asleep back at Newhope, Banks thought, if he hadn't decided to stay up and finish the Laphroaig and start watching movies. He was glad that he had drunk only two small whiskies, otherwise he might be nodding off himself. No chance of that. The St Mary's business was far from over. The killer might be dead, but there would be official inquiries, analyses of Edgeworth's motivation, questions in the house, more calls for stricter gun laws – all of which meant a lot more media attention focused on Eastvale over the next few weeks or months. They could also not rule out the possibility of an accomplice. The last thing they needed was a second gunman on the loose.

By this time, a few of the villagers had been woken by the mysterious comings and goings, and one or two inquisitive souls had even attempted to wander up the driveway and see for themselves what was going on, only to be turned back by the constables on duty. Tomorrow, they would all be questioned about Martin Edgeworth, but tonight they were civilians, and they had no place at a crime scene.

Banks and Annie sat with Dr Burns at the granite island in the kitchen, where they drank hot strong tea and nibbled on the sandwiches.

'So everything seems kosher to you?' Banks said, after Dr Burns had recapped his findings from the preliminary examination of Martin Edgeworth's body.

Dr Burns rubbed his eyes. 'I'd say so. Assuming we're not overlooking something so devastatingly obvious, like he was left-handed.'

'He's wearing his watch on his left wrist,' said Banks, 'but we'll be checking all that very carefully. I'd imagine his friends at the club would certainly know. Time of death?'

'You know I can't give you that with any reasonable degree of accuracy. All I'll say is it's within the time frame.'

'What time frame?'

'Of his committing the murders at St Mary's, driving back here and blowing his brains out. Rigor's been and gone. It was quite cool in here, which would have slowed the process down a bit, but I'd say offhand that our man has definitely been dead for longer than two days. It's Monday night now, or Tuesday morning, if you prefer, and I'm afraid the best I can estimate is between ten o'clock Saturday morning and five o'clock that same afternoon. Dr Glendenning may be able to narrow that down a bit in the post-mortem.'

'Has the body been moved at all?'

'No sign of that, as far as I can tell, but I'd need to get him on the table and check hypostasis to be certain. It appears to me as if he sat himself down against the wall and . . . well, you can see the blood spatter for yourself. From a cursory glance, I'd say his head was hanging a little bit forward when he put the gun in his mouth and pulled the trigger. The bullet took most of the back of his head off. He certainly got the angle of his shot right, otherwise the bullet might easily have gone through the roof of his mouth. It happens sometimes.'

'Ouch,' said Banks.

'Dr Glendenning will be able to tell you more, of course, including the exact trajectory the bullet took and whether the body was moved after death, but I'm pretty certain I'm right.'

'Why do it down there in a dank miserable cellar?' Banks asked.

'No idea,' said Dr Burns. 'I would assume it didn't matter to him where he did it, as he was going to die. And the gun cabinet's down there.'

'Fair enough. Maybe he didn't take the revolver with him to St Mary's. He certainly didn't use it there. Perhaps it was still in the cabinet.'

'Perhaps,' Burns agreed. 'But what does it matter now?'

'It probably doesn't. Just thinking aloud. Getting my ducks in a row.'

'Hmm. Well, the wound is definitely consistent with the position of the body and the hand holding the weapon,' Burns went on. 'I would imagine the rifle was too large and awkward to use as a suicide weapon, so he put the revolver in his mouth and pulled the trigger. He would have died pretty much instantaneously. No doubt your forensics lab will be checking for gunshot residue on his hands. When all you have to do is pull a trigger, it's sometimes all too bloody easy.'

'Now, now, doc,' said Banks. 'Remember: it's not the gun but the person who fires it.'

'Yes,' said Burns. 'But take the gun away from them and do you think they'd have the guts to do it some other way? A knife? A rope? Bare hands? I doubt it. When you've seen as many gunshot injuries as I have, you can't help but be a bit cynical about the whole thing. I know people argue it's a valid and enjoyable sport, like any other, but why the hell can't they just play golf or tennis like everyone else?'

Banks had forgotten that Dr Burns had worked briefly with the military in Iraq. 'At least this time it's not some innocent victim,' he said.

Dr Burns sighed. 'No. We had enough of those on Saturday.' He got wearily to his feet. 'I'm off home now. You'll have my report sometime tomorrow. Let's at least try and be pleased it's over, shall we?'

'We'll be drinking champagne before the night's through.'

Dr Burns glanced at Annie. 'I wouldn't be too sure of that,' he said. 'Goodnight.' Banks noticed that Annie was dozing with her head resting on the island. He nudged her gently and suggested it might be time to leave. The teams were professional and methodical, and it would be hours yet before they finished.

'Sir?' It was one of the search team come down from the study upstairs. 'I think you might be interested in this.' He held out a scrapbook. 'I found it taped underneath the bottom of one of the desk drawers in the study.'

Banks slipped his latex gloves back on and opened it. Most of the pages were filled with clipped newspaper and magazine articles about Laura Tindall and Benjamin Kemp, especially the reports of their upcoming wedding at St Mary's church,

Fortford. Here and there, a word or line had been underlined in red. There were newspaper photographs, articles, stories of Benjamin Kemp's heroism, grainy images of Laura in her modelling days, including one or two, clearly printed from an Internet site, in which she appeared naked. They were tasteful model's poses, the kind that could be called erotic rather than pornographic.

Banks handed back the scrapbook. 'It seems he had his sights set on Benjamin and Laura well enough. If only we knew why. Bag it and make sure it gets priority tagging.'

'Right you are.' The officer headed back upstairs.

Back out in the rain, Banks offered to drive, and Annie accepted.

'I can hardly keep my eyes open,' she said.

'Come back with me,' Banks said. 'You can have Tracy's room. It's made up. All fresh linen and everything. Harkside's a bloody long way, and it's half three in the morning already.'

Annie said nothing for a while. 'Mm,' she said finally. 'And one of Ray's famous fry-ups for breakfast. What a treat. How could a girl possibly resist?'

7

Eastvale was throbbing with excitement on Tuesday morning, from what Banks could see when he drove in with Annie through the throng of reporters and cameramen. Banks had not managed to get much sleep, and as a consequence he felt groggy as he dodged questions and headed inside. Annie didn't seem much more lively. At least Ray had done a bit of shopping the previous day and cooked them some eggs and bacon with their morning coffee. He said he would be out house-hunting most of the day, so not to worry about him.

The desk sergeant told Banks that Mike Trethowan, head of the firearms cadre, had left a message to meet him in the lab as soon as possible. Also, Dr Glendenning sent his regrets, but he was still busy with the victims of the wedding shooting and wouldn't be able to get around to Martin Edgeworth's post-mortem until tomorrow morning, if then.

They were lucky that the Eastvale Regional HQ was attached to a small forensic laboratory in the building next door, though the lab was constantly under threat due to budget cuts. Even though the technicians there handled jobs from all over the county, Banks could generally get priority on most matters. Unfortunately, the lab wasn't equipped to deal with ballistics. For that, Edgeworth's weapons, bullets and casings had to be sent to LGC Forensics in Wakefield.

Trethowan was chatting with CSM Stefan Nowak and Vic Manson, the fingerprints expert, when Banks and Annie dropped by.

'Good timing,' Trethowan said. 'Vic here has just confirmed Martin Edgeworth's prints on both weapons, and there was gunshot residue on his hand, too.'

'Good. No other prints?'

'None,' said Manson.

'What about the shell casings and the remaining bullets?'

'Clean.'

'You mean no prints at all?' Banks said.

'That's right,' said Trethowan. 'It doesn't mean much, though. People often wear thin gloves, latex or cotton, when they're handling explosive materials. Edgeworth made his own bullets.'

'Even so . . .'

'We're just waiting for the designated firearms officer to pick the guns up and take them to Wakefield for further testing,' Trethowan went on. 'I've had a quick shufty at them myself, and I honestly don't think there's much doubt that the rifle is the one used at St Mary's, and the Taurus is the gun that killed Edgeworth.'

Banks nodded. Trethowan led him and Annie over to the table where the guns lay sealed in carefully labelled plastic bags.

'Ugly things, aren't they?' Annie said.

'Do you think so?' said Trethowan. 'I think they have a sort of beauty all their own, a shapeliness, a form that perfectly suits their purpose. They're actually rather sleek and elegant machines, when you think about it.'

'It's not so much their form I think about as their purpose.'

'Don't you mean their owner's purpose?'

'Oh, we're back to that hoary old chestnut, are we?' Banks cut in.

Trethowan laughed. 'I suppose it's become one of the great conundrums, hasn't it?'

'Not to me it hasn't,' said Annie, fingering the scar on her chest where a bullet had entered her several years ago, narrowly missing her heart.

'Sorry,' said Trethowan.

'No matter.'

Banks stood over the two weapons, the one matte black, the other stainless steel with a hard black rubber butt. As per regulations, the Taurus had a barrel extension, which resembled a silencer, to comply with the twelve-inch legal requirement, and there was a long metal tubular extension sticking out from the butt, so that the gun as a whole was over twenty-four inches in length, also as required by law. Handguns were barely tolerated these days, and those that were had to be almost as long as rifles, far too long and bulky to hide easily in your pocket or stick down your trousers like the gangsters did on TV, but still easy enough to stick in your mouth and pull the trigger.

Trethowan stood beside them. 'Both perfectly legal and both registered to Martin Edgeworth,' he said.

'I assume all the regular checks were made when Edgeworth applied for his certificate?' Banks said.

'Certainly,' said Trethowan. 'I've verified the documents, and there's no doubt that Edgeworth was deemed fit to own firearms. No charges or convictions, not even a speeding ticket, and no health issues raised by his doctor. Solid guarantors. All above board.'

'What did he use the guns for? Hunting?'

'Competitive shooting, mostly. Targets more than clay pigeons, of course. For clay pigeons you'd generally use a shotgun of some sort.' He touched the bag with the revolver inside. 'This baby here is a Taurus 66 .357 long-barrelled revolver, using a .357 Magnum FMJ 158 grain bullet. One bullet fired and fragments dug out of the wall of Edgeworth's cellar.' He moved on to the AR15. 'And this daddy, as you know already, is an AR – Armalite Rifle – 15, emasculated for legal use under a firearms certificate in the UK.'

'Do you think you could stop referring to the weapons in familial terms, please?' Annie said. 'I mean, it makes me cringe to hear someone talking about guns as babies and daddies. And "emasculated"? Give us a break.'

Trethowan reddened. 'Sorry,' he said. 'Just a piece of AFO slang.'

'And you're still certain that Edgeworth would have been able to work the bolt fast enough to get off ten shots in under a minute?' Banks asked.

'Yes. Easily. There are ten bullets missing from the thirty-round clip of 5.56mm bore ammunition, which qualifies for small-bore calibre designation. But it's small-bore with full-bore performance, as they say, if it's loaded with the right ammo. In this case, he used .223 Remington 55 grain bullets. They travel at three thousand feet per second and carry eleven hundred foot-pounds of energy.'

'More than enough to do the job from that distance, I take it?'

'More than enough. Especially with the hollow points.'

Annie had wandered away to talk to Stefan Nowak. Banks couldn't blame her. He wasn't especially comfortable around firearms himself, though he had been through some basic training. And it did sometimes seem to him that the relish with which some AFOs talked about weapons was more than a little OTT.

The AFO charged with delivering the guns for ballistic examination arrived, signed the necessary papers, put the plastic bags inside a large messenger bag and headed out.

Banks couldn't think of anything else to ask Trethowan, so he made his farewells and they left.

Chief Superintendent Gervaise's office was set up in a similar way to Banks's, but everything was bigger, befitting her senior rank, even the conference table they sat around. And the chairs around her conference table were more comfortably padded.

Adrian Moss had joined Banks and Gervaise for a quick briefing. The young MLO was wearing so much black that he might have been going to a funeral, Banks thought. His gelled black hair shone and his perpetual five o'clock shadow and black-rimmed spectacles completed the style. Banks supposed his attire was appropriate for someone who had to face the media at a time like this. Much as he liked to criticise Moss, he didn't envy him his job today. The poor boy was stressed out enough already, and Banks doubted he had managed to get much sleep lately. There had been too much going on behind the scenes. For a start, the firearms cadre versus emergency services issue hadn't been resolved yet, and it probably wouldn't be without the appointment of a special commission and the preparation of a thousand-page report, which would cost the taxpayers a fortune and probably be so ambiguous as to leave all parties scratching their heads as to what to do after they had read it.

Moss crossed his legs and balanced a yellow A4 pad on his knee. He had a press conference coming up soon and was anxious for angles. He could handle the spin himself, but he needed something to work with in the first place, something suitable for spinning.

'It's the usual ending to this kind of saga, isn't it?' Moss began. 'Killer mows down a congregation then goes home and tops himself.'

'Is that what you think happened?' Banks said.

'Well, it is, isn't it?'

'I think what Superintendent Banks means,' said Gervaise, 'is that there could easily have been a number of different outcomes to yesterday's actions.'

Moss frowned, pen poised. 'Such as?'

Gervaise flashed Banks a wry smile, as if to tell him he had got himself into this and must get himself out. 'Alan?'

'Well,' Banks said, 'Edgeworth could easily have gone on a rampage and shot a lot more people before either forcing us to take his life or killing himself when we had him cornered.'

Moss made a few scratches on his pad. 'But he didn't, did he?' he said. 'I mean, he didn't get the chance. So we're golden, aren't we? We saved lives. It's win–win.'

Banks took a deep breath. 'I suppose you could say that,' he said. 'Apart from one or two minor ticks.'

'Minor ticks . . .?'

'Laura Tindall, Francesca Muriel, Katie Shea, Benjamin Kemp, Charles Kemp. Need I go on? Edgeworth killed five people and wounded four. He put Diana Lofthouse in a wheelchair. And he's ruined even more lives. Do you think people just return to normal, pick up and carry on, after something like this? Some of them never will. If you ask me, that's the story the media will be going with, the aftermath, the *human* story, not how it was a "win–win" situation for us. We did nothing. We got lucky.'

Moss scratched on his pad. 'I like that,' he said. '"The human story". But you're not being fair to yourself. You did track the killer down.'

'It was routine police work, a paper trail, and that's not very exciting to our friends out there. A helicopter and jeep chase over moorland terrain in zero visibility followed by a stand-off and shootout would have made much better copy.'

Moss tapped his pen on his pad and chewed on his bottom lip. A few of his abundant glossy curls were hanging over his creased brow above his glasses. 'That's what I was getting around to,' he said. 'I mean, when you get right down to it, it's all rather boring, isn't it? I mean, as a story.'

'Not for the victims and their families.'

'No, I know that. I didn't mean to be disrespectful or anything. But try to see it from my point of view.' He gestured towards the window. 'And theirs. We don't have much to give them, do we? I mean, the whole gun law business is getting rather predictable, for a start. They've just about done that one to death. No pun intended.'

'None heard,' said Banks. 'And since when hasn't a bit of blood and gore been enough for them?'

'I don't mean to be critical, Superintendent,' said Moss, 'but I don't think you fully understand the situation. I mean *my* situation. The media situation in general. I'm sensing resistance here. You underestimate them. They're not simply a bunch of children suffering from attention deficit hyperactivity disorder.'

'Oh, I see,' said Banks, with a questioning sideways glance at Gervaise. 'They're not? Do enlighten me, then.'

'There's no need to be sarcastic,' said Moss. 'We simply see the world in different ways. That's all. But we *do* need to be on the same page here.'

'And how do *you* see all this?'

'That there must be *another* story. A better story. This can't be the end.'

'Isn't it the bridal party they'll all be writing about?' Banks asked. 'That's where the glamour and tragedy lie. Laura Tindall was a sexy model; Ben Kemp a war hero. Martin Edgeworth was a nobody. A bloody retired dentist, for crying out loud. What are you going to do, dredge up the statistics about how many retired dentists become rampage killers?'

'A possibility,' said Moss, jotting down another thought, 'but they've already had enough of the victims. They've been running pictures of Laura Tindall on the catwalk and Benjamin Kemp in his fatigues holding a weapon that, in my opinion, is similar to the one the victims were shot with. People are getting tired of the ex-supermodel and the war hero.'

'And you say we're not dealing with a bunch of kids suffering from ADHD?' said Banks.

Gervaise gave him a warning glance. 'So, what's your suggestion, Adrian?' she asked. 'I assume you have an alternative in mind?'

'Yes.' Moss paused for effect before his pronouncement. 'It's Edgeworth's story now.'

'What?' said Banks.

'You said it yourself. The details of the investigation aren't very interesting. The manhunt wound down too soon, held no real excitement, and the weather's been too bad to do much location filming, anyway. You followed a paper trail. It led you to Edgeworth. Simple.'

'You're saying we solved the case and stopped a mass murderer too quickly?' Banks said.

Moss managed a thin smile. 'If you care to put it that way, yes. You've left the table bare, Superintendent. Well, not quite.'

'Once again,' said Gervaise, 'what do you suggest?'

Moss leaned forwards, put both feet firmly on the floor and tossed his pad on the table, where it landed with a loud slap. 'People are fascinated by what motivates killers like Edgeworth,' he said. 'What makes them tick. Look at all the books on mass murderers like Moat and Bird and the rest. Dunblane. Hungerford. Or Columbine and Sandy Hook in the States. The Pulse nightclub in Orlando. And serial killers? For crying out loud. Just pick one. They give them nicknames and make movies about them: the Yorkshire Ripper, Son of Sam, the

Moors Murderers, the Boston Strangler, the Zodiac Killer, the Green River Killer. I mean, why are we still fascinated with Jack the Ripper after all these years? How many people can remember the names of any of his victims? But how many books have been written about him and these killers? Most of them by journalists.'

'Mary Kelly,' said Banks.

'What?'

'Mary Kelly. One of the Ripper's victims.'

'Oh, I see. Right.'

'OK, Adrian,' said Banks, holding up his hand. 'I take your point. People are interested in the grotesque, in the aberrations, deviations from the norm. That's why they read *Silence of the Lambs* and so on. Why Hannibal Lecter and Norman Bates are such cultural icons.'

'Exactly! And they're interested because, no matter how much has been written, no matter how many of these monsters we've studied, no matter how many reports and learned dissertations there have been, we still don't understand them. There's still a need, a hunger, for more knowledge about such things, such people. What makes them tick. What went wrong. How they became defective. They can't be pigeon-holed, filed, put away in a box marked read and understood. They're still viable. No matter how much we *think* we know, the bloke next door could still be a serial killer or a mass murderer. That's the angle to exploit.'

'But that isn't our job,' said Banks. 'And to be perfectly honest, neither is this. I certainly didn't sign up to waste my time sitting around coming up with angles for the media to use.'

Banks moved to stand up, but Gervaise waved him down. 'Hang on a minute, Alan. Hear him out.'

Banks sat reluctantly.

'Please don't think for a minute that I'm trying to tell you how to do your job,' said Moss, 'or what your job is, but it's been my experience over the years that the boundaries have changed, and the media expect people like you to do a lot more than keep order and put bad guys away – in fact, half the time they criticise you for doing those very things.'

'What then?' asked Gervaise.

Moss leaned back and crossed his legs again. 'They want to understand, to explain to their readers, listeners, viewers, and they want us to help them to understand. Half the explanations the police come up with for what's happening in society are unbelievable. Hardly surprising, as they're cobbled together from lies and bullshit and obfuscated by the appalling use of language. Have you ever tried to read a chief constable's report? People would like to trust us, but they don't. They'd like to understand us, but we don't make ourselves clear. We come on as if we're always trying to cover something up, keeping our guilty secrets from the general public and failing to face up to things. As if we're some sort of superior private club. They think we know something they don't, and that we're deliberately keeping it from them. And they're right. They feel excluded. The only thing that dispels that feeling and is likely to bring us any closer together is if we attempt to publicly make sense of things like this. Of people like Martin Edgeworth.'

'So you're saying we should be psychologists as well as officers of the law?' Banks argued.

'You already are, to a large extent. One could hardly do your job without some understanding of the criminal mind. But there are criminal minds, and then there are people like Martin Edgeworth. He's not a drug dealer or a mugger or a burglar or a wife-beater. He passed all the psychological and physical tests he needed to acquire his firearms certificate. How many more people like him are out there? That's what people are interested in. They want to know what makes him different. Is that so difficult to understand?'

'No, Adrian,' said Gervaise. 'Not at all. It's just that we've been rather too busy catching the man to think very much about what set him off.'

'I know. Believe me, I understand your priorities. But now you've got him, one way or another, you can afford to direct your attention elsewhere. We all know that it was a terrible thing he did, but what we want to know now is why he did it. And maybe how we can stop something like that from happening again. You've already been using a profiler, Dr Jenny Fuller. I've met her. It's not as if you've had zero interest in what sort of person did this.'

'Not at all,' said Banks. 'That kind of profile can be very important. And if things had gone on much longer, and we'd had more information to feed Dr Fuller, then her work might well have been instrumental in leading us to Edgeworth. It just wasn't the way things worked out this time.'

'And now?' asked Moss.

'You said it yourself. Now we've got him.'

'So it's all over?'

'The killing is over, which is the main thing. And the killer himself has saved us the expense of a trial.'

'And your Dr Fuller? Do you just pat her on the head and send her home? You might not have noticed, but she also happens to be very photogenic. Perhaps a bit long in the tooth, but most presentable for a woman her age. She'll do well on *Newsnight* or *Panorama*. The media will lap her up.'

Banks held back from punching Moss. 'Don't be so fucking patronising,' he said.

'I'm sorry, but I think you know what I mean.'

Banks glanced at Gervaise then turned back to Moss and said, 'I, for one, am certainly still interested in Edgeworth's psychology, in who he is and why he did what he did. Just because it's over on one level doesn't mean we're going to stop studying him. All I'm saying is that our main job is over.' Banks knew that Jenny would continue with her profile, and he was intending to put Annie Cabbot and Gerry Masterson on the other angles of the case. Gerry was good at digging up stories and background, seemed to have a pretty firm grasp of basic human psychology, and she could use the experience. Annie could steer her. 'We also need to make absolutely certain that Edgeworth was acting alone,' he added.

'What do you mean?' said Moss. 'Are you suggesting he had a sidekick? Someone who helped him? Is there evidence of this? Why didn't you mention it before?'

'Don't get your knickers in a twist, Adrian,' said Banks. 'It's merely a box to tick. We have no evidence that anyone else was involved. It's just an avenue that needs to be thoroughly investigated and cleared.'

'Superintendent Banks is right,' Gervaise added. 'And perhaps the investigation is not as high-powered now as it was when Edgeworth was on the loose and a danger to the public, but it's not over yet. We are perfectly aware that profilers such as Dr Fuller often rely on us for access to information that may give them a deeper understanding of the killer's psychology.'

'Good,' said Moss. 'Then I think we're on the same page at last.'

That was a rather frightening thought for Banks, but he said nothing.

'But back to this business about the accomplice—'

'There *was* no accomplice,' said Banks, wishing to God he'd never mentioned the possibility. 'And I'd appreciate it if you didn't suggest that there was in any of your releases. We don't want a panic on our hands, do we? Especially one caused by an MLO who got hold of the wrong end of the stick?'

Moss swallowed. 'But you'll keep me informed on anything more you find out about Edgeworth?'

'We'll keep you informed, Adrian.'

'Including Dr Fuller's profile?'

'Including the profile.'

'Right. OK, then.' Moss gave them each a nervous smile and made his way crabwise out of the office.

'So can you clarify the point of all that for me?' Banks asked Gervaise when the door had closed. 'Am I to do anything different than I was intending to do?'

'No, Alan. Like it or not, we've been on the same page all along, as Adrian says. He just needed to vent his spleen a bit. He's under a lot of pressure. He needs a bit of babying every now and then.'

'Thought so.' Banks left shaking his head.

The river was not much more than a beck swollen with the recent rains where it ran through Swainshead village from its source high in the dale. The weather seemed to be offering a brief respite that afternoon. By the looks of the iron sky, though, that wouldn't last long.

Now that he could see them in daylight, Banks remembered the rows of limestone cottages with their flagstone roofs, facing one another across the river, the waterside benches and the stone bridge where the old men in flat caps stood talking, passing the time. Three of them were out there today, no doubt talking about the recent excitement, and Banks wouldn't have been at all surprised if they were the same old men who had stood there almost twenty-five years ago, when he had worked on his first case in Swainshead. Two major incidents in twenty-five years wasn't bad going for such a small village.

He ejected David Gilmour's *Rattle that Lock* and parked outside the whitewashed facade of the White Rose, founded in 1615, or so the sign proclaimed. Further up the road stood the empty Collier house, a Victorian pile of stone cluttered with porticos, oriels and turrets, with most of its windows boarded up. Banks glanced across the river. The Greenock Guest House, which had played a pivotal role in the first Swainshead case, was now a pottery centre and gift shop. Banks wondered what had happened to Sam and Katie Greenock, the former proprietors. Katie had been a natural beauty, he remembered, and an innocent, but a woman confused by her attractiveness and uneasy mix of sexuality and innocence, like Hardy's Tess. She had been in her twenties back then, so she would be fifty or more by now. He wondered where she was, what she was doing with her life. Was she still married to Sam? Or was she dead, like Emily and Katie Shea, her namesake at the wedding?

The pub was busy for a Tuesday lunchtime. Most of the customers were locals, Banks guessed by their easy manner and casual clothing, but there was a smattering of reporters, no doubt grubbing for the nitty-gritty on Martin Edgeworth. Adrian Moss had said that Edgeworth was their subject now, and Banks thought he was probably right. No doubt they were hoping to stumble across someone who had seen him pull the wings off a fly when he was five.

Banks was on his way to the Edgeworth house to meet up with Annie. The CSIs and search teams were still working there, packing anything that might be possible evidence of Edgeworth's actions or motives into boxes. He might be dead, but the reverberations of his deed lingered on, as Banks had told Adrian Moss, and if anything could be learned from his actions to prevent such a thing happening in the future, it needed to be discovered. Profilers such as Jenny Fuller, for example, were always interested in as much data as they could get on forms of deviant behaviour in order to build up more accurate and comprehensive profiles. Jenny hadn't had much to do this time before they found their man, but she might still be able to learn something useful from the case. Banks had phoned her on his way, and she had agreed to have dinner with him that evening. He couldn't deny, even to himself, that he was still attracted to her after all these years, but he also knew he could hardly forge ahead on the assumption that she felt the same way.

First, though, as the sense of urgency had disappeared with Edgeworth's suicide, Banks realised he hadn't eaten much over the past couple of days, so he decided to eat a pub lunch while he had a casual word with the landlord. The people in the village who had known Edgeworth – including friends, neighbours, shopkeepers and publicans – would all be officially interviewed over the next few days, but Banks saw no reason not to try to get a general picture of the killer, and what better means than through the landlord of his local pub?

The White Rose had clearly undergone a face lift since Banks had last been there. The dark wood panelling was still on the walls, but above it, the pale blue paint was much brighter and fresher than the previous dun colour. Perhaps the years of accumulated tar and nicotine from cigarette smoke had been scraped off the walls and ceiling, too, since the pub smoking ban. The lounge even smelled of air freshener. A number of framed photographs of local attractions hung on the walls: waterfalls, the hanging valley nearby, a panoramic view of the village, the mouth of a cavern. The tables were more modern and less wobbly than before, square with wooden legs rather than the old cast-iron type. There was a fire burning in the hearth, and along with the Christmas lights and decorations, it gave the place a warm, cosy atmosphere.

The man behind the bar was a lot younger than old Freddie Metcalfe, who used to run the pub, though he had old Freddie's craggy brow. It turned out his name was Ollic Metcalfe, Freddie's nephew. He was a broad-shouldered lad with a bristly beard and weathered outdoorsman's face, the type who would make a good second-row forward, and probably even had, as his nose seemed to have been broken more than once. Banks introduced himself, ordered a pint of Sneck Lifter and glanced over the menu, which was more gastronomically adventurous than its counterpart from twenty-five years ago. Not that he fancied anything adventurous right now. In the end, he went for a simple steak and mushroom pie and chips, introduced himself and indicated to Ollie Metcalfe that he would prefer to eat at the far end of the bar, away from the reporters, and would appreciate a quiet word when his food arrived. Metcalfe nodded and set off about his business.

Banks didn't recognise any of the reporters, though he prided himself on guessing who they were, if not exactly what newspapers they represented. It used to be a lot easier to tell them apart, but these days it wasn't even easy to find much difference between the newspapers themselves. He got a few suspicious glances, noticed several whispered exchanges, and assumed that he had been recognised, but nobody approached him. Now they had a bigger story, they were far less interested in any police investigation, unless it related to the now very public row between the firearms cadre and emergency services.

Banks had managed no more than a couple of pulls on his beer when his pie arrived, delivered by Metcalfe himself, who had left his young helper to handle the bar. The pastry was a puffy, crusty hat plonked on top of the stewed beef and mushrooms, but it would do. Anything would do at the moment. The chips were crispy and hot.

Metcalfe leaned on the bar opposite him. One or two reporters eyed them enviously – Banks could almost see their ears twitching – but nobody made a move to get any closer. If they knew Banks, they also knew his reputation. 'What can I help you with, Mr Banks?' Metcalfe asked.

'Nothing specific,' said Banks. 'I'm just after a spot of lunch and a nice chat. Case like this plays havoc with your meal times.'

'I'll bet it does.' He jerked his head. 'Up the road with that lot last night, were you?'

'Until about four.'

'I still can't believe it,' said Ollie. 'Nobody around here can.'

'Popular bloke, Mr Edgeworth?'

'Very.'

'Isn't that always the case with these mass murderers and serial killers?' Banks said. 'Butter wouldn't melt in his mouth, they say. Quiet as a mouse.'

'I wouldn't know about that. I've never met anyone who did such a thing before. Are you sure you've not got it wrong?'

'Everything adds up so far.'

'But *why*? Why would a man like Martin Edgeworth do something like that?'

'What sort of a man was he?'

'A decent one. Good sense of humour, took a keen interest in local events, clubbable, went to meetings and so on. He liked to cook. Said if he hadn't been a dentist he'd have trained as a chef. Keen amateur photographer, too.' He pointed to a picture of a landscape. 'And very good. He took that one over there. Even paid to have it enlarged and framed specially for our wall.'

Banks glanced at the photo. 'You mentioned clubs. What clubs?'

'Well, the shooting club, for a start. Swainsdale Rifle and Pistol. But I suppose you know all about that.'

Banks was intending to visit the club after stopping in at the Edgeworth house. 'Was he any good?'

'I think he must have been. He went in for competitions, won awards and so forth. They did a lot of shooting on the army range about five miles up the road, too. Proper supervision there, see, so you can use the real McCoy. Or so he said.'

'What about grouse and the like?'

'Occasionally. But he got rid of his shotgun a while back.'

'Why?'

'Lost interest in shooting defenceless little birds, I should imagine.'

'What did he do with it?'

'I've no idea. Whatever it is people do with used shotguns. Sold it, I suppose, or handed it in to some government agency.'

'Do you know if he had any strong political leanings or connections?'

Metcalfe laughed. 'If you'd known Martin, you wouldn't have got him started on politicians. Hated the lot of them. Thought they were only in it to line their own pockets.'

'So he had strong views?'

'I didn't mean to suggest there was anything unnatural about his ideas. It was just pub banter, blethering, like. A joke or two. He just didn't care much for politicians, that's all.'

'How long had Mr Edgeworth lived up at the house?'

Metcalfe scratched his head. 'Twenty years or more. He was here when I took on this place from my uncle, and that's seventeen years back.'

'Was he always a regular here?'

'Aye, certainly all the years I've been here. Dropped by most days for a jar or two. Not a big drinker, mind you. Just the odd pint or two now and then.'

'Beer man?'

'Occasional splash of single malt. Special occasions.'

'Was he popular?'

'Aye, I'd say that he was. Yes. Very.'

'Any particular close friends, drinking companions?'

'Geoff McLaren, manager of that gun club he belonged to. Nice bloke. George and Margie, a couple of friends of his from the club. Sometimes his old partner came in with him. Jonathan Martell.'

'Did Mr Martell come here often?'

'Now and then. He's retired now, too. Lives out Sedburgh way.'

'Did Mr Edgeworth bring any new friends in here during the past month or so, anyone you hadn't seen before?'

'Once in a while, aye. I mean, we didn't live in each other's pockets. He knew plenty of people, and I was quite happy if he wanted to meet any of them in here for a drink and a bite to eat.'

'So he sometimes came in with people you didn't know?'

'Now and then. Yes.'

'Singly or in groups?'

'Both. I mean, but not with groups that often, not unless the family was around, like.'

'Did he ever strike up conversations with strangers?'

Metcalfe considered the question. 'Sometimes,' he answered. 'Martin was sociable enough. He'd get chatting with other customers from time to time. Especially the ramblers. Martin liked walking, himself, and he knew a lot about local history, so if a customer had a question I'd usually point them in his direction.'

'Anyone in particular?'

'Not as far as I recollect. Certainly not in the past few months.'

'Anyone stand out for any reason at all shortly before the shootings? Say November, early December?'

'We get a lot of people in, believe it or not. And that's a busy time. I'm sorry, but I can't remember anyone in particular. I'm not saying he didn't come in with anyone just that no one stands out in my memory. Sorry.'

'Who else did he come with regularly?'

'Nobody special. I mean, most of my regulars knew him. I'm not saying he was a saint, but ask any one of them, and I don't think you'll hear a bad word.'

'We'll get around to that eventually,' said Banks. 'Had he been behaving any differently lately, say this past month or so?'

'Not at all. Same as normal.'

'When did you last see him?'

'Friday night.'

That was the day before the murders. 'And he behaved as normal?'

'Aye.'

'Was he with anyone?'

'No. He came in by himself and sat by the fire with Les and Barry most of the time he was here. They're regulars, like Martin. They'll be gutted.'

Banks made a note of the names. 'Did he say anything odd at all, anything that struck you as out of character or mysterious?'

'No. Like I said, he was the same as ever. Said good evening to me and the other regulars, ordered his pint and we chatted for a bit. It wasn't a busy night, as I remember. He didn't stay long after his drink with Les and Barry, though. Only had the two pints. Something on telly he wanted to see.'

'What did he talk to you about?'

'Oh, this and that. The weather. Christmas, how commercial it is these days. What everyone's holiday plans were.'

'What were his?'

'He was going to stop with his son and daughter-in-law in Derby. They've got a couple of wee ones. See, when Martin and Constance split, like, I know people say they don't take sides and all, but they do. Kids especially. The daughter, Marie, were always much closer to her mother. Not that she didn't come and see Martin now and then, of course, but when it comes to summat like Christmas, well, she's with her mother, isn't she? And she's divorced, like. Lives in Norwich, too, which is a bit of a bugger to get to and from.'

Banks thought about his own Christmas arrangements. It was coming up fast. He didn't think he would get to see either of his children this year, as it was his ex-wife Sandra's turn to have Tracy down in London, and Brian was still in LA with his band, the Blue Lamps. 'But his son stuck with him?'

'Aye, I suppose so. Nice lad. Colin, his name is. He'll be bloody heartbroken. And his wife Mandy. Pretty lass. Thought the world of Martin. They always used to drop in here for a pint and a pub lunch whenever they were up visiting.'

Officers in Derby, Norwich and Carlisle had called on the various members of Edgeworth's family early that morning, so they wouldn't have to read about what happened to him first in the papers, or see it on TV. According to their brief reports, there had been the predictable outbursts of tears and disbelief, and the upshot was that both his children said they'd be up in Eastvale to sort things out as soon as possible. His ex-wife in Carlisle had been stunned by the news, too, but she hadn't mentioned making the journey. By now, Banks calcu-lated, the media would be camping out in their gardens and their telephones would be ringing off the hook.

'Have you any idea what his movements were on Saturday morning?'

'What they usually were, I suppose,' said Metcalfe.

'What was that?'

'He usually went for a long walk along the tops on a Saturday and a Sunday morning, come rain or shine. It's a bit of a bloody hike to get up there from the back of his house, like, but he did it. You certainly wouldn't catch me trying it. But Martin kept himself fit. And he said the view's magnificent. You can see Pen-y-Ghent on a good day.'

'Any break-ins, or anything unusual happen in the village recently?' Banks asked. 'Crimes of any sort, unexplained events?'

'Nay, wouldn't you be the first one to know about something like that?'

'Only if it was reported. There's plenty goes on never reaches our ears. You must know that.'

'Aye, well, not that I can think of.' Metcalfe paused. 'Why are you asking me all these questions? I mean, Martin's dead. What does it matter?'

'We have to cover every angle, Ollie.'

'Well I can't think of anything along those lines. And he wasn't a nutter, if that's what you're saying.'

'That's not what I'm saying. We need to understand him, that's all. Did you ever see him get drunk, get involved in any trouble, any arguments?' Banks asked.

'Not in here. Like I said, Martin were no saint, and he did have a bit of a short temper, but I never saw him drink to excess. Well . . . maybe once.'

'Trouble?'

'Martin? No. Except . . .' He rubbed his beard.

'Yes?'

'Remember, I just mentioned that wife of his? Ex-wife. Constance. About two or three years ago, it were now, the split.'

'Not long after he retired, then?'

'Aye. Not long at all. It hardly seems to matter now, does it? I mean now that he's dead.' He gestured towards the group

Banks thought were reporters. 'It's just for them vultures to pick his bones clean now, isn't it?'

Banks glanced over. 'I suppose they'll do their jobs,' he said. Then he leaned forwards slightly. 'I'll give you a word of warning for when you're dealing with the press, Mr Metcalfe. Be careful what you say. Be very careful. They're experts at twisting the simplest thing. You could tell them you make meat pies and you'll come out sounding like Sweeney Todd. Know what I mean?'

Metcalfe laughed. 'Thanks, but I've dealt with their like before. Used to be in public relations for Newcastle United. You know footballers.'

'Well, you'll understand, then. We have to employ a bloke specially to deal with them. Media relations officer, he's called. I ask you. Course, we have to try and stay on their good side. It galls me to say it, but they *can* be useful.'

'That's the problem. And don't they know it?'

Banks drank some beer and held up his glass to inspect it. 'You keep a good pint, Ollie, I'll say that for you.'

'Thanks. But what use is a pub but for fine company and a decent pint of ale?'

'If only all landlords thought that. Now, about this bit of trouble . . .'

'It were summat and nowt.'

'Usually is, in my experience. What happened?'

'Martin was in here one evening enjoying his pint, like, keeping himself to himself, when this bloke Norman Lavalle came in.'

'Was he a regular?'

'No. I'd only seen him a couple of times before. And I didn't like him much. Too smarmy by half, too full of himself.'

'How long ago was all this?'

'About two years.'

'So what happened?'

'Well, we all knew what was going on, like, that this Lavalle bloke was having it off with Connie, Martin's wife. She were a bit flighty, like, but a nice enough lass, or so I thought. I suppose life with Martin was just too quiet and boring for her, especially after he stopped working and spent more time at home. Must've cramped her style. She were a good ten years younger than him. Anyway, she'd left him by then and was living down the dale a mile or two with a friend. This Lavalle bloke was panting after her. Well, Martin was none too pleased to see him. He'd been down in the dumps of late, a bit depressed, like, and who could blame him, so he makes some comment like, "What are you doing here? Can't you just leave me in peace?" or something innocuous like that. Lavalle replies, "What's it got to do with you? I'll drink where I want." At which point I'm about to come in and say not here you bloody well won't, but Martin shoves him, and Lavalle takes a swing at him. Misses by a mile. Then Martin takes his shot. Connects, too. Lavalle staggers back a bit, with a bloody nose, but by then I'm round the bar like a shot, holding them apart. I get Lavalle out and get Martin sat down again with his drink. He's a bit upset, so I leave him to it. He knocked back a bit more than usual that night, that's all.'

'Did he get angry when he was drinking?'

'No, not at all. Only earlier. Lavalle was long gone by then. Martin usually got a bit morose when he drank too much, if truth be told. Quiet. Subdued.'

'Did he say anything.'

'When I asked him later if he was all right, like, he just says summat like, "If Connie runs off with that slimy bastard, I swear I'll top myself."' Metcalfe gave a nervous laugh. 'It wasn't like he really meant it or anything, it were just the way he felt at the time. Sort of thing we all say sometimes.'

'So you didn't believe he meant it?'

'Certainly not.'

'But he did threaten to commit suicide if his wife left him?'

'That's the long and the short of it. But it were just sort of something you say, like, when you're upset. And he didn't. Top himself, that is.'

Not two years ago, he didn't, Banks thought. 'He didn't threaten to harm Lavalle or Constance?'

'Never anything like that.'

'Any further incidents?'

'None. That's just what I can't understand, Mr Banks. Martin Edgeworth just wasn't a violent man. Fair enough, he took a pop at the bloke who was bonking his wife, but what man wouldn't? And then he goes and does something like this out of the blue. I can't fathom it.' He scratched his head.

'What happened to Lavalle?'

Metcalfe snorted. 'He and Connie got married. Live out Carlisle way now.'

Banks drained his pint. He had eaten what he wanted of the pie and chips a while ago. 'Something caused Martin Edgeworth to snap,' he said. 'We don't know what it was, but that's what I'm after finding out. Maybe some people think it doesn't matter now that he's dead, but let's not forget, he killed five people and ruined a lot of other lives. I like to close my books, Ollie, and I like them to be properly balanced when I do.'

Banks picked up Annie at the Edgeworth house, where nothing new had come to light, and drove to the Upper Swainsdale District Rifle and Pistol Club, which was three miles up the road, then another half mile along a gravel drive.

The clubhouse was an old stone structure, much like a rambling country pub, and inside, beyond the small deserted reception area with its racks of brochures about shooting safely, was a bar. There were several wooden tables with blue-and-white checked tablecloths, only three of them occupied. The diners turned to see who had come in, then, not recognising Banks and Annie, went back to their conversations and their meals. The walls were bare, rough stone, and there were a couple of glass-fronted cabinets along one side filled with trophies and photographs of men holding guns. There were, however, no real guns anywhere in sight, for which Banks was grateful. A young man in a white jacket stood drying glasses behind the bar. Banks was surprised to find a fully stocked bar at a shooting club, but he realised there was no law against it.

'Can I help you?' said the young man, whose name badge identified him as Roger. 'Are you members? I haven't seen you here before. The bar's for members only.'

Banks and Annie flashed their warrant cards.

'Oh. I suppose it's about Martin, isn't it?'

'Boss around?' Banks asked.

'Mr McLaren isn't in today.' Roger gestured towards the grey weather outside. 'Not much point being open on a day like this, but some of the regulars like to come in for a bite and a natter, so we usually open for lunch.' He checked his watch. 'We'll be closing up for the day in half an hour.'

'Maybe we can have a quick chat with you?' Banks suggested, sitting on one of the high bar stools. Annie sat next to him.

'I can't tell you much,' Roger said. 'It's George and Margie over there you want.' He pointed to a man and woman sitting at one of the tables nearer to the door. 'George and Margie Sykes. They were close to Martin.'

Banks glanced over. The man had an almost full pint in front of him, enough to last him a while yet. Banks guessed that his wife's drink, with a piece of lime floating in it, was a gin and tonic. 'We'll talk to them in a minute,' he said. 'How long had Martin Edgeworth been a member here?'

'Dunno,' said Roger. 'Since well before my time. Ten years, say. Mr McLaren will be able to tell you.'

'You can't show us the membership records yourself?'

Roger shook his head. 'Mr McLaren always keeps the club office locked when he's not here, and I don't have a key.'

'OK,' said Banks. 'We'll deal with him later. Any trouble recently?'

'Trouble?'

'Yes. You know, disagreements, arguments, scenes, fights, shootouts, that sort of thing.'

'Good lord, no. Never. Mr McLaren wouldn't stand for anything of that sort. You'd be out on your arse.'

'When did you last see Mr Edgeworth?' Annie asked.

'Last week. Early on. Tuesday, I think.'

'Anything unusual about his behaviour? Was he upset, depressed, angry, anything like that?'

'No. Just normal.'

'And that was?'

'Cheerful, polite, generous with his tips.'

'Did you ever hear him mention the Tindall–Kemp wedding?' Banks cut in.

'No, never. Why would he?'

'I don't know. That's why I'm asking you. Did he ever mention Benjamin or Charles Kemp, or Laura Tindall?'

'No.'

'Were any of them members? Have they ever been here?'

'Not that I know of. And if they'd been in the last four years, I'd remember.'

Banks thanked him and slid off his stool. He turned to Annie. 'Let's go talk to George and Margie.'

They reached the table and introduced themselves. George and Margie made room while Banks pulled up a couple more chairs. 'Thought you were damned reporters at first,' said George apologetically. 'Was just about to give you a piece of my mind.' He had a shiny head, striped by a few dark hairs, and a handlebar moustache the likes of which Banks hadn't seen outside of an old TV programme about the RAF. Margie had a moustache, too, but it was far less well developed. She also had bottle-blond hair starched into place like Margaret Thatcher's.

'Been around already, have they?' Banks asked.

'First thing,' said George. 'I wouldn't mind, but it's the usual rot about should there be shooting clubs at all. What on earth can we get out of it? Isn't it dangerous? Very aggressive some of them are.'

'Well,' said Banks. 'They're men and women of great moral character.'

George guffawed. '"Great moral character". I like that. What can we do for you?'

Banks sat back and let Annie do some of the talking. 'I understand, according to Roger over there, that you were good friends of Martin Edgeworth?'

'Known him for years,' said George. 'Haven't we, Margie?'

'Years,' said Margie. 'George and I are absolutely devastated about what's happened. Just devastated.' There was the hint of a slur in her voice, and Banks guessed it wasn't her first G&T.

'I take it all this has been a great surprise, then?' Annie went on.

'You can say that again, love. Completely.'

'So neither of you would have considered Martin Edgeworth to be capable of something like this?'

'Never in a million years,' said Margie. 'He was a true gentleman, was Martin.'

'A true gentleman,' her husband echoed. 'Martin Edgeworth was one of the gentlest souls you could ever hope to meet. Wouldn't harm a fly. Mind you . . .'

'What?' Annie asked.

'He didn't like to lose. Did he, Margie?'

'No, he didn't like that at all.'

'What do you mean?'

'You know, competitions and the like. Got all huffy if he lost.'

'Why all the interest in guns and shooting?' Annie asked.

'Why?' said George, a suspicious gleam in his eye. 'You're not one of these anti-firearms lot, are you?'

'Not at all,' said Annie. 'Just wondering what the appeal is.'

'It's a hobby, that's all. Gets you out of the house. And I suppose it's a sport, too. At least it's competitive. In the Olympics, you know. We have regular competitions. Won a few trophies, as you can see. As far as I'm concerned, shooting's no more about hurting anyone, or anything, than darts or cricket. You've got to be careful around guns, no doubt about that, but if you follow a few simple rules, you're safe as houses. Martin just enjoyed the sport, getting out and meeting people. That's all there is to it.'

'Do you remember when he split up with his wife?' Annie asked.

George's expression darkened. 'Connie, that little minx. Oh, yes. We remember, all right.'

'He was upset about that, right?'

'Naturally.'

'Did he ever express any desire for revenge, to hurt her or the man she ran off with?'

'Not to me he didn't. Besides, that was over two years ago, and he didn't go anywhere near Connie again.'

'Was he angry about the idea of marriage?' Annie asked. 'Seeing as it had gone so wrong for him.'

'He never said as much. And as far as I can tell, he didn't know those people at the wedding from Adam, either, if that's what you're hinting at.'

'Why did he shoot them, then?' Banks asked.

George glanced back and forth from Annie to Banks and gripped his wife's hand. 'I've no idea,' he said in a quiet, trembling voice. 'He was my friend. I don't understand any of what's happened. To tell you the truth, I'm not even convinced that he did it.'

'Oh, why's that?'

'Just not in his nature.'

'But we know he had a short temper, and you said yourself he was a bad loser,' said Annie.

'Don't try to twist my words,' George said. 'I'm not saying he was perfect. There's plenty of people like that, and they don't go around killing strangers.'

'There was nothing on his mind, nothing erratic in his behaviour lately?' Annie asked.

'No,' said Margie. 'We saw him just last week, and he was the same as normal.'

'When was this?'

'Tuesday.'

'What did you talk about?'

'Nothing much. Just an upcoming competition, the prices in the new gun catalogue, membership fees going up. Nothing important. Club gossip.'

'Was that the last time either of you saw him?'

'Yes,' said George.

'Do you shoot, Mrs Sykes?' Annie asked.

'Me? Good lord, no,' said Margie. 'I just come along for the company. It's a bit empty here today, but it's usually more lively. Quite a few of the wives come along, and we have some fine female shooters as members. But me? I don't think I could hit a barn door at ten paces.'

'It's probably a good thing you don't shoot, then,' said Annie with a smile.

'Yes.'

'Was Martin any good?' she asked George.

'He was. Yes. Beat me nearly every time.'

'Do you know where or when he became interested in shooting? He didn't have any military training or background, did he?'

'Martin? Military? Heavens, no. Though he did go up to their range now and then. It's the only place you can fire the full-bore rifles, you see. Under strict military supervision, of course. Quite a few of our members enjoy the hospitality there from time to time.'

'Did you go, too?'

'Me? No. I'm happy enough with small-bore.'

'It was a small-bore gun Mr Edgeworth used at St Mary's.'

'Well, it would have to be, wouldn't it, unless he'd acquired something else illegally?' George leaned forwards. 'Now listen here, young lady, I respect that you have a serious job to do and all.' He glanced at Banks. 'Both of you. But if you're expecting me to imagine my friend, my best friend, getting up one day, heading out with his gun and shooting into a crowd of people from the top of a hill, then driving back home and blowing his own head off, then you're in for a disappointment. Because I can't. I can't relate to it. Don't you see. I just can't . . .' There were tears in his eyes.

Margie gripped his hand more tightly and patted it. 'Now, now, George,' she said gently. 'There, there.'

'I'm sorry if it's hard to take in,' Annie said, 'but we're just trying to understand why it happened ourselves.'

'I know. And I'm telling you I can't help you. I don't know. I don't even believe it. Martin was just an ordinary bloke. Sure, he had a bit of a temper. Yes, he didn't like to lose. I think he might have cheated on his income tax, too, if truth be told. But none of that makes him a killer. He was neither so quiet and polite you might be worried what was really going through his mind, or loud and violent and abusive. He was just Martin. And don't give me any of that guff the reporters tried on, like your neighbours not being what they seem. With Martin, what you saw was what you got, and it was *him*.'

'We're not just making it up, you know,' said Banks. 'There's often more to people than we think. We do have evidence that Martin Edgeworth shot those people, Mr Sykes. And himself.'

'I'm sure you do. All I'm saying is that I can't believe it. No more than you would if I told you . . .' He paused, then pointed at Annie. 'If I told you that *she* had done it.'

'So what do you think happened?' Banks asked.

'I don't know. All I know is it can't have been Martin Edgeworth. It must have been someone else.'

Banks pulled up outside Jenny's front gate at seven o'clock that evening and tooted his horn. The rain was coming down in buckets again. He thought perhaps he should dash to the door and hold his umbrella for her – it would be very gallant – but the door opened almost immediately, and out she came with an umbrella of her own. A large, striped one.

'Sometimes I wish I'd stayed in Sydney,' she complained as she slid into the passenger seat. 'Not that it never rains there. Mm, nice car. When did you get this? And how did you afford it? Been taking backhanders from drug dealers?'

'My, my,' said Banks, 'we do have a lot to catch up on, don't we? And I believe you've developed an accent.' He turned down the volume a notch on Van Morrison's 'Warm Love' and set off. Though not quite a match for the opulence and grandeur of the Heights, the Green was a pleasant and relatively wealthy enclave of Eastvale just south-east of the River Swain, where it curved through the town, opposite the terraced gardens and falls. Those fortunate enough to live in one of the detached Georgian houses by the water had a magnificent view of the castle towering above them on the opposite bank.

Jenny now lived only a street away from the house she had sold when she left Eastvale. Her semi overlooked the green itself, a swathe of parkland, dotted with poplars and plane trees, wooden benches, marked pathways and notices about cleaning up after your dog. Though the area attracted its fair share of tourists in season, especially with a famous ice-cream shop and a bakery nearby, it was far enough from the town centre to be quiet for the most part of the year. Professionals and some of the better-off academics lived around there, along with a fair number of retired couples and even a few successful artists and writers. It wasn't the sort of area that would suit Ray, though, Banks thought. Far too bourgeois for him, and perhaps too claustrophobic.

Luigi's wasn't far, just over the bridge and up the road past the formal gardens to Castle Hill, but on a night like this, it wasn't a walk anyone would care to make. The rain bounced in puddles on the road and pavement and ran like rills down the gutters, warping the reflections of the street lamps and the occasional green or red neon shop sign. Banks could hardly hear Van Morrison for the noise it made.

Even though it was a wet Tuesday evening, it wasn't long until Christmas, the shops were open late, and Banks was lucky to find a parking spot almost right outside the small restaurant. They shared Jenny's umbrella briefly on the way in and Banks smelled her familiar scent. He could swear it was the same she used all those years ago, and he still couldn't put a name to it. Whatever it was, it smelled fresh and natural as a perfume carried on a light summer breeze, and it reminded him of childhood trips to Beales with his mother. It seemed they always had to walk through the perfume and make-up department to get to the toys or children's clothing.

The maître d' fussed over them, took their wet things and led them to a corner table for two beneath a romantic oil painting of Venetian canals in a scratched old gilt frame. The white tablecloth was spotless, with two red candles at its centre casting shadows on the walls. It was still early, and there were only six other diners, one table of four and another of two, but it was a small and very popular restaurant, and it would soon fill up. The ambience was dim and muted, and Banks thought he could hear Elvis Presley singing 'Santa Lucia' in the background.

'Have you caught up on your sleep yet?' Banks asked.

'I don't think so. I don't seem to be sleeping regular hours, or for very long periods.'

'I imagine it takes a while.'

The menus were printed in italics. Jenny pulled her tortoise-shell reading glasses from her voluminous handbag, and Banks put on his own Specsavers specials. They both laughed and studied the menus in silence. The waiter came and asked about drinks, and after consulting with Jenny, Banks ordered a bottle of Amarone. Pushing the boat out, perhaps, but then, he reminded himself, it was a special occasion: dinner with a lovely woman he hadn't seen in over twenty years.

Jenny had been a friend, not a lover like Emily, but they had come close, and there was no doubt about their mutual attraction. Perhaps if he hadn't been married, things would have turned out differently. As the waiter poured the wine, Banks looked across the table at Jenny in the candlelight and thought how lovely she still was. As she studied the menu, she gently bit the end of her tongue between her front teeth. The candle-light was reflected in her eyes. She had a silk scarf around her neck and was wearing a V-neck rust-coloured top, which showed just enough cleavage. Her arms were bare, and she had silver bangles around her left wrist that moved and jingled as she turned the pages, and a tiny watch with a loose chain on her right. He had forgotten that Jenny was left-handed.

'What?' she said, flashing him a smile.

'I didn't say anything,' muttered Banks, flustered at being caught staring. He reminded himself that this was a working dinner, though he didn't think he could sneak the expense of the Amarone past AC Gervaise's eagle eye.

'My mistake. So what do you fancy?'

Banks buried his head in the menu again. 'I thought I might start with a small Caesar salad and then perhaps the lobster ravioli or spaghetti and meatballs. You?'

Jenny closed her menu. 'I'll have the same.'

'Are you certain?'

'Of course. I always find it easiest to do that when I'm out with somebody.'

'What if you absolutely hate what he orders?'

'Then I get a little more creative. But it's not always a "he". Honestly, Alan, spaghetti and meatballs sounds fine, and I'm sure it will go with the wine a lot better than lobster ravioli, delightful as that sounds.'

Banks closed his menu. 'Done, then.' They gave the waiter their orders and returned to the wine. 'Am I losing my mind, or didn't you used to be a redhead?'

Jenny laughed. 'Can't a girl change her mind? We women are arch-deceivers when it comes to things like hair colour. It was henna,' she said. 'Couldn't you tell?'

Banks had believed the red hair to be genuine. 'I never got close enough to find out,' he said.

Jenny arched her eyebrows. 'And whose fault was that?' She touched her head. 'This is my natural colour. I grew into it. You were going to tell me about the Porsche.'

'I'm afraid it's not a happy story. That's why I went for a diversion when you first mentioned it. It used to be my brother's.' Banks explained about Roy's murder and the new-found wealth for his parents that resulted from it, along with the Porsche for him.

'That is sad,' said Jenny when he'd finished. 'But you solved the case, found the killer?'

'Oh, yes. That's not always . . . I mean, it doesn't always help. You know. Whatever's lost, you can't quite make up for that.'

'True,' said Jenny. 'You know, I've often thought of this moment, or one like this, over the years. Us, meeting again. Wondering what it would be like. I was so nervous. Would it be awkward? Would we have moved so far apart we had no common ground? Other than murder, that is. Would there just be nothing at all, like two strangers?'

'And?'

Jenny laughed. 'In some ways it's like I've never been away. I know it's a bit of a paradox, that so much has changed, that we have both changed, but I honestly don't feel any different in your company than I used to do.'

Banks leaned back in his chair. 'Comfortable like an old pair of slippers, eh? But you're right that so much has happened. Sandra left me, for a start.'

'Oh, I know, but I'm not talking about that. Not the details. Just the essence. We have to be something more than the accumulation of things that happen to do us, don't you think?'

Banks worked on that one as he tasted some more Amarone. As he looked into her eyes again, he realised that what he thought had been sadness the other day was a depth of experience, an air of having *lived*, with all the suffering, joy, hope, loss, dreams, grief and occasional despair that living involved. Their salads arrived and they put their wine aside. The waiter quietly topped up their glasses. Banks had heard the door open a few times and he looked around to see that the place was now almost full.

'I hate it when they do that,' Jenny said. 'I get so pissed. I can't tell how much I've had to drink.'

'You'd rather count your glasses, mark your bottle?'

'Well, no. That's a bit sort of *anal*, I suppose.'

Banks laughed. 'At these prices, I don't think getting pissed is an option.'

'Then I won't worry about it again.'

'So what happened? In Australia. Why did you come back?'

'Just couldn't stay away, I suppose. The English weather, the healthy food, the politics. You. And then the job offer.'

'Seriously.'

'I got divorced.'

'I'm sorry to hear it.'

'Don't be. Anyway, the job offer was important. I'm not independently wealthy. But the marriage? The divorce wasn't nice. I don't suppose it ever is, is it?'

'No,' said Banks. 'Mine certainly wasn't. After all those years, you think you know somebody, then . . . they're strangers.'

'Yes . . . Well, I'm sure you've heard about Australian men. All they're interested in is beer, Aussie rules football and dwarf-tossing.' She shook her head. 'No. That's not fair. Henry was a dear fellow, a true thinker and a very creative type. Sensitive. Things just didn't work out for us, that's all. I don't know why. Listen to me, the psychologist who can't even understand her own psychology.'

'Physician, heal thyself?'

'Something like that. Mutually incompatible, let's say. That covers a multitude of sins. Best leave it at that.'

'There's no possibility of a reconciliation?'

'No. You?'

'Lord, no,' said Banks. 'It's been years now. Sandra's happily married to another man. They're living in London. They have a child together.'

'Do you ever see one another?'

'No. Not for years. I've lost track. I see the kids often enough, though. Brian. Tracy.'

'The Blue Lamps are pretty big down under, you know. You must be a proud father.'

'Don't tell him that, but yes, I am. And Tracy's had her ups and down, but she's turned out all right, too. Seems to have settled down. She's living in Newcastle now, working and studying at the uni.'

'You're lucky then.'

'I suppose I am. Kids?'

'No. It was a matter of choice on both our parts, so it's OK. I never thought of myself as the maternal type. Lovers?'

'One or two,' said Banks. 'You?'

'Three or four.' Jenny's expression was inscrutable.

The waiter delivered their main course and emptied the last of the wine into their glasses.

'You never wrote,' said Banks, when the waiter was out of earshot.

'Nor did you.'

'I didn't have your address.'

'You're a detective. You could have tracked me down.' Jenny stared at the table. When she looked up again, her mouth had taken a downward turn. 'You don't get it, do you?'

'What?'

'Never mind.'

'No, really.'

'I mean it. Never mind. It's nothing. I just needed to get away. Completely away. That's all. Now eat your spaghetti like a good boy.'

They tucked in. The food was good, the tomato-based sauce piquant and the meatballs moist and spicy.

'I don't suppose you'll be needing me any more, now you've got your man,' Jenny said after a while.

'That's one of the things I wanted to talk to you about.'

'Well, I must say, this is a nice way of giving someone the push. Do thank your boss for using the velvet-glove approach.'

Banks laughed. He had almost forgotten how much he laughed when he was with Jenny. 'You've got the wrong end of the stick. Yes, we've got our man – or he got himself – but there's so much we still don't know. I'd like you to keep working on the profile, if you'd be willing.'

Jenny's expression brightened. 'Of course. If nothing else, it might prove useful as research. One of the problems with this type of killer is that we don't have any useful profiles to work from. They're so few and far between, and most of them kill themselves before we get a chance to talk to them.'

'Well, this one's no exception to that rule.'

'In a strange way, not talking to them doesn't matter that much. I've always thought that talking to serial killers and mass murderers was overrated. All they do is whine and lie and blame society or their parents for their crimes. You don't learn very much. It's their behaviour and the way they present themselves in the world that I find more interesting. And the cracks, of course. What builds up to such a point that it bursts the dam, so to speak, sets them on an unalterable course with only one possible outcome. That's far more interesting.'

'I'm glad you think so.'

'So tell me everything you know about him.'

They finished their main courses, and Banks told her what he had discovered and heard so far about Martin Edgeworth, most of it that very day from Ollie Metcalfe and George and Margie Sykes at the shooting club. Annie and Gerry Masterson would be trying to dig up a lot more background, but that was all he had for now. While he spoke, Jenny rested her chin on her fists, elbows planted on the table. When he had finished, she seemed thoughtful, moved one hand to pick up her glass and drank some more wine. Her glass was nearly empty.

'Do we want another?' Banks asked. 'I can't. I'm driving. But . . .'

'I don't think I could manage it,' said Jenny. 'This tiredness just washes over me.'

'Want to go?'

Jenny waved her glass. 'Not just yet. There's still a mouthful or two left. So, basically,' she went on, 'everyone you talked to told you that Martin Edgeworth was sociable, generous, clubbable, uncomplaining, caring and successful?'

'Basically, yes,' said Banks. 'Apart from the broken marriage, the quick temper and bad-loser bit.'

'Well, we all know about broken marriages, don't we? If a difficult divorce were a trigger for mass murder, there'd be a lot more dead people in the streets. Same with a bad temper and being a poor loser.'

'Too true. We haven't interviewed his wife or children yet. The children – grown-ups now, actually – should be here tomorrow. The wife didn't mention coming over from Carlisle when Gerry spoke to her on the phone, so who knows? We may have to go there to talk to her.'

'Your man certainly doesn't fit any profile that I'm aware of,' said Jenny. 'Usually mass murderers tend to be profoundly alienated and embittered. They want revenge against the world, and they want to show everyone they're not failures, that they can't be used as doormats. There's no evidence that Martin Edgeworth was a failure, or even felt he was. Sometimes the revenge is specific, and sometimes it's just a sort of random rage against society in general. That doesn't seem to fit, either, unless Edgeworth was very, very good at hiding his true self. He wasn't a loner, and he wasn't a failure. True, he was divorced and probably felt angry with his wife for humiliating him, but that's hardly an indication of psychopathy. Some killers are good at hiding their true selves. I'm sure you've seen it often enough on the news, how the serial killer next door wouldn't harm a fly, according to his neighbours. Was just a quiet lad, never any trouble, and he's got five dismembered corpses buried in his back garden. Sure, it happens. But not that often. Most people demonstrate some clues as to what they are. I mean, there's been plenty of meek little men finally snapping and killing their wives and families and then themselves. But going out with an assault rifle and mowing down a wedding party? That's something else. We need to dig a lot deeper.'

'I think Raymond Chandler wrote something about meek little wives holding a carving knife and studying their husbands' necks, didn't he?'

'Yes,' said Jenny. 'But that was in Southern California during the Santa Ana. The hot wind makes people crazy.'

'Not only is the woman beautiful, but she knows her Raymond Chandler,' said Banks, before he realised exactly what he was saying.

Jenny didn't miss a beat. She fluttered her eyelashes and said, 'Of course, I'm not just a pretty face. You ought to know that by now.'

But Banks could see her blushing beneath the bravado. Yes, he thought, people do demonstrate clues as to what they are, or feel, or think. Most of us can only hide so much from the rest of the world. We have tells, giveaways. Body language. 'So what do you think?' he said. 'About Edgeworth.'

Jenny knocked back the rest of her wine. 'I'm not sure what to think,' she said. 'But from what you've told me, if I were you there's one question I would most certainly be asking myself.'

'What's that?'

'Despite all the evidence to support my position, am I sure, am I *absolutely* sure, that I've got the right man?'

'You're not the first person to say that to me today,' Banks grumbled. 'Shall we go?'

When he stopped outside Jenny's house to drop her off, the rain was still teeming down. They sat in silence for a while, then Jenny said, 'I'm not going to ask you to come in for a nightcap tonight, Alan. Partly I'm just too damn tired, and partly . . . I don't know . . . I'm still not quite sure where I am in the world yet. I'm out of sync. I don't know if it's day or night.'

Banks leaned over and kissed Jenny on the cheek. She smiled and touched his arm with her fingertips before moving away, grabbing her umbrella and dashing out into the rain. He waited until she had got her front door open. She turned, silhouetted by the light, waved to him and closed the door behind her. Van Morrison was singing 'Wild Children' as Banks drove back over the bridge, across the market square, where the cobbles glistened with rain under the coloured lights, and headed for home.

8

Christmas fell upon Eastvale like a knife-wielding mugger desperate for a fix, and with the St Mary's killer no longer representing a threat to the community, the investigation slowed down over the holiday period, and the town was able to get into the spirit of the season without that undercurrent of fear that a gunman on the loose inspires. The retailers loved it because people got out and went shopping rather than cloistering themselves indoors.

It might not have been a white Christmas – for the most part it was the colour of a puddle in a cow pat – but chains of festive lights lit up the market square, wound around the ancient cross and strung up over the numerous cobbled streets and ginnels nearby. The castle battlements and keep were floodlit, too, and many of the shopkeepers hung strings of lights over their signs, put up decorated Christmas trees or stuck red-and-white Santas to the insides of their windows. A huge Christmas tree arrived from the unpronounceable town in Norway with which Eastvale was twinned, and was duly set up and decorated beside the market cross. In the square, seasonal music overflowed from the pubs and filled the air. Even Cyril at the Queen's Arms entered into the spirit of things with his Christmas playlist which, Banks was pleased to hear, included a whole range of songs and carols from Nick Lowe and The Ronettes to Bing Crosby and Renée Fleming.

On working days, detectives returned to the Upper Swainsdale District Rifle and Pistol Club and interviewed more members who had known Martin Edgeworth. They also talked to just about everyone in the village of Swainshead. But they learned very little. He came from a normal middle-class background in Spalding, Lincolnshire. His parents, both deceased, were decent, law-abiding members of the community who did the best they could for their only child. Edgeworth was well behaved at school, the local comprehensive, and always came in the top five at the end-of-term exams. He showed some skill at cricket, a bit less at rugby. He came second in his graduating class at dental college. After a few years on his own, he started a successful partnership with Jonathan Martell, then retired three years ago. He gave generously to charities such as Save the Children and the British Heart Foundation, and his hobbies included military history, shooting, rambling, golf and photography.

All efforts to forge a connection between Edgeworth and any of the dead or wounded members of the wedding party came to nothing. The counter-terrorist officers and spooks packed up shop and went back home to London. They said they wouldn't be back unless something new came up to connect the St Mary's shooting with terrorism, though they doubted it would.

Edgeworth's son and daughter came to Eastvale to identify the body and kick up a fuss. Their father couldn't possibly have done such a terrible thing, they argued. The police must have got something wrong. They refused to talk to the media. Connie, the ex-wife, never showed up at all. Banks and Annie visited her in Carlisle and came away feeling they had wasted their time. She could shed no light on why Edgeworth might have done what he did, though she was quick to point out his deficiencies as a husband: 'selfish, pompous and lousy in bed'.

Most of all, she was terrified of being publicly connected with Edgeworth in any way. She had quickly forged a new life for herself with Norman Lavalle, a New Age chiropractor, who had a lucrative practice among a wealthy clientele of the north-west. She didn't want anyone to know about her previous existence as the wife of a dentist turned mass murderer. Unfortunately, less than a week after their visit, Banks spotted a well-illustrated feature on her in one of the less discriminating Sunday newspapers.

To the media, Edgeworth remained a fascinating mystery: an enigma, the mass murderer who defied all definition. To some of the more sensational reporters, he became the killer who made a mockery of criminal profiling, which hardly thrilled Jenny Fuller. Adrian Moss turned out to be right. As the bloodshed receded in people's minds, the media did their best to keep the story alive by asking questions about police actions on the day of the murders and by examining Edgeworth's life in detail for anything that might help to explain the grotesque act he had committed. They were no more successful than Gerry had been, though some of them were far more willing to play fast and loose with the truth when the occasion demanded it.

While Banks was as perplexed as the next person about Edgeworth's motives, certain aspects of the case nagged away at him – a small but insistent voice almost, but not quite, drowned out the louder cries. He didn't know what it was, but there was something fishy about the whole business.

On Christmas Eve, Banks attended the midnight service at St Agnes, in Helmthorpe. He wasn't especially religious – and nor was Ray, who went with him – but he enjoyed the sense of community in the crowded church, the fine organ playing, the choir and all the old familiar songs from his childhood – 'Once in Royal David's City', 'O Little Town of Bethlehem', 'Silent

Night' – rekindling his childhood memories of the tiny fake Christmas tree with its tinsel and lights, Uncle Ted having too much port and lemonade to drink, and Aunt Ellen's raucous laughter as they played charades.

Penny Cartwright and Linda Palmer were at the service, too, and afterwards Banks and Ray were invited back to Penny's for mulled wine, Christmas cake and a bit of a wassail. Some of Penny's folk-community friends turned up and sang traditional Yorkshire Christmas songs, one of them a favourite of Banks's from a Kate Rusby album, called 'Serving Girl's Holiday'. They continued singing and drinking well into the night, and Banks and Ray wandered home though the church-yard, both slightly tipsy, singing the schoolboy version of 'Good King Wenceslas'. When they got back, they rather fool-ishly poured another drink and put *A Christmas Carol* on the DVD player. Banks was asleep before the Spirit of Christmas Present appeared.

As a consequence, on Christmas morning Banks and Ray were both hung-over, but Ray still managed to cook an excel-lent Christmas dinner, turkey and all the trimmings, and Annie drove out to Gratly to join them. They pulled crackers, wore silly hats and read out bad jokes, and again they drank and ate too much. Annie spent the night in the spare room. On Boxing Day, Banks made time to visit his parents in Durham, feeling guilty as usual because he didn't go to see them often enough.

Whenever the commercial onslaught of the season sagged, and whenever Banks's thoughts about the St Mary's Massacre ebbed, Emily was waiting right there in the wings. Most of his memories of her were warm with summer sunshine and sweet air, lazy afternoons on the grass in Regent's Park or Hyde Park with her head on his lap and all well with the world, but they had also been together through two winters. He remembered in particular one magical bone-chilling night when they were both home for the holidays and escaped from their respective family Christmases to go for a walk over the rec. Despite the amber glow of the street lamps surrounding the field, the black velvet sky was scattered with bright stars and the frozen puddles crackled under their feet. They kissed for a while in the old bandstand, warming each other, smoked a cigarette or two, then went back to re-join their families. Whenever Banks heard the sound of ice cracking underfoot, and whenever he heard Simon and Garfunkel's 'For Emily, Whenever I May Find Her', he thought of that cold amber night all those years ago, and the memory warmed his heart rather than chilled it.

Things didn't start moving again at the station until a few days later. Naturally, there had been a number of incidents over the holiday period – domestics, a pub fight or two – but none of them had required the expertise of Homicide and Major Crimes.

Then, just a few days into the new year, Banks received a phone call from Dr Glendenning that brought the St Mary's case back to the forefront of his thoughts again.

The Unicorn, across the road from Eastvale General Infirmary, was a run-down street-corner Victorian pub clad in dull green tiles, with wobbly chairs and cigarette-scarred wooden tables inside. Most of its clientele consisted of hospital workers, including nurses and doctors, especially after a late shift at A & E. It was hardly the sort of place to impress a date, but the landlord kept a decent pint, and there was no loud music or video games to make conversation difficult.

On a Thursday lunchtime early in January, when Banks went there in response to the phone call from Dr Glendenning, the only other customers were a couple of orderlies and a table of pupils from the comprehensive school playing truant. They probably weren't old enough to be drinking, but it was hard to tell these days. He didn't care if they were underage; he had managed to get served in pubs and get in to X-certificate films when he was sixteen. Good luck to them.

Dr Glendenning was already waiting in the corner with a tumbler of whisky in front of him. Banks went to the bar and bought a pint of Timothy Taylor's Landlord Bitter and joined him.

'This bloody weather,' Glendenning grumbled. 'Chill gets in your bones. I'd rather have a bit of snow and ice and get it over and done with it.'

It was true that the rain seemed to have been falling non-stop for weeks now, and every day there was a new story in the papers about somewhere or other being flooded, or on the verge of flooding, from the Lake District to the far end of Cornwall. If you were to believe everything you read or saw on TV, you might be forgiven for thinking that the whole country was under water, and that it was just a matter of time before some present-day Noah would appear with his ark and start shepherding people and animals on board.

'What's on your mind, doc?' Banks asked. Dr Glendenning didn't usually request lunchtime meetings in quiet pubs; in fact, this was the first time Banks could remember having a drink with him in all his years in Eastvale. This seemed to be a case of firsts. He realised how little he knew the man behind the white coat, what his life was like, his family, even though they had worked together for close to thirty years. Glendenning must certainly be approaching retirement. Banks contemplated the craggy, lined face with its bristly grey moustache, brick-red complexion and head of neat thin grey hair. He could have been a leftover colonel from the Raj in some long-forgotten Saturday afternoon film on TV. The moustache was stained yellow close to his upper lip, and it didn't take a Sherlock Holmes to figure out that the good doctor was still sneaking a cigarette whenever the opportunity offered itself.

'Good holiday?' Glendenning asked.

'You know. The usual. Turkey, green paper hats, crackers that don't crack and too much to drink.'

'Aye. Only had two suicides this year, mind you. Usually a bumper time for suicides is Christmas.'

'So you say every year.'

Glendenning sipped some whisky and grimaced as it burned on the way down. 'That's what I want to talk to you about,' he said. 'In a way.'

'The Christmas suicides?'

'One suicide in particular. Martin Edgeworth.'

'I see.' Banks leaned back in his chair. It wobbled dangerously so he sat up straight again. It was uncomfortable no matter how he arranged himself. 'Go on, then.'

'It's a bit awkward,' Glendenning went on. 'Not that I missed anything, you understand. Not as such. Natalie, one of my most capable assistants, carried out the post-mortem. Under my supervision, of course. Definitely not her fault. It's more a matter of interpretation than anything else.'

'I understand.'

'Unfortunately, even we scientists have to connect the dots on occasion without any clear idea of the order they're in.' Glendenning seemed a little embarrassed, and Banks was careful not to tease or push him. After a few moments' thought, the doctor seemed to make up his mind to carry on. 'Well, the truth is that I had one or two niggling doubts when I read Natalie's report after post-mortem. Things I couldn't quite put my finger on. So I decided to go back and have a look myself, reconstructing the sequence of events in my mind. I even revisited the scene, then I re-examined the body.

Fortunately, the coroner hasn't released it for burial yet. Not a full second post-mortem, you understand, but just another look at one or two features that puzzled me. I had Natalie show me what she had done and what she had found, and she agreed.'

'And?'

'Well, perhaps our glee at believing we'd found a mass murderer might have put blinkers on us as regards considering any alternatives.'

'Such as?'

'That somebody else did it. Or killed Edgeworth. Or both.' Glendenning held his hand up. 'Now, I'm not saying that's what happened. First of all, I had a hard time trying to visualise how and why the man sort of flopped down backwards against the wall to shoot himself. There's a bruise on his left shoulder consistent with its bumping against the wall. Usually suicides are . . . well, more careful, more fastidious, even, in an odd sort of way. I mean, it's your last act, so you might as well make it as neat and tidy as possible. According to all the crime-scene photographs I looked at, his outer clothing was folded neatly beside him. The anorak, the waterproof trousers, the black woolly hat on top.'

'What are you saying?'

'I'm saying that on the one hand you have the signs of a careful, neat man, even on the verge of suicide, but slumping against the wall doesn't fit. It's sloppy. You'd expect him to position himself carefully, perhaps even on a chair rather than on a dirty cellar floor. Don't forget, this is a man who neatly folds an anorak. But he was sitting on the floor with his legs stretched out and his back against the wall when the shot was fired.'

'But what does it matter?' Banks argued. 'He was going to shoot himself. I mean, he'd just killed a number of people, and he was about to end his own life. He was no doubt agitated.'

'Why did he even remove his outer clothing in the first place, then?' asked Glendenning.

'Any number of reasons. He was too warm, too uncomfortable . . .'

'It was chilly in that cellar.'

'Perhaps he had been home for a while. The house upstairs would have been warm enough, with that big Aga. Perhaps he took his outer clothing off when he first came in?'

'In that case, why was it folded neatly beside him in the cellar?'

'I see your point. But none of that necessarily means anything. I should imagine he was in an unusual state of mind, perhaps not thinking clearly. Certainly not acting normally. He did take his boots off upstairs. We found them.'

'Balance of his mind disturbed? Yes. Even so . . . if it were only that . . .'

'What else?'

'I was curious, so I went and had a chat with the forensic chappies who examined the clothes and had them go over their findings with me.'

'We got their original report,' said Banks. 'No unexplained hairs or fibres.'

'Yes,' said Glendenning. 'Doesn't that strike you as odd? If he wore those clothes *over* the clothes he was wearing – and we've no reason to think he didn't – then surely there would have been traces of his sweat, fibres from the shirt itself, and perhaps other things? You can't tell me he climbed that hill and shot all those people without a shedding a single drop of sweat. Or hair. He wasn't bald, so you would expect hairs inside the woolly hat, wouldn't you, and perhaps on the shoulders of the anorak, but there are none.'

'OK,' said Banks, frowning.

'It was as if the outer clothes were new, as if they hadn't been worn. Fair enough, they were damp, there were a couple of grass stains and a streak of mud here and there, but again, anyone could have rubbed them on the ground. One of the CSIs suggested that if someone had worn those clothes to commit the murders, the stains were in the wrong places. Especially the knees, as they must have made contact with the earth when he got to his feet or lay down.'

'I get your point,' said Banks. 'There were no prints on the shell casings or the other bullets, either,' he said, almost to himself. 'Mike Trethowan didn't think it odd, but it bothered me. What are you suggesting?'

'Perhaps the clothes the killer wore were different altogether? The same kind, of course, and same colour, but not the ones found at the house. If anyone saw him from a distance, all they would see was dark outer clothing and a black cap of some sort. All he'd have to do was dampen the other set of clothes and rub them in the grass and mud. But there are no hairs inside the shoulders of the anorak, as there were on the shirt Edgeworth was wearing underneath, or in the woolen cap. You can't tell me that if he wore something on top it wouldn't pick up some hairs inside either piece of clothing.'

'So you're suggesting two sets of clothing? One set folded neatly by Edgeworth, unworn, and another worn by someone else? The real killer? If you're right, what happened to the outfit the real killer wore?'

'No idea,' said Glendenning. 'You're the detective. He probably destroyed it if he had any sense. Evidence. Damn. I swore I wouldn't, but I'm going to have another.' He glanced towards Banks's glass. 'You? And before you say anything, it's my day off, and I'm not going to be staggering over to the hospital to commit medical atrocities on an unfortunate corpse.'

This was a first, and Banks was certain he wasn't going to miss the opportunity of having the doctor buy him a drink.

'Things are pretty quiet for me, too,' he said. 'Same again, please. Landlord Bitter.'

Glendenning grunted and went to the bar, leaving Banks to think unwelcome and chaotic thoughts.

When the doctor came back, he plonked down the drinks and said, 'And there's another thing.'

'Yes?'

'It was impossible to tell at the scene or at the post-mortem, because the shot blew off the back of his head. Natalie is certainly blameless in all this. But when I managed to gather the skull fragments together – it was a bit like doing a jigsaw puzzle – I found something odd. Odd and very disturbing.'

'What?'

'A slight indentation in the area of the exit wound.'

'Indentation?'

'Yes. It was very difficult to see because of the fragmentation of the skull, not to mention the general mess the bullet made. Even then I might have thought nothing more of it, assuming he just banged his head on the wall as he flopped down, or when he pulled the trigger. Those old cellar walls are rarely smooth. They're full of bumps and pits.'

'Why couldn't it have happened that way?'

'When I revisited the scene, I concentrated on the spot where his head hit the wall. It was smooth as a baby's bottom. Hitting his head against it couldn't have caused the depth of indentation I found over the skull fragments.' He picked up his glass and took a long pull. 'I rest my case.'

'Are you trying to say what I think you are?'

'Don't try to stump me with riddles, laddie. What do you think I'm trying to say?'

'That someone hit Edgeworth on the back of the head and fired the gun into his mouth. Murdered him.'

Glendenning sat silently for a while, swirling the liquid in the bottom of his glass. 'Well, it's certainly a possibility, isn't it?' he said finally. 'But there could be other explanations. And I could be wrong. I'm a scientist. I'm uncomfortable enough speculating as much as I have done.'

'I understand that,' said Banks. 'But see it from my point of view. Imagination and speculation are almost as much use to a policeman as reason and scientific evidence. Often more so.' He took a swallow of beer. 'Besides, it fits with one or two things that have been bothering me.'

'All I'm saying,' Glendenning explained, 'is that it's possible – only *possible*, mind you – that someone hit Edgeworth on the back of the head before any shot was fired.'

'Hit with what?'

'I don't know. Some kind of hammer with a rounded head. A ballpeen, or machinist's hammer, for example. Did you find anything like that at the scene?'

'We've got everything from Edgeworth's cellar locked up in evidence. There was a work bench, and we can certainly check all the tools for traces of blood and try to match them with the wound.'

'The weapon would probably be among them,' said Glendenning. 'Or whoever used it might have brought it with him and taken it away.'

'We'll check,' said Banks. 'And then this person shot him?'

'Well, he could hardly have done it himself. But it might not have been the same person.'

'Possibly,' said Banks. 'But it makes for an odd sequence of events however you look at it. Someone hits him on the back of the head and leaves, then someone else comes and fakes his suicide. Or maybe Edgeworth came round from the blow and then decided to shoot himself?'

'When you put it like that, it does sound rather far-fetched. But there's more. The angle was off.'

'What do you mean? What angle?'

'It's a small thing in itself, but taking into account all the evidence of the possible trajectory of the bullet, the angle at which the weapon was held, it would have been ... well, perhaps uncomfortable is the best word, for Edgeworth to have held it the way it would inflict such a wound. He got it right. A lot of suicides don't realise you need to hold the gun at an angle, pointing up, not straight at the back of your mouth. That likely wouldn't bring about the desired result. I'm just saying that it would have been a bit of a twist for Edgeworth to hold it at the right angle from the way he was slouching against the wall. Not impossible, you understand, perhaps not even improbable, but *uncomfortable.*'

'I understand,' said Banks. 'What about time of death?'

Glendenning sighed. 'You know as well as I do that there's usually plenty of leeway there, especially in a body that's been dead as long as Edgeworth's had when we found him.'

'So he could have been killed earlier on Saturday morning, before the wedding?'

'He could indeed. That was apparent from the start. The chill slows things down a bit.'

'I'm just trying to get this all clear. The timing is such that the killer could have killed Edgeworth first and left the pile of clothes beside him, then used Edgeworth's gun and RAV4 to carry out the shootings at St Mary's, returned them to the house and left.'

'Indeed. What are these other things that have been bothering you?'

'First,' said Banks, 'there's the scrapbook we found with the pictures and stories about Benjamin Kemp and Laura Tindall's forthcoming wedding. I can understand why the killer might have kept such a record – it fits with his obsession – but why would he tape it to the underside of a drawer, where any police search was pretty certain to find it, if hc was going to commit suicide after the murders?'

'So in your speculative policeman's way,' Glendenning said, 'you're suggesting that someone else might have planted the scrapbook there, the real killer perhaps, to incriminate Edgeworth further, or to misdirect you?'

'Well, someone might have realised that it would help to convince us we'd got the right man if we had some evidence to link him with the people at the wedding, and not just physical evidence, ballistics and so forth. The thing is that other than the scrapbook we've got nothing, no links at all between Martin Edgeworth and anyone in the wedding party, the church itself, the vicar, verger, curate, you name them.'

'Maybe he'd just kept the scrapbook hidden so that no casual visitor would see it, and he forgot to move it before his suicide, or couldn't be bothered to. After all, he had other things on his mind. I mean, he'd hardly take it out of his hiding place and put it on the kitchen table, would he?'

'Well speculated, Watson. And we found no identifiable prints on the scrapbook, only smudges. But such things are notoriously difficult to get prints from, anyway. Edgeworth didn't leave a suicide note, either.'

'That happens so often, in my experience,' said Glendenning, 'as to be meaningless.'

'True. And perhaps even more often with mass murderers. But on the other hand, there's often a need to explain, or to demonstrate how clever he's been. None of these little things add up to anything until you start collecting them all together. And there's another thing. Nobody I talked to who knew Edgeworth believed him to be capable of committing such a crime. Oh, some people didn't like him much, especially his ex-wife, and some admitted he had a short fuse and he didn't like losing, but that's about as far as it goes. Now, I know in itself that means very little. If I had a penny for the number of times I've heard friends, family and neighbours describe a sadistic killer as a decent, normal, sociable chap with a few flaws, I'd be a rich man today. But still . . .'

Glendenning made a throaty, gurgling sort of sound Banks took for laughter.

Banks finished his pint. 'So the question is, I suppose, what are we going to do about it?'

'I'm not going to do anything,' said Glendenning. 'I'm simply trying to bring a few anomalies and alternative inter-pretations to your attention. I think the rest is up to you.'

'But you'll back me up if necessary?'

'Naturally. To the extent of my professional opinion.'

'What a waste,' said Banks. 'And you seem so promising at speculation.'

Glendenning polished off his whisky. 'Aye, well, I'll leave that to you. I would certainly be comfortable to go as far as mentioning the indentation, for example, and should you provide me with a possible weapon I would be happy to check it for fit. Now I've had my say. I'll be off.'

When Glendenning had left, Banks sat staring into his empty glass. Was there anything in what Glendenning had told him? Was Edgeworth really innocent, as most of his friends and acquaint-ances seemed to believe? He might have been involved tangen-tially, of course, then hoodwinked or double-crossed by an accomplice at the final hurdle, but he might also have been used, knowing nothing about the real killer's motives or intentions. The only bright spot in all this was that the two of them must have crossed paths at some point. The killer must have known about Edgeworth's membership of the Upper Swainsdale District Rifle and Pistol Club, about his guns. And that gave Banks a few places he could start searching for the connections he needed.

★   ★   ★

Banks hadn't given Annie and Gerry any specific instructions for interviewing Robert and Maureen Tindall again other than to play it by ear, go over some of the questions they had already been asked and note their reactions. Robert and Maureen were the only immediate members of the wedding party who hadn't been killed or wounded, which was interesting in itself to a suspicious detective's mind. If the killer had been aiming at specific targets, then why had they been spared? Why had he killed the groom's father, but not the bride's? Not that Annie thought the Tindalls had anything to do with the shooting, but it was odd, all the same. They had been standing with the main group but had escaped injury. Their witness statements had been taken as soon as they had recovered from the immediate shock, but neither had anything new to add. Had the shootings really been random?

The Tindalls' house came complete with double garage, gables, spacious gardens at front and back, and a bay window. It sat in one of the quiet streets a stone's throw from the Heights, Eastvale's Millionaire's Row, but lacked the panoramic view the large detached houses commanded, and wouldn't fetch anywhere near the same price. Even so, Annie would have given up her cottage in Harkside for such a home had she been able to afford it. Banking had clearly been as good to Robert Tindall as it had been bad to most customers.

They parked out front and walked up the path. Annie had phoned ahead, so they were expected, and Robert Tindall opened the door almost immediately she rang the bell.

'Come in, come in,' he said, taking their umbrellas and depositing them in an elephant's foot stand by the door. Annie hadn't seen such a thing in ages, if ever. She thought elephants were a protected species. Certainly, it was illegal to hunt them for ivory. Perhaps it wasn't a real elephant's foot. 'If you wouldn't mind removing your footwear,' Robert Tindall went on, 'you can put it on that mat there.'

Annie took off her red boots, not without some awkward-ness over the zips, and Gerry slipped off her pumps without even bending down. Annie felt decidedly underdressed in jeans and a plain grey sweatshirt under her raincoat, but Gerry appeared elegant enough in a dark green trouser suit over a russet top that matched her flowing waves of red hair. Tall and elegant, Annie thought, with a rush of irrational envy that occasionally rose in her chest when she worked with Gerry. It passed quickly enough. They had got off to a bad start, but Annie had now actually come to appreciate the many qualities of her occasionally difficult oppo over the past couple of years, even if they hadn't exactly warmed to one another on a personal level yet. It was her own fault. Women like Gerry Masterson and Jenny Fuller, always elegant, beau-tiful, well turned out, posh accents, walking around as if they had a stick up their arse, had always irritated her. It was a problem that probably had something to do with her uncon-ventional and Bohemian upbringing, but knowing that didn't solve it.

Robert Tindall led them into a high-ceilinged living room where a fire burned in the grate and a baby grand occupied one corner.

'Maureen's,' he said, as Annie stared at it. 'She's the musical one. Not me, I'm afraid. Tone deaf.'

'You couldn't fit one of those in my entire cottage,' said Annie, realising immediately that she had made Tindall uncomfortable. 'Bijou, they call it.'

'Ah, yes, the vagaries of today's language. Do sit down.' He gestured to a sofa upholstered in rough cream cloth printed with French wine labels. 'Maureen is resting. She hopes to be with us shortly.'

Annie hoped so, too. She had come to talk to both of them, preferably together. There was a whiff of camphor about the room, she thought, which gave it something of an old-fashioned atmosphere.

Robert cleared his throat. 'I'm afraid she's not been herself since Laura's death. It shook her to the core. I'm upset, too, naturally, we all are. But Maureen was always more fragile. Laura was our only child. You know.'

'Yes,' said Annie. 'I can hardly imagine how terrible it must be. Fragile? You say your wife is fragile?'

'Yes. Sensitive. Highly strung, as they say. But she's a wonderful wife, and she was a good mother to Laura. Strict but good: attentive, loving, supportive. Maureen helped her so much with her modelling career. Maybe she was over-protective, but there are some wily predators in that business, you know.' He shook his head slowly. 'Can I perhaps get you a cup of tea, coffee, or something while you're waiting?'

'Tea would be great, thanks,' said Annie.

'Any kind in particular?'

'Have you got any chamomile?' Gerry asked.

'Afraid not. It's Yorkshire Gold or Earl Grey.'

They agreed on the Yorkshire Gold and Robert Tindall went off to the kitchen.

'Bloody chamomile, indeed,' said Annie.

Gerry blushed. 'Well, he asked. And you're a one to talk. It was you got me into herbal teas in the first place.'

Before she could reply, Annie heard a soft rustling behind her and turned to see a woman walk into the room. In contrast to her husband, Maureen Tindall was painfully thin and pale, like an invalid, clutching a cashmere cardigan at her throat as if she were freezing despite the fire. Robert Tindall was tall, slightly stooped, silver-haired and distinguished, but his wife looked as if a puff of wind would blow her away.

'Good afternoon. I'm Maureen Tindall.' Her voice was a shaky whisper. She sat in the armchair closest to the fire and rubbed her hands together. 'This weather,' she said. 'When will it ever end?'

'Not until we've all been washed away,' Annie replied.

Maureen Tindall managed a thin smile. She was in her early sixties, Annie guessed, with short steel-grey hair plastered to her scalp. Her face was bony, blotchy in places, eyes sunken, dull with the numbing glaze of tranquillisers, and anywhere except on Annie or Gerry. Still, Annie thought, the poor woman had just lost her only daughter in the most horrendous circumstances one could possibly imagine. Who in her position wouldn't reach for the Valium? Maureen smoothed her skirts over her lap and leaned back. 'I can't imagine what you want with us now,' she said. 'Not now that it's all over.'

'We just want to make sure we've got everything right,' said Annie. 'The boss is a real stickler about reports and that sort of thing.'

Robert Tindall came back in with a tray bearing a teapot, cups and saucers, milk and sugar. 'Ah, darling, here you are,' he said. 'Feeling all right?'

'A little better,' said Maureen. 'I think my rest helped.'

Her husband put down the tray and patted her arm. 'Good. Good.' He glanced at Annie. 'I don't suppose this will take long?'

'Shouldn't think so,' Annie said. Gerry took out her notebook and pen.

Maureen Tindall peered at her wristwatch. 'What time is our appointment with Dr Graveney, darling?' she asked.

'Not until half past four. We've got plenty of time.'

'Only we mustn't be late. We'll have to set off in good time.'

'We will, darling, we will.'

'Dr Graveney?' Annie said.

'Outpatient care,' said Robert Tindall. 'Maureen is still rather very much in shock, as you may have noticed.'

'A psychiatrist, then?'

'Yes,' said Tindall, through gritted teeth. 'A specialist.'

He clearly didn't appreciate Annie's encroaching on their private affairs. Still, plenty of people were embarrassed about seeing shrinks. Annie had felt that way herself after her rape some years ago. In retrospect, though, she thought the visits had done her some good. They had at least speeded her reintegration back into some approximation of normal life. Had she been left to her own devices, she would probably still be wallowing in guilt, anger, anxiety, shame, alcohol and God only knows what else.

'I'm afraid I still find it very difficult to accept the reality of what happened,' Maureen said. 'I find myself constantly dwelling on those moments in the churchyard, reliving them. My dearest Laura. I don't sleep well. It always seems to be on my mind like those tunes you can't get rid of sometimes, only much worse. Dr Graveney is trying to help me overcome all that. To make the pictures go away.'

Good luck with that, Annie thought. 'Then I wish both of you every success. I can't imagine how terrible it must be reliving events like that over and over.'

'It's not even so much the images,' Maureen said, 'but the *feelings* that go with them.'

'I understand,' said Annie. And she did. 'I'm sorry if our visit causes you any more pain. There's a just a few small things we'd like to go over. Not the event itself, you understand. Just background.'

'But you've got the man, haven't you?' said Robert Tindall. 'The one who did it. He shot himself, didn't he?'

Annie noticed Maureen flinch at the word 'shot'. 'Yes,' she said. 'That's all pretty well cut and dried. What we don't have is any kind of motive. From all we've been told, Martin Edgeworth just wasn't the kind of man to do what he did.'

'Something must have pushed him over the edge,' said Robert Tindall.

'Exactly. That's what we're trying to find out. If he had some connection with anyone in the wedding party, for example. And if there was anyone else involved.'

'Anyone *else*?'

'Yes. There are one or two anomalies, and there's a remote possibility that he had an accomplice.'

'You must understand, we didn't actually *see* anyone,' said Robert.

'Everything was too confusing,' Maureen added. 'We didn't know what was happening.'

'Of course,' said Annie. 'I'm just trying to find out whether you had any sense at all of there being more than one person up there.'

'Well, the shots seemed to come rather fast,' said Robert. 'I can't say I've ever been under fire in a battle situation, but I rather imagine that's what it would feel like. So I suppose there *could* have been more than one. But surely your forensics people could tell you all about that?'

'What about the other matter, his connection with the wedding party?' Gerry asked. 'What might have pushed him over the edge?'

Robert looked at her askance. 'How could we possibly speculate on something like that?'

'What DC Masterson means,' Annie went on, 'is whether there's anything you can think of, anything at all, that might have given someone like Martin Edgeworth a reason to do what he did.'

'But we knew nothing about this Martin Edgeworth,' Robert protested. 'And it seems to me there was no reason any sane person could grasp what he did.'

'You mentioned predators earlier,' Annie said. 'Were you aware of anyone like that causing Laura problems?'

'No. At least she never said anything. Anyway, she'd left that part of the business behind, the modelling.'

'Fair enough,' said Annie. 'Is there anyone from Laura's past who you think might wish to do her harm, even after a very long time?'

'Revenge being a dish best eaten cold?' said Robert.

'Something like that.' Annie noticed that Maureen Tindall seemed distracted. It could have been the Valium, or the general state of her nerves.

'Mrs Tindall?' Annie said. 'Can you think of anything? Anyone?'

Maureen seemed to snap back from a long distance. 'Who, me? No, no, of course not. No one.'

'Are you sure?'

'Of course I'm sure,' she snapped. 'Laura was not the kind of person to go about making enemies.'

'That's not what I mean,' Annie said. 'And if I gave you the wrong impression, I apologise. I'm not saying she did anything wrong to attract the attention of someone like Martin Edgeworth. We don't even profess to understand his motivation. But it could have been a simple thing that set him off. Someone who did what he did doesn't exactly see the world in quite the same way as the rest of us.'

'We've never heard of the man before,' said Robert Tindall. 'And Laura certainly never mentioned him.'

'Would she have?'

'We like to think she would have confided in us if something, or someone, was bothering her, yes.'

'We do know that he seemed interested in the wedding,' said Gerry. 'He had newspaper clippings of the announcements. He put them in a scrapbook.'

Maureen took a handkerchief from her sleeve and put it to her mouth. 'Why would he do something like that? That's just sick.'

'Good lord,' said Robert. 'So he was stalking Laura?'

'Not necessarily. But he knew the details. It wasn't a spontaneous assault. That's what makes us think there could have been someone in particular in the wedding party he wanted to hurt, and hurt very badly, and he killed the others as a sort of smokescreen, to distract us from what he really intended. Naturally, we thought first of Laura and Ben, though Ben wasn't killed immediately.'

Maureen shook her head. 'It can't be,' she whispered. 'It can't be.'

Annie and Gerry exchanged glances. 'Can't be what?' Gerry asked.

'Wh–what you say it is. Something Laura did, or one of us did, or something he thinks we did. Obviously, I can't speak for everyone else, but as far as Robert and I are concerned, that just sounds ridiculous.'

'There are still so many things about all this we don't understand,' Annie said, 'but that's probably because we don't have all the facts yet.'

'Can't you just let it be, now it's over and he's dead?' said Maureen. 'Let *us* be? We just want to get on with our lives. To heal.'

'But someone may have put Martin Edgeworth up to it,' Annie said. 'Used him.'

'I don't see how that could have happened,' said Maureen. 'Surely people are not that manipulable?'

'You'd be surprised. With that type of killer, it could have been a minor slight, a build-up of pressure, even over years. Some insult or rejection he perceived or misread. Some past transgression, real or imagined.'

Maureen lowered her head and sniffled.

'Do you remember Wendy Vincent?' Gerry asked.

Maureen looked up sharply. 'Wendy?' she repeated. 'Yes, of course I do. How could I forget? But what's that got to do with anything? That all happened fifty years ago.'

'You were her best friend, weren't you?'

'I like to think so.'

'It must have been terrible for you. And so young.'

'Yes. I was fifteen.'

'Her killer was only brought to justice recently, a cold case solved by modern methods. DNA.'

'I read about it.'

'Did you know him? Frank Dowson?'

'I knew who he was. He was Billy Dowson's weird older brother.'

'Weird?'

'There was something wrong with him. He wasn't all there. We stayed away from him. But I still don't see what this has to do with anything.'

'We're just looking for connections,' Gerry said. 'However vague or distant.'

'Might Laura have unwittingly drawn attention from the wrong sort of person?' Annie cut in. 'Perhaps she declined someone's advances, something like that? Can you think of anyone?'

'We've been through all that,' said Robert. 'Racked our brains. I think someone already told your colleagues about that cyber-stalker a few years back. But he's in New Zealand.'

'We've checked him out thoroughly,' said Gerry. 'It wasn't him, or anything to do with him.'

'Something *could* have happened in London, I suppose, either recently or during Laura's modelling career, but if there was, it wasn't something she told us. And she usually told us most things.'

Annie doubted that very much. 'She may not have even known about it,' she said. 'The person might never even have approached her. Perhaps a perceived slight at a party, or something like that, was enough. A colleague. A waiter.'

'If she didn't even know about it herself,' said Robert Tindall, 'then she could hardly tell anyone else about it, could she? I'm sorry, but we can't help you any further. You can see my wife is upset. Perhaps if you talked to some of Laura's friends and colleagues down in London . . .?'

'We've already done that, Mr Tindall, but rest assured we'll stick at it.' Annie gave Gerry the nod and they stood to leave. 'I'm sorry for probing at painful memories, Mrs Tindall, but you've been most helpful. I shouldn't think we'll have to bother you any more.'

Maureen Tindall remained with her face buried in her handkerchief. Just as Robert Tindall was leading them to the door, his wife checked the time again and reminded him of the forthcoming doctor's appointment.

'Don't worry, darling,' he said. 'We've got ages yet.'

The market square outside was dark and deserted. As Banks glanced out after having recounted his earlier discussion with Dr Glendenning, he could see the reflections of the others gathered in AC Gervaise's office: Jenny Fuller, DCs Doug Wilson and Gerry Masterson and DI Annie Cabbot. The only significant person missing was Winsome, who had spent Christmas in Montego Bay with her parents, and would be there for another two weeks. Terry Gilchrist had gone to visit her over there, and Banks hoped the sun, sand and sea and long cool drinks with umbrellas were helping them get over the terrible ordeal they had endured at their friends' wedding.

After a brief pause, Gervaise said, 'As far as I'm concerned, Alan, I think we've got enough already to get started investigating possibilities beyond Edgeworth. But you'll have to proceed carefully. Don't tread on any toes or upset any of the bereaved. Most of all, we don't want the newspapers getting hold of our speculations until you get somewhere with the investigation. If there's anywhere to get. You know as well as I do how much they'd love the opportunity to tell the world how we got it wrong, or accuse us of harassing grief-stricken survivors.' She drank some coffee. 'On the other hand, they're all still hungry for a motive, for some sort of explanation, and we haven't been able to show them yet that Edgeworth was the monster they'd like to paint him as. Anyway, let's carry on. There must be more. Dr Fuller?'

Jenny Fuller cast her eyes over the group. 'I've been over and over my notes, back to the textbooks, reread all your statements and reports, read up on just about every spree killing and mass murder I can find, and I still can't make him fit. Naturally, there are so many variables. You can always get away by saying he was an exception to the rule, or that we've missed some vital piece of information, but in the light of what Alan's just told us, I don't think we have. I think it's a strong case for at least considering other possibilities. Edgeworth doesn't have a dysfunctional background, for a start. And if what you're telling me about his cleaning up after things is true, that doesn't fit the profile, either. Mass murderers don't usually bother to get rid of all the forensic evidence they possibly can. Admittedly, they rarely have the time, but it's certainly not part of the profile. Nor do potential suicides. Frankly, I'm stumped. Besides, you need more than a dysfunctional background to make a mass murderer. Plenty of people come from backgrounds of violence and abuse, for example, and never stray off the straight and narrow. You also need a series of triggers, or maybe something more like the series of numbers in a combination lock. Click. Click. Click. Until the tumblers align and it's all systems go. I've got no idea what that combination might be in Edgeworth's case. I'm not saying he didn't do it, just that he didn't do it as a textbook mass murderer, if you understand what I mean. With all the care he took to misdirect us, he could have had a more complicated reason than the need to kill a lot of people. But then why did he kill himself after taking so much care to cover his tracks? And why was it so easy to trace him through the firearms certificate? That kind of basic mistake doesn't fit with the other stuff, the extra set of clothing and so on.'

'So,' said Banks, 'the question is, if we're giving him the benefit of the doubt when it comes to psychology, and admitting the inconsistencies of forensic evidence, are we going to take the leap of faith and assume that the man who was up on the hill shooting at the wedding group outside St Mary's was *not* the same man we found slumped against the wall in Martin Edgeworth's cellar?'

'I can't see any other conclusion,' said AC Gervaise. 'If Dr Fuller and Dr Glendenning are right.'

The others nodded.

'If we're going to work on the assumption that someone else shot the wedding party and also killed Martin Edgeworth,' Gervaise went on, 'then it should open up new lines of inquiry. Now we have a second crime and all the fresh thinking and evidence that brings to the investigation. Where do you suggest we direct our attention next, Alan?'

'I'd like someone to have a word with his old partner, Jonathan Martell,' Banks said. 'After all, it's only a few years since they wound down the practice, and according to Ollie Metcalfe at the White Rose, Martell and Edgeworth often met up for a jar or two. They were still pals. Martell might know something, say if Edgeworth was in some kind of trouble or someone was trying to blackmail him, for example.'

'You think this Martell could be a suspect, sir?' DC Wilson asked.

'I wouldn't go that far,' said Banks. 'But keep an open mind. If it comes to it, if we think he merits it, we'll do a full work up on him. If there's any hint of a motive, then we'll have him in. After all, he was Edgeworth's partner for quite a few years. Edgeworth would have trusted him. Who's to say it wasn't Martell who came knocking on his door that Saturday morning, got him down in the cellar with the guns on some pretext or other, then bashed him on the back of the head with a ball-peen hammer and set up a phony suicide?'

'And then?' Wilson asked.

'Then he put the second set of outer clothes he'd bought beside the body, rumpled up a bit but not enough, went out in Edgeworth's RAV4 with Edgeworth's AR15 and shot up the wedding party, returned the people-mover, guns and all, and hurried off home.'

'So it was well planned?' Annie said.

'At a guess. If it happened that way. Whoever did it.'

'It's a possibility,' said Gervaise.

'It's still speculation, ma'am,' said Banks. 'But it's a place to start. What we need to do is find a link between the killer and Edgeworth, and some connection between one of the victims and the killer.'

'As I said in our previous meeting,' Jenny cut in. 'It could be that a war hero, a wedding, a model or some other ingredient of the event could have acted as a symbol of something to the killer, a trigger that set him off, so it doesn't even have to be a specific deed by a specific person he's avenging. I know that sounds vague, but . . .'

'OK,' said Banks. 'So maybe we're after someone who hated models, weddings or war heroes. Or bridesmaids. Even so, we do the best we can with what limited resources we've got.

Remember the scrapbook at Edgeworth's house? It was filled with cuttings and pictures of the Tindall family, more than anyone else. Not the Kemps, the bridesmaids, the maid of honour, but the Tindalls. Annie, you and Gerry talked to them this afternoon. What were your impressions?'

'On the whole, I'd say Robert Tindall is trying to put a brave face on things and having a tough time of it,' said Annie. 'Still, it's hardly surprising, given what they've been through. Are still going through.'

'And Maureen?'

Annie glanced at Jenny Fuller. 'Without being any kind of an expert in the field, I'd say she's still severely traumatised by what happened and still grieving for her daughter.'

'Isn't that only natural?' Banks said. 'Jenny?'

'Sure it is,' Jenny Fuller agreed. 'I don't quite get what point you're making, DI Cabbot.'

'It isn't easy to explain,' Annie went on. 'You're absolutely right, of course. There's every reason she should still be grieving, taking tranquillisers, spending half the day in bed "resting".'

'Don't you think you're being a bit harsh on the woman?' Jenny said. 'Given what she's just experienced?'

'If you'd let me explain.'

'Go ahead, Annie,' said Banks. Jenny leaned back in her chair and folded her arms.

'Naturally, I was sympathetic. Gerry and I both were. I kept telling myself this woman has been through a severe trauma. She lost her only child. What could be worse?'

'But?' said Banks.

'According to her husband, Maureen Tindall was always a bit fragile, fraught with anxiety.'

'That business with the time,' said Gerry.

'Yes,' Annie went on. 'She seemed obsessed with punctuality. They had a doctor's appointment later in the afternoon.

Dr Graveney. A psychiatrist –' she glanced at Jenny '– and she seemed obsessed with getting there in plenty of time. She was always looking at her watch. The appointment was at least a couple of hours away.'

'Punctuality isn't a bad thing,' said Jenny. 'Especially if you're going to see a doctor. But you're bandying about words like "anxiety" and "obsession" with probably very little understanding of their true technical meaning.'

'I'm just trying to give you my experience of the interview,' Annie said. 'I'm using the words as any layperson would. I mean, maybe you don't, but most of us know what it's like to be anxious, perhaps even obsessed, or consumed by grief. I'm not pretending to be a psychologist or anything. I'll leave that to you.'

'The pretending?'

'You know what I mean.' Annie sniffed. 'So that's the impression we got, and I think Gerry would agree that Maureen Tindall was edgy, nervous, always worried about the time, and maybe that wasn't all caused by the recent trauma. That's all. Not that it matters so much. And we checked with Dr Graveney. The appointment was genuine, and she kept it.'

'There was also that business about repeating "It can't be" when we were talking about the killer maybe having a reason to hurt someone in the wedding party,' said Gerry.

'Disbelief sounds pretty reasonable to me, under the circumstances,' said Gervaise.

'But it wasn't just that, ma'am.' Gerry glanced at Annie, who gave her the go ahead. 'It was the way she said it. It seemed to us that the mention of Wendy Vincent made her think of something, or make some sort of connection which she then refused to tell us about. She quickly became very eager for us to move on, to leave, even, and not come back. I don't know. Maybe I'm being fanciful.'

'You think there could be something in that?' said Banks.

'I don't know. I haven't been able to find any connection with Martin Edgeworth. He was a few years younger than Maureen Tindall, and he grew up in Lincolnshire, so I doubt there is any. And Laura wasn't even born then. But the direction of the whole inquiry seems to be changing now.'

'Indeed it does.' Banks finished his coffee, though it was a little too bitter for his taste. 'What do you think about Maureen Tindall?' he asked Jenny Fuller.

'I couldn't possibly say without talking to her, but people do get hung up on punctuality and such, for example, which is a little bit different from simply being on time. It's not especially abnormal. It may be a sign of general anxiety. As for the other thing, who knows? I imagine what Gerry here is trying to say is that she thinks there was something about Maureen Tindall's past, or her daughter's or husband's past, that she didn't want to touch upon, was maybe worried you would uncover, so she changed the subject.'

'That's what it felt like,' said Gerry.

'Well, we can't always trust our feelings on these matters,' said Jenny. 'It bears further examination, though, I'd say.'

'OK,' said Banks. 'Well done, the two of you. Gerry, do you think you can work your magic and get us some more background on that old murder, dig even deeper than you dug before?'

'I'll do my best, sir.'

'Doug, you can also keep working on the old dental practice for now, ex-patients and so on. Who knows, something could have happened there. Perhaps Edgeworth made a mistake and ruined someone's smile, or sexually assaulted a female patient under anaesthetic. It happens. I might wander back up to the club tomorrow and talk to Geoff McLaren the manager. According to Ollie Metcalfe at the White Rose, he was a drinking buddy of Edgeworth's. I keep thinking that if Edgeworth didn't do it but his guns did, then the club's a good place to start looking.'

'Another thing,' said AC Gervaise. 'You mentioned the extra clothes and the use of a hammer, Alan.'

'Yes. I was just about to get to that.'

'Well, let me pip you to the post. Show you I've still got what it takes.' Gervaise smiled. 'What brand were they? The clothes.'

'They're from Walkers' Wearhouse. Their own brand.'

'Then we need to check with all branches of Walkers' Wearhouse. I know it's a very large and popular chain, but we should be able to manage it. And someone needs to go down to the evidence locker first thing tomorrow and find out if Edgeworth had a ballpeen hammer in his tool chest, and if so, could it have been used to cause the blow on his head. DI Cabbot, can you supervise that? There may still be minute traces of blood.'

'Certainly,' said Annie.

'Let's call it a night, then,' Gervaise said. 'We've all got more than enough to keep us busy from tomorrow on.'

There was a letter waiting for Banks when he got home after the meeting, along with the circulars, bills and the latest copy of *Gramophone* magazine. It was handwritten, postmarked Scarborough, and there was an almost illegible address in the top left-hand corner that he could just about make out was in Filey. He didn't get many real letters these days. He put the junk on the table by the door and took *Gramophone* and the letter with him into the kitchen. Ray was stopping over with friends in the Lake District tonight, Banks remembered, and he was glad to have the cottage to himself for an evening. Not that he minded Ray staying there while he found a suitable home of his own, and the cooking was a definite plus, but it was good to have the conservatory to himself again, the chance to relax and listen to whatever music he wanted to hear. Ray wasn't much of a classical fan. He loved sixties' rock and jazz, mostly, which was fine, but Banks still missed his Schubert, Shostakovich and Beethoven. When he had tried to play a Borodin string quartet or some Chopin nocturnes, Ray hadn't grumbled or made any comment, he had simply talked all the way through it as if it were mere background music.

Luckily, there was some of Ray's excellent lasagne left over from the other night, and Banks stuck it in the microwave, then he poured himself a glass of Primitivo and walked through to the entertainment room. He hadn't bothered tidying up since Ray had been around, and there were books, CD jewel cases and DVD boxes scattered around on just about every available surface. He had recently bought a disc of Alice Coote singing French *mélodies*, so he put that on, making sure it was routed through the speakers in the conservatory. He couldn't understand sung French very well, except for a few lines of Françoise Hardy and Jacques Brel, but he enjoyed the music of the language. And the sweetness of the singer's voice, of course.

After the team meeting, he was more convinced than ever that there was something fishy about the whole St Mary's business. Even AC Gervaise seemed to agree, and he had expected more resistance from her. True, profiles aren't always accurate, and Jenny had quite reasonably complained that she didn't have enough to go on, but the comparison between what they knew of spree killers or mass murderers and what they had been able to discover about Martin Edgeworth's character, life and actions just didn't match up. Then there were the forensic and pathology details. It might be a long haul ahead, but there had to be a way of getting to the bottom of it.

In the meantime, Banks was curious about the letter, which lay on top of *Gramophone* on the table beside him. He turned on the reading lamp, which reflected in the windows, effectively blotting out the dark mass of the hills outside.

Banks held the letter in one hand and tapped its sharp edge on the palm of his other, stretching the anticipation. He didn't recognise the handwriting. Right now, it could be anything – good news, bad news, a death, a birth, a favour asked, an offer, a piece of news that could change his life – but as soon as he opened it, its promise would evaporate and it would simply be what it was. There would be no further room for speculation. It could be from one of his few surviving school friends, for example. Or maybe it was from someone he had come across on a case he had worked. Or a distant uncle leaving him a fortune. The longer he held it unopened, the longer the tension would last. Eventually, though, he gave up teasing himself and opened it as carefully as he could, in case he needed to decipher the address in the top left corner for a reply.

In the light of the lamp, he read the surprisingly clear script:

Dear Alan,

I hope you don't mind me writing to you out of the blue like this. It took me a while to track down your address, but I finally managed. Maybe I should have been a detective, ha-ha!

First let me explain. I'm Julie Drake, Emily's best friend from uni – or university, as we used to call it back in the day. You might remember me as we used to hang around together quite a lot in the pubs and at gigs. I remember you were with us when we saw Bowie live just days before Ziggy Stardust came out. The place was three-quarters empty and he invited everyone to come up to the front. I remember he sat on the edge of the stage at one point and sang 'Amsterdam' with only an acoustic guitar. We were so close I could have touched him. My boyfriend at the time was Andy Mathers, and I think the two of you got along OK. You had similar tastes in music, at any rate, and I remember you both enjoyed a pint or two when you could afford it. Andy and I split up in third year.

But that's enough about me. The reason I'm writing to you is that Emily and I remained close friends until the very end. I thought I saw you at her funeral, but when I came out after the service you were gone, and my eyes were bleary with crying. Still, I'm sure it was you I saw. I won't say you haven't changed, but it's odd how you can sometimes immediately recognise someone you haven't seen for going on forty years. At least it happens to me often enough. I even saw Andy a couple of years ago and recognised him immediately, despite his lack of hair and the extra stone or two around the middle.

I spent a lot of time with Emily in her last few weeks, even held her hand at the end, and I have to tell you first of all that she was unbelievably brave. The cancer had got to her liver by then and we knew there was no hope. Of course, most of the time I wasn't the only one there, her family was very supportive, but we did get a lot of time alone together, just the two of us sitting, listening to music sometimes. She still loved Bowie best of all and she cried buckets when he died, but she'd come to like classical music as well, and it was Schubert's string quintet she wanted at the end. Mostly we just spent our time talking, talking, talking (you must remember I could never shut up!). Sometimes because of the morphine she was given to rambling, and a lot of her thoughts seemed to go back to years ago when we all knew each other. She spoke about you a lot, both in her lucid and rambling moments. I think in some way she always had a special love for you despite the years apart. I remember thinking when I was around you all that time ago that as a couple you emanated a special sort of love, but that's just romantic old me being sentimental with hindsight.

I suppose by now you must be wondering when I'm going to get to the point. If there is a point. Well, there is. I just thought you'd like to know that she didn't forget you. She felt guilty about breaking up like that, and there are some things she wanted me to tell you, or at least she said it would be OK to tell you after she'd gone, but they're not things I can write in a letter. I retired from teaching a while ago, and my husband and I are running a B & B not too far from you, in Filey. If you get the chance to come out here sometime soon, I'd be happy to have a chat. Come anytime. It's off season. Just give me a ring first. My husband Marcel is a superb chef and he will cook us a fantastic meal.

In the meantime, I hope you think of Emily sometimes and remember her with as much fondness and love as I do. She was one of the special ones.

Best Wishes XX

Julie

She added her email, address and phone number in a post-script. Filey wasn't that far, and Banks was sure he could manage a quick visit. He remembered Julie Drake quite well. As best girlfriends often were, she and Emily were different as chalk and cheese. Julie was – or had been back then – a vivacious, flirtatious brunette who often seemed quite manic in proximity to Emily's cool blond presence. Julie had an attractive full figure: large breasts, a pert nose and big eyes. She favoured low-cut tops to reveal a tempting glimpse of cleavage. She also had a reputation for chasing the boys that Banks had often felt was undeserved. He had once seen her crying alone at a party when she thought no one was watching, while the boy she had come with was chatting up a prettier and more sophisticated girl, and more often than not, she went home alone. Banks felt that she probably tried too hard and set her sights on the wrong men. He could recognise the signs. After all, he had set his sights on the wrong woman often enough.

Banks felt his eyes prickle as he put the letter aside. Schubert's string quintet, the very same piece of music Mahler had asked to hear on his deathbed, or so Linda Palmer had told him. He wondered whether Emily had known that.

Reading Julie's words transported him back over forty years. Romantic and sentimental, indeed. He remembered the last time he had seen Emily. They had met in Hyde Park on a glorious summer's day in 1973. Everyone was out enjoying the sunshine. Lovers embraced on the grass, children kicked plastic footballs around, businessmen sat with their jackets off and shirtsleeves rolled up, reading newspapers, and shorthand typists adjusted their office clothing as tastefully as possible to get lunchtime tans.

Banks was propped up against a tree not far from the Serpentine reading a second-hand paperback edition of *The Exorcist*. When he saw Emily walking towards him, he felt an immediate sense of foreboding. She had been distant and moody of late, and there was something in her expression, in the way she smiled at him, that made him feel apprehensive. It wasn't long before she was telling him that she didn't think they should see each other any more, that things had run their course and they were going in different directions and neither of them would be truly happy if they carried on together. He didn't understand any of what she was saying. They hadn't had a fight – they rarely fought, in fact – and in his mind things had been going well, except for the moodiness. He guessed that perhaps there was someone else, but Emily swore blind there was no one. She just needed a break, some distance between them.

In the end, it didn't matter what Banks said, whether he understood it or not. The result was the same. It was over. Back to drunken nights at someone's party, half-hearted fumblings on a pile of lumpy coats in the spare bedroom. Hangovers and guilt in the morning. Then came the lonely nights of Leonard Cohen albums and cheap wine by candlelight. That went on pretty much until he decided to drop out of his business studies course and join the police. He wasn't even sure why he did that to this day. Maybe it started as an act of rebellion and a cure for heartbreak, like joining the Foreign Legion. His father hated him for it, and his mother only managed a fair job of pretending to approve until the first time he got his name in the papers years later. But it had turned out to be a good life for him; he couldn't imagine having taken any other course. He certainly wasn't cut out for business, and he'd made a mess of most of his relationships. Emily had no doubt been better off without him. He was convinced he had an emotional blind spot somewhere. He remembered that he had even thought all was well years later between him and his wife Sandra, up to the point when she left him for another man. He didn't know why that had happened, either. It wasn't that he had failed to lead an unexamined life, just that his life had failed the examination.

He put the letter aside and guzzled some wine. Alice Coote was singing 'Le spectre de la rose', one of his favourite songs from *Les nuits d'été* to the sound of rain running down the window outside. Banks drank and listened, mulling over the letter as he did so. Did he really want to talk to Julie Drake?

He decided that he did. He had to admit that he was curious as to what Emily might have said about him as she lay dying some forty years after they had been in love for a while.

When Alice Coote finished, he went back into the entertainment room to dig out his copy of the string quintet, one of the last pieces of music Schubert had written in his short life.

9

The Edgeworth house was still a crime scene when Banks pulled up the following morning, although the investigation had been scaled down. An officer stood guard in the taped-off drive, and Banks had to show his warrant card to get past him. Banks wondered who the young PC had pissed off to be given such a boring task.

'Anyone else been around?' he asked.

'Nobody, sir. The CSIs come and go, but that's about it. And the pathologist was here. Dr Glendenning.'

'Nobody trying to sneak in?'

'A couple of curious neighbours, but I sent them packing, sir.'

'Get their names and addresses?'

The young officer seemed horror-stricken. 'Nobody said to do that, sir.'

'Don't worry about it. Just remember in future, right?'

The young man swallowed. 'Yes, sir.'

Banks ducked under the tape and walked into the back garden, which was separated from the hill beyond by a wooden fence and a low hedge. There were no trees to spoil the view, which was magnificent, even in the gloom of the day. At least the rain had stopped.

The hillside stretched up gently at first, then became steeper and steeper until its summit was lost in the clouds. Banks noticed a gate in the back fence, and beyond it a well-worn path meandered up the hillside, disappearing into the mist like the hill itself. The scene reminded Banks of an ancient Chinese painting he had seen in an art gallery: tiny human figures walking on a similar path halfway up a huge mountain whose peak was lost in mist. Perhaps this wasn't on such a grand scale, but it was impressive enough.

So this was where Edgeworth went for his walks every Saturday and Sunday morning, according to Ollie Metcalfe. The whole village had been questioned, and nobody had seen Edgeworth since his visit to the White Rose on Friday night. Could he have gone for his walk on Saturday morning before the wedding and met someone up there, either by arrangement or by clever planning on the other's part? If so, what had transpired? Had he invited this person into his home? If so, why? Edgeworth's people-mover had been seen by a couple of villagers just after midday on Saturday, heading for the main Swainsdale road, which would have taken him eventually to Fortford and St Mary's. Nobody had seen the driver's face, as the windows were tinted, so he couldn't definitely be identified as Martin Edgeworth. It could have been anyone.

The house was locked, but Banks had brought a key, and after leaving his overcoat in the vestibule, he entered the kitchen. It was as he had last seen it on the night they had discovered Martin Edgeworth's body. Somebody had washed the cups they used for their tea, but other than that, nothing had changed: the granite-topped island, the big red Aga, the stainless-steel fridge and freezer units. As Banks remembered, it had been immaculate, all surfaces polished or sparkling. A faint hint of antibacterial cleaner in the air.

As he made his way quickly around the upstairs rooms, he noticed the CSIs had taken Edgeworth's filing cabinets, computer, printer, his clothes, the drawers from his study desk and just about everything else they thought might provide some evidence. But all Banks thought about was the neatly folded pile of dark clothing that yielded neither a hair nor a drop of sweat. Both Terry Gilchrist and Gareth Bishop had seen a slim man of medium height wearing dark clothing and a black cap, albeit from a distance. Edgeworth had been slim and of medium height. Did that mean the killer had bought two identical sets of clothes? It made sense. One set for him to wear and dispose of later at his leisure, and the other to leave beside Edgeworth's body to make him appear guilty. If he had been foolish enough to buy both sets of clothes in the same size at the same time, in the same branch, then there was a chance the sales clerk might remember him.

The killer had been a little sloppy, otherwise Banks wouldn't have been standing where he was, but whoever did it would no doubt have counted on the police being so over-joyed that they had solved their crime, caught their killer, that they wouldn't dig any deeper than they had to. In that, he hadn't been entirely wrong. Until now. The only real risk was that someone might have paid a call on Edgeworth while the shooting was taking place, and found the body. But that was most unlikely. He lived alone, and if someone had knocked on the door and got no answer, that person would have gone away, only adding to the evidence that Edgeworth was out shooting the wedding party. A visitor would hardly have entered the house uninvited and discovered a body.

Finally, Banks stepped down into the musty, dank cellar and gave a shiver. As he had told Dr Glendenning, all Edgeworth's tools had been taken away, but nobody had got around to scrubbing away the blood spatter yet, and it was easy enough for Banks to find the exact spot where the body had lain. On the surface, everything had been consistent with a self-administered gunshot. Banks could visualise Edgeworth sliding to the floor, leaning back against the wall, legs stretched out, putting the gun in his mouth and pulling the trigger.

Only it was beginning to appear very much as if it hadn't happened that way at all. Now Banks imagined a shadowy figure hitting Edgeworth from behind with a hammer, shifting him to the floor, into position, then placing the gun in his hand and carefully positioning it in his mouth so that the bullet smashed through that part of the skull he had hit with the hammer.

He bent to examine the spot on the wall where the back of Edgeworth's head had hit. The forensics team had finished their tests, so he knew it was OK to touch the surface, and he found that Glendenning was right. The whitewashed stone was smooth around there, certainly not rough or bumpy enough to cause an indentation like the one in Edgeworth's skull.

He stood back and tried to imagine what had gone on in the mind of Edgeworth's killer. He had probably taken Edgeworth by surprise, and if the killer intended to fake a suicide, he wouldn't want to risk poison or sleeping tablets in a cup of tea. He would have known that the police would carry out toxicology tests and that anything unusual would be a flagged. So he waited until Edgeworth's back was turned and stunned him with a blow to the back of the head, then arranged him on the floor against the wall and shot him. It was certainly a plausible explanation.

If someone else had done it and assumed Edgeworth's identity, then Edgeworth must have been killed *before* the church massacre. Even Dr Glendenning had admitted this could have easily been the case. There were no indications in the postmortem that his body had been restrained in any way. To make everything work, the killer must have got into the house in the morning, done his business in the cellar, then driven off in Edgeworth's RAV4, with his AR15, wearing clothing identical to that he had left in the cellar neatly piled by the body. And the odds were that Edgeworth had let him in, or taken him back there after meeting on a walk, for example, as there had been no signs of forced entry.

And if the killer had gone to such lengths and thought things out that much, Banks was probably dealing with a more intelligent person than someone who had simply snapped and started shooting people at random. Which meant there was likely to be a motive somewhere, something very important that he didn't know yet, hidden away in all this, however deep it may be buried and however tricky it might be to find.

Banks found Roger behind the bar again when he called at the Upper Swainsdale District Rifle and Pistol Club that Friday afternoon. 'Boss around today?' he asked.

Roger regarded him as if he were mad, then recognition dawned. 'Oh, it's you again,' he said. 'Sorry. As a matter of fact, Mr McLaren *is* in today. I'll just let him know you're here.'

As Roger disappeared through a door behind the bar, Banks leaned on the polished dark wood and waited. The dining area was much busier than on his previous visit, and most of the tables were occupied by late lunchers. Banks tried to pick out George and Margie Sykes among the diners but couldn't see them. He wondered what drew people to shooting, never having had much inclination or aptitude for it, himself, though he had completed a number of firearms courses both during his training and later. It was probably something you couldn't imagine people enjoying unless you actually took it up yourself, like trainspotting or running marathons. Maybe it was somewhere between the absorption and soothing influence of a hobby and full-throttled adrenalin-fuelled obsession with speed or distance.

'This way. Second on the left.'

Roger held the bar flap up and Banks walked through. The business section of the club wasn't quite as well appointed as the public area, but everything was recently polished, and the air smelled of fresh lemons. Not a whiff of cordite anywhere. Banks walked along the corridor past an open storeroom then tapped on the door marked MANAGER. A reedy voice bade him enter.

Geoff McLaren sat behind a large desk of imitation teak. At least, Banks assumed it was imitation. Real teak was prohibitively expensive these days. It was a tidy desk, and the laptop computer that sat on it was closed. McLaren's large bald head shone as if it had been polished as recently as the woodwork, and his handshake was a little too damp and limp for Banks's liking.

'Can I get you anything?' McLaren asked, when both were settled in their chairs.

'Nothing, thanks,' Banks said. 'I don't think I'll take up much of your time.'

McLaren's expression and voice turned funeral-director deep and sympathetic. 'It's about poor Martin, isn't it, I assume? What a terrible, terrible tragedy.'

'Did you know Martin Edgeworth personally, or was it merely in your professional capacity?'

McLaren made a pyramid with his fingertips on the desk. 'I'd like to think Martin and I were friends, or at least very good acquaintances. We lunched together on occasion. Not here, of course. My place of business. That wouldn't do. But at his local down in Swainshead sometimes. In Eastvale once or twice. When he had the dental practice, I was a patient. Martin was one of our longest-standing members, and he helped out with a lot of the committee work, competitions, legal paperwork, that sort of thing.'

'Vetting new members?'

McLaren pursed his lips, then spoke. 'On occasion. But only in the preliminary stages, you understand. The rest has been done with the correct legal authorities, by the book.'

'Of course.'

'We take law and safety very seriously here, Mr Banks.'

'I'm sure you do. Did Mr Edgeworth vet any new applications for you recently, or perhaps propose any new members?'

'It doesn't exactly work that way, but no, he didn't.'

'Anything unusual at all happen?'

'Not that I can think of.' McLaren frowned. 'What sort of thing were you thinking of?'

'Any unpleasant incidents. Arguments. Accidents. Threats. Thefts.'

'No, nothing of that sort. We run a tight ship.'

'So nobody got drunk and shot up the restaurant?'

McLaren's smile was little more than a polite flicker. 'Contrary to what a lot of people seem to think, it's not exactly the wild west out here. We don't permit any firearms in the restaurant and bar area. They have to be securely locked in the specified areas under the specified conditions when not out in use out on the ranges.'

'Very wise. What did you and Martin Edgeworth talk about when you met up for lunch?'

'Just things in general. Club gossip, politics, business, new products, that sort of thing.'

'Is there much club gossip?'

'Well, it's only the sort that's interesting if you know the members involved.'

'Affairs, that sort of thing?'

'Hardly. A few members do bring their wives for meals and functions and so forth, but we're not the sort to go leaving our car keys in a dish by the door.'

'Good lord, do people really do that?'

McLaren smiled. 'I wouldn't know. It's just something I remember from an old movie.'

'I think they have more sophisticated methods these days. Apps and the like.'

'I'm sure they do,' said McLaren. He was starting to shift in his chair and drum his fingers on the desk.

'All right,' Banks went on, 'I realise that all this probably has nothing to do with your club at all, and believe me, though I'm no fan of firearms, I have no desire to cause any discomfort for those who are. But if Martin Edgeworth *did* take his AR15 rifle to Fortford on the day in question, if he did kill five people and wound four, then I'm sure you can understand that it would be in all our best interests to know why.'

'Of course. But I'm afraid I don't believe he did what you say.'

'You don't?'

'Not at all. You didn't know him. If you had done, you wouldn't even be suggesting anything of the kind.'

'Appearances can be deceptive, Mr McLaren. People found Ted Bundy charming.'

'For heaven's sake, it wasn't like that. I've heard all about the charming and convincing psychopaths. We've had one or two people of that ilk attempting to join even during my time here. People I wouldn't trust with a firearm as far as I could throw them. But not Martin. He was straight as a die.'

Banks had resigned himself for yet another eulogy on Martin Edgeworth, and maybe, he realised, he was simply visiting the club again for reassurance that he was right to believe in Edgeworth's innocence himself, that he was pushing at people like McLaren to test the strength of his own belief. But there was still the matter of a point of contact between Edgeworth and the real killer, and the club seemed to fit the bill nicely for that. Here were plenty of people who both knew Edgeworth and knew their way around weapons. 'I'd like their names, if possible,' he said.

'What names?'

'These people you wouldn't trust with a firearm as far as you could throw them.'

'Oh, for heaven's sake, that was just an off-the-cuff comment.'

'So there haven't been any such applicants?'

'I'm not saying we don't turn people down, but there's usually more to it than my personal feelings about them.'

'If you have a record of the names of these people you've turned away, or if you remember any of them, I'd still very much appreciate a list, along with a list of your active members. Remember, I can get a court order if I need one.'

'That won't be necessary. I'll see what I can do. I'm as concerned as you are that we get to the bottom of what happened that day.'

'Thank you. Did Martin Edgeworth ever put forward any of these applicants you rejected?'

'No.'

'Did he ever recommend anyone for membership at all?'

'Not that I recall.'

'And you know most of your members personally?'

'All of them. Not as well as I knew Martin but well enough. It's not that large a membership.' He leaned back in his chair. 'Am I to take it that you're thinking along the same lines as I am? That Martin is, in fact, innocent?'

'The investigation is still ongoing,' said Banks. 'There are a number of issues we have to clear up for ourselves, seeing that Martin Edgeworth committed suicide and can't explain his actions or motives to us. I can't really say much more than that at this stage.'

'Of course,' said McLaren. 'But I'm afraid I can't help you. And I believe you know that I would if I could. If it would help Martin's reputation in any way.' He paused. 'There was only one little thing that struck me as at all odd lately.'

'Oh? What was that?'

'I wouldn't want you to get your hopes up. It's probably nothing. But once, over lunch, Martin asked me if it was possible for someone with a criminal record to get a firearms certificate and join the club, if he'd paid his debt to society and so on, and his crime hadn't involved firearms or violence, of course.'

'I'm not that well up on the law in this area,' said Banks, 'but I would assume that it isn't. All right, that is.'

'And you'd be correct. Though if the sentence was under three years and the police and doctors offer no objections, then it can be done. Which is what I told Martin. It's not even a matter of the letter of the law. As a club, as a respectable organisation, we wouldn't accept as a member anyone with a criminal record, and nor would we be required to.'

'Do you have any idea who he was talking about?'

'No. The subject was never mentioned again. I'm not sure he was referring to anyone in particular.'

'Then why ask?'

'I don't know. Just wondering, I suppose.'

'When was this?'

'Not very long before . . . you know. Say, early last November.'

'Where?'

'Over lunch in the White Rose.'

'Was he with anyone?'

'There were only the two of us. I mean, there were others in the pub, of course, but no one else was a party to the conversation. And, as I said, he never mentioned the subject again. I'm sorry I can't be any more helpful, but that really is all I can tell you.'

'No, that's fine,' said Banks, standing to leave. 'You've been very helpful, Mr McLaren.'

And, in a way, Banks thought as he made his way across the gravel to his car, he had. McLaren might not have been able to supply any useful practical information, but the simple fact that Edgeworth had been asking about a man with a criminal record joining the shooting club went a long way towards confirming that Edgeworth had probably been a victim rather than the perpetrator. It also implied that the killer might have been grooming him, befriending him and asking for his help. One sure way of gaining someone's confidence, if you were charming and devious enough, was to be honest with him about something like a prison sentence.

DC Gerry Masterson parked her lime-green Corsa behind Banks's Porsche and walked towards the front door. It was going on for ten o'clock, and the lights were still on inside Newhope Cottage, as well as the one over the front door, so she could see her way. She rang the bell, and a few seconds later Banks opened the door. He seemed surprised to see her.

'Gerry,' he said. 'What brings you all the way out here?'

'I need to talk to you, sir. And I thought it might be better to come in person.'

Banks stood aside. 'Come in, then. Let me take your coat.'

Gerry handed him her coat, which he hung on the back of the door. They were in a small room, a sort of den or study, with a two-seater sofa and reading lamp, an iMac on a desk and a small bookcase overstuffed with books. The walls were cream with light blue trim. Banks was casually dressed in jeans and black crew-neck jumper. Gerry followed him through the kitchen, where she could smell the lingering remnants of a curry, and into the dimly lit conservatory. She didn't recognise the music that was playing, a woman singing to piano accompaniment.

'It's Lorraine Hunt Lieberson,' Banks said. 'Singing Mahler's "Liebst du um Schönheit". He wrote it as a gift for his new bride, Alma. Ray here's a bit of a philistine when it comes to classical music, and I'm trying to educate him. Don't you like it?'

'I . . . er . . . Yes, sir. It's very beautiful, haunting.'

The other man in the room stood up and held out his hand. Gerry shook it. 'Take no notice of him, love, he's a music snob. Give me Pink Floyd any day.' He smiled, and with a little bow, added, 'Ray Cabbot, at your service.'

'This is DI Cabbot's father,' Banks said. 'He's staying with me until he finds a place of his own.'

He was older than Banks, Gerry noted, and with his ponytail and lined face, he reminded her of a picture of Willie Nelson she had seen on a magazine cover recently. He wore ugly baggy trousers with pockets up and down the legs and a grey sweatshirt that said MIAMI DOLPHINS in bright red letters on the front.

Ray peered at her. 'Has anyone ever told you how closely you resemble Jane Morris?' he said.

'I can't say I've ever heard of her.'

'Famous artists' model. Pre-Raphaelite.'

'Sorry, she's a new one on me.' Gerry had heard of Lizzie Siddal, and she was sick to death of hearing about her resemblance to the most famous Pre-Raphaelite model, mostly because of her slender 'wand-like' figure and long red hair. It wasn't so much that she thought such comments inappropriate, though they often were, but she wished men could be a bit more original in their compliments, if compliments they were meant to be.

'Fascinating subject, artists' models,' Ray Cabbot went on. 'You could write a book about them. They invariably slept

with the artists, you know. It can be a very intimate relationship, being painted. Very erotic. Rossetti and Fanny Cornforth,
for example. Have you ever posed?'

'I can't say it's a line of work I've ever wanted to pursue.'

'Oh, you should. With your bones and colouring, you
could—'

'Er, Ray,' Banks cut in, tapping his watch. 'Weren't you
about to head off to the Dog and Gun? Folk night.'

'Is it? Was I?' Ray scratched his temple. 'Ah, yes. Of course.
Right. See you later, Jane. I mean Gerry.' And he shot off
through the kitchen and out of the front door.

'He's an artist. What can I say?' Banks picked up a remote
and turned off the music.

'You didn't have to do that for me, sir. I was enjoying it.'

'Sure you wouldn't prefer Pink Floyd?'

'I wouldn't know, sir,' said Gerry. 'I haven't heard Pink
Floyd. Not that I know of. I mean, I know the name, but, you
know . . . I'm pleased to hear that Mahler wrote the song for
his wife. It must have been a wonderful gift to receive.
Nobody's ever written a song for me, let alone one as lovely as
that.'

'Me, neither,' said Banks. 'And next time we're in the car
together, remind me to play you *Ummagumma*. So what can I
help you with? Would you like a glass of wine? Cup of tea?
Coffee? Perhaps a wee dram of whisky?' He turned the CD
player on again with the remote and the beautiful music
continued quietly in the background.

'Nothing, thanks, sir. I can't stay. I just . . . well, I found
something I thought was interesting, and I wanted to tell you
in person.'

'You've got my attention. Go ahead.'

Gerry sat in the one of the wicker chairs. Outside, the dark
humps of the fells stood out in silhouette against the lighter

night sky. Banks sat on the angled chair beside her and picked up a glass of purplish-red wine from the table between them.

'You know you told me to dig a bit further into the Wendy Vincent business?'

'You were working late on that tonight?'

'Yes.'

'Then don't keep me in suspense.'

Gerry turned slightly to face him. 'Do you remember anything about the Wendy Vincent murder, sir? December, 1964.'

'Even I'm not so old that I've been on the force that long,' said Banks. 'But I do believe I heard the name in the news not long ago.'

'That's right. I'll get to that.' Gerry went on, 'Wendy Vincent was a fifteen-year-old girl who was sexually assaulted and murdered in some woods near her home in Leeds. There were rumours that she could have been an early victim of Brady and Hindley, and more recently the press threw Jimmy Savile and Peter Sutcliffe in the mix.'

'How old would Sutcliffe have been in 1964?'

'Eighteen, sir. It's not beyond the bounds of possibility. If they hadn't caught the real killer, that is. Frank Dowson. A couple of years back there was a piece in the papers on the fiftieth anniversary of fifth December, 1964. Just a simple retelling of an unsolved crime. That's probably why you remember the name. The murder took place in the same part of west Leeds where Maureen Tindall lived at the time with her parents. Maureen and Wendy Vincent were the same age, went to the same school and were best friends. According to one of her teachers interviewed for the TV programme, Wendy had been playing hockey for the school team that morning, and she took a short cut through the woods on her way home. Apparently, she had taken a bit of a knock on the field, so she wasn't feeling too great.'

'And that's where she was killed? The woods?'

'Yes, sir. Raped and stabbed repeatedly. Her body was found hidden under some branches and bracken under a bridge over the stream. There was no mention of Maureen Tindall in the articles that coincided with the fiftieth anniversary, or on the TV footage about it, but I found one passing mention on a website, quoting a local newspaper back at the time, in 1964. The newspaper is no longer published, but the website had scans of back issues, and I found mention of Wendy's best friend there: Maureen Grainger.'

'Maureen Tindall's maiden name.'

'That's right. It was the usual sort of human interest story you'd get in a small local weekly – what was the "real" Wendy like, what was her taste in clothes, music, did she have a boyfriend, what was she like as a friend, that type of thing.'

'As I remember, that anniversary article you mentioned and the accompanying TV documentary sparked a reopening of the case, and that's where Frank Dowson comes in, right?'

'Yes. First on DNA evidence, connected with a series of rapes, then he confessed. Some of the papers accused the original police investigation of a massive cock-up, sir. Please excuse my language.'

'I remember that. But there's no question that they got the right man?'

'Not as far as I can tell. Everything was done by the book. The confession was solid, the DNA evidence admissible. They'd found traces of blood and skin under Wendy's fingernails that they were certain came from her killer. Of course, DNA typing didn't exist at the time, but the samples were properly stored. After the case was reopened in 2015, they were checked against other cold-case samples, and a match was found for a suspect in several rapes. He was also on the database. Frank Dowson. He'd been twenty-one at the time of Wendy's murder, and in the merchant navy. He admitted to a number of other unsolved rapes when they brought him in. And to Wendy's murder. He got life, but he died in the prison hospital early this year. Respiratory failure.'

'That's all very interesting, Gerry, Maureen Tindall, or Grainger, being the best friend of a murder victim fifty years ago, and the killer finally being caught after all that time, but it happens these days. You know that. How could there possibly be any connection between the Wendy Vincent murder and what happened at Laura Tindall's wedding? I mean, Frank Dowson could hardly have done it. He's dead.'

Gerry's shoulders slumped. 'I don't know, sir, but I think we should talk to Maureen Tindall again, and maybe do a bit of digging around in the West Yorkshire archives for whatever files they've still got. People who were around at the time. You never know. Someone might remember something. There might even be a connection with Edgeworth.'

'Edgeworth was just a child in 1964.'

'Later, then. Some point over the last fifty years.'

'That's stretching it a bit,' said Banks.

Gerry could sense his frustration. She felt it, herself, but she also felt she was on to something. 'It's the only angle I've come up with so far, sir. I drew a blank with the bridesmaids and the maid of honour. You've already interviewed Katie Shea's boyfriend and the father of her unborn child, Boyd Farrow, and his alibi stands up. The Wendy Vincent murder is all we've got so far. However tenuous the link may be. Otherwise, it's back to Martin Edgeworth. And Maureen Tindall was definitely strange when we talked to her, as if she was remembering a long way back and seeing a possibility she didn't want to admit.'

'Are you sure that's not just your imagination after the fact?'

'Maybe, sir. But if her best friend was murdered, and we were asking her if she could think of anyone, no matter how long ago, who might want to do her family harm, and she seemed to remember something she wouldn't tell us, don't you think it's worth following up on?'

She watched as Banks leaned back and drank more wine.

'I'm still curious as to why you came all the way out here to tell me this,' he said. 'What you've told me is interesting, yes, but surely the telephone would have done?'

Gerry hesitated. There was something she hadn't told him yet that had made her irrationally determined to put the facts of the case before him in person. 'Well, you'll have to be the judge of that, yourself, sir,' she said. 'It was just that a name came up once or twice in the old newspaper reports from 1964, someone we might want to talk to.'

'A name?'

'Yes. One of the investigating officers. I did a bit of checking around and found out he's someone you know. I just wanted to run the name by you before going off half-cocked. I mean, with all the press criticism of the original investigation and so on.'

'Don't tell me it was DI Chadwick again?' Banks said.

'No, sir. Definitely not Chadwick. It was someone called Gristhorpe. A DC Gristhorpe. Apparently, he used to be your boss.'

IO

Banks and Jenny Fuller drove down the rutted drive to ex-Detective Superintendent Gristhorpe's farmhouse outside the village of Lyndgarth late the following morning. The sky looked like a pot full of boiling oily rags, and the air was so moist that it was hard to breathe, but at least it wasn't raining. Which was just as well. All the meteorological reports stated that the ground was so waterlogged already that one more spell of heavy rain would cause even more serious flooding.

The car splashed up water from the puddles, and Banks finally brought it to a halt outside the back door. He hadn't been to visit the old man in quite a while, but not much had changed. The drystone wall that went nowhere and fenced in nothing still ran through his large back garden, but ended jaggedly and abruptly. There had been no decent weather for working on it lately. It was Gristhorpe's hobby – he said it was therapeutic, kept him calm and focused – and whenever he came to the end of his allotted pile of stones, he dismantled the wall then mixed them up like a bag of dominoes, adding a few new ones, and started all over again.

The green paint on the heavy back door was so fresh Banks could smell it. He rang the bell. They didn't have long to wait before it opened and the tall, bulky figure of Detective Superintendent Gristhorpe stood there beckoning them in, wearing a pair of old brown cords and a dark woolly jumper.

'Well, look at you, lass,' he said to Jenny. 'It's been years since I last saw you, and you've hardly changed at all. You're still a right bobby-dazzler.'

Jenny blushed and gave him a hug. 'You silver-tongued old devil. It's been a long time. How are you?'

'Can't complain, though I wouldn't recommend old age,' said Gristhorpe as he led them into his wood-panelled, book-lined living room and bade them sit in the worn leather armchairs. There was a fire crackling in the hearth and a book on the table beside Gristhorpe's chair. Thomas Hardy's *The Mayor of Casterbridge*, Banks noticed. So the old man was still rereading the classics. 'First, tea.' Gristhorpe rubbed his hands together. 'Then talk.' He disappeared into the kitchen.

Jenny smiled at Banks. 'It brings back so many memories, just seeing him again. Hearing his voice.' Her eyes were shining.

'How long *has* it been?' Banks asked.

'More years than I'd care to remember.'

Banks stared into the flames in silence, thinking about time and age and Emily and death, then Gristhorpe reappeared with the tea and mugs on a tray. He moved his book and set the tray down on the table, rubbing his hands together. 'We'll let it mash for a while first.'

Gristhorpe eased himself into his chair. Banks thought he noticed a grimace of pain flash briefly across his features. The old man always did suffer from back problems and a touch of arthritis. Otherwise, he seemed hale and hearty. He had the same weathered, pock-marked face, and the unruly thatch of hair might have turned a bit greyer and thinner since the last time they met, but it was still mostly all there.

When the tea was ready, Gristhorpe poured them each a mug, opened a tin of ginger nut biscuits and sat down again, cradling the mug on his lap. 'You mentioned something on the telephone about the Wendy Vincent case,' he said to Banks.

'Yes. It came up in some research Gerry – that's DC Masterson – was doing on the wedding shooting.'

'Nasty business that. But I thought it was all over and done with. I thought you got your man?'

'We're not exactly sure about that.'

'The man we found didn't match any profile I could come up with for a mass murderer or spree killer,' Jenny added. 'Not that such things are always an accurate guide – I'd be the first to admit – but there are certain parameters.'

'Exception to the rule?'

'Could be,' Jenny admitted. 'But I think Alan also has a number of forensic issues and other concerns.'

'When you add it all together,' Banks said, 'I think the case merits further investigation.'

He told Gristhorpe about Dr Glendenning's doubts and added a few of his own. Gristhorpe took a mouthful of tea and dunked his ginger biscuit as he listened.

When Banks had finished, Gristhorpe frowned. 'I'll go along with you for the time being,' he said. 'Maybe it does deserve a bit more attention. But where does Wendy Vincent come into it? I remember that case well. It was one of my very first, and it was a complete bloody disaster. It still galls me to this day, even though they finally caught the bastard. We should have had the gumption to question Frank Dowson back at the time of the crime – it's not as if he was unknown to us – but he was a merchant seaman, and nobody told us he was in the area at the time.'

'When your name came up,' Banks said, 'Gerry found your connection with me, and she thought I might want your name kept out of it. So she came to me with the story first, in person.'

'She thought I might resent my failure being broadcast around again?'

'It may have crossed her mind. She's young. And she doesn't know you like I do.'

'She'll probably go far, then.' Gristhorpe slurped some tea. His eyes twinkled.

'One of the members of the wedding was Maureen Tindall, née Grainger,' Banks went on. 'DC Masterson's discovered in the course of her research that she was Wendy Vincent's best friend.'

'That's right. I remember her. Pretty young thing in a flower-patterned frock. Nervous as hell. And clearly very upset. She was at the wedding?'

'Mother of the bride.'

'Dead?'

'Unharmed.'

'Then why make the connection?'

'I don't know,' said Banks. 'All I know is that I suspect there might be one, and I'm not a hundred per cent convinced that Martin Edgeworth was responsible for the shooting.'

'You're not trying to say that someone shot Maureen Grainger's daughter because of what happened to Wendy Vincent over fifty years ago, are you?'

'I'm not sure what I'm saying. Why don't you tell me about it?'

'We worked on the assumption that it was a crime of opportunity.'

'Most likely it was,' said Banks. 'But why did Frank Dowson kill Wendy Vincent after raping her?'

'You know as well as I do, Alan,' said Jenny, 'that rapists often kill their victims.'

'Not always,' Banks said. 'Unless they're sexual psychopaths. And usually, if they do, it's a matter of identification.'

'Which is exactly what it was in this case,' said Gristhorpe. 'Wendy Vincent did know Frank Dowson. Not well, but certainly well enough to recognise him, to know who he was. He lived on the same estate. He was the older brother of some-one she knew. When they finally caught up with Dowson a couple of years ago, he confessed to a number of other rapes, but denied any more murders.'

'The others were strangers?' Jenny said.

'Aye.'

'Was there any gossip about Wendy Vincent?' Banks asked. 'Did she have any sort of a reputation to make Dowson think she'd be easy, or asking for it? Anything that might make him believe she was sexually available?'

'Good lord, no,' said Gristhorpe. 'Quite the opposite. Young Wendy was an angel, by all accounts. Sunday school, Brownies, the whole kit and caboodle. Did well at school, good at sports. Pretty much held a dysfunctional household together by herself. There'd been problems, social services involved, that sort of thing. The parents were alcoholics. But Wendy was a nice kid. Everyone said so.'

'Is it possible that he might not have intended to kill Wendy Vincent, but that she surprised him by struggling?'

'He was certainly a strong lad, and one of those who didn't know his own strength. But he raped her then stabbed her five times, Alan. There wasn't much of a struggle. I'd hardly say he didn't know exactly what he was doing. You were right first time. He knew she'd be able to identify him. And that's what the court believed as well, fifty years later, despite the sneaky defence barrister trying to claim diminished responsibility.'

'Frank Dowson was mentally challenged?' Jenny asked.

'He had a very low IQ. But he knew what rape and murder were. At least he knew how to commit them.'

'Can you remember what happened that day?' Banks asked.

'As if it were yesterday. Happens when you get older, you know, Alan. Yesterday becomes a blur, but the distant past comes sharp into focus. I remember all my cases, and Wendy Vincent was one of the first, like I said. I was a callow DC working in West Yorkshire.'

'Do you remember anyone called Chadwick, a DI? Was he involved in this case at all?'

'I knew Chadwick, but he wasn't on the Wendy Vincent case. I never worked with him, but I heard things. I don't even think he was around at the time. Always thought he was a bit iffy. Detective Superintendent Lindsay was running the investigation, and I was working mostly with DI Rattigan and DS Saunders. Decent coppers, all of them. Of course, there were plenty of others involved, plainclothes and uniformed. There was a huge search for the girl, then a manhunt for her killer, but by then Dowson was back at sea, and as far as we knew he'd always been there.'

'How did it begin?'

'We got a phone call from Wendy's parents. Her father, if I remember rightly. They didn't have a phone in their house, so he had to walk to the nearest telephone box. That's before they all got vandalised.'

'When was this?'

'About seven in the evening. They'd been expecting her home to make their tea. She was playing hockey for the school in the morning, then there was a lunch afterwards at school for the team. Teatime at home was half past five. Regular as clockwork. They assumed she'd be knocking about with her mates in the afternoon, but when she wasn't home by then, they got worried. By seven they were even more worried. It wasn't like her. Wendy was a good girl. They got in touch with Maureen's parents, who said that Maureen hadn't seen Wendy that day. Maureen wasn't a hockey player, by the way, so she'd been visiting her gran in Thornhill, near Bradford, and not at the game. Then they got really worried. Being December, it was dark by late afternoon, of course, and it had started raining.'

'Then what?'

'The usual. Naturally, as the family was known to us through social services, we searched the house and questioned the parents pretty thoroughly. You know as well as I do, Alan, that as often as not it's the best place to start, however callous it might seem. But they were convincing, even though it was obvious to anyone they were drunk. Pretty much everyone who talked to us believed that Wendy would never run away from home or do anything like that. She was a good kid, despite her tough home life. You could tell. You can almost always tell. Next we checked with all her school friends and teammates. Nobody had seen her after she left the school canteen to go home. We mapped out the route, and instead of taking the main roads and residential streets, she took the short cut through the woods. This involved walking down a narrow treelined lane with houses on one side set well back and high up, hidden by the trees. We did a house to house there, of course, but nobody saw her. On the other side there was a small church, empty that afternoon. The lane petered out at the woods. There's a stream runs through it, quite wide in parts and there's an old stone bridge, been there since Dick's day as far as anyone remembered.'

'What did you do next?'

'There wasn't much more we could do that night except search the streets, knock on doors. It was dark and rainy, turning to mist. It wasn't much better by morning, but by then we thought we'd found a witness. A local dog-walker from one of the houses on the lane had seen a man going into the woods shortly before we think Wendy would have been there. That's why we thought it was a matter of bad timing and opportunity, not premeditation. Nobody could have known she would take that route, as far as we could discover. Not that it made much difference to the outcome. Trouble is, we didn't get a good enough description to put out an identikit. It was a gloomy afternoon, and he was in shadow. It got us nowhere. Someone else saw a lad on a bicycle passing the edge of the woods, maybe a delivery boy of some sort. Same negative result.'

'And Wendy?'

'We began a search of the woods. It covered a fairly extensive area so it took a while. Her parents had told us it wasn't unusual for her to take that route, depending on whether she was with friends who lived close to the main road or not. This time she wasn't. The woods didn't have a bad reputation. Nothing terrible had ever happened there, and there was no reason to think anything would. The conditions weren't much better for the search as far as the rain was concerned, which made it pointless to bring in the canine unit, but at least it was daylight. It took about three hours, but by the early afternoon, one of our uniformed lads found the body under the old stone bridge, covered by a makeshift pile of leaves, twigs and bracken, on the narrow path beside the stream. She was only about a hundred yards from home, poor thing.'

'But you said Frank Dowson was thick. It sounds a bit sophisticated for someone like him, hiding the body like that.'

'I only said that his lawyer *claimed* diminished responsibility. And I said he had a low IQ, that's all. It doesn't mean he had no self-preservation instinct. He wasn't without a certain low cunning. And you'd better watch it. You'll have the political correctness squad after you if you go around calling intellectually challenged people thick.'

'Even the least intelligent of us can be quite cunning under the right circumstances,' said Jenny.

Gristhorpe sighed. 'Aye, lass. You can say that again. He managed to elude our grasp for fifty years, at any rate. And he committed more rapes during that time. They said that was one of the things that finally led them to him. The crimes corresponded with the periods of his leave from the navy. That and his conviction five years ago for handling stolen goods and committing actual bodily harm. Only God knows how many rapes he committed on his travels around the world.'

'Do you remember anything else about Wendy Vincent's family background?' Jenny asked.

'From what I could gather,' said Gristhorpe, 'the parents weren't abusive, just neglectful. It was the drink, of course. They could hardly take care of themselves, let alone two kids. Her dad was a bit of a wide boy, too, in and out of work, Beatles' style haircut, fancied himself as a musician. The mother was a hard-working charlady when she had a job, but she got fired as often as not for absenteeism. There was a younger brother called Mark. He was only eleven at the time of the murder and, naturally, he was pretty shaken up, but maybe still a bit too young to take it all in. Frank Dowson came from an even more dodgy family on the same estate. His old man was a fence. Kept a lock-up across town full of stuff that "fell off the back of a lorry". Small stuff, but we kept an eye on him. Frank had a younger brother called Billy Dowson, about Mark Vincent's age. They were mates, as far as we could gather. Part of the same gang. And I don't mean "gang" like you hear it used today. They never did owt more than knock on a few doors and run away and lather a few doorknobs with treacle. Typical Mischief Night behaviour. Mostly I should imagine they sat around in some den or other and smoked Park Drives and pored over dirty magazines and felt grown up. There was a sister, too. Cilla. She was sixteen and already on the game. But Frank Dowson didn't live with his parents at the time. Like I said, he'd joined the merchant navy, and he only dropped by occasionally, when he was on leave. That's one reason we didn't follow up the way we should have. Nobody told us he was in the area when the murder occurred, so we neglected to check with the naval authorities to see if he had an alibi. It was sloppy police work. No excuses. Except there were more villains on that estate than you could shake a stick at. But I still can't see how any of this is connected with your wedding shootings.'

'Nor can I,' said Banks. 'What we need is a connection between Martin Edgeworth and the shooter, but we don't know who the shooter is. All we have so far is a connection, however tenuous, between one member of the wedding party and this fifty-year-old crime. I think we'll try to track down some of the people who were involved, if they're still alive. Billy Dowson, maybe his sister, Cilla, Wendy's brother, any other members of the gang. See if anyone remembers something that might help. Do you know what happened to them?'

'I didn't keep in touch,' said Gristhorpe. 'And as far as I know both families moved away from the estate fairly soon after the investigation ground to a halt. I know Wendy's mum and dad split up not long after and the lad, Mark, was packed off to live with an aunt and uncle in Ferry Fryston or some such place, but don't quote me on it. I can give you some names, and you should be able to find them easily enough with your modern methods.'

'Gerry should be able to take it from there,' said Banks. 'She's good with computer research.'

'And now,' said Gristhorpe, looking towards Jenny, 'what have you been doing these past few years?'

'Why is it people always seem to retire to places like this?' asked Annie as Gerry drove along a narrow, winding road just beyond Sedburgh. They were almost in the Lake District, and the change was apparent in the shapes of the mountains and rolling hills, much older here, bigger and more rounded.

'I suppose they're after a bit of peace and quiet after fifty years of the daily grind, commuting and what have you,' said Gerry.

'It's either somewhere like this or some seaside hellhole like Bognor or Blackpool.'

'Nobody retires to Blackpool.' Gerry swung the wheel at a particularly awkward corner. The tyres slipped on the shiny road surface.

'Watch it,' Annie said as they almost scraped a drystone wall. 'When my time comes, I'm going to retire to London,' she announced. 'Spend my days in the art galleries and my nights in the theatres and pubs. After that, I'll be out clubbing until dawn.'

Gerry laughed. 'Better hurry up then.'

Annie gave her a sideways glance. 'You think I'm too old, don't you?'

'Maybe if you just put in your thirty. Do you think that's what you'll do, or will you follow in the boss's footsteps?'

'Depends on whether I win the lottery,' Annie said. 'Ah, here we are. Village of Little-Feather-up-the-Bum.'

'It's Featheringham,' said Gerry. 'Little Featheringham.'

'Thank God Alan isn't here or we'd be getting a lecture about how Wordsworth wrote some stupid poem sitting up on that hill over there.'

'We're not quite in Wordsworth territory yet. And I got my A-level English. I know a thing or two about Wordsworth, myself.'

'Spare me the details. In love with his sister or something, wasn't he? Pervert. But it's a fine place for a dentist to retire. Maybe he's got a cellar full of reclining chairs and slow drills, those pointy things they try and pull your filling out with, and those scrapers they use to clean your teeth? Could be a real torture chamber down there. Nobody could hear you scream. Are you sure you're ready for this?'

Gerry pulled up outside the squat cottage. A thin column of smoke twisted from the chimney. 'I don't suppose we need to worry about parking around here,' she said. 'Or the Krook lock.'

'Doubt it,' said Annie, slipping out of the car.

A short path led from the red wooden gate to the front door. Jonathan Martell answered almost immediately after Annie rang the bell, and she had to admit that he wasn't quite what she had expected of a retired dentist. Slim, trim and handsome in a white V-neck cricket jumper over a blue button-down Oxford, jeans and Nike trainers, he appeared a lot younger than she had expected, for a start. He also had a fine head of wavy brown hair and a nice smile. She found herself wondering if he was married. He was wearing a ring, she noticed, but experience had taught her that didn't always mean anything. They shook hands, and he led them through to the living room. The ceilings were low and criss-crossed with weathered wooden beams, but it was a cosy space, and the fire burned in the hearth. The walls were dotted with local landscapes, some of them quite good, in Annie's eyes, and a number of framed photographs on the mantelpiece above the fire: Martell on a beach somewhere with an exotic dark-haired young beauty, Martell standing in the garden with his arms around the shoulders of two young children; a professional portrait of the beautiful woman, no doubt his wife, whose teeth were far whiter than Annie's. She ran her tongue over molars. They felt furry and jagged. It was odd, she thought, as she settled into the comfortable armchair perhaps just a little too close to the fire, but it was as if a whole lifetime had flashed in front of her eyes when she entered the cottage. Not her own lifetime, necessarily, but a lifetime, nonetheless.

'Can I get you anything?' Martell asked. 'I know you're driving, but I'm sure a small port or sherry wouldn't do any harm.'

'Tea, please, if you've got any,' said Annie.

'Do you have herbal?' Gerry asked.

'What a healthy pair of coppers,' said Martell. 'Peppermint? Chamomile?'

They agreed on peppermint, and Martell disappeared into the kitchen to make it. Annie glanced around the room, its mullioned windows offering a fine view of the open fields across the lane, a range of mountains rising beyond, their summits lost in cloud; the hiss and crackle of logs burning; whiff of woodsmoke and warm leather in the air. Annie shifted her legs away from the heat. She felt that she could almost fall asleep here.

Martell came back in no time with a teapot and mugs on a tray, along with a glass of amber liquid. 'Whisky,' he said. 'I'm not driving anywhere today.' He gestured to the window. 'I was supposed to be playing a round of golf later, but it looks like rain.'

A golfer, then, Annie thought. Still, nobody's perfect. 'You never know around these parts,' she said.

'Too true.' Martell sat down and crossed his legs. Annie noticed that his jeans had creases, which meant they must have been ironed. Which meant he *was* married, after all.

As if to confirm her suspicions, Martell went on, 'I'm sorry my wife Françoise isn't here to greet you, too, but she's gone into Carlisle to do some shopping.'

Françoise, Annie thought. *Shopping*. She tasted the bitter ashes of defeat. Françoise had no doubt borne him two adorable children and still managed to keep her gorgeous figure without exercise or diet. Or maybe she was the replacement model, the trophy wife he took up with after he dumped his first wife, the one who helped him pay his way through dental college? She decided to banish any further speculation from her mind and stick with Nick Fleming. He might be a bit humdrum, but he was handsome enough, they had a good laugh, and he did take her to the pictures and to plays and galleries and nice restaurants in York and Harrogate. They had even been to the First Direct Arena in Leeds once to see Morrissey. Nick would do. For now.

'I don't suppose your wife knows a great deal about your dental practice, or about your partner Martin Edgeworth,' Annie said.

'Ex-partner. And no. Not a lot. Though Françoise did know Martin, of course. We had many good times with him and Connie before they split up.'

'How long were you in partnership?' Gerry asked.

'It must have been about twelve years.'

'And before that?'

'We each had our own private practice. Martin in Eastvale and me in Durham.'

'The partnership worked well?'

'Very well,' said Martell.

'So there was no particular reason for packing it in?' Annie asked.

'No. It was just time. We had both made plenty of money. In addition to some NHS work, we had private patients, too. Martin specialised in cosmetic dentistry, and the NHS doesn't cover a lot of that, of course. And I'm afraid it's also a matter of the old cliché. It really does get rather dull poking and prodding about in people's mouths day after day. Unpleasant, even.' He smiled. Dazzling white. He leaned forwards and passed them their tea from the table and picked up his whisky.

'Don't worry,' he said. 'The other dental cliché doesn't apply. I'm not an alcoholic. I just enjoy a dram or two of whisky before lunch.'

Annie shrugged to indicate that she didn't care whether he liked a tumbler or got pissed to the gills. Maybe he had a cylinder of nitrous oxide in his den, too. 'I understand that you and Martin Edgeworth also remained friends after you gave up the partnership?'

'Yes,' said Martell. 'We didn't see one another every day, of course, like we used to do at work, but we'd get together every now and then for a couple of drinks or a meal, or a trip to Headingley for the cricket. We're both big cricket fans. Were. I mean, he was.'

'This was during the last three years?'

'Yes. After the practice wound down, and after Connie left him, which was a little over two years ago.'

'I should imagine he was devastated by the break-up?'

'Not really. By the time it happened, I think he'd prepared himself for the worst, strengthened his defences. Deep down, he knew he was better off without her.'

'What was wrong with her?'

'Connie? She was manipulative, unfaithful, a spendthrift and a liar.'

'And those are just her good points,' said Annie with a smile.

'I'm sure you get the idea.'

'I do. You didn't like her very much.'

Martell laughed. 'Actually, that's not completely true. Connie was also a lot of fun. A great hostess, wonderful conversationalist, and she had a wicked sense of humour. People are complicated. Sometimes you have to take the good with the bad. But surely Connie doesn't have anything to do with all this?'

'No, not at all. I suppose we're still trying to build up a picture of Martin Edgeworth. He seems rather elusive.'

Martell laughed. 'Elusive? Martin? He was one of the most open and honest people I've ever met.'

'Perhaps it's just my suspicious nature. I always get the impression there's more hidden beneath the surface.'

'Not with Martin. And I've known him for nigh on twenty years. That's why I can't believe any of this.'

'Any of what?'

Martell tasted the whisky and seemed to enjoy it. 'The shootings. That Martin could have had anything to do with them.'

'But he did like his guns?'

'In the same way I like my golf clubs.'

'You could kill someone with a golf club, too.'

Martell laughed. 'True, but that's not what I mean. It was a sport, for each of us. Something we enjoyed and, if I say so myself, were good at. When you spend every day doing what we did, you appreciate something that takes you far away from it. And Martin had a very competitive nature.'

'Shooting never appealed to you?'

'No. I've nothing against it, per se, but I never felt the inclination to get involved.'

'What we're thinking,' Gerry said, leaning forwards, 'is that Mr Edgeworth may have had some sort of accomplice, perhaps even someone who tricked, forced or blackmailed him into doing what he did. This is in complete confidence, of course. We have no evidence. We're just trying to cover every possible angle.'

'Well, that's very open-minded of you, I must say. Naturally, it makes far more sense to me than the idea that Martin simply decided it would be a good idea to go and shoot a few people.'

'If there was someone who forced him or blackmailed him, have you any idea who this person might have been?'

'You think *I* would know?'

'One of the possibilities we have to consider,' Annie said, 'is that it was someone he met while he was practising, or at least someone who had befriended him in the last while and whom he might have mentioned to others. A patient, perhaps, or another dentist, a supplier. We thought that seeing as you spent quite a bit of time with him he might have mentioned someone?'

'Not that I can think of.'

'Do you know whether anyone would have had reason to blackmail him?'

'Martin? You must be joking.'

'Just trying to get things straight, that's all.'

'No. I don't.'

'Nothing odd or unusual happened over the past while, the period leading up to the shootings? No sudden new friends? He wasn't worried or upset about anything. Distracted? Concerned?'

'Not as far as I could tell. Everything seemed normal the last time I saw him.'

'When was that?'

'About a week or so before the . . . incident.'

'You're sure there was no one bothering him, no one new in his life? A woman, perhaps?'

'Martin wasn't especially in the market for a new wife. His experience of the previous one was still a bit raw, and he liked his life the way it was. No, I can't think of anyone. I knew most of his friends and acquaintances, at least in passing.'

'You're sure there was no one else?'

'The only one I can think of is that he mentioned a bloke Gord a few times. That was quite recent. And someone I never met.'

'Gord?' said Annie. 'Who was that?'

'Someone he went rambling with on the weekends some-times. I didn't get the impression that it was regular – I know

Martin used to appreciate his walks alone – but he did mention meeting this bloke up on the moors one morning, and they got chatting. You know what it's like when people share enthusiasms?'

Annie nodded. 'Yes. Yes, I do. Do you know anything more about this Gord? His last name, where he lived, what he looked like?'

'I'm afraid not. It's just someone Martin went rambling with occasionally.'

Annie made a mental note to have Banks ask about this person at Edgeworth's local and around his shooting-club friends. The name had never come up before, though the idea of someone approaching Edgeworth on one of his walks had certainly crossed Annie's mind.

'There was one little thing,' said Martell, 'though I doubt it's of any relevance.'

'You never know,' said Annie. 'Best tell us.'

'It was funny, but Martin once told me he thought he was being followed.'

'When was this?'

'Last November sometime. You know, when the days were getting shorter and the winter gloom was moving in.'

'Did he give you any details?'

'He laughed it off. We both did.'

'Where did he think he was being followed from?'

'From the club to his home.'

Annie leaned forwards and tried to put a sense of urgency in her voice. 'This could be important, Mr Martell. Can you remember anything else, anything at all, about what he said?'

'Just that he said he'd seen the same car on two or three occasions when he left the shooting club. It's a quiet road up there. You don't get much traffic.'

'Did he say anything about the car?'

'I never asked. I do believe he mentioned it was a bit beat up, but that's all I can remember.'

'Was this before he first mentioned this Gord person, or after?'

'Before.'

'Neither you nor Mr Edgeworth ever linked the two?'

'Good lord, no. Why?'

'Why would he even tell you about this if he pooh-poohed it so easily?'

'I think he just wanted to tell me so that he could convince himself he was being silly about it, so I could help him laugh it off. I obliged. I told him it was probably nothing. Just a coincidence. It seemed to help. He said he'd thought it might have been the club keeping an eye on its members, or even the military from the base they used to shoot at. You know, some sort of cockeyed terrorist alert. But nothing came of it.'

'Maybe not,' said Annie. 'Or perhaps *everything* came of it.'

Because it was a Saturday, and because they were hungry, Banks, Jenny, Annie and Gerry met up in the Queen's Arms at lunchtime. There was a lot of information to share and sort, and Cyril, the landlord, opened up the old snug for them and even turned the heat on. It was a tiny room without windows, and perhaps a little chilly and musty at first due to disuse, but it was private, and they wouldn't have to worry about being seen or overheard by the media, who were leaking hints that the 'Red Wedding' investigation, as they called it, was far from over, that the police had discovered new evidence revealing that Martin Edgeworth had possibly not done the shooting, or had not acted alone. There were enough 'ifs' and 'possibles' to cover a stadium of arses, but the message was clear enough: the cops had screwed up, and the real killer was still at large.

Things seemed to be fast approaching conspiracy-theory level.

The radiators rattled and clanked for a while, then settled down to exude a pleasant warmth. Pat, the Australian barmaid, brought in two large platters of nachos, and while Gerry and Jenny abstained, Banks and Annie both went for pints of Black Sheep bitter.

As soon as everyone had eaten a few nachos and washed them down, Banks suggested they try to put some sort of order to the things they had found out so far.

'OK,' he began. 'We don't have a connection between Edgeworth and someone who might be the real killer yet, but we do have four important pointers. First of all, Ollie Metcalfe in the White Rose said Edgeworth was sociable and often talked with non-locals in there, which means he might have had a drink there with the killer at some point. Second, Geoff McLaren, the manager of the shooting club, told me that Edgeworth had asked him about whether it was possible for someone with a criminal record to join the club. That could mean he was asking on behalf of this new acquaintance who wanted to acquire a gun. Third and fourth, Jonathan Martell told Annie and Gerry this morning that Edgeworth confided in him that he felt he was being followed, and that he later mentioned a fellow called Gord who he sometimes went walking the moors with. They managed to laugh off the bit about being followed between them, and neither made a connection with Gord, but why would they? I don't think we can do that too easily ourselves. It's quite possible that if someone *was* after a gun – someone who either didn't want to or couldn't acquire one illegally, and who couldn't get one legally because of health reasons or a criminal conviction – might wish to befriend someone who already owned one. But perhaps it's even more likely that whoever did it wanted someone to use as a scapegoat more than he wanted the gun itself. And if he needed a scapegoat, he needed one with a gun that would be traced back to the scapegoat. There'd be no point in all the subterfuge if Edgeworth's gun didn't match the murder weapon.'

'So someone stakes out a shooting club?' Annie said. 'Good idea.'

'But why pick Edgeworth?' Gerry asked. 'By chance?'

'Why not?' said Annie. 'Maybe Edgeworth was the first one out of the drive the first day the killer was there, or maybe the killer tried a few others first and they weren't what he wanted.'

'Which was?'

'His location, I'd say. Edgeworth lived alone and his house was nicely isolated. And perhaps the guns, too. They were weapons that suited the purpose the killer had in mind.'

'OK. And then? How does he find out all this?'

'He follows Edgeworth a few times, just to make sure there is no Mrs Edgeworth, then perhaps strikes up a conversation with him in the White Rose on a busy night when no one would remember. OK so far?'

'Go on,' said Banks.

'Maybe the killer finds out Edgeworth is a keen rambler. He meets him "by chance" on a walk on the moors once or twice. They become pally. At least pally enough for Edgeworth to invite him in for a coffee when he comes knocking on the morning of the wedding.'

'Do you think it's possible that he had a grudge against Edgeworth rather than against someone from the wedding group?' Gerry asked. 'Or both? Someone from his past?'

'That might be pushing it a bit,' Annie said, 'but I suppose it's not beyond the bounds of reason. He was certainly out to frame Edgeworth, once he'd killed him, but as to whether that was his primary motivation, I don't know. We can dig a bit more into

Edgeworth's past, see if we come up with any possible candidates, but we might have to accept that he was chosen simply because he had what the killer wanted. But going back to the story, as soon as they get pally, our man is all set. He's now got a contact who owns a Black Rifle and a Taurus automatic. I can't say how far ahead he's been planning things, but at least he's thinking clearly in terms of saving his own skin. He has no desire to end up dead at the end of the day, like most mass murderers. Or in prison. So what does he do? He buys two identical sets of outdoor clothes. He visits Edgeworth, or accompanies him back from a walk for a cup of tea or something, manages to wangle a trip to the cellar to play with the guns, hits Edgeworth on the back of the head with a hammer, stuffs the gun in his mouth and shoots him, careful to emulate a suicide and careful to obliterate the traces of the hammer blow.'

'Have we got anywhere with the ballpeen hammer we took from Edgeworth's cellar yet?' Banks asked.

'I've had a word with Jazz,' said Annie. 'She's come in today specially to deal with it, so I'll check with her when we're done here.'

'Excellent,' said Banks. "Someone needs to check Edgeworth's credit and debit cards. Make sure it wasn't him who bought the two sets of clothing.'

'He could have used cash,' said Annie.

'Not much we can do about that, is there? I should imagine if the killer bought the clothing for that purpose, which is most likely, he probably used cash, but there's no reason to think someone like Edgeworth would. He had nothing to hide, and these days it's pretty much second nature for most people to use plastic. At least we should try to rule out the possibility that clothing is a red herring. Anything else?'

'That's about it,' Annie went on. 'He leaves one pile of outdoor clothes beside the body. That's a black anorak and black waterproof trousers, the sort you put on over your other trousers if you go walking in the rain. That makes it appear as if Edgeworth came back from St Mary's and took them off before killing himself. Maybe the real killer's in a hurry, so he neglects or forgets to make sure the clothes have any trace evidence from Edgeworth himself, or enough to convince our forensic team, at any rate. Then he heads out in Edgeworth's RAV4, Black Rifle and all, and does his business. Afterwards, he returns the RAV4 and the AR15, checks that all is as he wants it to be, then goes home.'

'Which is probably why the clothes were placed downstairs, next to the body.'

'What?' said Annie.

'Something I discussed with Dr Glendenning,' said Banks. 'Wouldn't you think that if Edgeworth came home from the shooting, he would take off his outer clothing upstairs, the same as he did with his muddy boots? Let's assume the pistol was in the cellar, so he had to go down there to shoot himself, but wouldn't he still most likely have taken his anorak off, and maybe even the waterproof trousers? But if the real killer simply brought the clothes with him and went down in the cellar with Edgeworth *before* the shooting, and killed him, then it would be perfectly natural to leave the clothes there. He probably wouldn't think about taking them upstairs and putting them in the hall cupboard. A small point, but one that bolsters up our theory a bit, I think. And there's another thing. He knows something about firearms if he realises that Edgeworth's guns suit his purposes, especially the AR15.'

'That's right,' said Annie. 'Maybe a military background?'

'Or police,' Banks added. 'Worth checking, at any rate. It's something we would have done by now if we hadn't thought Edgeworth was the killer. That was an excellent riff on what few facts we have, by the way, Annie,' he said. 'Our only problems are that we don't know who this person is or where he came from and returned to. And nor do we know his motive. Rather big problems, unfortunately.'

'What about the club?' Gerry said. 'Why choose that one in particular to stake out? It might have been because it's the nearest one to where the killer lives. It's not as if such places are abundant around the dale. They're few and far between.'

'It makes sense that he would choose somewhere fairly close to home,' Banks said. 'Though it might have simply been a temporary base. Either way, let's check who's been renting or buying property in that area of the dale since, say, last summer. B and Bs and hotels, too, for good measure. He must have stayed somewhere for a few days, at least. Maybe he's still here. Maybe he hasn't finished yet. Good thinking, Gerry.'

'And we should ask a few questions about this mysterious Gord,' said Annie. 'Maybe Edgeworth mentioned him to someone else. And we can check with other members at the shooting club, see if any of them remembers being followed by a beat-up car.'

'I'll put that in motion,' said Banks.

'What about the Wendy Vincent murder?' said Jenny Fuller. 'Where does that fit in? Or does it?'

Banks swallowed a mouthful of Black Sheep and leaned back in his chair. He'd had enough of the nachos, which were already burning their way through however many feet of intestines he had. 'We don't know that it does,' he said, with a glance at Gerry. 'Not for certain. But I think it's worth doing a bit more digging. You might carry on with that, Gerry, seeing as it was you who came up with the possibility in the first place.'

'Yes, sir,' said Gerry.

'And I suppose I should keep working on the profiles?' Jenny said.

'Perhaps,' said Banks, 'you could attempt a profile of the sort of killer who does the things we've just been talking about.'

'I can tell you one thing right away,' Jenny said, rolling her eyes. 'He's a mass of contradictions. I say "he", but let me correct myself. He could just as easily have been a she.'

'Don't forget the lad from the youth hostel – what's his name?'

'Gareth Bishop, sir,' said Gerry.

'Yes. Gareth Bishop. Let's not forget that he told us he was certain it was a male figure he saw scampering down the hillside to the people-mover.'

'Because he didn't see a pair of tits,' said Jenny. 'I've read his statement. Just for your information, one of my bosses over in Oz was skinny and titless, and she was as much a woman as any woman can be.'

'All right, Jenny,' said Banks. 'Point taken. I know you'll proceed with caution.'

'Indeed I will. Opportunistic and premeditated. Careless and extremely cautious. Devious and—'

'You might start with the fact that he may have a prison record,' said Annie.

'Along with how many other members of the local population? How would that help me?'

'And he may have done some sort of military or police training,' Annie continued, ignoring her.

'It's not as if we're exactly a million miles from Catterick Garrison,' said Jenny. 'Half—'

'Jenny, why don't you go and talk to Maureen Tindall with Annie tomorrow? You might be able to read between the lines.'

Annie gave Banks a look and glared at Jenny. Banks drank some more bitter. Gerry studied her fingernails. Banks couldn't tell whether she was disappointed at not being included, especially as the Wendy Vincent business was her discovery to begin with, but he suspected that she was. Still, it was a matter of teamwork, and Banks thought that Annie and Jenny might benefit from working on something together. Jenny was a skilled psychologist, and she ought to be able to spot what it was that seemed to get Maureen Tindall wound up so tightly.

Pat the barmaid walked into the ensuing silence and asked if anyone wanted anything else. Nobody did. She picked up the empty plates and left. Gerry reached for her coat, and Annie did likewise. Banks still had a little beer left, so he stayed where he was, as did Jenny, who seemed to have something she wanted to say.

'Blood on the hammer, let there be blood on the hammer,' thought Annie as she inserted her police ID card in the slot then walked through the sliding doors that led to the forensic lab next door. When it came right down to it, a bloody hammer was what mattered most right now, not the half-baked theories of some airy-fairy psychological profiler, despite what Banks seemed to think. He clearly still fancied Jenny Fuller; that was obvious enough to all and sundry. Whatever had remained dormant all those years, since before her time, had certainly come back to life. She just hoped he didn't embarrass himself. In Annie's view, Dr Fuller was in all likelihood a high-maintenance prick-teaser with an inflated opinion of herself.

As usual, Annie was impressed by the pristine appearance of the lab and all its inhabitants, buzzing around in their Persil-white coats. She had no idea what the various machines that sat on the benches and desks actually did, but she respected the results they spat out.

The lab was open plan for the most part, though some of its most sensitive equipment was housed in special rooms or chambers, and Annie found Jazz Singh in her cubbyhole staring at a large computer screen full of strange dots and coloured lines, as far as Annie could see.

'Good timing,' Jazz said, keeping her eyes on the screen. 'Just about time for a coffee break. Join me?'

'Of course.' Annie realised that Jazz, short for Jasminder, must have seen her reflection on the screen.

The lab had a decent Nespresso machine, like Banks's office, and Jazz and Annie walked over, made their drinks and went into the common room. A couple of other members of the department sat around reading the newspapers or poring over laptops, and people mumbled their greetings. Jazz and Annie took a corner table with two comfortable orange chairs.

'The ballpeen hammer, right?' Jazz said.

'That's the one. Any luck?'

'Well, I'd hardly call it luck, myself,' Jazz said. 'More like the application of consummate skill of the blood specialist.'

Annie laughed.

'But I don't expect you want a lesson in the science of blood detection, do you?' Jazz went on.

'Only if you think it'll help.'

'Help you appreciate my skills more?'

'Jazz, I couldn't appreciate your skills any more than I do already. You know that. Now give.'

'OK. Naturally, the first problem is to determine whether there's any blood present at all. That hammer had been well washed and wiped. Second, it's then important to discover whether it's human or animal blood. And finally, while you're doing all that, you have to be damn careful you don't contaminate the sample so much that you can no longer determine whose blood it is, should you need to do so.'

'That makes sense,' said Annie.

'It's science,' said Jazz. 'Logic. Reason. Of course it makes sense.'

'Like the Higgs boson and Schrödinger's cat?'

Jazz laughed. 'They make perfectly good sense, too, if you have a bit of patience.'

'So in this case?'

'In this case I used good old Luminol. Favourite of *CSI* and a thousand other cop shows because it lights up nicely when it comes into contact with blood. But you have to be careful not to overuse it on the entire stain, which is rather difficult when you can't see the stain, or the reaction could destroy any sample needed for further analysis. I used very effective masking, and the area I sprayed came up positive.'

'For human blood?'

'For blood. The only problem is that Luminol can also give false results. It can light up on certain plant enzymes, and even metals. But you can usually tell by the colour and kind of luminescence what you're dealing with. Blood doesn't sparkle, for example, and it gives a steadier, longer glow.'

'OK,' said Annie. 'I think I get it. We have blood. What next.'

Jazz took a hit of espresso. 'Mm, that's good. After getting a positive human antigen-antibody test, which isn't always the case with invisible stains, I think I can safely say that we have *human* blood.'

Annie clapped her hands together.

'This was mostly around the region of the ball and the top of the shaft. It's almost impossible to wash every trace of blood from that area where the head and shaft join. There are also minuscule cracks in wood that trap blood, though they render it invisible to the human eye.'

'So we've cracked it? Edgeworth was hit with the hammer?'

'Don't jump to conclusions. The blood on the hammer is consistent with Edgeworth's blood group, but that's all I can tell you right now.' Jazz looked at her watch. 'It'll be a few hours before the PCR DNA results are available, and I'll probably need another hour or more to interpret and compare the results. Say if you call back around five or six I might have something more positive for you.'

'Thanks,' said Annie, standing up to leave. 'I think I can manage to wait that long. And I appreciate your coming in on a weekend.'

'It happens more often than you think,' said Jazz. 'We get behind. I had a batch to run and it's a good time to catch up with my paperwork while I'm waiting. Plays havoc with my social life, though. And talking about that, five will be around my knocking-off time today, so you can buy me a drink in appreciation of all my sacrifices and tell me how wonderful I am.'

'OK,' she said. 'You're on. Five o'clock it is.'

'Thanks for that, Alan,' Jenny said as soon as the others had left the snug. 'She hates me.'

'She doesn't hate you,' said Banks. 'You're the new girl on the team, that's all.'

'Girl?'

'They're all saying it these days. Book titles and all. That woman on the train was far from being a girl.'

'Are you saying I'm too old to be a girl?'

'I . . . I . . .'

Jenny laughed. 'You're too easy to bait, Alan. But as for DI Cabbot being "an old friend of yours", come on, give. Did you two have a thing?'

Banks sighed. 'Once,' he said. 'Briefly. A long time ago. After Sandra and I split up. We decided that work and dating didn't mix.'

'Very wise of you, I'm sure.'

'Seriously, Jenny. Give her a chance. She's a good cop and a good person. She's just a bit insecure, that's all, and she can be abrasive.'

'Insecure? Abrasive? I'd say the ropes have just about pulled away from the moorings.'

'It's not that bad.'

Jenny took a few deep breaths then seemed to relax and smile. 'I don't know how you manage to do it,' she said.

'Do what?'

'See the good in everyone after so long on the job.'

'It's not that,' Banks protested. 'I know my team. Strengths and weaknesses.'

'And do you know me?'

'Not any more, apparently.'

'Oh, don't be such a sensitive bastard. I'm only teasing. Remember that?'

Banks dredged up a weak smile. 'I remember.'

'Besides, I haven't changed that much.'

'Come off it. We both have. We've already discussed that. A lot's happened.'

'I'm not so sure about that. You've become a bit more grumpy, true, but I don't think people change all that much, deep down.'

'We learn nothing from experience?'

'Well, it certainly seems that mankind learns nothing from history, so why should individuals learn anything from their own experience?'

'I'm no expert, but that sounds like spurious logic to me.'

Jenny wrinkled her nose. 'It is,' she said. 'Rhetoric, to make a point. I know we shouldn't, driving and all, but do you fancy another pint? It's quite cosy in here, and I don't much like the idea of hurrying home to an empty house so soon.'

'I'll have another,' said Banks. Jenny went to the bar.

He planned on going back to the office and getting through some more paperwork after lunch. By the time he'd finished with that, he planned on heading out to Filey to see Julie Drake. He had phoned, and she had invited him to dinner. In the meantime, why not enjoy another drink in a nice warm snug with a beautiful and intelligent woman? The music Cyril was playing through his sound system was muted in the snug, but Banks could make out Ray Charles singing 'I Can't Stop Loving You'. It seemed a good omen.

Jenny returned with another pint of Black Sheep for him and a glass of white wine for herself.

'What happened with DI Cabbot,' she said. 'Do you think it's serious? I mean, could it affect the case?'

'Just teething troubles,' said Banks. 'We've all been under a lot of pressure.'

'She doesn't seem to have much time or use for profilers.'

'Forget about Annie,' Banks said, raising his glass. 'Here's to solving the case.'

They clinked glasses.

After a long pause, Banks shifted in his chair and said, 'Don't take this the wrong way, but do you think, maybe after all this is over, you and I could, you know, maybe get together for a drink or dinner or something?'

'What on earth do you mean?' Jenny said. 'Aren't we having a drink now? And as I remember we've had dinner since I've been back.'

'I know that, but . . .'

'And how many ways are there to take it?'

'Jenny, don't make it more . . . awkward . . .'

Jenny gave him a thoughtful stare. 'It's all right,' she said. 'I know what you mean. I shouldn't tease. But do you have any idea why I went away in the first place all those years ago?'

'Your work, I assumed. Or you'd already met a fellow you wanted to follow halfway around the world.'

'Neither of the above. You can be so thick sometimes, you know. Though I won't deny moving did my career no harm. No, it was because of you.'

Banks felt his chest tighten. 'Me?'

'Yes. Maybe you thought I was just a frivolous young slut making a pass at you, but I was in love with you, Alan, and I knew it was hopeless. Christ, I was young and idealistic, and you were married with kids. I knew you were a decent man, that you wouldn't cheat on your wife or leave her and the kids for me. What was the point in me hanging around and feeling like crap every time I saw you, going home crying every night after we'd worked together because you weren't going home with me?'

'Australia was a long way to go just to get away from me.'

Jenny laughed, the lines around her eyes and mouth curving as she did so. 'You're incorrigible. That was just what came up, where I settled. I'd probably have gone to Antarctica if there was a job there. In fact, I did go to Antarctica once with Sam. No, my career was certainly a part of it, but if you'd been free, and interested . . . Who knows? Maybe things would have turned out differently.'

'Maybe they still could. I was interested. I just wasn't free.'

'And now?'

'Both.'

'Are you sure? What about Annie?'

'Old friends.'

'And the poet?'

'A newer friend.'

Jenny stared at him as if trying to make her mind up whether he was telling the truth.

'I'm not being difficult,' she said. 'I just don't know what I want, Alan. I might have left because of you, but I certainly didn't come back for you.'

'Someone else?'

'No, you idiot. I'd just got divorced, I felt alone and I wanted to come home. Simple as that. And let's face it, you haven't exactly been the world's best correspondent over the years. I had no idea what your situation was. Married, single. Even if you were still here. Still alive.'

'And now you know?'

Jenny drank some wine and looked down at the table. 'You can't just pick up where you left off, you know. Maybe our time has passed. Maybe we didn't take the chance when it was there.'

'I wouldn't exactly say we'd be picking up where we left off, would you? We didn't leave off anywhere.'

'You know what I mean. Maybe *you* didn't. Maybe you regretted not taking what you could have had. Maybe I'm the one that got away. How do you know you're not just chasing a memory, making up for what you didn't do the first time around? I suppose what I'm saying is I just don't know any more. I don't want to piss away what's left of my life, Alan. Maybe it doesn't mean so much to you, but I'm well turned fifty, and I know damn well that most men prefer younger women. From what I've heard, you're no different. I don't want a toy boy, but I don't want a fling with someone I care about, either. I still have feelings for you. I think that much is clear. Can't we just leave things as they are? The occasional dinner? Drinks like now? No pressure. I may not want a fling, but I'm also not sure I want commitment yet, either. I'm still stinging from the divorce. I don't even know if I like men any more – and if you make one crack about me turning lesbian, you've lost any chance you might ever have had.'

'You mean I'm in with a chance?'

'That's not what I said.'

'She said, weakening?'

Jenny flicked a little wine at him. 'Besides,' she went on, 'we'll be working together. You said work and dating didn't mix.'

'It wouldn't be the same. You're a consultant. You'd be doing other work, teaching, work for other crime units. We wouldn't be work colleagues. And I'm not your boss.'

Jenny rested her elbows on the table and cupped her chin in her hands. 'God, it *is* good to see you again. To sit and talk like this.'

'So you'll give it a go?'

'I didn't say that. I don't know. Like I said, I still care about you, but I don't want a fling. I've only been here a month or so. I'm still settling in.' She sighed. 'To be perfectly honest, I don't know what I want.'

'Me, neither. At least we're agreed on that. Neither of us can predict where we'll end up, but as the bard said, "Our doubts are traitors / And make us lose the good we oft might win / By fearing to attempt".'

'Oh, you smooth-talking bastard. That your poet's influence?'

'She's not *my* poet, but yes, it is.'

'Aren't you just saying, "nothing ventured, nothing gained" in fancy language?'

Banks laughed. 'I suppose I am. Though I'd argue that the Shakespeare quote does have more of a ring to it.'

Jenny lifted her head from her hands. 'You're right,' she said, leaning forwards slowly. 'Of course you are. But please do me a favour, for now at least. Don't push it. Just leave things as they are.' She held up both her hands, palms out.

Banks didn't know where his next thought came from, and he had the good sense and quick enough wits to stop before he spoke it out aloud, but as he leaned back and reached for his beer glass, it flashed through his mind, as clear as anything: *I don't want to grow old alone.*

II

'This is a dead loss,' Doug Wilson complained as Gerry manoeuvred into yet another narrow parking space later that afternoon. 'The last sales clerk I talked to said it wasn't so unusual for people to buy two or more sets of items they liked. I've even done it myself with shirts and stuff, especially when they're on sale two for one. And like I said before, he might have gone to different branches. I know I would have if I'd been worried about getting caught. They didn't even have to be exactly the same, just like that from a distance.'

'But maybe he *did* buy two outfits in the same branch,' said Gerry, 'because it would have meant another expedition to find the same of everything in another one. Time might have been a factor. You checked Edgeworth's debit and credit cards yourself before we set out and we know *he* didn't buy them, at least with plastic. Don't be so negative. I'm just happy to get out of the office for a while. We've even got a few patches of blue sky. Enjoy it while you can.' She knew Doug wanted to be at the football match, a local derby, and she wouldn't have minded a bit of time off to tidy her flat, as there wasn't much more digging she could do on the Wendy Vincent case until after the weekend, but that was the way the job went. She didn't want to have to put up with Doug sulking all afternoon, at any rate.

'Besides,' she went on, 'the killer had no reason to think we'd end up traipsing around every bloody branch of Walkers'

Wearhouse in Yorkshire asking after someone who bought two pairs of everything. He clearly thought his plan would work and everything would end with Edgeworth's suicide. We'll do Relton and Lyndgarth, then call it a day. OK?'

Doug glanced at his wristwatch. Gerry could see him calculating whether he'd make the second half or not. 'Right,' he said, opening the door and stepping out. 'Let's get on with it, then.'

They turned up nothing in Relton, but things started to get more interesting in Lyndgarth.

The doorbell of the Walkers' Wearhouse branch jingled as they entered, and immediately Gerry was hit by the smells of leather, wet wool, warm rubber and that peculiar chemical odour that seemed to emanate from waterproofed garments. Doug slunk in behind her, having clearly written the place off before they even got out of the car. Gerry spotted a young woman towards the rear of the overstuffed room sorting out a table of lumberjack-style shirts. She glanced up when she heard the bell and moved forwards, smiling as if she were pleased at the interruption of a customer. 'Yes? Can I help you?'

Gerry showed her warrant card. 'I hope so.'

'Police? Is it about the shoplifting we reported?' The woman smoothed her hair, which was smooth enough to begin with, as it was tied back in a tight ponytail. She looked to be in her forties, short, mousy-haired, and pleasantly round. Her complexion was ruddy, but not weather-beaten like many keen ramblers. Gerry guessed this was just a job to her rather than a way to be close to her passion.

'It's not about shoplifting,' Gerry said.

'So you haven't caught them?'

'Shoplifters are notoriously difficult to track down, unless you catch them in the act.'

'Yes, yes, I see that. That's what the local bobby said, too. We've been vigilant – that's Sue and me. She's not in today. But you can't have your eyes everywhere at once, can you?'

'Unfortunately not, or it would make our job a lot easier.'

Doug Wilson grunted in what might have been a minor guffaw or an indication of impatience.

'My name's Paula Fletcher, by the way. What can I do for you, then?'

Doug lingered in the background pretending to examine a pair of thermal socks. 'It may seem an odd question,' Gerry began, 'but we were wondering if you can remember a customer, say, last November or early December. Someone who bought two sets of exactly the same items.' Gerry showed her the photocopied list of articles, colours and sizes.

The woman chewed on her lower lip as she read through before handing it back. 'We have quite a few customers who like to buy a couple of sets of their favourite walking gear,' she said. 'After all, unless you put on a lot of weight you don't grow much after you reach a certain age, do you?'

'I suppose not,' Gerry said, disappointed. She couldn't fail to notice the 'I told you so' smirk of triumph on Doug's face. 'This might not be a regular customer,' Gerry went on. 'In fact, he's far more likely to have been a one-off, a stranger.'

Paula's face scrunched up in a frown of concentration. 'That's when we had our last two-for-one sale. When exactly would this have been, did you say?'

'Towards the end of last year. November or early December, most likely.' She realised it could have been long before then, but there was no sense in giving anyone such broad parameters, or they wouldn't even bother trying to remember.

'Can I have a peek at that list again, please?'

'Of course.' Gerry handed it to her. As she waited while Paula went laboriously through the items, she first heard the patters, and then saw the rain trickling down the plate-glass window. It had started again; the blue sky had only been a tease. Please let this be the last stop of the day, she begged silently. Now all she wanted was a long hot bath and a few chapters of the new Rose Tremain novel. She'd tidy up her flat later. After all, it wasn't as if she was expecting company, or had a hot date this Saturday night. Or any night for that matter. Work took care of that. She didn't know how DI Cabbot and Detective Superintendent Banks managed relationships, if they did. Banks certainly must have had, because he had a family, and Gerry had heard rumours that he'd had one or two youngish girlfriends of late. She had always got the impression that he would fall for someone more his own age, like the poet Linda Palmer, but what did she know about romance?

When she let herself think about it, which wasn't often, she realised that she wouldn't mind at all going out with someone like Banks, if he wasn't her boss, that is, that age wouldn't really be an issue. He seemed healthy and young enough in body and spirit, was handsome in that lean and intense sort of way, and she certainly got the impression that he was interested in a wide range of subjects, so conversation wouldn't be a problem. He also had a sense of humour, which she had been told by her mother was essential to a happy marriage. Not that she was having fantasies about marrying Banks, or even going out with him. Just that the whole idea didn't seem so outlandish. She knew that he and DI Cabbot had had a thing because DI Cabbot had told her once after a few drinks, and warned her that it was a bad idea to have relationships with people you worked closely with, especially your boss. Gerry thought she already knew that, but she thanked Annie for the advice.

Paula tapped the list with her forefinger. 'You know, there is something here that rings a bell.'

'Any idea what?' Gerry asked.

'It's just . . . well, it wasn't quite the way you said it was.'

'What do you mean?'

'Someone buying two sets of the same clothes.'

Gerry frowned. 'It wasn't? Then what was it?'

'It was this fellow who *wanted* to buy two sets – you know the black anorak, black waterproof trousers, the black woollen cap.'

'When was this?'

'Around the time you said. Well, it must have been during the last two weeks of November because that's when we had our last big two-for-one sale. It helps at that time of year to get people in, a sale, you know, something special like that. Usually business is a bit slow in November.'

'Yes, I understand,' said Gerry, rushing on. 'But what about this particular man? What stood out about him?'

'Stood out? Oh, nothing. He was ordinary enough, I suppose, except for his eyes. They were deep set, like, and a bit scary, if you know what I mean. Like they'd seen things you wouldn't want to see.' She gave a slight shudder.

'Go on,' Gerry encouraged her.

'Well, he came up to me with an armful of clothes, which turned out to be two sets of the same, except for one jacket. We'd had a run on the black anoraks and were completely out of them. I remember he asked me if we had any more in the storeroom and I told him I was sorry but that was it. I even went and had a look. I said we did have orange or yellow if he'd like, but he just shook his head impatiently, like, then I said if he'd care to leave his name and address and a contact number, we could perhaps order some in from the warehouse, or get some from another branch, and let him know, though it might take a day or two. I assured him he'd still get the same deal, even if took a few days.'

'How did he react to that?'

'Well, that's it. That's why I remember. He just grunted, put the items down on the nearest table and left. A bit rude, I thought, but it takes all sorts. He could at least have thanked me for trying. I understand he was disappointed, but it would only have been a matter of a day or two.'

No, thought Gerry, her excitement rising. It would have been a matter of him having to leave a name, address and telephone number. He needed to buy the two-for-one items at the same time in the same place. 'He didn't buy anything, then?' she asked.

'Not a thing.'

Gerry cursed under her breath. No chance of a credit-card transaction, then. And why hadn't he bought the one set? Her guess was that he wanted to make sure both outfits were the same, and until he could do that, he wasn't going to lay out cash on one of them. Either that or he was flustered and frustrated at not being able to succeed easily. 'Can you give us any idea of what this man looked like?'

Paula took a deep breath. 'It was a long time ago. I mean, I told you about the eyes, didn't I?'

'Yes. What colour were they?'

'I don't remember. I'm not even sure I noticed. But piercing, like. Maybe blue.'

'Did he have a beard or moustache?'

'His face hadn't seen a razor in a week or two, but you get a lot like that these, days, don't you? I don't know why—'

'Was he tall or short, fat or thin?'

'Medium.' She pointed at Doug, who was five foot ten. 'About his height, give or take a couple of centimetres. And about the same shape. You know, slimmish. And he had bad skin, sort of rough and pock-marked, like he'd had acne or chicken pox when he was a boy.' She blushed and looked at Doug Wilson. 'Not that he resembled you in that, of course.'

Wilson nodded in acknowledgement. Gerry smiled to herself. The woman fancied Doug; she was sure of it.

'Anything else, Paula? You're doing very well. Your powers of recollection are really good.'

Paula wiggled with embarrassment. 'Thank you.'

'Any scars, moles, distinguishing features?'

'He did have a tattoo. I could see the top of it where his shirt button was open. The hair, too.'

'Hair?'

'Chest hair. It came up almost to his throat.'

'What kind of tattoo?'

'I don't know. You see so many these days, don't you? If you knew how many young lasses around here have tattoos all down their arms or legs and God only knows where else. I mean, what will they do when they grow up and want a job?'

Gerry smiled to herself, imagining what AC Gervaise would think if she saw *her* tattoo. 'You didn't see what the tattoo depicted, what it was of?'

'Not all of it.'

'What, then?'

'I only saw the top bit. Some red, blue whorls, like the tops of wings or something. Maybe a bird. Or a butterfly. I don't know. All I can say is I had the sense it was part of a bigger one that went down his chest.'

'OK, thanks, Paula,' said Gerry. 'That really is helpful. Would you be willing to spare the time to work with a police artist on trying to put together a sketch of this man?'

'Ooh, I don't know. I mean, I've got the shop to look after.'

'It wouldn't take long,' Gerry said. 'It would be a real help. And we can bring the artist here, to you. Or we can do it on the computer if you want.'

'But what if I get it wrong? What if I can't remember things?'

Gerry put her hand gently on Pat's shoulder. 'You mustn't worry about that. You've done fine so far. Besides, people usually remember much more than they think they do when they start to see the beginnings of an image. The shape of the head, hairline, that sort of thing. It's all important.'

'He had short curly hair,' Paula said. 'Turning grey. Just like on his chest. I remember that.'

'See,' said Gerry, 'you're remembering already.'

Paula blushed. 'Well, I suppose I can try, if you think it's important. What did he do, this bloke?'

'I'm sorry, but I can't tell you that. We don't even know if he's done anything, yet. But it might be very important to us, so thank you. There's just a couple more things. Have you ever seen this man before or since? Do you have any idea who he is, where he lives at all?'

'None at all. Never seen him before in my life.'

'Did you see what kind of car he was driving?'

Paula laughed. 'Even if I had, I wouldn't be any use to you there, love. Can't tell a Rolls-Royce from a Mini.'

'Do you remember what he was wearing?'

'That I do,' said Paula, clearly pleased with herself. 'If there's one thing I know, it's clothes. That's my business, after all.'

'What was it?'

'A cheap grey windcheater.'

'Any emblems on it?'

'Emblems? You mean like badges and stuff.'

'Yes. Decals, symbols, things like that.'

'I don't remember any, no.'

'You mentioned a shirt.'

'Yes. He kept his jacket zipped up most of the way, so I just saw the button-down collar like, when I noticed the tattoo. Pale blue. And jeans. I think he was wearing just ordinary blue jeans.'

'Thank you, Paula,' said Gerry. 'See you remember far more already than you thought you could. We'd better go now, but we'll be back with an artist as soon as possible.'

'That's all right, love,' said Paula. 'I'll be here.'

As they hurried back to the car, Gerry wondered where the hell they were going to scrape up a police artist at such short notice. Doug was still sulking as the second half of his game ticked by, so she didn't imagine she'd get much help out of him. Then she had an idea, took out her mobile and called Annie.

It was only a couple of hours drive to Filey, if that, Banks thought as he skirted the southern edge of the North York Moors, and drove through Malton. In the early darkness, the town centre was almost deserted and the roads had been quiet all the way so far. In season, he would probably be stuck in a traffic jam by now. Almost as quickly as they had appeared, the stars had been obscured by clouds, but the rain was still holding off.

He listened to Maria Muldaur's *Heart of Mine* as he drove, probably his all-time favourite album of Dylan covers, mulling over the thought that had leapt unbidden into his mind in the snug with Jenny. He was glad he hadn't spoken the words out loud. She would probably have taken them as a kind of begging pitch, and the last thing he wanted was for her to feel sorry for him. Like her, he didn't know what he wanted out of a relationship these days. 'I'll Be Your Baby Tonight', which Maria Muldaur was singing at the time, seemed enough for now.

Naturally, he had thought before about growing old alone, as one does in the wee small hours with only the darkness and a tumbler of whisky for company. Some men, he knew, were so desperate for someone to care for them as they aged, that they deliberately sought out young and healthy women. 'A Man Needs a Maid', as Neil Young once put it. But that wasn't what Banks wanted. However he ended up, it would be for love, not for comfort and convenience. Over the past few years, since he had moved to the more remote Newhope Cottage from what had been the family home in Eastvale, he had been content to shore up his loneliness with music, books and wine, an evening out now and then at the pub, especially on folk night, and the occasional concert at the Sage or Opera North performance in Leeds. He took his holidays alone, too, usually long weekends in interesting cities he loved to explore on foot – Berlin, Stockholm, Krakow, Barcelona, Paris. And he had girlfriends from time to time, though they never seemed to last. He was so used to his settled way of life that the stray thought had taken him unawares and unnerved him. He didn't know where it was likely to take him, or even whether he wanted to go there. Maria Muldaur finished and he put on Luna Velvet for the last mile or two.

As Banks entered Filey, he concentrated more on the roads and found the hill that sloped down to the seafront. He had suggested that he and Julie meet in a pub or restaurant, but Julie had insisted that he dine with her at the B&B. It was off season, she had said, and there were no paying guests. Besides, it would be more private. Her chef husband loved nothing more than a chance to show off his skills, she told him. Banks agreed. Why argue against a meal cooked by a fine chef?

There seemed to be quite a squall out on the water, with the wind whipping things up and the waves slapping hard against the sea wall, cascading spray on to the road. Julie had given him clear directions when he phoned to inform her he was coming, and she told him he could park on the front by the row of houses. When Banks saw the sandbags, though, he decided to find a more sheltered spot and parked back up the hill, around the corner, where the houses themselves provided a barrier. The wind tugged at his coat as he walked along the promenade towards the B&B, one of a terrace of similar guest houses, and he could taste the salt on his lips, feel its sting in his eyes.

He walked up the path and rang the doorbell. He would have recognised the woman who had answered his ring even if he hadn't known who she was. She still looked young for her years, and though she had filled out quite a bit, the plumper version was similar to the one he remembered, except it had rather more substance, more chins, the eyes more deeply buried in puffy cheeks. Her husband's cooking, perhaps.

She stared at him, a distant smile on her face. 'Alan Banks, as I live and breathe. Come in, dearie. Do come in. Marcel is busy preparing dinner for us. He'll be out later to say hello, but he has to go out to a business meeting tonight. We've got the place all to ourselves.'

Banks followed her inside and took off his coat in the hallway.

'We'll eat in the guests' dining room,' Julie said. 'There's a nice window table with a view of the sea, or as much as you can see of it in this weather.'

'If you like,' said Banks.

'I'm sure you'll enjoy the view. It's a bit wild tonight, isn't it?'

'Just a bit.'

'It's just through here.'

Banks followed her into the front room, where a table in the bay window was already laid for two with white linen cloth, serviettes in silver rings, gleaming cutlery and two candles flickering in cut glass holders. The rest of the room, filled with bare tables, was in semi-darkness and shadow except for a small dimly lit bar at the end where they entered. Julie asked him if he wanted an aperitif. Banks knew he would have to be careful, but one aperitif and one glass of wine with dinner wouldn't put him over the limit. He asked if she had Pernod. She did. He watched the clear liquid cloud up as she added a little water and ice. She poured a sherry for herself then led the way to the table, giving Banks the place with the best view of the raging sea.

When they sat down, she raised her glass and proposed a toast. 'To absent friends.'

'To absent friends,' Banks repeated.

It felt strange sitting opposite Julie in the candlelight, surrounded by the dark, deserted dining room, waves crashing against the sea wall and splashing over the road. Christmas lights still strung along the prom between the lamp posts danced and flickered in the wind, and the streetlights themselves reflected and rippled in the undulating water just off the shore. The whitecaps stretched a long way out to sea. Banks felt apprehension. What was he doing here? It all seemed so *arranged*. Did she have something special in mind? The place to themselves, the candlelight, the view of the sea. He dismissed the thoughts. Her husband was cooking for them.

'Don't worry,' Julie said, clearly noticing an expression of concern on his face and misinterpreting it. 'The waves rarely come as far as the garden gate. Even on a night like this. We've only been flooded once since we moved here over ten years ago. The sandbags are there mostly to reassure people. The squalls come and go. You wait and see, it'll be all over by the time we've finished dinner. The starters should be here soon.'

As if on cue, a man carrying a tray walked into the room. He wasn't dressed as a chef, but was wearing dark trousers and an open-neck checked shirt. Julie introduced him. He put down the tray, and Banks stood up to shake hands. Unlike his wife, Marcel was tall and rangy. 'Just a little appetiser,' he said, gesturing to the plate. 'Foie gras, figs and crusty bread.' Then he excused himself and returned to the kitchen.

'Do tuck in, Alan,' said Julie, taking a couple of figs. 'I'm afraid I can't touch the foie gras myself, not with the state my heart's in these days.'

'Serious?'

'No. Well, yes, I suppose. I mean, anything to do with the heart is serious, isn't it? I'd been getting a bit short of breath, so I had some tests done. The upshot was that the doctor gave me some pills, told me to lose a few pounds and to cut back on the fatty stuff.'

'I've been told the same,' said Banks, spreading a little foie gras on a slice of crusty bread.

Julie laughed. The skin around her eyes wrinkled. 'But you're skinny as a rake,' she said. 'You must be one of those enviable people who can eat what they want and not add an inch to their waistline.'

'I suppose I've been lucky that way, yes,' said Banks. 'I didn't mean the weight, though. Just the fatty stuff.'

'Ah.'

A wave hit hard against the sea wall, and Banks could swear a few drops of water splashed on the bay window. Julie didn't seem concerned.

Marcel delivered their main courses next: roast cod with a light watercress sauce and roasted cherry tomatoes, buttered new potatoes and haricots verts. 'Try the white Rioja with it,' he said. 'I think you'll enjoy it . . .' He turned to Julie. 'I have to go now, love. There's a nice cheese plate on the kitchen table for later, along with a drop of Sauternes, and there's fruit and ice cream if you want sweet stuff.' He bent forwards to kiss her lightly on the cheek. 'I won't be late. Nice to meet you, Mr Banks.' Then he was gone. Banks felt as if he were being deliberately left alone with Julie to put forward some sort of business or romantic proposal. Again he felt a twinge of apprehension.

'Don't be so nervous,' Julie said.

'I must admit I hadn't expected such a feast when I invited myself,' Banks said, picking up his knife and fork.

'Oh, he loves it,' said Julie. 'Any excuse to spend time on his creations, and make a mess in the kitchen. Honestly, sometimes I think he does it just to get away from me.'

'I doubt it,' said Banks.

'Well, maybe not. He's one of the good ones, Marcel is. A keeper.'

'This is excellent,' said Banks. 'Nice wine, too. Be sure to pass on my compliments to the chef.'

'You can do it yourself. He won't be late back.'

'Now what was it you wanted to tell me?'

'Did I say I wanted to tell you something?'

'You certainly hinted at it.'

'Yes. Yes, well, I suppose I did.' Julie paused. 'I believe I mentioned in my letter how I spent a lot of time with Emily towards the end.'

'Yes. It must have been a terrible ordeal.'

'Not half as bad as it was for her, despite the morphine. A lot of the time we just sat in silence. I held her hand. She stayed at home as long as she could, but the last few days . . .' Julie shook her head at the memory. 'She had to go into hospital. She was skin and bone at the end. The skull beneath the skin.'

Again, Banks remembered the young and beautiful girl he had loved all those years ago: her spontaneity, her rebellious spirit, her fearlessness. They'd go on marathon night walks – St John's Wood, Notting Hill, Holland Park, Hampstead, Camden – pass by desperate late-night partygoers trying to hail a taxi already taken, or hear strange stirrings in the dark bushes of the Heath, see a homeless person bedded down in a shop doorway, walk around an aggressive drunk. Once they got chased by two drunk yobs and ended up panting, breathless and laughing. Streets so busy in day were dark and empty at night. They would go home to lie down and make love as the dawn chorus swelled, then drift to sleep, maybe missing their first lectures of the day and not caring.

'But we also talked a lot,' Julie went on. 'About life, death, old times. She loved you very much, you know.'

'I loved her, too,' said Banks. 'I never could understand why things didn't work out.'

'You wanted different things, that's all. You were both too young. Emily was a free spirit. She wanted to travel, live life to the full.'

'So did I.'

'Maybe. But you were also set on a career, even then. You didn't like business studies, I remember that, but you had mentioned the police once or twice.'

'I did? Is that why . . .?'

'No, that's not what I'm saying. If it wasn't the police it would have been something else. It's just that in Emily's eyes you wanted to settle down. You know, the semi-detached, steady job, healthy pension, mortgage, two point five children, little dog, but Emily, well, Emily—'

'Didn't really know what she wanted.'

Julie laughed. 'Yes, I suppose it's fair to say that. She only knew what she didn't want.'

'Why didn't she tell me? Maybe if she had I could have . . . you know . . . changed.'

'No, you couldn't. People don't. Not deep down.'

Banks remembered hearing almost the same words from Jenny Fuller only hours ago.

'Besides,' Julie went on. 'Things hadn't reached crisis point. You were still in your honeymoon period, willing to overlook a lot. Neither of you were thinking very much about the future. You were living in the present.'

That was true, Banks remembered. And it was exciting, just going where your fancy led you. It might well have been the last time he had lived for the moment, he thought sadly. Not long after the break-up had come career, promotion boards, marriage to Sandra, children, financial struggles, then the mortgage, the pension, the semi-detached, the move up north. Everything except the little dog, and that was only because Sandra was allergic to dogs.

'Do you remember the last time you saw her?' Julie asked.

'As if it were yesterday,' said Banks. He could remember the texture of the tree he leaned against, the red-and-white striped ball two young boys were kicking on the grass, a blackbird's song, a dark stain on the page of the book he was reading, the heat of the sun on his face, the shouts of rowers from behind him on the Serpentine . . . 'Why?'

Banks noticed the faintest of smiles pass across Julie's features. 'She said she thought you would,' she said. 'She remembered, too. It was a hot day in Hyde Park, wasn't it? You couldn't understand why she was finishing with you.'

'That's because she wouldn't tell me why.'

'Did you really not guess?'

'No.'

'Do you want to know?'

Banks speared a thick flake of cod. 'After all this time? I don't know that it matters. Why? Did she tell you?'

'Oh, yes. I've known all along. She was pregnant, Alan. That's why she split up with you and she couldn't tell you why. Emily was pregnant.'

★   ★   ★

'You won't catch me working with any of those computer facial recognition programmes,' said Ray Cabbot as Annie and Gerry sat with him on the wicker chairs in Banks's conservatory. Banks was nowhere to be seen. Annie had already tried to get him twice on his mobile, but the first time he didn't pick up, and the second time it was switched off. She wondered what was going on with him, what mysterious mission he was on, but she wasn't especially worried. He was a big boy; he could take care of himself. Maybe he was on a hot date with that profiler, she thought, and didn't want to be disturbed.

Annie wasn't too thrilled at first about being dragged away from her date with Nick, but that was the way the job went sometimes, and if anyone could understand, Nick could. She and Gerry were admiring the sketch Ray had done of the man Paula Fletcher had described.

'You're a natural,' said Annie. 'It's brilliant.'

'You don't know that, not until you find him,' Ray said. 'It might be total crap.'

'Paula Fletcher said it was accurate,' Gerry said.

'Memories fade.' Ray got up and headed for the door to the entertainment room. 'I'm off to find something to drink.'

Annie rolled her eyes. It had been a successful evening so far. After Gerry had rung, Annie had met her at Banks's cottage, and they had persuaded a reluctant Ray to go with them to Lyndgarth and try his hand at a police sketch. After a few false starts, Ray and Paula had seemed to develop a rapport, and the end result was amazingly lifelike, Annie thought. Though Ray was right, of course; they wouldn't know for certain until they found the man.

First came the music, a little too loud for Annie's liking, then Ray came back brandishing a bottle of Macallan and three glasses. He seemed disappointed when both Annie and Gerry declined and poured himself a large one.

'Driving,' Annie said.

'Me, too,' said Gerry.

'You can both stop over if you want,' Ray said. 'He's got plenty of room.' He glanced at Gerry. 'We can have our own party. Maybe I can do a couple of preliminary sketches?'

'In your dreams,' said Annie. 'Grow up. And you'd better be careful, knocking back Alan's expensive single malt like that.'

Ray held up the bottle. 'I bought this one, myself,' he said. 'Sure you won't join me, love? I don't like drinking alone.'

'You could have fooled me.'

'*Ummagumma.*'

'What's that?'

'The album. Pink Floyd. *Ummagumma.* The live disc. "Astronomy Domine" is the song. Classic. He's got a fine music library, your boss.'

'Can you turn it down a bit?' Annie asked.

Ray muttered to himself but fiddled with the remote, and the volume dropped a couple of decibels. 'Philistines,' Annie heard him grumble.

Ray was in his element with Gerry for an audience, the old goat, she thought, smiling to herself, all old-school charm and romantic roguishness. Mad, bad and dangerous to know. If she heard about the mesmerising texture of Gerry's red hair and the smooth creaminess of her complexion one more time she thought she might accidentally knock his drink into his lap.

Gerry tapped the sketch. 'We don't even know if he's the one we want yet, remember,' she said. 'So perhaps we'd best not get our hopes up.'

'Fair enough,' said Annie. 'But that doesn't mean we shouldn't get this circulated pronto and see what happens. We could add that he may be called Gord, or Gordon, too. Maybe that'll help.'

'But we don't know for sure it's the same person Jonathan Martell mentioned.'

'We don't know anything for certain. It's probably not even his real name, if he is the killer. But sometimes you just have to take a shot.'

'Doesn't the artist have any rights here?' Ray cut in. 'I assume I've got some sort of copyright on this, or do you lot take that, too?'

Gerry ignored him and went on. She's learning, Annie thought. 'We'd be playing our hand, though, if we got it in the media. Tipping him the wink. He might scarper, if he's still around.'

'I don't think so,' said Annie. 'If he's still around, he's around for a reason . . .'

'But why?'

'To watch us look like fools,' said Annie. 'Or because he hasn't finished.'

'Finished what?'

'I don't know.'

'Even so, we should get the sketch out there. We still need to know who he is.'

'We could just say we're anxious to speak with him in connection with a recent occurrence,' Annie suggested. 'Something vague like that. Covers a multitude of possibilities.'

'But he could still go to ground if he sees his likeness in the papers or on telly.'

'It's a risk we've got to take. But I don't think he's going anywhere. I reckon he thinks he's safe. Besides, how else are we going to find him? Do you have any better suggestions?'

'Not really,' Gerry admitted. 'I suppose we could always do it more discreetly. Door to door.'

Annie rolled her eyes. 'Just think how long that would take. And think of the manpower. The AC would never authorise the budget.'

'Even though we're pretty certain what happened?'

'Even so. And just how certain are we?'

'Well, thanks to Jazz we now know that the blood on the hammer is Edgeworth's,' said Gerry. 'And that probably proves that Edgeworth didn't shoot up the wedding party, hit himself on the head with the hammer and then shoot himself.'

'It's possible the blood might have got there earlier,' Annie said. 'A cut or something. I don't want to muddy the waters, but after all, it *was* Edgeworth's hammer and Edgeworth's blood. He could have hit his thumb banging in a nail or something.'

'I know we always have to bear in mind the possibility that we might be wrong,' Gerry said, 'but in this case I think the odds are pretty good that we've got it right. Remember, there's what Dr Glendenning said about the blow to the head to factor in, too, and according to Paula Fletcher the man in the sketch was after buying two sets of the same clothes – the same brand and colour that we found in Edgeworth's cellar.'

'There's another thing we haven't followed up on yet,' said Annie.

'What?'

'He couldn't buy the two outfits he wanted at Paula's branch of the shop, so he didn't buy anything. Where *did* he get the clothes? He had to have got them from somewhere. Another branch, perhaps?'

'Right,' said Gerry. 'They were on sale that week. It's worth checking, and we do have the sketch to show around now. Maybe someone will recognise him, and we'll find a credit-card receipt after all. Does this mean Doug and I have to carry on with our shop crawl?'

'So this is how you two like to spend your Saturday nights, is it?' said Ray, who, Annie noticed, had been glancing from one to the other as they talked the way people watch a tennis ball going back and forth.

'I thought you'd been quiet for too long,' Annie said. 'What is it you want to do? Go dancing, go clubbing or something?'

Ray topped up his glass. 'Well, as I'm in the company of two lovely young women, my muse and my wonderful daughter, I do think we could come up with something a bit better than sitting around talking about bloodstained hammers and murder.'

Annie jerked her head towards the entertainment room. 'Why don't you go in there and listen to the music on Alan's headphones, loud as you want, then we wouldn't have to put up with it blaring in our ears while we're trying to work.'

Ray studied his drink and narrowed his eyes. 'You can be cruel sometimes, you know. I don't know where you got it from. "How sharper than a serpent's tooth . . ." Your mother didn't have a cruel bone in her body.'

Annie sighed. '*Dad*. Just let us finish. Please? We'll join you in a while. OK? Then we'll have a party, a dance or two. Gerry might even let you sketch her. She'll be keeping her clothes on, though.'

Gerry gave Annie a look of horror. Ray seemed to brighten at the possibility of fun later, picked up his bottle and glass and headed for the entertainment room singing along with Pink Floyd as he went. The music in the conservatory stopped. He'd found the headphones.

'I quite liked it,' Gerry said.

'What?'

'Pink Floyd. They're good. The boss said he was going to play me *Ummagumma* in the car some time, but Ray beat him to it. But why did you tell him he could sketch me? I'd be so embarrassed.'

'Don't worry, he'll have forgotten in half an hour, and I'll get you out of here without the slightest stain on your honour. You have to know how to deal with Ray. Now you know what it was like for me growing up.'

'How did you manage it?'

'He's my dad. I love him.'

'I know. I'm sorry. I just don't understand your relationship at all,' she said. 'I mean, my parents are . . . well, just normal.'

Annie laughed. 'Well, you certainly couldn't say that about Ray.' Growing up in the artists' colony, her mother dying young, she and Ray had never perfected a normal father–daughter relationship, whatever that was, and in some ways Annie regarded Ray as the child while she played the indulgent parent. But that was too complicated to explain to Gerry. Just then the music came on again, a loud scream followed by thumping drums and screeching guitar feedback.

'Oops,' said Gerry. 'Perhaps I spoke too soon about liking the music.'

Annie glanced at her watch. 'The headphones have come off. He's getting impatient. Honestly, he's got the attention span of a two-year-old, except when he's working. Then you can't budge him for love nor money. Let's get out of here. Leave him to it. He probably won't even notice. Come back to mine. I've got a couple of bottles, and we can have a nice quiet natter. You can crash there if you like. You won't have to drive home.' It was a step, she thought, the hand of friendship outstretched, beyond the job.

Gerry seemed to consider the option, then she stood up and said, 'Why not? Let's do it.' And they tiptoed through the kitchen to the front door, got their coats and drove off.

Banks felt as if someone had pulled the floor from under him. He was spinning, in free-fall, the sea outside was deafening, the waves threatening to engulf him. For a while he couldn't speak, couldn't breathe, couldn't get back his hold on reality. Then he heard Julie's voice cutting through the roaring. 'Alan? Alan? Are you all right, Alan? I'm sorry I didn't mean to give you such a shock. I was so certain you must have suspected.'

'I can be very thick sometimes,' Banks mumbled. 'Or so I've been told.' The world began to settle back into its proper order. Even the sea sounded calmer. The candle flames reflected in the bay window like two bright eyes. Banks took a gulp of wine. Julie refilled his glass.

'But why didn't she tell me?' he asked when he found his voice.

'Think about it. You'd have done the decent thing. You were halfway there already. You'd have persuaded her to have the baby and get married. I think you may underestimate how persuasive you could be. And how malleable Emily was. She seemed strong, determined, but she was so uncertain about what she wanted to do with her life that she'd have taken direction from someone as solid and resolute as you. Someone as *dependable*. And she knew that. That's why she didn't tell you. She didn't want to give you the chance to persuade her to change her mind.'

'About what?'

'About the termination, of course.'

Somehow, Banks had known that was coming, but it still felt like yet another blow he hadn't had a chance to protect himself from. He didn't reel quite as much as he had from the first piece of news, but he felt a tightness in his chest and a burning sensation behind his eyes. He gulped some more wine, was vaguely aware of Julie opening another bottle, red this time. He had almost finished his main course and didn't feel like eating any more so he pushed his plate aside.

'She knew you'd do your best to talk her out of it,' Julie went on. 'It was an awful period for her. Not physically, there were no medical problems, but . . . the depression afterwards, the self-loathing. I was there with her through all that. Later.'

'She didn't have to go through with it.'

'Well, she was right, wasn't she? You *would* have tried to talk her out of it.'

Banks considered the comment. 'Yes,' he said. 'I probably would have tried to dissuade her from having an abortion. But if she was so determined . . . I mean, I wasn't anti-abortion, pro-life or anything. It would have been *her* choice.'

'Emily wasn't anywhere near as strong as you thought she was. Believe me, it took almost all she had to do what she did. But she knew where it would lead if she had a baby, knew the life it would pull her towards, and that wasn't the life she wanted.'

'But she had children later.'

'Yes, when *she* was ready. Face it, Alan, neither of you were ready back then, in 1973.'

'We could have made it work.'

'Perhaps. And perhaps Emily would have believed you. But think about it. Think about it now, after the passage of all that time, the children you do have, the life you've lived, the things you've achieved. Would you have wished it to be any different?'

'Well,' said Banks after a brief pause. 'There are some days I could definitely have done without.'

Julie smiled. 'I don't mean that sort of thing. There's events we all wish had never happened to us, things we regret. A drop of red? It's Rioja, too.'

'Please.' Banks held out his glass.

'Do you want a clean—'

'It doesn't matter.'

Julie poured. Banks sat with his chin in his hands trying to get a grasp on his feelings. He couldn't. For some reason he heard a few snatches of 'Gliders and Parks' in his head. It seemed to offer some oblique comment on his last meeting with Emily in Hyde Park. He tried to imagine having a baby with her, a life together wholly different from the life he had lived. He couldn't. And the other alternative would be having a child out there he hadn't known about all these years. He wondered how that would feel?

'Is this why you invited me for the condemned man's last meal?' he said finally. 'To give me this news?'

'Oh, don't be so melodramatic. Or sarcastic. You're not being condemned to anything except the truth. And you always did have a sarky tongue on you, Alan Banks. I told you, Marcel loves to cook for people, and I thought you might enjoy it, having driven all this way. Is it just your job, or have you never been able to see any charitable motives in anyone?'

'Such as Emily?'

'It's true that she did what she did to spare herself a lot of grief, but even though you might not realise it yet, she was sparing you, too.'

Banks said nothing, returned to his wine.

'What are you thinking?' Julie asked.

'Nothing much. I'm a bit too stunned to think, if truth be told.'

'It was all for the best, Alan.'

'Maybe it was. We were very young. I . . . I just wish . . . Oh, never mind.'

'I know you wish it could have been different. But it couldn't be. It was what it was. Don't hold it against Emily. Don't let it taint your memory of her. Don't hate her.'

'I could never hate her. I just wish I'd known, that's all. I wish she'd told me. Even if she had wanted to go through with

the abortion, I could have been with her. At her side. I could
have comforted her. She wouldn't have been alone.'

'She needed to be alone. And I've told you why she couldn't
tell you.'

'I know. And you're probably right. But that doesn't help.'

'Let me bring the cheese plate.'

Julie got up and left the room. The candles flickered and
the sea continued to rumble and smash against the wall, like
Banks's thoughts, sucking back the water like an indrawn
breath. He drank some Rioja. And some more. Julie reappeared with the cheeses. Runny Camembert, old Cheddar,
blue-veined Stilton. Banks didn't have much of an appetite
left, but he cut himself a chunk or two, took some water
crackers and grapes. He was feeling a bit dizzy and realised
that he had had far too much to drink. Driving home was out
of the question. Too late to worry about that now. He'd find a
hotel in town.

As if reading his thoughts, Julie said, 'You can't drive all the
way back to Eastvale like this. The front guest room's made
up, just in case we had any last-minute customers. It's yours
for the night if you want it.'

'Thank you,' said Banks. 'I'll take you up on that.'

'The squall,' Julie said, pointing. 'Look. It's receding.'

Banks followed her gaze and, sure enough, the sea had
stopped battering the wall, and there were even one or two
gaps in the clouds towards the horizon, like tears in fabric,
where the stars and a hint of moonlight shone through. Banks
thought he could see the lights of a fishing boat far out at sea,
but he realised it must be a buoy of some sort; it would be
madness for anyone to go out fishing in this weather.

'Someone mentioned at the funeral that Emily worked for
Médecins Sans Frontières,' he said. 'How did that come
about?'

'It was just something she wanted to do. She travelled through most of her twenties and early thirties, did temp office work to make money, then she married Luke and raised two children. She and Luke were happy for many years, but they split up when the kids went to university. That's when she took the job.'

'But she didn't train as a doctor, did she?'

Julie laughed. 'Good lord, no. She wasn't a doctor. She worked in administration. The doctors' doctor, she called herself. They need someone to keep the wheels rolling – food, supplies, medicines, personnel, soap, towels, accommodation and so on. Training local people to do the job. That was Emily's job. She worked in every hellhole in the world, from South Sudan to Afghanistan. I can't imagine how awful a lot of it must have been. But her letters and emails were funny and insightful. Never self-pitying. I wish I'd kept them. She loved what she was doing, though it took its toll on her. Depression was never very far from the horizon. Witnessing so much of man's inhumanity to man can do that to you. But it didn't break her spirit.'

Banks took in what Julie had said, tried to imagine Emily under fire in a tent in a desert somewhere. 'Why tell me about the pregnancy now?' he asked. 'After all these years. You said you knew all along.'

'Yes, but it was my secret to keep, not to spread around. In the end, it was something Emily wanted, a favour she asked of me. Her last wish, if you like. Not to hurt you. She'd just felt guilty about it her whole life. She wanted you to know. That's all. I think because she knew she was dying she got caught up in the past, her youth, and you were a big part of that, an unresolved issue, if you like. Unfinished business. She wanted to put things right. She knew she couldn't turn back the clock, but she wanted to do what she could to reveal what happened.

Believe me, she didn't ask me to do this to hurt you. That was the last thing on her mind. I think she wanted your forgiveness. She talked most of all about the good times and good feelings. She said people often forget about that as love grows older and colder over time. That first days feeling. The sheer joy and ecstasy of falling in love, when everything seems new and possible. Do you forgive her, Alan?'

'Of course I do,' said Banks. 'I would never have wanted to hold her back, to stand in her way. I just wish things . . .' He felt his eyes prickling and swigged more wine. 'Oh, never mind.'

'Wish things had been different?' Julie paused. 'Let me ask you a question. Where would you have gone from there? If things *had* been different. If she had told you at the time. If you had persuaded her against having the abortion. If you had got married. Where would you have gone from there?'

'I don't know. I tried to imagine it just now, our life together, but I couldn't.'

'Whatever it would have been, Alan, the moment's gone. You had your time, you and Emily.' She got up and walked over to the bar, took something out of a drawer. 'And don't forget it was a good time. She wanted me to give you this to remind you.'

It was a photograph. Banks held it by the candlelight. He and Emily in the early seventies. He was wearing a denim jacket over a T-shirt, and bell bottoms, and his hair was much longer than it was now. Emily was wearing the embroidered white cheesecloth top she had favoured so much, along with her jeans, also bell bottoms. Banks had his arm around her and her head rested on his shoulder, her long blond hair hanging over his chest, that little sleepy satisfied smile on her face. Banks felt a lump in his throat.

'Turn it over,' Julie said.

Banks turned it over. Written on the other side, in shaky handwriting, were the words, 'Better by far you should forget and smile / Than that you should remember and be sad.'

'Christina Rossetti again,' Banks said.

'Yes, that's the one,' Julie whispered. 'Forget and smile.'

'I love that line, "with magic in my eyes",' said Banks, sitting in the Low Moor Inn with Linda Palmer on Sunday lunchtime. They both had the traditional roast beef and Yorkshire pudding lunch before them, but while Linda sipped at a glass of red wine and tucked in with gusto, Banks stuck to copious amounts of water and picked at his food.

The Low Moor Inn, which Banks had discovered by accident a couple of years ago, was one of those old sturdy and badly lit Dales pubs high on the moors, well off the beaten track. Its enormous fireplace blazed like a smithy's forge, quickly erasing memories of the damp and chill weather outside. Prints and framed paintings of the local hunt and sheep-shearing scenes hung here and there on the rough stone walls. Some were for sale and had price tags stuck below them. Bottles of spirits stood on shelves behind the polished bar and reflected in the long mirror behind them. A brass footrest ran along the bottom. The legs of the old wooden chairs scraped on the flagstone floor when anyone moved.

Banks had woken early, disoriented and hung-over in Filey, to the squealing of seagulls and the smell of bacon and eggs. Marcel, of course, had provided a hearty full English breakfast, including black pudding and baked beans. At first Banks hadn't thought he would be able to manage it all, but he found himself staring at an empty plate when he was on his second cup of coffee. He thanked Marcel, gave Julie a quick peck on the cheek and left. 'Don't be a stranger,' Julie had called out after him. But he didn't think he would be back there again, no matter how good the food.

'It is magnificent, isn't it? *Magic,*' said Linda. They were talking about Hardy's *Poems of 1912–1913*, which Banks had read over the new year, before his meeting with Dr Glendenning in the Unicorn, though the quotation that appealed so much to Banks came from a musical setting of an earlier Hardy poem, 'When I Set Out for Lyonnesse', by Gerald Finzi. Banks was feeling a little better after his long drive, but he was still finding it difficult to concentrate. The things Julie had told him the night before kept running through his head. Emily. A baby. Abortion. But Emily was dead now, and she had wanted his forgiveness. Thinking back to the first flush of love with Emily made Banks think of Sandra, whom he had married a few years after the split. Sandra. His ex-wife. Mother of Tracy and Brian. Now remarried to Sean, and a mother again. He tried hard to remember the early days, when they were poor but happy, living in Kennington, but the details eluded him. Their break-up had been acrimonious, and relations were still strained between them, so much so that they rarely met unless it was an important event involving Brian or Tracy.

Hardy captured that sense of first love so well, Banks thought, yet his relationship with Emma Gifford had been troublesome, and the couple had grown more distant over the years. Only when she died could he resurrect the magic of those early days, the places they had been and emotions connected with them. That was the thread that ran through the sequence. The poems were a true marriage of place and memory, Linda had said, and Banks had to agree, though he found Hardy's syntax and diction rather awkward sometimes, as if he were willing to twist the English language into any shape just for the sake of a rhyme or a rhythm. Not like the relaxed conversational flow of Larkin, for example, whom they had discussed at their last meeting, where Banks hardly even noticed the rhymes and meter.

'You seem a bit distracted today, Alan,' said Linda. 'Is it the hangover or the case you're working on?'

'Sorry,' said Banks. 'Bit of both. Is it so obvious? I *am* having difficulty concentrating. Other things. The poems . . . I mean, I've just lost someone and . . . I mean, it ended very abruptly, without explanation. A long time ago. I hadn't seen her in over forty years, and she died last December. It's not the same situation as Hardy and Emma at all, but the feelings. Somehow they seem similar. I'm remembering things we used to do, the way she looked, her clothes, places we used to go.'

Linda closed her book and put it down on the table. 'In some ways Hardy felt he hadn't seen Emma for forty years, either,' she said. 'They were hardly talking by the time she died. You don't have to talk about it if you don't want.'

'I know,' said Banks. 'This isn't a therapy session. Poetry isn't therapy. That's what you told me the first time we talked like this.'

'This person you lost. It was serious, at the time?'

'Yes. First girl I ever loved, as the song goes.'

'And the case you're working on?' Linda asked.

'No connection. Except I think it reaches back into the past, too. For different reasons, with different intentions.' Banks gulped down some water. 'In fact, I've been thinking that it might be something you can help me with.'

'Me?'

'Yes. If you don't mind thinking back.'

Linda narrowed her eyes and gave him that 'don't treat me with kid gloves' look.

Banks held up his hands in surrender. He knew that he sometimes avoided certain topics with her because she had been raped by a well-respected TV celebrity at the age of fourteen. But he also knew that she had not let it ruin her life. She had even written up her recollection of events for him in a journal during the case they had met through. 'OK, OK,' he said. 'I know you told me not to pussyfoot around the past. It's just that in my job I come across some of the worst things people do to each other.'

'I know that. How do you manage it?'

'You should know. You visit the dark side often enough. I've read your poetry.'

'I've been there,' said Linda, 'but it's different.'

'Why? Because I see real dead bodies and you see only imaginary ones? You know as well as I do it's not the bodies but the people who do such things. They're in your poems as much as they're in my life. We both spend far too much time down there in the dark. Alone.'

'You know I have my reasons,' said Linda softly.

'So do I,' said Banks. After a short pause he went on. 'Anyway, I seem to remember you told me you went to Silver Royd girls' school in Wortley.'

'That's right. Why?'

'Does the name Wendy Vincent mean anything to you?'

'Yes, of course. She was the girl who was murdered when I was at school. She was raped and stabbed. It was terrible.'

Banks looked away. He couldn't help it, knowing the things that had happened to Linda, but she seemed unfazed. 'That's right,' he said.

'And there was something about her in the papers a couple of years ago. The fiftieth anniversary. Right?'

'That's the one.'

'It seems a strange sort of anniversary to celebrate. A murder.'

'Media. What can I say? It wasn't a celebration of the murder, as such, and it did lead to the reopening of the investigation, the identity of the killer and his eventual capture. So we can't complain. One of the triumphs of DNA evidence in cold-case work. Turns out Frank Dowson, the killer, was on leave from the merchant navy at the time of the killing, and nobody knew he was in the area. Of course, some people might have known and been lying to protect him. His family, for example.'

'Dowson? I can't say I remember anyone by that name.'

'What about Wendy Vincent? And Maureen Grainger?'

'If they're the right ones I'm thinking of, they were ahead of me. I didn't know either of them. I was just starting in the first form, and they'd have been in the third or fourth. Older girls like them wanted nothing to do with us younger ones back then.'

'I don't doubt it's still the same. Boys, too. Except for a bit of bullying.'

'Well, I certainly don't remember either of them being spoken of as bullies. Wendy Vincent was famous for hockey. She was the star of the school team. I saw her play lots of times. Do you remember *The Prime of Miss Jean Brodie*, where all the girls were "famous" for something?'

'What was Maureen Grainger famous for?'

'I don't know if she was famous for anything. I didn't know her. I only remember Wendy Vincent because she was murdered. Isn't that a terrible thing?'

'It's perfectly normal.'

'Now, do you want to talk about Hardy or don't you?'

'Yes, ma'am. I've done my homework.' Banks glanced through the window. 'I liked that line about the rain being like "silken strings". Here, it's more like rough old rope.'

Linda laughed. But even as they talked about the poems, about the mysterious ghost figure and the way Hardy revisited places where he and Emma had been happy years ago, Banks couldn't get Maureen Grainger and Wendy Vincent out of his mind. Was Gerry right, and was that crime of over fifty years ago linked to the St Mary's shootings in any way at all?

Banks wasn't the only one feeling the effects of Saturday night that Sunday morning. Gerry had been reasonably abstemious back at Annie's cottage – she could be annoying that way – leaving Annie to polish off most of the wine by herself. At least Gerry had made tea and toast in the morning before leaving, after what must have been an uncomfortable night on the living-room sofa, and she had the good sense to keep small talk and noise in general to a minimum when Annie finally lumbered downstairs. And she left as soon as she decently could after breakfast.

Annie was never much of a morning person, and on Sundays she usually hunkered down with the papers, at least with the *Mail on Sunday* and the *Sunday Express*. She missed the old *News of the World* – nothing like a bit of gossip and scandal with your Sunday morning hangover – but that was long gone now.

By midday, she remembered she was going to interview Maureen Tindall with Jenny Fuller, and her spirits fell. It was an important interview, too, so she needed to be at the top of her game. Maureen Tindall might hold the key, or one of the keys, to the events that had happened in Fortford last December, though as yet nobody could quite imagine how. She had certainly been nervous when the talk got around to past events in their last interview. Annie took a quick hot shower and threw on some jeans and a sweatshirt before going out to her car. She hoped Jenny Fuller would stay in the

background and keep her mouth shut. The last thing she
wanted was some damn uppity profiler interrupting with
pointless questions whenever she felt she was getting
somewhere.

Annie phoned Jenny to tell her she was on her way and picked
her up outside her posh house in The Green, then drove on to
the Tindalls' posh house opposite The Heights. That was about
as much posh as Annie could handle for one day. Fortunately,
it was all she had signed up for. Naturally, Jenny Fuller was as
well turned out as usual in closely fitting black silk trousers and
loose white top and tailored jacket. Why did she always make
Annie feel like such a slob? It wasn't as if her own outfit was
especially cheap, just that she dressed casually and Jenny had a
way of wearing clothes as if they were made for her. Some
women had it, and some didn't. Annie felt that she didn't. No
matter what she wore – Primark or Versace, jeans or a skirt –
she felt as if she'd just come out of the Oxfam shop.

Annie had wanted to catch Maureen Tindall off guard, so
she hadn't phoned ahead to say they were coming. It was a
risk, she knew; people often go out to visit friends or relatives
on a Sunday. But this time it paid off far better than she could
have hoped. When Maureen eventually opened the door on
the chain and peered nervously through the crack, it became
clear that she was alone. Her husband was at a church meeting, she explained, when Annie had finally persuaded her to
open up and let them in.

To Annie's relief, Jenny Fuller settled herself at the far end
of the sofa, out of Annie's line of sight, and took out a large
Moleskine notebook. She would, Annie thought, putting her
regulation police notebook on the arm of the sofa beside her.
She didn't trust Jenny to make the right sort of notes, and two
people in her house were almost more than Maureen Tindall
could bear.

Though it was afternoon, Maureen was still wearing a pink quilted dressing gown over her nightdress and her hair was flattened on one side where she had clearly been lying down. Annie tried to dredge up some sympathy for her; after all, it wasn't long since Laura's murder. It was difficult, though, as she seemed so full of self-pity to start with. It was a nasty thought, and Annie immediately felt ashamed for having it, but she couldn't help herself. Maureen didn't offer any refreshment, even though it was a damp and chilly day. Annie thought herself lucky that there was a fire in the hearth, no doubt started by her husband, and that Maureen herself was obviously cold enough to add a couple of logs.

Maureen sat closest to the fire and leaned forwards in her armchair, hugging her knees. 'I've not been very well,' she said. 'I'm not sure I'll be up to this. I took one of my pills and fell asleep. What time is it?'

'Half past two,' Annie said.

Maureen seemed to relax a bit at that piece of news. 'Robert will be back soon,' she said. 'He said he would be home by half past three, and he's never late.'

Wouldn't dare be, Annie bet, given Maureen's obsession with punctuality.

'Would you like me to make you a cup of tea or coffee or something?' Jenny Fuller asked from the far end of the sofa. There was a note of kindness and concern in her voice that even Annie noticed.

Maureen's face brightened. 'Would you?' She fingered the collar of her dressing gown. 'I'd do it myself, you know, but . . .'

'No problem,' said Jenny with a smile. 'Annie?'

'Er, whatever's going, please,' Annie said.

'I'll make a nice pot of tea,' said Jenny, and patted Maureen's shoulder before heading into the kitchen. She seemed to know instinctively where it was, Annie noticed. Maybe these posh houses were all the same inside.

Maureen smiled after Jenny, then it faded like the Cheshire cat's when she turned back to Annie. 'She's nice, isn't she?' she said.

'Very,' said Annie. 'Do you know why we're here?'

'No. Should I? Something to do with Laura? The wedding?'

'Sort of.'

'You must think it's very odd, me being in bed at half past two in the afternoon.'

'That's not for me to comment on.'

'But Dr Graveney says I need plenty of rest after, you know, the trauma of what happened.'

'Of course,' Annie said. 'We won't disturb you for very long.'

Maureen consulted her watch again. 'Robert will be home soon,' she said, as if to herself.

Jenny Fuller reappeared with a tray. 'We'll just let it brew a few minutes, shall we?'

Even as she played mother with the tea, Jenny didn't have a hair out of place, didn't spill a drop as she passed over the cups and saucers. When she had done, she sat down in her corner again and set her Moleskine on her lap, as if she were signalling Annie to get started.

'The last time I talked to you,' Annie began, 'I noticed that you seemed a bit anxious when I mentioned the possibility of something from your past being connected with the shootings.'

'Did I?' said Maureen.

'Yes. Wendy Vincent.'

'I can't imagine why.'

'It would be only natural. Wendy Vincent was your best friend, and something terrible happened to her.'

'How could that possibly have anything to do with what happened to Laura?'

'We don't know that it does yet, but it's the kind of coincidence that makes us prick up our ears. Wendy was murdered, wasn't she?'

'Yes,' Maureen whispered. 'I'm sorry.'

'Why should you say that?' Annie asked.

Maureen glanced between the two of them. 'You know, don't you? I should have known you'd find out. Who told you?'

'Know what?' Annie said. She was sure the exasperation sounded in her tone.

'It wasn't in the papers. I never told anyone.'

Annie felt as if she were struggling to land a particularly slippery fish. 'What happened, Maureen?' she asked. It was all she could think of to say. 'Were you there? Did you see something?'

Maureen clutched her dressing gown at her throat. 'See something? Oh, no. Nothing like that.'

'Then what is it?'

Annie thought the silence was going to last for ever, then Maureen said in a barely audible voice, 'I was supposed to meet Wendy at the bus stop after lunch. I'd been to visit my granny in Bradford. We were going to go shopping in town. Clothes and records. We'd arranged to meet in secret because Wendy's parents didn't like us being friends.'

'Why?'

'Oh, I don't know. I suppose I was a bit more grown up than Wendy. I'd matured quickly. Her father tried to kiss me once. He was drunk and sloppy and I slipped out of his grasp easily enough, but he remembered. He never liked me after that. Wendy was fifteen and never been kissed. A bit of a goody two-shoes, I suppose, and sporty, but she could be a laugh and . . .

well, what can I say, we got along really well. We were different, but we were friends. I didn't lead her astray or anything. I wasn't really a bad influence.'

'We're not saying you did, Maureen. Go on. You were supposed to meet on the day she disappeared?'

'That's right.'

'And you didn't tell your parents or her parents where you were going?'

'No. Not even after. And not even later when the reporters came talking to all her friends. And Susan Bramble didn't tell anyone, either.'

'Susan Bramble?'

'Another girl from school. From the hockey team. Another friend. She told me later she saw Wendy at the bus stop, and Wendy admitted she was waiting for me, but to keep it secret in case the Vincents found out. Susan knew how to keep a secret.'

'But you didn't meet Wendy?'

'I was late. By the time I got to the bus stop, Wendy was gone. She must have taken the short cut through the woods. It was my fault.'

'Listen to me, Maureen.' It was Jenny talking again, and this time her voice was concerned but authoritative. 'Nobody's blaming you for anything. Anything at all. Do you understand?'

Maureen nodded, but Annie doubted that she was convinced.

'What DI Cabbot needs to know is what happened that afternoon. What stopped you from meeting your friend? This might be important. Why does remembering that day make you feel so anxious?'

'It was a terrible day,' Maureen said. 'Wendy was . . . stabbed and . . . I . . . it was the worst day of my life.'

'I know,' said Jenny moving forwards, going on her knees and taking Maureen's hand. Annie could only look on. Jenny was good with people, she had to admit. 'All these years you've been blaming yourself, haven't you?'

Maureen hesitated, then said, 'It *was* my fault. I was selfish. I *should* have been there to meet her.'

'Where were you, Maureen?' Annie asked. 'What happened that afternoon?'

Jenny let go of Maureen's hand and went back to her place on the sofa. After what seemed an eternity, Maureen picked up her tea. The cup and saucer were shaking in her hand.

'I was with a boy,' she said.

Having got nowhere in the squad room checking out property rentals and purchases in the Swainshead area for most of the morning, Gerry decided it was time to go out and visit a few Walkers' Wearhouse branches. There was no sign of Doug Wilson, but that was only to be expected as he had Sunday off. She did, too, but she was working anyway. She was better off doing it by herself, she thought. Doug would only sulk or complain and slow her down. Before she left she phoned Paula Fletcher at the Lyndgarth branch to ask her whether the two-for-one sale had extended to all branches. She said it had.

Gerry studied the photocopy of Ray's sketch. She still didn't know how closely it resembled their man, but it was a hell of a good drawing. Ray was a talented artist, despite the drinking and childish behaviour. The thought passed through her mind that perhaps she should let him paint her in the nude, then her modesty pushed it away quickly. She wasn't prudish – far from it – but the idea of posing nude in front of Ray Cabbot held no appeal. She didn't even think her body was worth the canvas. She was too skinny by far, had no true womanly curves like Jenny Fuller, or even Annie. She was all bones and planes.

And while she was quite willing to believe in the purity of
Ray's artistic intentions, or at least suspend her disbelief, there
was something just a bit too *louche* about him for her liking.
And he was old enough to be her father. Christ, he was Annie
Cabbot's father. He was old enough to be Gerry's *grand*father.
Why couldn't some clean-cut handsome young artist come
along and want to paint her, or a composer write a song for
her like that Mahler had for his Alma?

She took out the list of branches they had already visited,
wondering whether it was worth calling again on any of them
with the sketch of the man Paula Fletcher had described.
Someone had already talked to the press, and word was getting
around that the police now had an Identikit picture of their
person of interest. While this wasn't quite accurate, it was enough
to make her feel a sense of urgency. She decided it definitely was
worth visiting the shops again. On previous visits, they hadn't
had the sketch to show around. It might jog someone's memory.

She decided on the branches closest to the one in Lyndgarth,
where Paula Fletcher had encountered him, guessing that he
probably wouldn't have travelled as far afield as York,
Harrogate or Leeds. If she had no luck, then the larger centres,
each with two or three branches, would be her next stop, but
she hoped it wouldn't come to that. Buying the clothing would
have been a job he wanted to get over with as soon as possible.
As far as Gerry could make out, there were three branches
nearby: one in Helmthorpe, one in Eastvale and another in
Northallerton, east of the A1. She started there but had no
luck. She also drew a blank in Eastvale. The third branch was
on Helmthorpe High Street, opposite the Dog and Gun.

The first young man Gerry spoke to had only been working
at the branch since Christmas, but the manager Henry
Bedford also happened to be in the shop that day preparing
for stock-taking. He had worked there for over eight years and

prided himself on knowing all his regulars, including Martin Edgeworth, who had shopped there often for all of his outdoor needs. 'Terrible tragedy,' he said as he examined the sketch.

'If it helps,' Gerry said, 'he was wearing a cheap grey wind-cheater and an open-neck shirt, showing a bit of chest hair and the top of a tattoo. Maybe a bird or something.'

'Yes,' said Bedford, tapping the sketch. 'Yes.'

Gerry felt the tingle of excitement ripple up her spine. 'You remember him?'

'I do. He seemed to be in a hurry, rather brusque, a bit rude, if you ask me. You tend to remember people who act that way. Impatient, imperious. He wanted two sets of identical items. Anorak, waterproof trousers, woolly hat.'

It was their man, Gerry thought. 'Is this sketch a good likeness?'

The manager peered at it again. 'Yes,' he answered. 'Pretty good.'

'How did he pay?'

'I'm afraid I don't . . . yes, just a minute. Yes, he paid cash.'

Gerry's hopes faded. 'I don't suppose you got a name or anything?'

'No. Sorry.'

'It's all right. Tell me,' she went on. 'You said Martin Edgeworth shopped here for his outdoor clothes?'

'Yes. He was a regular.'

'Did he know this man? I mean, did you ever see them together? Did he mention Edgeworth?'

'No,' said Bedford. 'Whoever he was, he was a complete stranger to me. I never saw him with Martin, or anyone else, for that matter.'

'Thank you, Mr Bedford,' said Gerry, heading for the door. 'Thank you very much. You've been a great help.'

★　　★　　★

'A boy?' Annie repeated. 'What boy? Who was he?'

'It doesn't matter who he was. He doesn't have anything to do with it. I think he was called Danny. He was older than me. He'd already left school.'

'Danny who?'

'I don't remember. Honestly. He was just a local boy. He worked for Sammy Ledgard's, driving.' She turned imploringly to Jenny.

Annie knew it was time to slow down. 'OK,' she said. 'We won't worry about that for the time being. Was Danny your boyfriend?'

Maureen was plucking at the stitching of her quilted dressing gown. She managed a weak smile. 'Sort of, I suppose. I was quite pretty back then. I was fifteen. I had a lot of boyfriends.'

'I'm sure you did,' said Annie. 'The boys liked you?'

'Not like that. I wasn't like some girls. Not like they said at school. There were some houses on the old estate over the road, all boarded up. We knew how to get into one of them. It was the only place you could go, you know, to be by yourselves. We were just kissing and cuddling. It was all quite innocent. I lost track of time, and I was late to meet Wendy. She'd set off home. They said later that her leg was hurting from where someone had whacked her with a hockey stick. If she had been feeling better, maybe she would have waited and we'd have got the next bus. You can't believe how sorry I am for being so selfish.'

'You mustn't think that way,' Jenny said.

'But if I'd been there, like I should have been, we'd have both gone into town, and it would never have happened. Don't you see? If it wasn't for me, Wendy would still be alive.'

'You don't know that,' said Jenny. 'Perhaps she would have told you she didn't feel like going, and you'd have gone by yourself, then she would have still walked through the woods alone. After all, neither of you thought there was anything to be afraid of there.'

'But it didn't happen like that, did it?'

'Had you arranged this meeting with Danny before?' Annie asked.

'No. I just bumped into him in the street. I was early to meet Wendy, so I went with him. I thought I still had enough time. My watch . . . stopped. I didn't realise. But we didn't do anything wrong. We were just kissing and holding hands.'

'Nobody's suggesting you were doing anything wrong,' said Annie, smiling. 'I liked a kiss and cuddle with my boyfriend when I was that age, too. It's only natural.'

'But I lost track of the time,' said Maureen, clutching at the neck of her dressing gown. She consulted her watch again. 'Robert will be home soon. He *will* be home soon.' Annie thought it sounded like a kind of mantra she was saying to calm herself down as she struggled to hold back the tears.

'It's all right, Maureen.' Jenny's velvety comforting voice came from the far end of the sofa. 'You've nothing to blame yourself for.'

'But I do!' Maureen said. 'Don't you see? I was kissing a boy while Wendy . . . Wendy was . . . Oh, my God.' She held her face in her hands and cried. In a flash, Jenny was kneeling beside her, a tissue materialising from nowhere. Annie wondered how she did it, but she got Maureen calmed down quickly enough and went back to the sofa.

'It's all right,' Maureen said after a while, looking at Annie now. 'Ask me what you want to know. It's all right. I'll tell you. Then you can take me away.'

'Nobody's going to take you away, Maureen,' said Annie. 'Robert will be back soon. He'll take care of you. Why didn't you tell anyone about this before?'

'Because Wendy and I weren't supposed to be friends. Because I was ashamed. Because I felt guilty. I thought if they knew, they'd blame me. They already said I was a bad influence.'

'But you've blamed yourself all these years,' said Jenny. 'Maybe if you'd told your parents or someone, you'd have been able to get the help you needed.'

'What good would it have done? Nobody can undo the past. Wendy was dead and it was all because of me. What does it matter now? Laura's dead, too. I thought you'd got the man who did it?'

'We have to follow up on things that come up, even if they don't seem connected.'

'Do people have to know?'

'Have to know what?'

'That I lied. What I was really doing.'

'I don't see any reason why they should. Nobody knew about this but you and Danny?'

'Only Mark Vincent.'

Annie ears pricked up. 'Mark Vincent?'

'Wendy's younger brother. He was on his way to the gang meeting in Billy Dowson's garage. He must have seen me and Danny holding hands, but he didn't say anything. He was only eleven. He probably didn't know what holding hands meant.'

Annie tried to work it out. Susan Bramble had seen Wendy at the bus stop shortly before she was killed, but had said nothing to anyone. Mark Vincent had seen Maureen walking hand in hand with this Danny, and he had also said nothing. But why should he have? He didn't know that Maureen was supposed to meet his sister. The meeting between Maureen and Wendy for the trip into town was a secret. Only Susan Bramble knew about it. Annie wasn't sure what it all meant, if anything. 'Where is Danny now?' she asked.

'I don't know. We lost touch. I haven't seen him since then.'

'You knew Frank Dowson, right?'

'I knew who he was. He was Billy Dowson's older brother. But I didn't *know* him.'

'You knew his brother?'

'Only because he was mates with Wendy's brother Mark. They were both eleven. They were in some sort of silly gang, and they used to meet in Billy's dad's garage. He never used it to keep his car in there. It was an old banger and he left it in the street. People said he had a lock-up across town where he stored stolen goods, but I don't know if that was true or not. Billy had a key to the garage. They just used to sit around and smoke and tell dirty jokes. He thought we didn't know about it, but Wendy and Susan and me listened outside once.'

'Who else was in this gang?'

'Just local kids. Mark, Billy, Ricky Bramble, Susan's younger brother, Tommy Jackson and Mick Charlton. Maybe others. I don't remember. They wouldn't let girls in. As if we'd want to be a part of it. They were just little kids.'

'Maureen, you do know that Frank Dowson was arrested for Wendy's murder just a couple of years ago, don't you? And that he died in prison last year?'

'I saw it on TV.'

'Was Frank in the gang?'

'No way. He was a grown-up. Maybe twenty-one or something. And he didn't come home very often. We hardly ever used to see him. He was in the merchant navy. We were all a bit scared of him.'

'Why?'

'I don't know. The way he looked at us. How he was so big and quiet. We'd heard there was something wrong with him. You know, in his head.'

'Did you see him that day you were supposed to meet Wendy?'

'No. Wendy and I had arranged to meet at the bus stop just before half past one. That was when the bus went. There wasn't another one for twenty minutes. It was nearly quarter to when I got there. I thought she might still be waiting and we'd get the next one, but she was gone. I just thought she'd gone home. I didn't see anyone around.'

That was something that simply couldn't happen today, Annie realised, in the age of mobiles, of constantly being in touch. When she found out she was running late, Maureen would probably have texted Wendy and got a response – either she would wait or she was going home. They would probably have been in touch earlier, too, and Wendy would have texted Maureen that she'd taken a nasty hit on the hockey pitch and didn't feel too well, so she'd have to cancel the trip to town for today. It might not have made any difference to the outcome, if she had taken the short cut and bumped into Frank Dowson, but communication might well have brought about a different course of action entirely. Still, it was pointless speculation. With today's methods, Frank Dowson would have been caught pretty quickly, too – but it hadn't happened in the twenty-first century; it had happened in 1964.

'What did you do when you found Wendy wasn't there?' Annie asked.

'I went home. I didn't feel like going into town by myself.'

'Did you walk through the woods?'

'No. Our house was in the other direction. I walked along the main road.'

'And you're sure didn't see Frank Dowson or anyone else you knew?'

'*No.*'

'What about afterwards? Did anyone ever say anything to make you think Frank Dowson might have hurt Wendy?'

'No. We moved away not long after, and I never saw any of the old crowd again.'

'And you've been blaming yourself all these years?' Jenny asked.

'It was my fault,' said Maureen. 'I shouldn't have lost track of time. I can't be trusted. If I hadn't been so selfish, Wendy would still be alive.'

Annie couldn't help but notice the helplessness in her voice as it cracked, and as Jenny came over again to mutter more words of sympathy and comfort, Annie also couldn't help thinking that if Maureen had carried her guilt with her through her whole life, and if it were somehow linked with her nerves and obsession with punctuality, then maybe someone else had been nursing a festering blame for her for just as long, and perhaps that, too, had had deep psychological effects. But who? Wendy's younger brother had seen Maureen with Danny, and Susan Bramble had spoken with Wendy at the bus stop and seen her walk towards the woods. Did someone else know Maureen's secret? If so, how? And why wait fifty years before taking any action? Why bother now that the killer had been brought to justice? And why not shoot Maureen herself, if she was to blame? To make her suffer?

It was always possible that Frank Dowson hadn't killed Wendy Vincent, that despite the DNA evidence, someone else had done it. Maureen? She certainly couldn't have committed the rape, but who was to say that the person who had raped Wendy was the same as the person who had killed her? There was no apparent motive for anyone around at the time – not, as far as Annie knew – but sometimes motives don't become clear until much later. In addition to Maureen, there were

Billy Dowson and Mark Vincent to consider, though they were very young at the time of Wendy's murder.

Whatever had happened, Annie thought, Banks would want to know about this new information as soon as possible. She took out her mobile.

13

The first old 'gang' member Gerry had managed to trace for Banks was called Mick Charlton, or Michael, as his wife had insisted on calling him when Banks dropped by the house later. Mrs Charlton had told him that her husband was at work and had given him directions to the workshop. Michael Charlton had done well for himself since leaving Armley Park Secondary Modern for an apprenticeship as an electrician, and he now ran his own business not far from the estate where he grew up.

Gerry had trawled through the case files and newspaper articles for Banks quickly again after Annie and Jenny had passed on Maureen's story, and, as expected, she had found no mention of Maureen's secret meeting with Wendy, or of her tryst with anyone called Danny. Clearly, Banks thought, the most important details of that day were not in the public documents, or even in ex-Detective Superintendent Gristhorpe's memory, but were known only to those in the two close-knit groups – the eleven-year-old boys, on the one side, and the fifteen-year-old girls on the other.

As Banks drove to Leeds, listening to Al Stewart's *Love Chronicles*, he couldn't help but dwell on what Annie and Jenny had told him about Maureen Tindall's secret meeting with Wendy Vincent, and the reason why it had never happened. He also wanted to know whether the sketch of the man described by Paula Fletcher rang a bell with anyone, and

Michael Charlton was someone who might know. He might even know who 'Gord' was. All Banks knew so far was that Maureen had said Mark Vincent saw her and Danny holding hands and heading for an old house where the kids went to kiss and canoodle. What he would have made of that at the age of eleven, Banks had no idea. He wasn't sure what his own feelings towards girls were at that age. Had he ever held a girl's hand, other than his mother's? He couldn't remember for certain, but he felt all that had come a bit later.

Banks turned off the music in the middle of the title track, just after some nice guitar work from Jimmy Page. As he parked in front of the low brick office block on Stanningley Road, he reflected that some people never move far from where they started out. That was certainly the case with Michael Charlton. His old estate was no more than a couple of miles up the road, and Armley Park Secondary Modern School was even closer, only a hundred yards or so from his offices just beyond the busy junction with Crab Lane and Branch Road. Of course, it was no longer a school but an office complex. According to Mrs Charlton, he had been running his own business there for over forty years.

Though the area had been given a facelift not so long ago, it was starting to become shabby again, Banks thought. That was partly because the renovations had never been completed. Some of the buildings condemned ages ago were still clinging on, a boarded-up pub, an empty shop, though the old Clock School, like Armley Park, had been converted into offices.

'I'd like to speak to Mr Charlton, please,' Banks said to the receptionist in her little alcove.

'Who may I say is calling?'

Banks flashed his warrant card. 'Detective Superintendent Banks.' He had almost said DCI, having still not got used to referring to himself as 'superintendent'. There was no decent abbreviation for the rank, either. Det. Supt. didn't sound right, and DS already stood for Detective Sergeant, so he was lumbered with the full moniker.

'Just a minute.' The receptionist picked up the phone and announced him.

'He says to go through,' she said, pointing to the door marked M. CHARLTON ELECTRICAL. Banks found himself in a large open-plan area with work benches, various pieces of electrical equipment, testing machines and wires and a desk in a corner by the window for the boss. It wasn't much of a view, just the estate over the road. People worked at the various benches, and another desk was occupied across the room. Banks could smell solder and burned rubber.

'Superintendent?' said Charlton, waving him over. 'Do sit down. There, move those files.'

Banks picked up the batch of files on the chair.

'Just dump them on top of that cabinet there, if you don't mind.'

Banks did as Charlton asked and sat down.

Charlton tapped his fleshy lower lip with his pen, contemplating Banks, then said. 'Well, it's not every day we get a visit from the boys in blue. What can I do for you?'

No point beating about the bush, Banks thought. 'It's about what happened in 1964. The Wendy Vincent business.'

'Wendy? I thought that was all over and done with now you finally got your man.'

'I still have a few questions. Would you prefer to go somewhere more private?'

Charlton leaned back in his chair. 'It doesn't matter to me. I've got nothing to hide. I must admit I'm curious what it is you're after, though.'

'Just information,' said Banks.

'Then I'm your man. I was there, got the T-shirt.'

'Did you know Wendy Vincent and her friend Maureen Grainger?'

'Not very well, no. I knew who they were, of course, but they were older than us and, well, when you're eleven or so, you're interested in other things than fifteen-year-old girls, aren't you?'

'Like cricket and model aeroplanes?'

'And stamp collecting, trainspotting. That sort of thing, yes. Anything, in fact. And they don't want anything to do with you, either. It's all pop stars and *Jackie* and make-up.'

'And there was the gang, wasn't there? You and your mates.'

Charlton laughed. 'I'd hardly call that ragtag collection of misfits I belonged to a gang. At least not in the sense that people use the word today.'

'Who were the members?'

'There was Mark Vincent, Billy Dowson, Ricky Bramble, Tommy Jackson and me.'

'Just the five of you?'

'Most weeks, yes.'

'Frank Dowson?'

'No. Too old for us.'

'Did you ever have a member called Gord? Or Gordon?'

'No.'

'Did you follow the reports in the papers when the case came back into the limelight a couple of years ago?'

'Of course.'

'Did it surprise you, Frank Dowson being found guilty?'

'Not at all. I always thought he was creepy.'

'In what way?'

'Just creepy.'

'Did you see him often?'

'Hardly ever. It was Billy's gang, mostly because it was his dad's garage we used to meet in, but Frank was away at sea most of the time. Besides, like I said, he was too old to be interested in anything like that, anything we were doing.'

'Still, you knew him, didn't you, and he raped and murdered a girl you knew. It must have had some effect on you?'

'Oh, I'm not saying I wasn't shocked or upset. Horrified. Creepy as he was, I never thought of Frank Dowson as a murderer. But the more I thought about it, the less surprised I was.'

'Because he was creepy?'

For the first time, Charlton seemed to become guarded in his responses. Banks could sense a curtain closing, and he wanted to wrench it open. 'That's a part of it. Yes. He hardly ever spoke, and when he was around, he had a habit of just appearing there out of nowhere. Like, he was a big bloke and all, but quiet as a mouse.'

'Did he ever come to your gang meetings?'

Charlton glanced towards the wall. 'Like I said, he was too old to be in the gang.'

'That's not what I asked,' Banks said.

Charlton sighed. 'There's a pub up on Town Street,' he said, glancing at his watch. 'Maybe we could talk more comfortably there.'

Banks stood up. 'Your choice.'

Gerry Masterson stood alone in the boardroom of Eastvale Police HQ with a huge Ordnance Survey map of the area spread open on the desk. She was used to the large space being filled with officers for a briefing, the sort of thing she had done at the beginning of what was now becoming known as the Edgeworth Case. Though she could hear occasional voices and various office noises from the corridor outside, the boardroom seemed to have a muffled atmosphere all of its own, partly due to the wainscoting and the long polished oval table with its matching high-backed chairs, not to mention the silent and disapproving stares of the men with mutton-chop whiskers and red faces in gilt frames around the walls. The woollen merchants who, along with the lead miners before them, had been responsible for whatever prosperity and population Swainsdale possessed.

The lead mines were all in ruins now, tourist attractions, and though you'd be hard pushed to go very far without bumping into a sheep in North Yorkshire, the cloth and woollen industries had long fallen victim to cheap imports; first, legitimately from India, but more recently from Asian sweat shops or child labour. It had also lost a lot of ground to synthetics over the years, though sheep-shearing was still a regular occurrence – and another tourist attraction – it was the meat rather than the wool that people were interested in these days.

Gerry rested her palms on the smooth wood and scanned the map. When it came to maps, she thought, you could only get so far with computers. They were great for the details and for suggesting or calculating routes, but for sheer scale you needed real sheets, not a computer screen, and to get that effect she had spread out the large OS Landranger map on the table and marked the perimeters according to places the killer was known, or highly suspected, to have visited. Maps told you a lot if you could read them well enough, and Gerry had learned that skill at school, then honed it later on country walks. She could follow the contours of a hill, the boundaries of a field and the progress of a footpath with the same ease that most people could read a book.

Close to the River Swain were Fortford, where it all started, Helmthorpe, where the matching sets of clothing were bought, and Swainshead, where Martin Edgeworth had lived. North of there was the Upper Swainsdale District Rifle and Pistol Club, to which Edgeworth had belonged, and to the east, over the moors, was Lyndgarth, the first place the killer had tried to buy his clothing.

If Gerry drew a line linking all these places she ended up with a wonky rectangle. None of its sides were exactly the same length, but the west–east lines were the longest sides. She also pencilled in an extension from Fortford to include Eastvale in the bottom south-cast corner and joined that line to Lyndgarth.

The area she had marked off covered a lot of ground, though much of it was wild moorland, and she also had to accept that the killer might have been living at least a short distance outside the boundaries she had drawn. But it was a start. The only places of any real size were Eastvale, Helmthorpe, Swainshead and Lyndgarth. Even Fortford and Gratly were not much more than small villages. Eastvale, though there was no proof the killer had ever set foot there, was by far the largest settlement, being close to twenty thousand in population.

Somewhere, in the midst of all this, lived a killer, Gerry was certain. The problem was how to find him. He might have lived in the dale for years, of course, but Gerry doubted that. She believed that he had come specifically to carry out the shooting at the wedding. Of course, he might have left the area immediately after – most sensible assassins would – but that was a risk she would have to take. She could hardly search the whole country for him, but she could do a thorough job of covering her own part of it. Even if he had left, there was a chance that, by finding out where he had lived when he was in Yorkshire, they could possibly find some evidence that would lead to his identity and perhaps help track him to his new location.

But Gerry felt he was still close. She didn't know why, and it wasn't a feeling she would share with DI Cabbot or the boss, but she felt it, nevertheless. He was nearby, watching, enjoying the results of his handiwork. There was even a chance that he hadn't finished yet. She had no idea whether he had planned any more killings, or even whether he had managed to get his hands on any more firearms, now that Edgeworth's AR15 and Taurus were in the police evidence locker, but she somehow felt he hadn't finished what he came to do.

So she was trying to find someone who lived a relatively hermit-like existence – but not too reclusive as to be suspicious – for perhaps only a short while. That set some limits. She would first check the out-of-the-way places, including empty properties where he might squat without being discovered. There probably weren't many, but there would be a few decrepit barns and old shepherd's shelters if he didn't mind living rough. Of course, he would need somewhere to park his car, and he might have used a nearby public car park. But on second thoughts, she quickly ruled them out. Given the magnitude of his intended crime, she didn't think he would want to take even the slightest risk of being seen to break the law before he got started. On the other hand, she had decided from his shopping habits that he was either parsimonious or short of money, so she could also rule out any higher priced properties or rentals. That should whittle the list down a bit; prices being what they were in the area these days, it was difficult to find an affordable cottage or flat. There were a few converted barns, but even they were pricey, and he would have stood out like a sore thumb in a student flat in Eastvale. His needs would probably be simple: a roof over his head, a bed or somewhere to set down a sleeping bag – though she ruled out camping because of all the rain – and solitude. The sort of place a poor writer or artist might be able to afford. Ray Cabbot might be able to help there. His resources weren't exactly limited, but he had been checking out properties all around the county since before Christmas. He didn't make her as nervous as he had when they first met. Somehow, hearing Annie talk about him and watching the way she dealt with him gave Gerry confidence. Ray Cabbot might not be a pussy-cat or a saint, but he was no abusive predator either.

There were certain routine things that could be done fairly quickly by telephone, such as checking the voters' registry at the council offices – though a man on the verge of mass murder might be expected to be relatively uninterested in who his next MP or councillor was going to be – and the land registry, which would give her the name of the owner, from which she could also perhaps get the names of anyone who had rented from him. Then there were the utilities that just about everyone had – gas, electricity, Yorkshire Water – and after that telephone companies, Internet providers, the Department of Vehicle Licencing, the post office, HMRC and many more.

She wasn't stupid enough to imagine that he would have used his own name or real previous address, but whatever details he had given the seller or renter might also help determine who he was and help locate him. And she had the advantage of Ray's sketch.

The problem was that Gerry didn't have time to do all this work herself. It would mean hours on the phone, perhaps even traipsing about the countryside, visits to out of the way places, false trails galore. And she had other things to do. Would AC Gervaise authorise the manpower? Doug Wilson could help, for a start. He didn't seem to be doing much these days. And maybe with the addition of a couple of ambitious uniformed officers, that would be enough to get things in motion. Surely the AC couldn't object to that.

There was only one way to find out.

Banks and Charlton crossed the road and walked up Branch Road, past the Western and back of the Tesco Express, on to Town Street, where most of the shops had foreign names. The pub had clearly seen better days, but they found a quiet corner in the lounge bar, where the noise of video machines and dreadful pop music was distant. Charlton offered to get the drinks. Banks asked for a coffee and wouldn't be talked out of it. He didn't want to be driving in Leeds traffic with even one alcoholic drink in him. He had let DCI Ken Blackstone know he would be on his patch that day, and they had arranged to meet in the city centre later for dinner and drinks. There was a good chance they would take a taxi and Banks would spend the night in Blackstone's spare room.

'It's not so bad here during the day,' said Charlton, 'but it gets a bit edgier by night. It's almost all Eastern Europeans these days, as you could see from the shops. First the Poles, now it's Romanians and Bulgarians.' Banks had been in the area before on more than one case over the past couple of decades, and he was aware that now the once Northern English working-class neighbourhood was very much domi-nated by Eastern European immigrants. There was even a new mosque not far away, on Brooklyn Terrace.

When they were settled in the corner, Charlton seemed nervous. 'You must think it's odd, me asking if you wanted to go somewhere more private after I said I'd nothing to hide?'

Banks gave a noncommittal shrug.

'I mean, it's true. I don't have anything to hide. Nothing at all. But some things . . . well, you know, office gossip and the like. After all, I am the boss. I do have a reputation to live up to, a standard to set. I don't want all my employees knowing about my misspent youth.'

'What is it that you don't have to hide, then?' Banks asked.

Charlton took a long pull on his pint of Guinness and licked the foam from his lips. 'Mm, nectar,' he said. 'I don't mean misspent in a criminal way, you understand. Just that I suppose I could have spent more time on my books, more time at school listening to teachers. The usual. I failed my eleven plus.'

'You don't seem to have done badly for yourself.'

'Not at all. I've nothing to complain about. If you show a bit of application you don't have to worry too much about the education. The world will always need plumbers and electricians. That's what I say. Elbow grease and a bit of savvy.' He touched the side of his nose. 'That's what it takes, superintendent. Hard graft never did anyone any harm.'

It was a variation on the Samuel Smiles self-help philosophy that was engraved in pithy sayings inside the Victorian town hall dome, and Banks had heard it many times before, almost as often as 'where there's muck there's brass'.

The coffee was bland. Banks added milk and sweetener. They didn't help much. 'Frank Dowson,' he said. 'What can you tell me about him?'

'Not much more than I have done,' said Charlton. 'I meant what I said. None of us really knew him. Maybe Billy, I suppose, being his brother, but he wasn't a topic of conversation. We were all a bit scared of him, like we were of Billy's dad. Frank was definitely strange. Retarded, I think. Or whatever they call it these days.'

'But there's something else, isn't there, or you wouldn't have wanted us to leave the office?'

Charlton started playing with an extra beermat, first manipulating it between his fingers, then picking it to bits.

'The day it happened,' he said finally. 'You know, the day Wendy . . . the murder.'

'Yes?'

'We had a gang meeting. All the members were there.'

'But not Frank Dowson?'

'I told you. Frank wasn't a member. Not that we did anything serious. A bit of mischief, you know. Boys will be boys. The occasional scuffle with the Sandford gang. But nobody ever got seriously hurt. No knives or bicycle chains involved. A bloody nose or a black eye at worst.'

'And Frank?'

'Right. I was getting to that. He was supposed to drop by that afternoon.'

'Why?'

'As a guest, like. You know. Billy had asked him.'

'Again, why? Did he have something to say, something to tell you, or show you?'

'You could say that.'

'Are you saying that?'

'Well, er, yes, I suppose I am.'

'Go on, then. I'm listening.'

'You're not making this easy.'

Banks leaned forwards. 'Then let me simplify things, Mr Charlton. If you don't tell me what it is you have to say, we'll go up to Eastvale HQ, find an empty interview room and talk there until I'm satisfied. Is that easy enough for you?'

'You don't have to be like that.'

'What do I have to be like to get you to tell me what it is you have to say? I'm being as patient as I can.'

'All right, all right. Billy told us his brother was going to drop by the garage during our meeting that afternoon, like, to show us something he'd got off a darkie in Marseilles.'

'What was this something?'

Charlton swallowed. 'A knife. A flick-knife. But don't go taking it the wrong way. He was just going to show it to us, that's all. We were kids, superintendent, fascinated by exotic things like that. A hint of danger, the forbidden.'

'And what was it like, this knife? Did it live up to your expectations?'

'I don't know.'

'Why not?'

'Frank didn't turn up.'

'What was that? I couldn't quite hear you.'

'I said he didn't turn up. Frank Dowson.'

'But he was in the area?'

Charlton seem to panic a little at that. 'I don't know, I tell you. How would I know? I didn't see him. I hadn't seen him for ages. I assumed he probably got leave from the merchant navy, like, and hadn't been able to come to the meeting for some reason. Maybe he'd been called back to his ship? Maybe his leave got cancelled.'

'So let me get this straight. Frank Dowson was supposed to drop by the garage and show you this exotic knife he'd picked up in Marseilles, but he didn't turn up, and around the same time Wendy Vincent gets raped and stabbed in the nearby woods. Stabbed, mind you, with a flick-knife, perhaps, and none of you thinks it's worth telling the police about it. You don't even think he was in the area. Am I right?'

'You didn't know Billy's dad. He was a holy terror was Mr Dowson. Like one of them Krays, he was, or that crazy mafia bloke in *Goodfellas*. You didn't want to get on his bad side. And Frank *was* family, after all.'

'Are you telling me that Billy Dowson's father told the gang members not to mention that Frank Dowson was supposed to show up with a knife that afternoon but didn't? That you were all protecting him? Protecting a possible killer?'

'No, it wasn't like that. He told Billy that Frank couldn't get leave. Simple as that. He didn't talk to us. He didn't even know about our gang. Billy was scared shitless, and he just asked us, like, not to say anything, or his dad would kill him. After all, Frank hadn't turned up with the knife. Nobody had seen him. For all we knew, he might have been having us on, or he could have been still at sea. There might not have been any knife at all.'

'Did Billy believe his father?'

'I don't know. He was just scared. He told us what he'd said.'

'Did you ever think the father could have done it, raped and killed Wendy, not Frank?'

'I was only eleven. I didn't think about things like that at all.'

'But there must have been conversations. At school, perhaps. I know what kids that age are like. I was one myself, too, don't forget.'

'It honestly never crossed my mind.'

'And did you believe Billy?'

'I don't know. I hadn't seen Frank, had I? He could have been anywhere, for all I knew.'

'Like in the woods?'

'I didn't mean that.'

'But Frank must have been at the house with the knife some time recently, mustn't he, if Billy knew about it, had persuaded him to come and show it to the gang, and if their father was worried about the police finding out? He must have known something. Frank *must* have been in the neighbourhood the day Wendy Vincent was murdered.'

'I don't know. I never saw him. Honest I didn't.'

Christ, give me strength, Banks thought, gritting his teeth. 'So tell me, how did you feel when they finally convicted Frank Dowson of Wendy Vincent's murder fifty years after the fact, along with several violent rapes he committed *after* he killed her?'

Charlton swallowed. 'I don't know what you mean.'

'Come on, Mr Charlton. It's not that tough a question.'

'Well, I suppose I thought about that flick-knife and that it really might have been him. But I didn't know at the time. How could I? I hadn't seen him anywhere around. We didn't even know what had happened to Wendy Vincent until well after the meeting. The next day. Later, even. And even then you lot didn't tell us all the details, like exactly when or how it had happened, or what weapon was used.'

'But Billy Dowson had warned you not to mention Frank and the knife?'

'Yes. Because of his dad.'

'So why didn't you manage to put two and two together? Or suspect the dad?'

'We were only kids, eleven years old, for Christ's sake, and Frank was always getting into trouble with the police. He was the kind of person you lot pick on, on account of he wasn't too bright, and he'd probably confess to things he didn't do, you know, clear unsolved crimes off your books, thinking he was being clever, like.'

'So you didn't think that Frank Dowson might have actually murdered Wendy Vincent?'

'I'm not saying it never crossed my mind. But no. Not seriously. I mean, it's not as black and white as you're making out.'

'Oh, for Christ's sake, just shut the fuck up and let me think. Will you do that for me?'

Charlton's jaw hung open, but he did shut up. Drinking some Guinness helped him with that.

'You should have told the police at the time,' said Banks after a brief pause. 'But you know that, don't you? Because of you, more innocent girls had to suffer at Frank Dowson's hands. None of them were stabbed, the way Wendy was, but that's probably because they couldn't identify him. Some of them might have wished since that they had been killed. Either way, you've got blood on your hands, Mick.'

'That's not down to me! You can't blame me for you lot not doing your jobs properly.'

Banks took several deep breaths. He was beginning to wish he'd ordered a real drink, driving or not. 'Just a couple more points before I go,' he said, as calmly as he could.

'Anything.'

'Where's Billy Dowson these days?'

'He's dead,' said Charlton. 'Ten years or more. Drug overdose.'

So Billy Dowson could hardly be involved in the wedding shootings, Banks thought, mentally scratching his name off the list. But could one of them – Ricky, Mark, Tommy, even Charlton himself – for some reason he didn't yet know? 'And his sister, Cilla?'

'Who knows. Probably dead, too, the state she was in back then. Went off to London, didn't she? And before you ask, Billy's father's dead, too.'

'Shot? Stabbed?'

'Natural causes. He had a massive stroke.'

'Hallelujah. So there is divine justice, after all. How about Wendy's brother, Mark Vincent?'

'I've bumped into him one or twice over the years. He joined the army. Paras, I think.'

'When did you last see him?'

Charlton broke eye contact.

'You'd better tell me the truth, Mick.'

'It was a while ago. We didn't keep in touch.'

'How long ago?'

'March last year.'

'Around the time Frank Dowson died in prison?'

'Just after.'

'Why did you meet him then?'

'He just happened to be in town. Passing through. He dropped by the office, asked about the others, suggested we could all maybe get together one evening for a few bevvies, like.'

'And?'

'Well, it sounded like a good idea to me. I was in touch with Ricky Bramble and Tommy Jackson, so I suggested to them and they were both keen, too.'

'Where did this get together of yours take place?'

'Pub in town. Whitelock's. In the—'

'I know where it is. How did the evening turn out?'

'Fine. Mostly.'

'You all still got along?'

'Well, people change, you know. Mark was sort of different. He'd seen action overseas. It changes you, that sort of thing.'

'In what way?'

'It's hard to explain. You get harder, maybe, less caring. The way he talked about the people in those countries he fought in, as if they were subhuman. To be quite honest he looked as if he'd just come out of prison.'

'How do you mean?'

'Pale, scruffy, down on his luck. It's kind of an aura. I've had plenty of ex-cons applying for jobs, and I've even employed some of them. You get to know the signs.'

'Did Mark Vincent want a job?'

'As a matter of fact, he did, but I didn't have any openings. And he didn't have the qualifications. He hadn't learned a trade in the army, either, certainly no electrical stuff.'

'So you turned him down?'

'Gently.'

'How did he take it?'

'A shrug and a sneer, like he was letting me know he knew I was saying no because he was down on his luck, because he seemed like a desperate bum.'

'What did you talk about that night?'

'The past, mostly. See, Mark was always devoted to his big sister. To Wendy. He came from a tough family, his parents were always at each other's throats, and his, and she was like some sort of guardian angel to him. Protected him when his father got pissed and violent. Fed him when their mother spent the grocery money on ciggies and gin. That sort of thing. Stood up for him against bullies. She was a fairly strong lass, fine hockey player. He was devastated when it happened, young as he was. Never really got over it, if you ask me.'

'That why he joined the Paras?'

'Maybe. I don't know. We weren't in touch a lot by then. His parents split up not long after Wendy's death and farmed him out to some aunt and uncle or other out Castleford way. What I heard was he kept on getting in trouble with the police and it was either jail or the army. He was sixteen when he joined up.'

'Anything interesting happen that night?'

'As a matter of fact, it did. Mostly we were talking about old times. Mark was asking about people we'd all known back then, what they were doing now. We mentioned Maureen, and Ricky happened to know she'd got married to some banker and changed her name to Tindall. And that her daughter was Laura Tindall, the model. Ricky's sister Susan still keeps in touch with Maureen on and off.'

'You told Mark Vincent this?'

'It came up in conversation, that's all.'

'Did you talk about Laura's forthcoming wedding?'

'No. We didn't know about it then. At least, it hadn't been announced, and Susan hadn't mentioned anything.'

'Go on.'

'Anyway, we got on to talking about Wendy taking the short cut through the woods and all, and Ricky Bramble said Susan told him she saw Wendy waiting at a bus stop. She asked her where she was going, and Wendy said she was supposed to be going in town shopping with Maureen Grainger, but Maureen hadn't shown up. She said not to tell anyone because she wasn't supposed to hang out with Wendy, but this was years later, like, so Susan didn't think secrecy mattered any more. Anyway, Susan just walked on, heard the bus come and go, turned and saw Wendy hadn't got on it. Instead, she was crossing the road to the lane that led to the woods. That was all.'

'Was this the first time you'd heard that story?'

'Yes,' said Charlton. 'Ricky said his sister had thought it was best not to tell the police. You know how kids can be about keeping secrets. It all seems so important. The cops talked to all of us, like. Susan didn't want to tell them she was probably the last person to see Wendy alive, did she? You didn't get involved with the law. It was that kind of estate. We took care of our own.'

'You didn't do a very good job with Frank Dowson, did you?'

Charlton stared into his glass.

'How did Mark Vincent react?'

'He left. Just like that. Turned very pale, even paler than before, drained his pint, plonked his glass down on the table almost hard enough to break it, and left without so much as a goodbye, lads, nice to see you again.'

'And did you have any idea why he did that?'

'Course. I might be a bit thick, but I'm not stupid. It must have been a hell of a shock to his system, like, finding out that maybe if Maureen Grainger had turned up to meet Wendy like she said she would, they'd have gone into town to shop, and none of the rest would have happened. Wendy would have still been alive and his life wouldn't have been ruined.'

Banks could do nothing but shake his head slowly at what he was hearing. '"A hell of a shock",' he repeated. 'Yes, I suppose it must have been. Do you know where Mark Vincent lives now?'

'No idea. Probably living rough somewhere.'

Banks took a copy of the sketch Ray had done out of his briefcase. 'Could this be him?'

Charlton studied it then handed it back. 'Could be, I suppose. The hair's right. Short and curly. Nose and eyes, too. Yeah, it could be Mark, all right.'

'Do you know if Mark Vincent had a tattoo?'

'Yeah. On his chest. He had it done in the army. He showed us it in Whitelock's. Wings with a parachute superimposed. Really cool.'

In itself, Banks thought, the story was nothing much. A young girl went off snogging with her boyfriend instead of turning up to meet her friend. But that friend got killed, and her brother, who had seen Maureen with a boy, was devoted to his sister. What happened brought his whole life crashing down. His parents split up, he was sent to live with relatives and he became a troubled young man before joining the army at an early age. If Mark Vincent had enough psychological damage to begin with, he could have had a motive for the shooting. The triggers were all there: the new attention given to his sister's murder in the media, the conviction and death of Frank Dowson, the revelation that Maureen had been supposed to meet Wendy, and the publicity surrounding the forthcoming Tindall–Kemp wedding. He already knew Maureen's married name, and the odds were pretty good that if he saw a photo of her in the paper, it wouldn't take him long to put two and two together. There were also ways of checking.

Was it enough? Banks was beginning to think they had a possible suspect in Mark Vincent and needed to find out as much about him as possible. They also needed to find him. They had Ray's sketch, which was a start, but a real photograph would be even better.

14

AC Gervaise had offered Gerry only DC Doug Wilson and PC Neil Stamford to help trace Mark Vincent, and while Stamford worked the phones from the incident room downstairs, and Doug Wilson questioned Edgeworth's friends at the White Rose and the shooting club, Gerry cracked her knuckles and tilted the screen to suit her angle of vision. Where to begin? That was the question. She needed to find out as much as she could about Mark Vincent as quickly as possible, so they could make an assessment as to whether they were dealing with the killer or a red herring. Detective Superintendent Banks had phoned from Leeds and told her that Mark seemed to resemble Ray's sketch, and why he might have had a motive for the shooting.

In the first place, no matter what tricks PC Stamford tried, he couldn't come up with a current address for a Mark Vincent. Gerry had half-expected that and assumed he was operating under an alias. Gord, perhaps? It would be Wilson's and Stamford's job to see if that were the case and they could get past that little problem and find out what name he was using.

Banks had already told her the basic details of what happened to him after Wendy's murder. Digging a little deeper, she found that he had been born on 24 April 1953 and in 1964, after failing his eleven plus, he had attended Armley Park Secondary Modern School. Not long after his sister's murder, his parents split up and he was sent to live with an aunt and uncle near Castleford, where he attended a local secondary modern.

In the army, after basic training at Catterick, where he was apparently discovered to be an excellent marksman, Mark assumed active duty as a private in the 1st Battalion. Shortly after his eighteenth birthday, he was posted to Northern Ireland. His history there was sketchy. Gerry also discovered that the emblem of the regiment was a pair of wings with a parachute at their centre, and that many soldiers had this tattooed on their upper arms or chests, sometimes with the words PARACHUTE REGIMENT tattooed in a semi-circle above or below the emblem. Banks had told her that Michael Charlton, one of the old gang members, had seen this tattoo less than a year ago.

As Gerry went through the main points, she made notes. Later she would make some phone calls. The forces could be very cagey about giving out information, but she knew a major in the army equivalent of Human Resources at Catterick who had helped her in the past. Aunt Jane would be able to fill a few gaps, she was certain. It might cost Gerry a posh meal, as Aunt Jane loved her gourmet food, but it would be worth it. She was also good company.

Mark Vincent later turned up as a corporal in the Falklands War at the age of twenty-nine then disappeared again until he was promoted to sergeant in 1988. That didn't last long, and he remained a corporal from then on. He would have been forty-seven by the time he turned up in Kosovo in 2000, Gerry reckoned. It didn't seem like a very distinguished career, and the details of his discharge were vague to the point of being useless. Reading between the lines, Gerry guessed at best dishonourable, and at worst something to do with a massacre of innocent women and children, but again, perhaps Aunt Jane would be able to help.

Vincent had been in Iraq for just a few months, in Basra, when he finally parted company with the army in 2003 at the age of fifty. The silences were beginning to tell her a lot more than skimpy details at this point. In the early noughties, it seemed that Vincent turned to a life of crime. He spent a short term in prison between 2008 and 2010 for burglary, then another, longer sentence for arson in 2012. Apparently, he had set fire to a failing business on the owner's instructions for a share of the insurance money. He had also been suspected of involvement in people-trafficking young girls from the Balkans for sex, but the police had insufficient evidence to charge him. He didn't come out of jail until February 2016, shortly after Frank Dowson had been convicted of Wendy Vincent's murder.

Jenny Fuller might be able to fill in some of the psychological insights once Gerry had managed to flesh out Vincent's biography, but the skeleton of it was already in place. With any luck, Aunt Jane would be able to provide some illumination on the army's role. And there would certainly be more details of his criminal activities in the West Yorkshire police files. She had called Banks to ask if he would get DCI Blackstone to dig around in the records a bit. Banks said he would. Gerry was beginning to think that the super was as convinced as she was that Mark Vincent was their man, and that he was still somewhere within their reach.

Perhaps the most important thing Gerry had learned was that Vincent had a criminal record, which meant there would be a photograph of him in the online archive.

All in all, she thought, turning away from the screen and scribbling more notes on her pad, it hadn't been a bad afternoon's work.

★   ★   ★

Ken Blackstone remained a staunch curry fan, though Banks found that spicy food was giving his digestion more gyp the older he became. He made sure to take an acid reducer before they settled down in the Indian restaurant on Burley Road that evening, on the southern fringe of the University of Leeds student area, and ordered a couple of pints of lager, samosas to start, then vindaloo for Blackstone and a lamb korma for Banks, with aloo gobi, rice and plenty of naans. Streetlights reflected in the wet dark streets through the plate-glass window. Passing cars sent up sheets of water from the gutters. Inside, the mingled smells of the cumin, cardamom and coriander overcame all Banks's initial reservations, but he tapped his pocket to make sure he had more antacid tablets with him, just in case. Blackstone smiled.

'It's all very well for you to smirk,' said Banks. 'We don't all have cast-iron stomachs.'

'Obviously not.'

'Anyway, cheers.' They clinked glasses.

'What brings you down to our fair city?' Blackstone asked.

Banks explained about Martin Edgeworth and how an old murder had turned up in the background of the mother of the bride.

'So you didn't get the right man?'

'I don't think so. I think he was set up, poor sod.'

'And this old murder is the answer?'

'Could be. It might help provide us with one, at any rate. I was sceptical at first. Gerry's apt to go running after any new idea that comes her way. But she's sharp, and she has good instincts.'

'So what can I do?'

'It was on your patch, quite a bit before your time, but you might have heard of Frank Dowson.'

'Of course. One of our big cold-case successes. He raped and stabbed a teenage girl in 1964.'

'Right.'

'But he's dead,' said Blackstone. 'Died in prison last March.'

'I know that. It's not him I'm after. It's the victim's brother.'

'Wendy Vincent's brother?'

'Yes. Mark. He was eleven at the time.'

Blackstone bit into a samosa and washed it down with lager. 'Why now, after so long?'

'I've thought about that a lot,' said Banks. 'It was one of my first objections against Gerry's theory. But people do nurse grudges. Feelings do fester. All they need is the right trigger, or triggers, and there were plenty of those.'

'The trial?'

'Among other things.' Banks told him about his chat with Michael Charlton and Wendy waiting for Maureen at the bus stop. 'And after him,' he went on, 'I tracked down a second old "gang" member. A bloke called Ricky Bramble. Quite happily retired, and devoted to his allotment.'

'Was he any use?'

'Well, he confirmed what Charlton told me about his sister talking to Wendy Vincent at the bus stop, and about Mark Vincent's reaction. He also confirmed that Mark Vincent doted on his big sister.'

'Nobody dotes on their big sisters,' said Blackstone. 'Believe me. I know. I have two.'

Banks laughed. 'Well,' he went on, 'everyone knew that Wendy did sort of take care of her little brother, look out for him. Their parents weren't always a lot of use, especially when they'd been drinking, which was most of the time, and Wendy took Mark under her wing. Protected him. But it seems that it was the memory of Wendy that haunted Mark. According to Bramble, after the murder, and years later, when they met up again only a year or so ago, Mark used to talk about places he and Wendy had been when they were kids, hiding places from their parents, the little kindnesses she'd done for him, how she made him laugh and how angelic she was. He carried a photograph of her in his wallet. He even tried to describe what he thought she would look like today if she were still alive. It's pretty weird stuff. And Ricky Bramble also verified that the sketch looked a lot like the Vincent he met last year.'

'So her brother idolised her after her death?'

'Yes,' said Banks. 'Like Thomas Hardy did with his first wife Emma. They hardly talked for years, but when she died, he wrote some beautiful poems about their early days, being in love, travelling around the Cornish coast.' As he spoke, Banks thought about Emily Hargreaves. Was he doing the same with her, despite what Julie Drake had told him? Perhaps. He certainly found it impossible to blame her for the action she had taken, hurtful though it was to him. And when he pictured her, it was the youthful, beautiful 'first girl I ever loved' that he saw. Life can push people in unexpected directions, but he thought he would probably always feel that way about Emily. She was one of those rare girls that you just felt you wanted to be always happy, even if you weren't going to be the source of that happiness.

'And then Ricky Bramble comes out with a story about Wendy and Maureen that Mark never knew before,' Banks went on, 'and it knocks him for six.'

Suddenly, Banks thought, Maureen was a slag who was snogging some kid in an old house instead of meeting her friend to go shopping, and that cost her friend her life. Mark had made a paragon of Wendy and a pariah of Maureen. The angel and the whore. And as much as Wendy had become a symbol of purity to him over the years, enshrined in loving memory, the more easily Maureen now became the harlot, the betrayer, the destroyer. At least that was how Banks saw it. And the last straw: the wedding announcement. Maureen

Tindall, mother of the happy, affluent, successful bride, marrying not just an ex-soldier, but a successful one, a true hero. All the things Mark Vincent had never had or had never been. That must have hurt.

Banks picked up his briefcase. 'Gerry found out that Vincent has picked up a criminal record since he left the Paras.' He told Blackstone about Mark Vincent's prison terms for burglary and arson and suspicion of being involved in the traffic of young girls from Eastern Europe. 'It happened on your patch, so I'm hoping you've got something on him in records. Particularly a good photograph.'

Blackstone flipped through the file. 'I'm sure we do,' he said. 'We photograph everyone we charge, and it should all be on the national database, along with DNA and fingerprints. But you already know that.'

'I was just hoping you might be able to dig out something a bit better than the mugshot from the archive.'

'I suppose we could try. We might have something. It's not as if you're asking about a fifty-year-old case this time, the way you usually do. Our recent records are actually in pretty good shape. And I even know where to get my hands on them.'

Banks scooped up a mouthful of korma with his naan. 'I'm sure you do,' he said, when he had eaten it. It burned all the way down, even though the waiter had assured him it was mild. Banks glugged some chilled lager.

'When would you like this information?'

'Tomorrow morning will do.'

Blackstone made a mock salute. 'No problemo, sir. I'll have one of my lads get right on it. Would you be requiring a scan, JPEG or courier job?'

'What a bewildering array of choices. What's fastest?'

'JPEG, probably. I can email it to you.'

'That'll do nicely, then.'

'Your wish, my command.'

Banks grinned. 'Thanks, Ken. I owe you.'

'I'll add it to the list.'

They ate and drank in silence for a while, then Blackstone ordered a couple more pints of lager. Banks could use another one by then; his gut was burning. The nachos had had the same effect the other day. He wondered if there was something seriously wrong with him. Cancer, or something. Or a heart attack. Didn't they sometimes start with what felt like indigestion? Maybe he should get checked out. On the other hand, it could just be a simple case of indigestion. In fact, the more he thought about it, the more he felt it easing off, fading into the distance. He'd take another antacid later.

'So tell me about your love life,' Blackstone said.

'What love life?'

'A little bird tells me that your profiler is back in town. Jenny Fuller.'

'Are there no secrets?'

'Word travels fast, old son. So? Is it true?'

'That she's back? Yes. She's been gone a long time, Ken. A lot of water under the bridge.'

'Oh, don't try to fob me off with clichés.'

'I'm not. There's nothing to tell.'

'You must know whether you're in with a chance.'

'I don't, Ken. Really, I don't. I don't even know if I want to be.'

'But you've talked about it, haven't you? I can tell. That's how it starts, you know.'

'She's still finding her feet. She thinks our moment may have passed.'

'Bollocks. I doubt it's her feet you're interested in, though who knows? It takes all sorts. But I'd hurry up if I were you, mate, or believe me, someone will get there before you. From what I heard she's still a bit of all right.'

'A bit of all right? Christ, Ken, I haven't heard that expression in years. Not since I was a teenager, at any rate. *A bit of all right?*'

'OK, sorry. Getting carried away. But you'd be a fool not to go for it, you mark my words. Unless you're too busy dallying with that poet of yours.'

'She's not mine, and I'm not dallying with her.'

'"Had we but world enough, and time . . ."'

Banks laughed. 'Who's the poetry fan now?' He realised that he sometimes got too lost in morose thoughts and memories when he was alone for too long, and someone like Ken brought him out of himself. Banks was a man who took his life and his job very seriously indeed, but he was able to laugh at himself, too. He was tempted to tell Blackstone about Emily, and what Julie Drake had revealed to him on Saturday night, but that still felt too close to home, too private, too raw. He didn't think he could bear to tell anyone. Not yet. Maybe not ever.

'It's one of the few I know,' said Blackstone. 'I've even tried it out a couple of times on dates but it's never worked.'

They finished their food, paid the bill and lingered over their drinks for a while longer. Eventually Blackstone said, 'You're obviously not driving home tonight. Let's get a cab, go back to mine and have a nightcap. I just picked up a jazz CD that might interest you. Maria Schneider, *The Thomson Fields*. Heard it?'

'No.'

'You'll like it. But let's go, before it gets too late. I don't know about you, but I'm not the night owl I used to be any more. You can come to the station with me in the morning before you set off home, and we'll see what we can find on your Mark Vincent.'

Banks finished his pint. 'Sounds like a plan to me,' he said.

★   ★   ★

Gerry made her way up the A1 for her meeting with Aunt Jane that evening. It was full dark already, and the road was busy with the last of the rush-hour traffic. Her windshield wipers were whipping back and forth at top speed to clear the filthy spray thrown up by the lorries ahead of her. The A167 through Northallerton would probably have been a more pleasant drive, Gerry thought as she slowed down for the roadworks north of Scotch Corner. Though the rain had stopped for now, for which Gerry was grateful, when she looked out from side to side, she saw lights gleaming on lakes where there should be fields. This was the danger point. The ground was so waterlogged that it couldn't absorb any more moisture. One more heavy shower and banks would be broken and barriers breached. Low-lying neighbourhoods would be flooded, streets evacuated, and perhaps even people would be killed.

She pulled into the village of Hurworth-on-Tees and parked outside the church opposite the Bay Horse, where she had arranged to meet Aunt Jane for dinner. It was an expensive restaurant, she knew. She had been once before with a potential boyfriend who had been trying to impress her. The meal had impressed her very much, but unfortunately the suitor hadn't. Her girlfriends had always said she was too fussy when it came to boyfriends, that she never gave anyone long enough to get to know them, but from Gerry's point of view, she wasn't so desperate for a man that she was willing to take the second rate. And in her experience the second rate didn't take long to spot, and was second rate for good reason.

Aunt Jane was already waiting at a table Gerry had reserved in the warm, soft glow of the dining room. The voices of the other diners were muffled and the servers came and went without fuss. She hoped she might be able to get some useful information tonight. She had been disappointed by the mugshot on the police Internet archive. It *resembled* the person in Ray Cabbot's sketch, but not enough.

Aunt Jane stood up to greet her, all six foot two of her. Gerry thought herself tall at six foot, and indeed she seemed so at work around her colleagues – only Winsome Jackman matched her – but Aunt Jane put her in the shadow. She was broad-shouldered and full-figured, clearly fit and sturdy, but in no way unfeminine. In fact, Gerry noticed a number of men in the dining room sneak an admiring glance as she stood up. Jane also looked a good ten or more years younger than fifty. Her blond hair was piled high, and that made her seem even taller. Statuesque was the word that came into Gerry's mind. She wasn't wearing a uniform tonight, but a simple black dress with a high neckline and a red waistcoat buttoned up the front. Bangles jingled like wind chimes around her wrists, and a simple string of pearls hung around her neck. The hoop earrings were just the right size. As usual, Gerry marvelled at her elegance just as much as she had marvelled years earlier.

Aunt Jane was an honorary title. There was no blood relation between the two. She was Gerry's mother's best friend from their schooldays and, though the two had gone in very different directions, the friendship had endured. When Gerry was younger, they didn't see much of Aunt Jane, who, she later learned, had been serving in both Afghanistan and Iraq, but when she did come to town it was like Christmas. Her energy and enthusiasm for just about everything were infectious, and although Aunt Jane and Gerry's mother were the same age, to Gerry, Aunt Jane always seemed more vibrant, more fun and far, far more cool. That was unfair to her mother, she now realised, but back then she had just been an impressionable child. Aunt Jane had taught her a few martial arts moves to use against the boys who pulled her hair at school; Aunt Jane had taken her for a pillion ride on her motorcycle and made her promise never to tell her mother; Aunt Jane had helped her choose the colours that suited her and showed her how to apply lipstick, eye-liner and mascara before she was officially allowed to wear make-up by her parents. And then, of course, she had disappeared back to Afghanistan again as suddenly as she had arrived. A leg injury caused by an IED had put paid to her active service, and she now walked with a slight limp, like Terry Gilchrist, but the army had found her a suitable desk job at Catterick, and she had seemed happy enough to leave the world of action behind.

'Well, look at you, stranger,' Aunt Jane said as they both sat down. 'It's been too long. Why haven't you been to see me? It's not as if I'm far away now you're up in Eastvale.'

'I know. I'm sorry,' said Gerry. 'Just, you know, being the new girl and all . . . it's a hard job.'

Aunt Jane smiled. 'No need to tell *me* that,' she said. 'I just miss my old friend Geraldine, that's all. You must come and see me more often.'

'I'd like that,' said Gerry. Aunt Jane was the only person apart from her mother who called her Geraldine.

'How's Tess – I mean your mother. I haven't heard from her in ages, either.'

'She's fine,' said Gerry.

'Still lecturing at the poly?'

'It's a university now,' said Gerry. 'They all are. Have been for years. But, yes, she's still working.'

'Dad still drafting wills?'

Gerry laughed. 'He's still working, yes.'

'Good for him. Aidan's still carrying a torch for you, you know.'

Gerry felt herself blush. Aidan was Aunt Jane's son, and they had been out together a few times in their teens. 'I thought he was married now.'

'Oh, he is,' said Aunt Jane. 'Mariette. Nice enough girl. But it doesn't stop him pining for you.'

'Oh, stop it,' said Gerry. 'You're embarrassing me.'

'You always did embarrass easily. Shall we study the menus? Wine?'

Jane already had a glass full of red wine in front of her, and the bottle stood open on the table.

'Just a drop,' said Gerry. 'I'm driving.'

Jane poured her some wine. A bit more than a drop, in Gerry's opinion, but she said nothing. 'And in case you're wondering,' Jane said. 'I'm not. Driving, that is. One of the perks of rank.'

They clinked glasses and Jane put on her reading glasses to examine the menu. In the end they both decided to have moules marinière for starters and settled on pan-fried halibut with black carrots and various foams, ketchups and sauces for Gerry, and for Jane a 28-day matured fillet steak, cooked rare, with hand-cut chips, onion rings and vegetables. They put in their orders and leaned back in their chairs.

'You were asking about a Mark Vincent,' Jane said finally. 'May I ask why?'

Gerry leaned forwards and lowered her voice. She had known when she set up the meeting that if she expected to get information she had to be willing to give some, and she trusted Aunt Jane as much as she trusted anyone. More than most, in fact. 'He's a suspect in a case we're working on,' she said.

Jane narrowed her eyes. 'Well, I assumed that much,' she said. 'What case? And don't try to weasel out of it.'

'A shooting. A mass shooting.'

'The Red Wedding?'

'Shhh,' said Gerry, glancing around nervously. 'Yes.'

Jane topped up her glass and offered to pour more for Gerry, who declined. 'You're working on that? How exciting. I thought you'd got your man, though. How much of a suspect is he?'

'Hard to say just yet. That's why I wanted to talk to you.'

'You know I can't give you any details? National security and all that. The army likes its privacy. We don't like to be held too accountable for our actions. We don't like to let people know what we're up to. We always have a get-out-of-jail-free card up our sleeve.'

Gerry laughed. 'I know,' she said. 'I'd just like to know anything you *can* tell me about his military career.'

'Oh, there's plenty I *can* tell you. I had a good nose around after you phoned, even talked to some people who knew him. And if it helps you, that's all well and good, as long as nobody else knows where it came from.'

'I've got no problem with that,' Gerry said. 'If it helps, I'm just trying to get some kind of confirmation that we're on the right track. I'm pretty sure of it, but we have no real evidence yet.'

Jane swirled the wine in her glass. 'Well, I can't answer that question for you,' she said. 'Mark Vincent was nothing unusual. He had a few problems, but who doesn't?'

'So how did you, or the army, deal with his problems? And what were they?'

Jane sighed. 'You have to understand, dear, that in addition to other things, we're quite tolerant of our own. As you know, we have internal systems of discipline, rules and regulations. They're as much meant to protect us from the outside as they are to enforce justice and punishment within the services. To put it bluntly, no matter what the recruitment adverts and friendly websites tell you about careers and what have you, all that goes out of the window in wartime. In wartime, a soldier's job is to kill people, and we will forgive him an awful lot if he just does that one job exceptionally well.'

'And Mark Vincent did?'

'There was a war of some sort or another throughout most of Mark Vincent's army career. Like many other soldiers in his position, he saw far more action than any human being should have to see, and he endured it. Don't you think that takes a sacrifice, maybe rips out a little part of your soul? We also asked him to do things that no decent human being should ever have to do. Whatever we may be, us soldiers are not automatons. We are not without conscience, human feeling, compassion even. At least we start out with those things. In some cases, they get knocked out of us over the years. That may have been the case with Mark Vincent.'

Their moules arrived and both sat in silence for a while to enjoy them. 'What was the general consensus on Vincent?' Gerry asked.

Jane paused with her fork in mid-air. 'Mark Vincent was a violent and disturbed young man when he joined up. He had a lot of anger, and we taught him to channel and direct that anger and violence. Which, when you think about it, is hardly unusual in the army. As a rule, we can direct violence against the enemy, but if you're asking me whether I think he's the kind of man who could direct it against someone he thought had betrayed or crossed him, then I'd have to say yes. But that's just an opinion based on an afternoon spent reading files and talking to people about him. And I'm not a psychologist.'

'Don't worry. I'm not going to quote you,' Gerry said. 'Did he ever train as a sniper?'

Jane hesitated before going on. 'The army doesn't like to talk about things like that,' she said, 'but yes, he did. He was an excellent shot, and he had no compunction about killing strangers from a distance. It would have been a waste not to train him. And use him.'

'Did he have mental problems?'

'Of course he did. Show me a soldier who doesn't. Sometimes mental problems can be valuable assets in the military. Oh, we have our psychiatrists and so on, but it's not like you can patch up a psyche in a field hospital the way you can a gunshot wound or an IED injury. And it's not as if our shrinks have the time it takes to spend on fixing these minds. Years of therapy? No chance. Many of them go undiagnosed. PTSD, for example. There's been a lot of talk about that recently.'

'Did Vincent suffer from PTSD?'

'Hard to answer. I'd reckon that he probably did – at least he suffered some of the symptoms. He was never diagnosed – he never spent long enough with a psychiatrist for that – but in my layperson's opinion, from what I've read, and what people have told me, I'd say he did. According to one report I saw, he suffered from headaches and insomnia, and he had difficulty controlling his emotions and forming relationships with others. There were also issues of substance abuse, again not uncommon in PTSD cases, or in combat, for that matter – just think *Apocalypse Now*.'

Gerry had never seen *Apocalypse Now*, but she didn't want to let on to Jane. 'Drugs?' she said.

'In Mark Vincent's case, the doctor thought it was mostly alcohol, though other drugs may have been involved. You should remember that pretty much all of this was only discovered towards the end of his military career, shortly before his discharge. He never underwent any serious psychiatric evaluation.'

'I got the impression, reading between the lines,' said Gerry, 'that the discharge was dishonourable.'

'Well, that's true to some extent,' Jane said, 'but we prefer a mutual parting of the ways, if we can work one out. I'm sure you have the same policy with bent coppers when you can get away with it. Far less headline-grabbing. And Mark Vincent had certainly served long enough to retire gracefully.'

'He didn't object?'

'No. He took the package, as they say in business.'

'Did his discharge involve anything to do with a civilian massacre?'

'I know of no such massacre.'

'Kosovo?'

Aunt Jane remained silent for a while. 'It takes a long time for these things to come out, for the investigation into allegations to be completed, probably much like your business.'

'So he was?'

Aunt Jane merely smiled.

'I also think he made connections there he used later when he was involved in people-trafficking,' Gerry went on. 'Especially young girls in the sex trade.'

'Well,' said Aunt Jane. 'I wouldn't deny that such things happen. Soldiers do sometimes come into contact with criminal elements.'

'But he was also promoted to sergeant at one point. How on earth did that come about?'

'How do these things usually come about? Deceptive appearances. Human error. He was good at getting people to do things, and that's one trait you want in a sergeant. Leadership quality. Unfortunately, as we discovered too late, Vincent was only good at getting people to do things that benefitted himself, not the army as a whole. I never came into contact with him, you understand, so I'm speaking very much as an outside observer here, based on official reports and a couple of off-the-record conversations, but I'm pretty good at reading between the lines, and I'd say Vincent was charming and manipulative when he wanted to be. And he did have a bit of a temper.'

'How did it manifest?'

'Bar brawls, that sort of thing. Fighting in general. Again, that's not so unusual for a soldier. He was quite a decent boxer in the ring, too. Controlled and disciplined.'

They finished their moules just as the main courses arrived. Jane worked her way through the wine as she ate her bloody steak. Gerry had only taken a few sips of her first glass. Mostly because she was driving, but partly because the rich and complex red wine didn't go very well with moules or halibut. 'What kind of state was he in after he left the army?'

'I've no idea what became of him. Maybe you can fill me in on that?'

'Petty crime,' said Gerry. 'Assaults, arson, prison, that possible involvement in people-trafficking I mentioned earlier.'

'Not surprising. It's what I would have predicted from what I've read. At least the army gave him a rudder to steer by and a structure and shape to his life. Without them, he'd have been lost. I've seen his type before, far too often. When they first come to us, it's generally because someone has told them – either you lot or their parents – that it's either prison or the army. And when they leave us, as often as not it's prison they drift towards.'

'I thought the army was supposed to make men out of boys?'

'You can't make a silk purse out of a sow's ear, Geraldine. You ought to know that in your line of work.'

'But was there a specific incident? He was in Iraq at the time, wasn't he?'

'Yes. Basra.' Jane finished her steak, pushed the dish away. She had finished her wine, and the alcohol seemed to be having no effect on her. 'But as I hinted earlier, it was mostly a matter of the Balkans catching up with him. In Iraq it was petty crime, mostly. Black market, that sort of thing.'

'And in Kosovo?'

'Other things. Many just rumours. Most not proven.'

'What sort of things?'

'That he was rough with women. Certain kinds of women. Rumour has it he beat up a prostitute once. There were several unexplained murders. Nothing we could pin on Mark Vincent, of course, but in retrospect . . . One way or another, Mark Vincent became a liability. You can argue that it should have happened sooner, but . . . what can I say? Hindsight makes visionaries of us all.'

'What was the problem with women?'

'Same problem as with so many men. Women were all sluts to him. Except his dear dead sister, of course. She was an angel.'

'How do you know about that?'

'According to one of the men I talked to, someone who knew Mark Vincent, he used to go on and on about her, showed her photo around. It seems she died when he was quite young. Is this of any use?'

'Yes. We think this may all be connected with his sister's death.'

'How?'

The waiter arrived with the dessert menu. Jane studied it and decided on a cream cheese and vanilla mousse, while Gerry settled on a herbal tea. Jane gave her a pitying look. 'Oh, Geraldine, Geraldine,' she said. 'What *are* we to do with you?'

When the waiter came by, Jane ordered the mousse and a double Remy. Gerry thought about the bill and swallowed.

When the waiter had gone, Gerry told Aunt Jane about

what had happened to Mark Vincent's sister, and of Maureen Tindall's role in it.

'And he naturally thought that if this Maureen had turned up, his sister wouldn't have died?' she commented.

'Yes. I think so.'

'In his eyes, then, she was perhaps as responsible for the loss of his sister as the actual murderer himself?'

'That's about it.'

'Well that'd certainly do it, wouldn't it?'

'It seems so. But don't say anything, Aunt Jane. It's only a suspicion. I'm not supposed to talk about it.'

Jane put her hand on Gerry's arm. 'Don't worry, my dear, your secret's safe with me. But I'm puzzled. I read about that wedding, of course, and the mother of the bride survived, didn't she?'

'Yes. But he did kill her only child.'

'Good lord,' said Jane. 'How little we really know about people.'

Indeed, thought Gerry. The dessert arrived, along with Jane's double Remy and Gerry's chamomile tea. While Jane tucked into her sweet, Gerry sipped the tea and watched her with fascination. She didn't think she had ever met anyone before who gave herself so wholeheartedly to the act of eating.

'What are you going to do?' Jane asked.

'Now? First we have to find him.'

'He knows the area. He's spent time at Catterick on and off over the years.'

'Right.'

'And he's got survival skills. Done all the courses. You know, dropped in the Scottish Highlands with only a Mars bar and a compass. That sort of thing. Passed with flying colours. He could probably live in a box at the bottom of a lake with nothing but cold gravel for breakfast if he had to.'

'Thanks for that, Aunt Jane. He's been in jail since his army days, though, and it's more than likely he's gone a bit to seed.'

'Just letting you know what you're up against. Never mind the killing skills we taught him. Be very careful. And I think you can ditch the "aunt" by now, don't you?'

Gerry agreed, but she would always think of Jane as 'Aunt Jane'.

'My driver won't be here for another three-quarters of an hour,' Jane said, 'so I might as well have another cognac while I'm waiting, and you can entertain me with stories about your life in the police force until he gets here. Are you sure I can't tempt you to anything stronger than another herbal tea?'

'I'll have decaf coffee,' said Gerry in a small voice.

'How daring. By the way.' Jane reached for her bag. 'I've got a photo of Mark Vincent for you. It's not a very good one, I'm afraid, and it's a bit old, but it's all I could come up with at such short notice.'

15

'It's him. There's no doubt about it,' said Banks as they studied the four images stuck to the whiteboard the following day. The whole team had gathered in the boardroom as if for the unveiling of a significant new portrait. In a way, that was exactly what it was, confirmation that Ray Cabbot's sketch – up there with the three photographs – was of the man they were after, Mark Vincent, possibly the killer of six people, and certainly a person of interest.

It was mid-afternoon on Tuesday 12 January, and Banks had just got back from Leeds. First Gerry had filled everyone in about her meeting with Aunt Jane, keeping her identity secret, and then Banks told them all about what he had learned from Michael Charlton and Ricky Bramble.

Banks had been lucky in Leeds that morning. When he had accompanied Ken Blackstone to Elland Road after a late breakfast, they had managed to dig out a photograph of Mark Vincent from their files, a photograph taken by a CSI officer after Vincent had been arrested for assault. His injuries were insignificant compared to those of his victim, and it was his bruised and bleeding knuckles the CSI was most interested in. Nevertheless, he had managed to capture Vincent full face, in a far clearer image than the mugshot, and when all four images were tacked up together, it was clear to anyone that the mugshot, CSI photo, artist's impression and army photo were of the same man at different ages, the earliest of which, the army photograph, was twelve years old and the most recent, Ray's sketch, was based on a description given by someone who saw him last November, roughly a couple of months ago. Vincent had lost some weight in the interim, perhaps as a result of his term in prison, but the greying curls, the intense eyes, the beetle brows, the crookedness indicating a nose broken more than once were all giveaways.

Definitely Mark Vincent.

'Which brings us to the question of what we do next,' Banks went on.

'We bring him in for questioning, surely?' said AC Catherine Gervaise.

'First we have to find him. Gerry?'

'Still working on it, sir,' said Gerry Masterson. 'We have a list of properties within the boundaries I marked off according to Vincent's movements. Doug and Neil have been checking these out and showing Mr Cabbot's sketch around to landlords, neighbours, local shopkeepers and so on, but nothing yet. We can extend the boundaries if we draw a blank. Doug's also questioned some of the regulars at the White Rose and members of the shooting club. Nobody recognises the photograph or had heard Edgeworth mention anyone called Gord or Gordon. Three other members reported noticing a beat-up car behind them on the way home from the club on occasion, though they didn't seem especially perturbed by it. One said he thought it was an old Clio badly in need of a paint job.'

Banks laughed. 'I'll bet there are a few of those around. Thanks, Gerry. Keep at it.'

'About all we've got so far,' added Adrian Moss, 'is more reporters sniffing around. They've got wind of something, and the rumours that we're on to someone have already hit the early editions. Some bright sparks are even making a link with the Wendy Vincent case, so they know we've been investigating that somehow. We'll have to give them something soon. Maybe a press conference.'

'We're not ready for that yet,' said Banks. 'Can't you keep them at bay?'

'I can only do so much. The only thing they seem to find more interesting is the weather. Apparently, we're due for more rain tonight. Can't we use them, perhaps?'

'For what?'

'To help us find him. Let them print a photo, or the sketch. Give them his name. It might speed things up.'

'I don't see how it would,' Banks said.

'Well, we've got to give them something,' Moss said. 'Once they run out of rumours they'll simply start making things up.'

'Most of them wouldn't know the difference between the truth and fiction if it bit them on the arse,' Annie muttered.

Gervaise gave her a sharp look. 'I think we'd better find him before they make up anything close to the truth, hadn't we?' she said.

'And maybe we should be asking ourselves just how they get hold of these little snippets of information they make so much of,' Banks said.

Moss sniffed. 'That's easy. Most police stations have more holes than a sieve. These are experienced information gatherers, not thickies with a notebook and a pencil. They overhear things. They buy off-duty coppers a pint without revealing who they are. There are any number of ways they can get hold of information. There's no—'

'If I may say something,' Jenny Fuller interrupted.

'Go ahead, Jenny,' said Banks. Moss shuffled sulkily in his chair.

'In my opinion,' Jenny said, 'he's not going to scarper or go to ground because he hasn't finished yet. I think we can agree, after DC Masterson's military information, that this Mark Vincent was an excellent shot, a sniper, in fact. That being the case, if he had wanted to kill, or even wound, Maureen Tindall at the wedding, he could have done so quite easily. But he clearly didn't. Why? In my opinion, it's because first he wanted to hurt Maureen Tindall, to cripple her with loss and grief, so that she could feel what he felt when his sister was killed all those years ago. But that's not enough. If it *is* Mark Vincent, and if those are his motives, then it's not enough for him. It's not over yet. Wendy died, so Maureen Tindall has to die. He'll go after her. And remember, we also know that he has good survival skills, however rusty, and facility with firearms, which could be very dangerous indeed if he has managed to get hold of another pistol or rifle.'

'So what's he likely to do next?' Gervaise asked. 'Is he a psycho?'

'It would take far too long to go into the ins and outs of that diagnosis,' said Jenny. 'But the short answer is no, I don't think he's a psychopath, but I do think there's a very good chance he's the one you're looking for. At least he's not a "psycho" in the sense most people understand the term. He's certainly suffering from some sort dissociative disorder, and he appears to lack a conscience, or he wouldn't have been able to do what he did at the wedding. But perhaps his experiences in Kosovo, Afghanistan, Northern Ireland, Iraq and wherever else he fought did that to him. Dehumanised him. There may be reasons for that desensitisation in his military training and experience. After all, DC Masterson's source has already told us not only that Vincent trained as a sniper, but that he had no compunction about killing complete strangers from a distance, a positive quality in the army's eyes, but perhaps not so in civilian life. And we know that Vincent couldn't make the adjustment to civilian life. His criminal activities and prison record show that to some extent. He also exhibited some symptoms of PTSD, though he was never diagnosed or treated for it. The lack of ability to form and maintain relations is an important factor here.'

'But PTSD doesn't make murderers, does it?' said Gervaise.

'We don't know what makes murderers. If we did, we'd all be out of a job. I'm simply talking about the sheer mental burden this man is walking around with, not speculating on what it might cause him to do. And at the root of all this, or tangled up in it somehow, is his sister's murder. That's something he doesn't appear to be able to let go, even fifty years after it happened. And I think we are all agreed that the triggers were there in the cold case, Frank Dowson's imprisonment, finding out that Maureen didn't turn up as promised and, finally, the news about the forthcoming wedding. More than enough for someone in as fragile a state of mind as I imagine Mark Vincent is. Gerry, do you know what happened to the Vincent family in the immediate aftermath of the murder?'

Gerry shuffled through the pages of her notes. 'The parents split up three months after Wendy's murder. The father moved to Sheffield and remained on the dole. He died of cirrhosis in 1988. The mother went home to her own parents in Salford and sent Mark to live with an aunt and uncle in Ferry Fryston, near Castleford. There was an incident recorded in 1967. The details are a bit vague, but Mark Vincent was taken into care for a while.'

'Abuse?' said Gervaise.

'Sounds very much like it, ma'am. Naturally, the details are scrappy after so long, but the police and social services were involved, and there was an investigation of sorts before he was returned to the family. His aunt and uncle, that is. That's when Vincent first started getting in trouble with the law. Small stuff at first, shoplifting, handling stolen goods, starting little fires, then graduating to more serious stuff like muggings and the occasional burglary. As my source said, it was jail or the army. His mother cleaned up her act. Detox, AA. She died of a stroke in 2004.'

'Any brothers or sisters still living?' Jenny asked.

'Not according to my records.'

'Drugs? In connection with Vincent.'

'No mention,' said Gerry. 'Neither dealing nor using. Though my source did say that alcohol abuse was a significant factor in his later violent behaviour, and other drugs may have been involved. But there's no evidence, or even suspicion, that he was a heroin addict, for example, or a cokehead.'

'So what exactly do we do now?' asked Gervaise. 'Take Maureen Tindall into protective custody?'

'I'd suggest discreet surveillance,' said Banks. 'It gives us more chance of nabbing him in the act if he goes after her. But it's not without risk of scaring him off.'

'Maybe you should give her a choice,' Jenny said.

'She's not in good enough shape to make one,' said Annie. 'She's in a state of constant anxiety, she's scared all the time, jumps at shadows, feels guilty, ashamed. I know I'm not a psychiatrist, but there you are, that's my opinion, for what it's worth.'

'You're probably quite right,' said Jenny. 'And those issues would certainly throw her decision-making ability out of whack, to use a technical term.'

Even Annie smiled at that.

'Get an unmarked car to the Tindall house now,' said Gervaise. 'Tell them to park down the street and try to remain unobserved,' Gervaise said. 'And arrange to have someone watching the back, if there's access that way. You know the lie of the land better than I do.'

'Should we tell Mrs Tindall what we're doing, ma'am?' Gerry asked.

Gervaise glanced at Jenny, then at Annie. 'Well, you two?'

'No,' they both said at once.

'It would only alarm her, cause her to panic,' Jenny said.

'I think we should get her and her husband out of the house,' said Banks. 'Panic or not. Put them in a hotel or somewhere to make sure of their safety. Unless he's watching at the time, he won't know they're not there. If he is watching, maybe that'll give us a chance of capturing him. At least that way nobody's in danger, and we still stand a chance of getting our man.'

'But not of catching him in the act,' Annie said.

'It doesn't matter. We're not going to use Maureen Tindall as bait. And don't forget, all we have is circumstantial evidence and a very strong suspicion of Vincent's guilt. We'll need more than that if we want to get a conviction, and I'm hoping we'll get it when we have him in custody and question him, search his premises. I think we're all agreed that right now the main thing is finding him, right?'

They all agreed.

'Good,' said Gervaise. 'Make it so.'

Before they could all return to their respective tasks, a soft tap at the door was followed by the entry of a uniformed constable.

'Yes?' said Gervaise, shoving her files into her briefcase.

'Ma'am.' The constable took a deep breath, then said, 'Just heard from dispatch that they've had a 999 call from a Robert Tindall. He's the hus—'

'I know who he is,' said Gervaise. 'What did he want?'

'They couldn't make out what he was saying, ma'am. Not all of it. Said his voice sounded funny. But they think he said something about being hurt. They've sent an ambulance and a patrol car, but I just thought—'

'Thank you, Constable. Good thinking,' said Gervaise, and glanced at Banks. 'Better get over there, hadn't you?'

Banks and Annie set off for the Tindalls' house as the rain started to fall again, gently at first, then harder. Behind them were two patrol cars with their lights flashing and sirens blaring. It wasn't far, but by the time they got there the uniformed officer on duty outside the house informed them that Robert Tindall had been taken to A & E on the orders of the paramedic. He couldn't say whether Tindall's injuries were life-threatening or not, but his partner, who was still inside the house, had felt for a pulse and found one, and when the paramedics had pushed him out on a gurney, his head had been bandaged. So he was alive when they took him to hospital.

Banks noticed that the front door was splintered around the chain, which was hanging loose. It looked as if the door had been on the chain when Robert Tindall, or Maureen, had answered it, and whoever was standing there had kicked it open. There was something resembling a scuff, possibly made by someone's foot, on the front of the door.

The second patrol officer, who had remained inside the house, led them along the hall and showed them into the kitchen, where Tindall had been found. Banks and Annie stopped in the doorway to avoid contaminating the scene any further. There wasn't much to see, though there had clearly been a brief struggle, as a few plates lay broken on the floor, along with slices of some oranges and bananas, knives and forks scattered among the wreckage. There was also a pool of dark blood.

'Where's his wife?' Banks asked the constable. 'Maureen.'

The constable shook his head. 'There was no one else here when we arrived, sir. Just the man lying on the floor there.'

'This blood come from him?'

'It looked that way, sir.'

'Was he unconscious?'

'Not quite, but I'd say he was definitely stunned.'

'Could you tell how he'd been hurt? Gun? Knife?'

'No, sir. Nothing like that. From what I could tell, he was most likely hit on the head with that heavy wooden chopping block. You can see the blood on it if you look closely. I tried to touch things as little as possible.'

Banks looked and he did see blood on the chopping block. It was certainly heavy enough to deliver a nasty wound. He knew that head wounds bleed a lot, so the amount no longer seemed so significant as it had at first. On the other hand, a blow to the skull can cause any amount of damage, not all of it immediately apparent. 'Did he say anything?'

'He was struggling to speak, sir,' the constable said. 'But I couldn't make out any of it. It seemed like he was trying to say something important but it just wasn't coming out. Then the paramedic got to work and I got out of the way.'

Banks and Annie next made a quick search of the rest of the house but found nothing of interest. There was no blood to be seen anywhere else, and no signs of a struggle in any of the upstairs rooms. Whatever the interloper had done with Maureen Tindall, he hadn't done it in the house. Maureen was gone. Someone had taken her.

Back outside, Banks told the constable to organise a house-to-house of the neighbourhood and show Vincent's photo to everyone, and to pay particular attention to getting information on the car he was driving.

After the meeting, Gerry went back to her maps with a heightened sense of excitement. She felt a little annoyed at being left out of the trip to Eastvale General Infirmary, but realised there was no point in all of them being there. According to Banks, Robert Tindall would tell them what he could when he was able to talk. It might mean a lot of waiting around, hospitals being what they were, and she had important work to do, especially now that Maureen Tindall was missing, presumed abducted, according to Banks.

DC Wilson and PC Stamford were out interviewing local estate agents and farmers who rented out rooms and converted barn accommodations. It seemed a fairly thankless task, Gerry thought, especially in this weather, but it had to be done. Now they had a good likeness of their man – of Mark Vincent – they might get a more positive reaction to their enquiries.

Gerry looked over the OS Landranger map with a magnifying glass, feeling a bit like Sherlock Holmes as she scanned the squares for anything she might have missed. At one and a quarter inches to a mile, it was a fairly detailed sheet, but she decided it might be worth having a look at an Explorer map, two and a half inches to a mile. It would be less cluttered.

She spent a few minutes in the tiny station library looking through the racks, eventually found the area she wanted and took it back to the boardroom, where she tacked it gently with adhesive putty to the whiteboard. That was better, she thought, standing back to admire the precision draughtsmanship, translating the whirls and blobs into images of a vital, living landscape in her mind's eye. The symbols were larger and less likely to be obscured by contour lines, footpaths or village streets, and after a while of simply standing looking at it as she might a painting in the National Gallery, she spotted something she had overlooked. Pausing only to make a few jottings of locations in her notebook, she dashed back to the squad room, grabbed her raincoat and went down to the car park.

★   ★   ★

Robert Tindall had been moved to the head of the queue for immediate attention, and nobody would be allowed to see him until the doctors had determined the extent of the damage. So far, none of them had given away a thing.

The coffee was weak and the decor drab. It was bad enough that you had to be in a hospital, Banks thought, without having to put up with weak coffee and drab decor, too. He vaguely remembered a funny quote about wallpaper. Oscar Wilde, he thought it was. Wilde had all the best funny quotes. Still, Banks didn't suppose that patients in need of serious attention cared much about the decor, or the coffee, though no doubt an expensive survey would one day prove that a little colour in a patient's life could work miraculous cures.

He looked out of the window through the 'silken strings' of rain to the jaundiced streetlight in front of the Unicorn across the road. That would be an improvement, he thought. The decor was just as bad, but the beer was decent enough. He found himself wondering what Emily's hospital had been like, her last days, whether she'd been aware enough to notice or care. As he remembered, she was always very fussy about furniture and paint colours. Julie Drake said Emily spent as long as she could at home, but when the pain got too much, and a visiting nurse could no longer provide the level of care she needed, they took her to hospital. He thought about the other hospital, too, where she had had the abortion all those years ago. What had she felt like after that? Empty, he supposed. Wasn't that the cliché they always used in movies? Perhaps she had felt free, elated. But he doubted it. Empty was more like it. And he hadn't even known. Hadn't even been able to hold her hand or offer her any comfort, let alone suggest having the baby, getting married. Julie was most likely right. He would have tried, and he might have succeeded, and it would probably have been a big mistake. Let go with both hands. Smile and forget.

Banks became aware of the doctor talking. He hadn't noticed him walk in. 'It's not as serious as we thought,' he went on. 'He's lost some blood, and he's weak, but there's no skull fracture and no brain damage as far as we can make out. Mild concussion. We'll keep him in and monitor him overnight, carry out some tests. What was he hit with, by the way?'

'We think it was a chopping block,' said Banks. He had placed it in an evidence bag and passed it on to one of the uniformed officers before leaving for the hospital. 'Can we talk to him?'

'I don't see why not. But just for a few minutes. He's very tired.' He glanced at Annie. 'Just one of you, though, I'm afraid.'

'I'll wait here,' said Annie.

The doctor led Banks down the corridor and up in the lift to the private room where Robert Tindall lay on a plumped-up pillow with bandages around his head and various tubes and monitors attached to him. They seemed to subject you to that indignity even if all you came in with was a cut finger. 'And don't overexcite him,' the doctor admonished Banks as he walked off.

'God forbid,' Banks muttered under his breath.

The light was dim and the curtains closed. Banks could hear the wind-blown rain lashing against the windowpane, along with an annoying beep inside the room itself every two or three seconds. That was another thing he had noticed; there was always an annoying beep in hospital rooms.

Tindall's eyes were open, and Banks noticed signs of recognition. It was a good start. Tindall tried to sit up but couldn't make it. He reached out and grabbed Banks's wrist. His grasp was surprisingly strong. 'Mr Banks,' he said. His voice was soft but the words were formed clearly enough, and the anxiety and urgency in his tone were obvious. 'Can you tell me anything about Maureen? Please. What's happened to her? Where is she? Did he hurt her?'

'We don't know much yet,' said Banks, 'but there are no signs that he hurt her. Now calm down. The doctor says you need rest and shouldn't become too excited.'

'But I'm worried about her.'

'Of course you are. It's only natural. But we're doing everything in our powers to find her and bring her back home safe and sound.'

'Thank God. Are you sure she's not hiding in the house?'

'I'm afraid not. We searched the whole place and she's not there.'

'Where is she?'

'We don't know yet.' Banks took the West Yorkshire photo of Vincent out of his briefcase. It had been taken recently enough that it could definitely be matched to the man in Ray Cabbot's drawing, but it was far easier for people to make identification from an actual photograph rather than a drawing, Banks had found. Somehow, art makes us expect distortion and exaggeration, yet we take photographs as representations of the real.

'Do you recognise this man?' Banks asked.

Tindall fumbled for his glasses on the bedside table. He had a hard time getting them on with the bandages over his ears, but he managed it well enough to study the photograph and say almost immediately, 'Yes. That's the man. That's the man who hit me and grabbed Maureen.'

'Thank you,' Banks said. 'Do you know who he is?'

'No. He was a stranger. It was . . .' he paused and frowned, as if trying to think clearly. 'It was odd. As if Maureen seemed to recognise him just a split second before he grabbed her. Who is he?'

'His name is Mark Vincent.'

'Vincent? Vincent? Isn't that the name of that girl who was murdered? Maureen's friend. She made me watch the programme on TV, the fiftieth anniversary.'

'That's right,' said Banks. 'He's her brother.'

'But what's he . . . I mean, why would he . . .?'

'It's a long and complicated story,' said Banks, 'and I think your wife would be the best person to tell it to you. For now, though, it's enough for us to know this was the man.'

'Do you know where he lives?'

Banks had to admit that he didn't, and Tindall's face fell at that. 'Oh,' he said. It was little more than a sigh.

'But we've got men out all over the dale searching for her. Don't worry, Mr Tindall. We're closing in. We'll find her.'

Tindall seemed to listen to the rain. 'On a night like this?'

'Even on a night like this. Is there anything else you can remember that might help us? Did Vincent say anything?'

'No. He just kicked the door, broke the chain and rushed. He pushed me aside and headed straight for the kitchen. The light was on, so I suppose he must have realised Maureen was in there. It's right at the end of the hall. I ran after him as quickly as I could. I was a bit winded. But when I got there he picked up that heavy chopping block, whirled around and hit me. I felt this terrible pain on the side of my head and everything flashed and then went dark. Just before I lost consciousness, I saw him grab Maureen and start to drag her away, out towards the front door. That's when I thought she recognised him. I tried to shout, but I couldn't move, not even my vocal cords. I must have lost consciousness, but it was only for a short while. I used my mobile to call 999, then . . . Well, you know the rest.'

Banks hadn't expected that Vincent had told Tindall where he was taking Maureen, but he still felt disappointed at the lack of information. Most of what Robert Tindall had told him he had already surmised. Maureen was probably still alive, and Vincent had most likely tied her up and stashed her somewhere. If so, where? And what was he going to do to her? Stab her, like his sister was stabbed? Or did he have a better idea? One thing was for certain, if Vincent had carried out the shootings at the wedding, which it appeared he had, and had not killed Maureen then, it was perhaps only because he had a worse fate in mind for her now.

It was time to leave Robert Tindall to the ministrations of his doctors and get back to the station.

16

Gerry could have kicked herself for not thinking of caravan sites before. If she had, she could simply have googled 'caravan parks in Swainsdale' and saved herself some time. But she hadn't. She had insisted on using maps, the old technology. Well, that would teach her. It wasn't as if the sites weren't marked clearly enough by little blue symbols on the OS maps, but she had overlooked them. A caravan was the ideal type of anonymous, easily transportable home that would suit Vincent. And his wallet, if money were indeed a problem. It was possible that he had picked up a used car and caravan somewhere cheap, no questions asked, cash in hand.

Even though Gerry had drawn a blank at the first two sites, she still felt optimistic as she pulled into the gates of the Riverview Caravan Park around half past four. It wasn't the first time Gerry had visited Riverview, about half a mile west of Eastvale across the river from Hindswell Woods. Only a couple of years ago she had been there with Banks around dawn on a miserable March morning watching the smouldering remains of a caravan.

The site stood on the north side of the River Swale, and when Gerry got there, the place was like a fairground packing up and leaving town. Car headlights and high-beam torches lanced through the darkness like searchlights as the cars crawled to the narrow gates, some of them pulling caravans behind them. Dark shapes stood in the rain waving their arms about and shouting instructions. It was an exodus in the wake of flood warnings, Gerry realised, and she was driving against the flow. She could hardly get through the entrance to park outside the main office building no matter how much she leaned on her horn.

Some good Samaritans were directing the traffic towards higher ground, and helping to get out the cars that got stuck in the churning mud. Several caravans had also got bogged down, one of them almost on its side. When Gerry finally managed to squeeze through and park outside the office, she grabbed her umbrella and put on the wellington boots she had kept in the boot of the car in the event of just such a situation. You didn't go far without a pair of wellies in the Yorkshire Dales, no matter what the time of year.

The scene inside the office wasn't any less chaotic, with the poor manager inundated by worried residents asking him where the hell they should go. As there was a fair slope down to the river, then a steep bank leading down to the water itself, Gerry wasn't convinced that the site would be flooded, but perhaps it was better to be safe than sorry.

The manager seemed almost relieved to see Gerry and excused himself to come over and talk to her, leaving his poor receptionist to deal with the anxious crowd.

'I remember you from before,' he said. 'Harry's my name. Harry Bell. What's up?'

Gerry slipped the photo of Vincent out of her pocket and showed it to Bell. 'Have you seen this man?'

Bell studied the photo for a few seconds, then said, 'That's him. Mr Newton. Gordon Newton. Can you tell me what it's all about?'

Gord, Gerry thought. At last. 'How long has he been here?'

'Over two months. Since last November, I think. Quiet as a mouse. I must admit I had my concerns at first. He's hardly

Mr Sartorial Elegance, if you catch my drift. His car's a right old banger, too, a clapped-out Renault, and the caravan's an eyesore. Mind you, he keeps it clean and tidy. So what's he done?'

'We don't know that he's done anything yet. I just need to talk to him.'

Bell gestured towards the outside. 'Must be serious if you've come out here in this weather.'

Gerry smiled. 'I'm only a detective constable,' she said. 'I'm out in all weathers. Now if it was my DI or the super, you might have a bit more cause for concern.'

Bell laughed.

'Is he here now?' Gerry asked.

'I'm afraid he's gone out. Drove off earlier this afternoon, before the rain was quite so bad. I try to keep an eye on the comings and goings. It passes the time.'

'Any idea where he was heading?'

'No. I just remember seeing his car leaving.'

'With or without the caravan?'

'Without.'

'Which way did he go?'

'Turned right at the top.'

That meant he was most likely heading for Eastvale, Gerry thought. On his way to abduct Maureen Tindall. 'Would it be possible for me to have a look inside his caravan?' she asked.

'Well, I—'

'As I said, we just want to talk to him, but it *is* quite urgent that we find him as soon as possible.'

'Bad news, is it? A death in the family?'

'Something like that,' Gerry said. 'There might be a clue in his caravan as to where he's gone.'

'Of course.'

'Do you have a key?'

'Er . . . no. Is that a problem?'

'We'll see,' said Gerry. In her experience, caravan doors were pretty easy to open.

Bell accompanied her outside on to the porch, where the chaos was starting to abate, and pointed down the rutted track to his right. 'Down there, towards the river. Second left, fourth caravan along, on the right side as you're walking. You can't miss it. It's quite small and could definitely do with a paint job. You'll see what I mean. Pardon me if I don't accompany you but . . .' He gestured back to the office. 'Bit of a crisis. We'll probably be fine, but people get all wound up listening to the weather forecasts.'

Gerry stood on the porch, scowled up at the sky, unfurled her umbrella and trudged off into the mud, fumbling with her mobile as she went.

Banks looked out of his office window at the blurry lights in the town square, listening to a Philip Glass string quartet on Radio 3. Gerry's phone call had him a little worried. If Harry Bell was wrong and Vincent *was* home, or if he suddenly came back, it could be dangerous for her. He had told her to wait at the site office for backup, but he was pretty sure she had already set off for the caravan when she phoned, and she wouldn't go back. There was a kind of hard-headed fearlessness about Gerry that he much admired, but it caused him concern for her safety. He called the duty sergeant and asked him to send out the nearest patrol car, just to be on the safe side. The sergeant said he'd do what he could, but the roads were a major concern. Banks stopped short of saying 'officer in need of assistance', the way he'd heard it on American cop shows, but raised the level of urgency in his voice and made it quite clear that Gerry's welfare took precedence over bloody traffic problems, thank you very much.

Next, he phoned Annie in the squad room.

'DI Cabbot,' she answered.

'Found out anything yet?'

'Not much,' Annie said. 'I talked to Doug back on the Tindalls' street. Neighbour across the way three doors down is the best bet. Says he saw someone leading Mrs Tindall by the elbow out of the house and shoving her into a beat-up old car about three o'clock. Thought it looked suspicious. He did phone it in, by the way, but Robert Tindall called us first.'

'Did he get the make?'

'He didn't get the number plate, but he said he thought it was a Renault. An old Clio. He couldn't see the colour because the light was poor, and the streetlights just reflected. But it was a dark colour, and there were rust patches, or lighter patches at any rate, around the wheel rims, and what looked like spray jobs elsewhere. All in all, it looked as if it had been around the block a few times too many. Seemed to know his cars.'

'Good.' Banks paused. 'Gerry's hot on the trail. She thinks she's found him. Vincent.'

'The little devil,' said Annie.

'Riverview Caravan Park.'

'That hotbed of crime.'

'Seems so. Anyway, the site manager says he's not in his caravan but has no idea where he might be. Drove off earlier this afternoon.'

'In time to nab Maureen Tindall?'

'Yes,' said Banks. 'According to my calculations.'

'So what next?'

'I think we'd better get out there as soon as possible. I've got a bad feeling about this. You know how impulsive Gerry can be. I've already dispatched a patrol car, but you can't rely on them tonight. They're very thin on the ground.'

'I'll meet you downstairs.'

Banks went back to the window, then walked over and turned off the radio. Philip Glass's edgy repetition was doing nothing to dispel his sense of unease. He grabbed his raincoat, switched out the lights and headed down. The sooner they got out to the Riverview Caravan Park, the better.

The door proved as easy to open as Gerry had expected, and when she switched on the light she found herself inside a cramped but cosy room. The single bed was made, the top sheet tight enough to bounce a coin off, and there were no dirty socks or underpants on view. Mark Vincent certainly knew how to take care of himself. It must be his army training, Gerry thought. But the place looked lived in, nevertheless. There were dirty dishes in the sink, for a start. Not disgusting old mouldy dishes, but recently used ones, probably left out that morning after breakfast. It indicated that Vincent probably planned on coming back before too long.

Gerry started her search slowly and methodically, from the end where the bed was. There was nothing of interest on the small bedside table, only a cheap clock radio, and in the one top drawer was the usual jumble of small change, blank notepad, pens and pencil stubs, a few rubber bands and a post office savings book that showed Vincent with a balance of £52.40. The bottom drawer was reserved for socks and underwear.

Gerry could find no correspondence in the small writing desk in the living area, not even a bill or a circular. A few clothes hung in the wardrobe, but not the black anorak and waterproof trousers he had been wearing during the shooting. Gerry guessed he was wearing them again now, along with the black woolly hat. There were several shirts, jeans, a couple of pairs of worn trainers and a sports jacket.

In the recycling box beside the door were newspapers, neatly folded and piled, that morning's on top. Gerry bent and picked it out. It was open at the crossword, which Vincent seemed to have completed in ink without corrections. Gerry was impressed. It was one of those difficult cryptic ones filled with anagrams and synonyms and the names of plants she'd never heard of.

In the tiny fridge she found milk, margarine, some cheese slices and a loaf of white bread. A box of bran flakes stood on top, along with teabags and a jar of instant coffee. The cutlery was in a drawer below the hot plate, along with a plate and a bowl. Frugal, indeed. Gerry looked in vain for any traces of Maureen Tindall, but there were no signs of a struggle.

Rain beat down on the flimsy roof as she searched, and she noticed a leak above the door. Water was trickling slowly down the inside wall. Outside, car headlights flashed by the windows now and then, and engines whined as wheels spun uselessly in the soft mud. Occasionally she could hear someone shout above the hammering of the rain.

At the opposite end to the bed was a breakfast nook, and beside it a small armchair with the stuffing leaking out, a reading light angled beside it. There was no TV, nor any kind of entertainment device, unless you counted the clock radio. A row of second-hand paperbacks stood on the single book-shelf over the desk. Old thrillers: Ken Follett, Robert Ludlum, Jack Higgins, Alistair MacLean. Well, she wouldn't have expected Vincent to have a taste for Jane Austen or Zadie Smith.

Gerry noticed something else on the bookshelf and pulled it towards her. It was an old WH Smith wide-ruled exercise book, battered and dog-eared. She sat down carefully in the chair and opened it up. The first thing that caught her attention was a newspaper cutting that slipped on to her lap, a photograph of Maureen Tindall cut from a larger group shot. Across it, someone – Mark Vincent, most likely – had written 'GRAINGER' in angry pen strokes.

Gerry shivered and flipped through the pages. She saw a list of names, three of which had been crossed out, and the second one, Martin Edgeworth, ringed in ink. She recognised the other names from the list of shooting-club members Doug Wilson had interviewed. Over the page were Edgeworth's personal details – his address, telephone number, date of birth, bank, estimate of height and weight. Later came a list of places, including the White Rose, a pub called the Moorcock in Eastvale, and the names of several local restaurants and country inns, presumably places where Edgeworth liked to dine. There was also a list of all the Walkers' Wearhouse branches in the dale.

Over the page was yet another list, this time of books: *The Making of the British Landscape*, *The Pennine Dales*, *High Dale Country*, *Yorkshire Villages*, *Walks in Swaledale and Wensleydale*, *A History of Cricket*, along with books on military history by Antony Beevor, Ian Kershaw, John Keegan and others.

Gerry put the exercise book down and leaned back in the chair. So Vincent had been grooming Martin Edgeworth. He had staked out the shooting club and spied on several members, finally deciding on Edgeworth, no doubt because he lived alone in an isolated house. After that, he must have made it his business to meet Edgeworth, get chatting, probably on long walks so they were less likely to be seen together. He had found out about the guns Edgeworth owned, which suited his purposes, and the more he learned about Edgeworth's tastes and interests, the more he could read up on and feign an interest of his own; hence the books on local history and geography, military history, rambling and cricket.

There were no signs of any of the books in the caravan, so Gerry assumed he must have either borrowed them from a local library or perhaps skimmed them in the library. There were pages of notes about the various subjects covered by the books, so he had clearly done his homework and turned himself into someone who had a lot in common with Martin Edgeworth. And he had done it all fairly quickly. The longer Edgeworth remained alive, the greater the possibility of something going wrong. It was a cruel and calculating thing to do to get revenge, a dish served very cold indeed. Gazing down the length of the caravan to the neat bed, she could see nothing out of place. She would bring in a team of experts to take the place apart, and they might find something else. But that would take time. Besides, she thought what she had found was incriminating enough, though it didn't tell her where he had taken Maureen Tindall. On a whim, she nipped outside and bent to check underneath the caravan. Nothing there, either, except the water rising.

There wasn't much she could do now but wait for Banks and Annie to arrive, and that could take a while, given the worsening state of the roads. Gerry lay the newspaper on the table before her and noticed something interesting. The way it was folded highlighted an article about local flood danger spots in the weather section above the crossword puzzle. Mark Vincent could have been reading this before or after he had worked on the crossword. The report showed a map of the River Swain's course, with attention drawn to potential flood trouble spots, places in danger when the Leas, a wide swathe of meadowland on both sides of the river just west of Eastvale, became waterlogged. The closest one marked on the map was Swainsford Bridge and there was a circle of ink around it. It could just be coincidence, of course, Gerry told herself, or a pointless doodle he'd done when filling in the crossword. But it chimed with something in her memory, something she couldn't quite grasp immediately. It was there, she knew, and it would come.

Gerry also knew from previous experience that the Leas wouldn't hold out much longer. The water would then spread further north and south, over and beyond the meadowland towards some of the houses that faced the riverside beauty spot. But that wasn't the worst of it. The water was rushing down from becks and streams high up in the hills at an alarming rate, all of it joining the Swain and swelling its already bursting banks. There were certain spots where the river narrowed and became shallower for a stretch, and as the water couldn't soak into the waterlogged swathe of the Leas, it would back up and overflow at those narrow points with some force, creating flash floods as unpredictable and as certain to burst as aneurysms. One of those spots, marked in a newspaper Vincent had been reading, was Swainsford Bridge.

The bridge was a single arch over the Swain, a bugger to cross because you couldn't see if anyone was coming the other way, and it was less than a mile east of the caravan site, right in the thick of Hindswell Woods.

Suddenly, the phrases ran like a mantra through her mind and she knew what connection she was looking for.

In the woods. Under the bridge. In the rain.

Wendy Vincent had been killed in some woods and her body hidden under a bridge beside a broad stream. What if Vincent were, in his way, trying to emulate that murder, or at least the scene of the crime? What if Swainsford Bridge was his chosen spot? What if he had left Maureen Tindall under the bridge by the riverside for the flood to take her? *Under the bridge. In the rain.* Was that the place from where she was meant to contemplate her own death arriving? Vincent hadn't intended to rape and stab Maureen Tindall, as Frank Dowson had done to his sister, but he had a twisted sense of poetic justice, and perhaps this was how he had planned things to work out.

It was a guess, of course, but Gerry thought it was an inspired one. She could find out whether she was right easily enough by driving to Swainsford Bridge and checking it out. The road running west from the caravan site was nothing but a narrow unfenced track for over a mile or so before it came to the turning for the bridge, and it wasn't likely to be busy now, not with everyone heading east. The only question in her mind was that, if she was right, where had Vincent gone after abandoning Maureen Tindall to her fate? Wouldn't he want to stick around and see what happened? But she couldn't let thoughts like that hold her back. The main thing was that Maureen's life might be in danger, if she hadn't been killed already.

When Gerry got back up to her car by the site office, the chaos had diminished enough for her to manoeuvre her way out easily enough. Fortunately, someone had found some boards and laid them across the muddiest sections of the road. Gerry picked up her mobile as she drove, squinting at the short stretch of road her headlights illuminated in the rain and darkness.

This time she got through to Banks, told him where she was going, what she was thinking and what she was doing.

'It's far too dangerous,' Banks said. 'Stay where you are, and I'll send the emergency services out to the bridge, in case you're right. The patrol vehicle should reach you soon. We're on our way, but these diversions are taking time. We'll be there as soon as we can.'

'There's no time,' said Gerry, narrowly avoiding a caravan that seemed to materialise out of the rain and darkness in the middle of the road. 'The emergency vehicles won't be able to get here any faster than you can. And if I'm right, it may be too late already. I'm almost there. It makes more sense this way.'

'Not if you get yourself killed, it doesn't.'

'I'll be careful. Come straight to Swainsford Bridge.'

'Don't do anything foolish,' said Banks. Gerry ended the call. She saw the turning for Swainsford Bridge ahead, to her left, the sandwich-board warning sign knocked on its side, yellow police tape across the road to the bridge broken in the middle and trailing in the rain.

Gerry was about a quarter of a mile away from the bridge itself when she went through the first dip in the road. It was filled with water, which splashed up in broad sheets on either side of the car. She could feel its drag, slowing her down as she ploughed through. Not far now, she told herself. Hang on.

Soon she could see where the river narrowed, a mass of churning foam to her right, and she knew the waterlogged Leas lay not far to her left beyond the bridge. The water that gushed faster and faster down from the mountain streams into the Swain would soon have nowhere left to go. It would back up and swell the river to bursting, fill the bridge's arch, perhaps even take the bridge with it. It had happened before.

There was a steep bank on the side of the river. Gerry drove to its edge, where her car would be safe from any flooding, and got out, taking her torch from the boot. The bridge stood ahead, about fifty yards further along the road, which was all downhill. She could see from where she was standing that it was blocked by more official boards declaring it unsafe. As far as she could tell, there were no other vehicles in the area. There were no houses for some distance, either. She levelled her torch and made her way slowly down to the riverside in its beam. The water was almost level with the top of the riverbank now, and it was swirling and swelling at an alarming rate as the mountain streams that fed it poured on relentlessly.

Gerry's progress was difficult because she was trying to walk down at a steep angle on mud and slippery grass in heavy rain and near darkness. She fell on her backside a couple of times and slid, but managed to hang on to everything except her dignity, and this was no time to worry about that. The lashing rain was practically blinding her. At the river's edge was a narrow footpath, like a towpath by a canal. It was already under half an inch of water. Gerry moved along it towards the bridge on her left carefully, in the light of her torch. The path was muddy, too, and water lapped over her feet. Here and there, the path had disappeared completely into the water, and she had to back up the slope a few paces to get by. If she lost her footing, that would be the end.

She shone her torch around, scanning the banks for anything that might be Maureen Tindall. Finally, the beam picked out a bundle of some sort under the bridge, on the narrow ledge between the inside of the arch and the river. The water was slopping over the bundle but hadn't covered it yet, or dislodged it at all. As the currents twisted and turned in the gushing stream, glinting dark and light in the moving torch beam, water occasionally splashed over it. Gerry hurried as best she could along the narrow, broken path in the weak light of her torch. She was scared. The noise of the water filled her ears and cut out all other sound. Vincent himself could be lurking somewhere nearby, even aiming a gun at her right now. And if she missed her footing and went into the river, that would be the end of her. Under the bridge, the noise was even louder, and the water hit the stone in such a way that it splashed up the walls and rained on the bundle she was slowly edging her way towards, moving sideways, hands against the stone.

Finally, she got there and saw that the bundle was indeed Maureen Tindall, gagged and tied up in such a way that, if she moved, the rope would tighten around her neck and strangle her. Gerry held her torch in her right hand and fumbled in her pocket for her Swiss army knife, the one her father had given her for her fourteenth birthday and told her to carry with her always. She found it and got it open, then bent and cut Maureen Tindall free, shouting in her ear for her to keep still and not to move an inch. When the ropes were loosened and Maureen could stretch out her legs and move her arms without choking, Gerry yelled to her that the ledge was narrow and fast disappearing under the rising water, and that the only way to get her out was for Gerry to grab her legs and slowly drag her backwards. Maureen had to remain completely still. Even so, it would be dangerous. Gerry knew that she could easily slip on the wet path, and they could both tumble to their deaths in roaring waters, but she bit her lip and concentrated as best she could.

She gave Maureen the torch to hold, but the light in her eyes didn't help at all as she shuffled slowly backwards, feeling for every step with her foot before advancing. It was slow and painstaking work. Luckily, Maureen had got the message and lay still, let herself be dragged. Finally, they cleared the arch of the bridge, where the path widened a few inches. But the river's flow seemed to be getting faster and noisier. It had swelled even more since Gerry had gone in, and now there was less of the muddy path to follow.

Gerry glanced back at the bridge and saw the water was now covering the ledge where Maureen had lain. Smashing to and fro against the sides. There was only one way to safety, and that was up the bank. Up there, on the higher ground, they would be safe. She would get Maureen into her car with the heater on, then drive her to the hospital. But the only way to get Maureen up the bank was to drag or carry her, and Gerry wasn't sure she had the strength left. Maureen was so frozen with fear and her circulation had been cut off by the tight ropes, so she could hardly do anything but whimper.

The fireman's lift wouldn't work. Not that Gerry couldn't bear the weight – Maureen was a slight enough figure – but carrying her like that would unbalance her, and she would surely slip back or sink into the bankside mud and slide down to the water. She couldn't make it up the slope walking upright. The only way was to get Maureen to cling around her neck without strangling her, and for Gerry to crawl on her stomach and claw her way up the slope with her hands, feel for foot-holds with her feet. It was slow going, even slower than the journey back from the arch. Once, they slid back and almost went over the bank into the water. But Gerry held on and set off again.

At last, she felt she had got far enough and had sufficiently dug in with her feet to take a breather. The water still roared in her ears. She glanced over her shoulder, past Maureen, and saw that it now almost filled the whole arch of the bridge.

Gerry took a deep breath, gathered all her strength together and grabbed on to whatever she could find in the bankside for the last haul – clumps of grass, a half-buried rock, an exposed tree root. Finally, they made it. She dragged herself and Maureen on to the roadside, unhooked Maureen and rolled over on her back, where she lay gasping for breath. Maureen lay still, a few feet away, also on her back. It was only twenty yards of easy paved path to Gerry's car now, but she wasn't sure whether she could make it. Her whole body hurt, every muscle, every joint. She had to struggle just to fill her lungs with air on every breath. The water roared in her ears. She felt her head spinning, the world receding from her. She wanted nothing more than to sleep.

Then she heard what she thought was a slow handclap and turned her head sideways to see a figure dressed all in black standing over her.

'Well done,' Mark Vincent said. 'That was a heroic effort. Pity it all has to come to nothing.'

17

Banks cursed under his breath and drummed with his hands on the steering wheel. They were stuck in a long line of cars at a set of makeshift lights west of Eastvale, the already narrow country road down to one lane. They were on the north side of the river, as the main dale road was now closed. At the front of the line, beside the temporary red light, a man in a yellow slicker stood holding a lollipop sign that said STOP. Just a few yards beyond the traffic disruption, they would be able to turn left along the lane towards the Riverview Caravan Park and Swainsford Bridge. But the red light seemed to be taking for ever to change. A patrol car had spotted a beat-up old Clio with two people in it heading west towards Swainsford Bridge not long before. Banks guessed that had to be Vincent and Maureen Tindall, and that Gerry was either already there or on her way.

'Calm down,' said Annie. 'There's nothing we can do. Gerry's a big girl. She can take care of herself.'

'But what if she can't?' Banks said. 'Vincent's had survival training. He's seen action, for crying out loud. He may be armed.'

The rain was pattering on the car roof in time with Banks's nervous tattoo. The patrol car in front of him had its light flashing, but that did them no good. Even if they tried to jump the queue, there was not enough space to manoeuvre without ending up in the ditch.

'There's no reason to think he'd still be hanging around,' Annie argued. 'He's probably miles away by now.'

'She's not answering her phone.'

'Maybe there's no signal out where she is. You know what Yorkshire's like. Or maybe she can't hear it for the rain.'

'I don't like it. Ah, here we go.' The gears crunched as Banks revved up too fast and set off, almost rear-ending the patrol car in front. When they had got through the one-lane closure, both he and the patrol car pulled out and speeded up, over-taking the other cars that had been in the queue and both turning left so sharply that the lead car had to brake so fast it almost skidded into the ditch. The driver honked his horn furiously. Banks ignored it and carried on following the patrol car towards Riverview.

'Be careful!' said Annie. 'It'll do nobody any good if you drive us or the lads in front off the road and get us killed. Slow down.'

Banks drove on, but not much slower.

'Look,' Annie said. 'There's the caravan site. Shall we go in?'

'No point,' said Banks. 'She was on her way to Swainsford Bridge. Gerry's like that. She only tells you she's going to do something dangerous when she's already past the point of no return.'

Annie quietened down and Banks drove on. Once again, he tried Gerry on both her mobile and the police radio. Nothing.

It didn't take him long to cover the mile and a half from Riverview to the turning for the bridge, and he slowed briefly to take in the overturned sandwich-board and the broken police tape. 'She's here,' he said. 'The only question is whether he's here, too.'

Then he turned left and drove on.

★　　★　　★

Gerry was too weary to fight. The rain fell in her eyes and flowed like tears down her face. She thought this blurred view of the dark figure against a background of darkness might be the last thing she would see.

'I was never far away,' he said.

'Don't do this,' Gerry said, dredging up all the energy she could to even speak. 'Please. There's no point. It's over now. The police will be here any moment.'

'Do you think I care about that?' He moved closer. 'Once she's gone, I'm finished anyway.'

Gerry felt a small ray of hope that he meant he was only going to kill Maureen Tindall, and spare *her*. The surge of relief made her also feel guilty and ashamed, but she didn't want to die, not like this, in the rain, covered in mud, at the hands of a mass murderer, the man who had killed Katie Shea and her unborn child.

Then she realised that what Vincent had said had merely been a figure of speech, and there was no way he was going to spare her. He had killed innocent people before, both in the army and at the wedding, and he would do it again with no compunction. Aunt Jane had told her as much.

She desperately cast around in her mind for a means of escape. There were no weapons to hand, not even a brick or a stone. Only her Swiss army knife, and that was in the depths of her pocket. Any attempt to reach for it and open it would surely alert him that she was up to something. She strained her ears and thought she could hear the sound of a patrol car in the distance above the roaring of the water below. *Please let it be them*, she thought. How could she keep him from killing Maureen until they got here?

'Can you hear it?' she said. 'The police. They're coming. Give it up, Mark.'

'I can't hear anything,' he said, now almost so close she could reach out and touch him.

Then he did something she hadn't expected. Maureen was lying on the edge of the bank just a few feet away. Gerry wasn't sure whether she was still conscious, but she hadn't moved or spoken since they had made it up the slope.

Mark Vincent walked slowly over to her and kicked her hard in the ribs. She cried out. He swung back his leg to kick her again, and Gerry seized her chance. With all the power she could muster, she thrust her leg up under his ankle, where it met the foot, and lifted it higher. As Vincent seemed to totter and lose his balance, Maureen Tindall found enough strength to swing both her legs at the shin of his other leg, whipping it from under him. He seemed to hang there for a moment, then scratched at the air as he pitched forwards over the bank.

Gerry dragged herself right to the edge and saw him sliding and bouncing down the steep slope, desperately reaching out for handholds but finding none. Finally, his head hit the stone path and he made one last attempt to clutch at something solid before he sailed over the edge. But the water and his own momentum were enough to carry him off now, and the stones were slippery with mud. He screamed as he plunged into the water and the surge carried him away. Gerry heard a loud crack as his head hit the inside of the arch, then she heard nothing more but the sound of the water and Maureen Tindall's whimpering beside her.

She closed her eyes and felt the soothing rain on her lids. Soon she could hear the siren coming closer. She reached for Maureen's hand and held it tight as the cars screeched to a halt and doors slammed. Then she let herself drift.

As soon as Gerry had managed to satisfy the paramedics that she was suffering from nothing more than physical exhaustion after her trip down to the bridge and up the steep bank, and that all she wanted was a shower and a good night's sleep,

she agreed to Banks's suggestion that they should all go back
to his house, which was not far away, and was safe on high
ground. The thought of driving all the way back home to
Eastvale didn't appeal to Gerry at all, and she didn't particularly want to be alone after her ordeal. Banks said Tracy had
left a few of her clothes at the cottage for when she visited,
and Gerry was welcome to wear them while he put her stuff
in the washer. Happy to be pampered for once, Gerry thanked
him. She said she would drive her own car up to Gratly to
avoid messing up the inside of his Porsche with her wet and
muddy clothes, but he told her not worry about it and get in.
They could pick her car up tomorrow.

There would be questions, of course. Lots of them. There
would have to be some kind of internal investigation into what
happened at Swainsford Bridge that night, as a man was dead.
Mark Vincent's body had washed up on the edge of the Leas
only a short while after his tumble into the fast-flowing river.
If his skull hadn't been cracked open, he would have drowned
anyway. Naturally, Dr Glendenning would perform the post-
mortem as soon as he could. Banks had talked to AC Gervaise
on his mobile, and she had given permission for them all to
dry out and rest before facing their questioners the following
morning.

Banks phoned home on the way, and back at the house, Ray
Cabbot hurried to meet them at the door to make sure that
everyone was all right, giving Annie an especially big hug.
Then Annie took Gerry upstairs, led her to the shower and
left her to herself.

When Gerry had finished, she came out of the en suite,
brushing her long wet hair, to find a selection of Tracy's
clothes laid out on the bed. Though the tracksuit bottoms
were too short on her, the elastic fitted fine around her waist,
and the sweatshirt was just right. Hair brushed but still wet,

she headed back downstairs and was surprised at the sight of Banks and Ray in the kitchen putting together plates of cheese, cold cuts, chopped vegetables. She could already smell the curry simmering on the range. As soon as she saw and smelled the food, she realised she was starving.

Ray turned as she entered, and she noticed a bottle of champagne on the table, the familiar yellow label of Veuve Clicquot. 'I know the timing's awful,' he said, 'but I was planning a little celebration. I found the perfect cottage today. Made them an offer they couldn't refuse. It was too good to get gazumped over.'

'That's wonderful,' Gerry said. 'Where is it?'

'Not so far from here, just over the other side of the hill, a little village called Beckerby.'

Gerry remembered it from one of her walks. 'I know it,' she said. 'It's lovely. Congratulations.'

'You'll have to come and visit me there.' Ray's expression darkened. 'I'm sorry. I know you've had a terrible experience tonight. Do you think a little champagne might help?'

Gerry managed a crooked smile. 'There's nothing in the world that a little champagne won't help.'

Ray poured a glass for them all, and the four of them ate at the breakfast nook in the kitchen, mopping up the lamb korma with naans. Champagne and curry had never tasted so good.

The mood was subdued, but Gerry did her best to convince them all she was fine and that they didn't need to tread softly around her. When they had finished, Banks phoned the hospital. Gerry could hear only his side of the conversation, but when he sat down again he told them that Maureen Tindall was suffering from two broken ribs, shock and exposure. She would recover eventually, they said, but they were going to keep her in hospital for a while longer. Her husband was up and about and already sitting at her bedside holding her hand.

It might be a long haul for her, Gerry thought, given the shock she had also suffered in the graveyard after the wedding shooting. Maureen Tindall had taken a hell of an emotional beating lately. Gerry also felt that there might be a hard road ahead for Maureen in legal terms, as the law doesn't take well to people getting killed, even in self-defence. She doubted, however, that there would be any form of prosecution. The CPS wouldn't touch it with a bargepole. She thought that she might have consequences to face, herself, too, but all that could wait. In her heart, she was certain that there was nothing else they could have done. She was only glad that Maureen had seized the time and delivered the *coup de grâce*, otherwise they might both be dead and Mark Vincent would be languishing in a cell having achieved his goal.

Gerry started to feel a little tired after eating, but Ray had other ideas. He ushered them all into the entertainment room and once there presented Gerry with a large sheet of paper. When she turned it over, she saw it was a sketch. Of her.

'I did it from memory,' Ray said.

Gerry was so overcome, so lost for words that all she could do was cry, and that made her feel like an idiot after all that had happened that evening. 'It's beautiful,' she said. 'I don't mean me, I mean, the work, you know, the way . . . the lines . . .'

'We know what you mean,' said Annie. 'He was going to do a full size nude but I talked him out of it.'

'I was not,' said Ray.

Gerry blushed, then laughed. 'Well he wouldn't have been able to do it from memory, I can assure you of that. But this is perfect. Lovely. Thank you.' She gave Ray a peck on the cheek and sank back gratefully into an armchair. It seemed to enfold her as she did so, and she wasn't sure she would ever be able to get up again. She could hear Gratly Beck roaring outside the house, and the noise reminded her of the Swain earlier tonight at Swainsford Bridge. She gave a little shudder. But that was over now. She'd done it.

She suddenly noticed that Banks wasn't in the room. Ray had put a CD on and he and Annie were chatting away about his new-found home, oblivious. Gerry put her empty glass down on the little table beside her and managed to drag herself up. Nobody noticed her as she headed out of the room.

She found Banks in the conservatory, just standing there, looking out of the window at the rain. She could see his reflection distorted in the dark glass, and she thought his expression was incredibly sad. He didn't even notice she was there until she spoke.

'Sir?'

Banks turned. Gerry thought he still seemed sad, then his expression brightened. 'By all rights, I should give you a serious bollocking for disobeying my orders,' he said, walking towards her. 'Maybe put you on report. But you and I both know that would only be for form's sake, and neither of us is that kind of copper. Well done, DC Masterson. You saved a life tonight, young lady. I'm only glad you're safe. Don't pull anything like that again. Are you sure you're all right?'

Gerry felt herself blush. 'I'm fine,' she said. 'That's David Bowie singing, isn't it?'

'Indeed it is,' said Banks. '"Blackstar". Do you know it?'

Gerry shook her head. 'Vaguely, perhaps. From the radio. Mostly I just recognise the voice. My dad likes David Bowie. I never really had much time for music.'

'You should make some,' Banks said. 'It helps keep you sane and human in a crazy world, especially after a night like tonight.'

'Will you come back through, sir? Join the group?'

Banks smiled. 'All right,' he said. 'That's a nice drawing Ray did of you. You should be honoured. He's a bit of a pain in the arse, but he's got quite a reputation, you know.'

'I know, sir,' said Gerry. 'And I am.'

Banks followed her back into the entertainment room, and Gerry wondered why he had been so sad, though she knew she would never dare ask.

Ray clapped his hands and said, 'Ah, here they are. Drinks all round? No more champers, I'm afraid, but there's a nice Macallan here waiting to be finished. Or there's beer in the fridge.'

For once, Gerry didn't refuse. She wasn't driving anywhere tonight. 'I'll have a large whisky, if that's all right.'

She noticed Banks raise his eyebrows. 'Hidden depths,' he said approvingly, reaching for the bottle and a glass.

Gerry took the drink Banks handed her and peered at the sketch again. It was a simple head and shoulders, the head slightly tilted, but Ray had caught her all right, and it had only taken him a few strokes. After his previous comment, she had checked out some Pre-Raphaelite paintings and decided she didn't resemble Jane Morris at all. Or Lizzie Siddal.

'We should all watch a movie,' Ray said. 'Something funny. Something silly.' He pointed towards Banks. 'You might not believe it, but this man has a complete box set of Carry On films. Which one shall we start with?'

They watched *Carry On Cleo* and laughed themselves silly. Just after Kenneth Williams uttered his immortal line, 'Infamy, infamy. They've all got it in for me', Gerry put her empty glass down. Much as she was having a good time drinking whisky and watching a daft movie with Banks and Annie and Ray, she found the sounds and sights of the world were slipping away from her for the second time tonight, and this time she welcomed oblivion, welcomed it with open arms.

ACKNOWLEDGEMENTS

Many thanks to Carolyn Mays, my editor at Hodder & Stoughton, for her insightful and helpful comments on the manuscript. Also thanks to Abby Parsons and Thorne Ryan for all their assistance, and to Justine Taylor for her clear, thorough and reliable copy-editing. At McClelland & Stewart, I would like to thank Jared Bland and Kelly Joseph, and at William Morrow my editor Daniel Mallory and assistant editor Margaux Weisman. I would also like to thank my wife Sheila Halladay, who read the manuscript when I thought it was ready to submit and convinced me that it could be much improved.

Thanks to my agents Dominick Abel and David Grossman for their continuing encouragement and efforts. Also thanks to the invaluable publicists – Kerry Hood and Rosie Stephen at Hodder, Ashley Dunn at McClelland & Stewart and Julie Paulauski at William Morrow.

I would also like to thank Jenny Brierley, ICT Archivist at the West Yorkshire Archive Service, whose input is invaluable when it comes to cold cases and lost files.

Thanks again also to Nicholas Reckert for the interesting North Yorkshire walks that, despite their beauty, somehow always seem to suggest to me a possible crime scene.

Last but not least, thanks to the sales and marketing teams who work behind the scenes to make the deals and set up the special promotions, to the reps who get out on the road and sell the book to the shops, and to the booksellers themselves, without whom you wouldn't be holding this volume in your hand. I would also like to add a special thank you to libraries everywhere. They are an endangered institution these days, and they deserve our support. And thanks, of course, to you, dear reader.

Do you wish this wasn't the end?

Join us at www.hodder.co.uk, or follow us on
Twitter @hodderbooks to be a part of our community
of people who love the very best in books and reading.

Whether you want to discover more about a book
or an author, watch trailers and interviews, have the
chance to win early limited editions, or simply browse
our expert readers' selection of the very best books,
we think you'll find what you're looking for.

And if you don't,
that's the place to tell us what's missing.

We love what we do, and we'd love you to be part of it.

www.hodder.co.uk

 @hodderbooks

 HodderBooks

 HodderBooks